"ASK ME IF I'VE EVER TRIED THE POSITIONS I'VE DESCRIBED IN MY BOOKS. THAT'S WHAT EVERYONE WANTS TO KNOW."

Joan's words were husky as she ran an index finger lightly over the hand Ronald used to grip his empty beer mug. She could tell she wasn't the only one feeling the heat from this game.

"I haven't read them."

"I won't hold that against you later."

Ronald's eyes flared. "That's very generous of you." His voice had deepened.

Her ability to get a reaction from this man amazed her. Joan had felt an instant attraction when she'd shaken Ronald's hand, and she hadn't wanted to let it go. . . .

Also by Patricia Sargeant

On Fire

You Belong to Me

Published by Dafina Books

Sweet Deception

PATRICIA SARGEANT

Kensington Publishing Corp.

http://www.kensingtonbooks.com

DAFINA BOOKS are published by

Kensington Publishing Corp.
119 West 40th Street
New York, NY 10018

All Kensington Titles, Imprints, and Distributed Lines are available at special quantity discounts for bulk purchases for sales promotions, premiums, fund-raising, and educational or institutional use. Special book excerpts or customized printings can also be created to fit specific needs. For details, write or phone the office of the Kensington special sales manager: Kensington Publishing Corp., 119 West 40th Street, New York, NY 10018, attn: Special Sales Department, Phone: 1-800-221-2647.

Dafina and the Dafina logo Reg. U.S. Pat. & TM Off.

ISBN-13: 978-0-7582-3143-7
ISBN-10: 0-7582-3143-1

First mass market printing: June 2009

10 9 8 7 6 5 4 3 2 1

Printed in the United States of America

To my dream team:

- *My sister, Bernadette, for giving me the dream*
- *My husband, Michael, for supporting the dream*
- *My brother Richard, for believing in the dream*
- *My brother Gideon, for encouraging the dream*
- *My friend and critique partner, Marcia James, for sharing the dream*

And to Mom and Dad, always with love.

Chapter 1

"Can you fulfill a woman's sexual fantasy?" Joan Brown challenged Ronald Montgomery. She felt confident confronting the arrogant thriller writer in her role as Cleopatra Sinclair, newly published erotic romance author, as they participated in this writers' conference author panel.

Ronald stared at her blankly. "I beg your pardon?"

He even sounded like an uptight, elitist author. Her disappointment escalated. Joan channeled her Cleopatra persona to turn up the heat. She gave the best-selling author a sultry stare. Her gaze stroked him from the top of his close-cropped natural hair to his dark and chiseled features, piercing coal black eyes, and broad, hold-me-tight-against-you shoulders.

"You look as though you could make a woman's sexual dreams come true. In fact, while we've been sitting here on this panel, I've been fantasizing about you."

"Excuse me?" Was there a touch of interest in his shocked response? That was probably her imagination. Her very vivid imagination.

"You look great in jungle print, by the way. But you

ruined the image when you insulted the romance genre."

She was amused and annoyed as Ronald shot a look at the now silent audience, a standing-room-only crowd of aspiring and published male and female authors.

He seemed uncomfortable. "This isn't the right time or place to discuss your fantasies, Ms. Sinclair."

Joan regretted that he couldn't use her real name, but she managed to stay in character. "Your mother should have warned you not to play with fire if you don't want to get burned, Mr. Montgomery." She licked her lips to turn up the heat.

Ronald wasn't the only author on the panel to tweak her temper, though. She'd come to this conference thirsty for acceptance. She'd been looking forward to this once-a-year opportunity to share experiences with other authors. Instead, Ronald and their fellow panelists—a tough-talking female mystery writer, a patronizing male science fiction author, and an irreverent male horror novelist—had condemned the romance genre with halfhearted disclaimers of "nothing personal." Those authors now shrank into their seats behind the long wooden table. *Wise.*

But Ronald was the one at whom Joan had taken aim. She'd been gathering her nerve to ask him to share a drink—maybe even dinner—after the panel. Well, hell hath no fury like a romance author insulted.

Joan propped her chin on her fist and sent him a steamy look. "I know you're *just* a thriller author." She paraphrased his earlier words and threw them back at him. "But tell me, do you have the imagination to fulfill a woman's sexual fantasy?"

Every muscle in Ronald Montgomery's body went on red alert at that question. Cleopatra Sinclair's velvet voice taunted him. Ronald had asked himself that same thing every day for the past three months, ever since his breakup. He was still looking for an answer. "Yes, I do have the imagination to fulfill a woman's sexual fantasy." *Don't I?*

Shocked laughter popped like champagne corks around the room, magnifying his self-doubt. Female authors—approximately 90 percent of the audience—watched with glee. Their male counterparts regarded him with pity, shaking their heads as though to say, "Buddy, you've brought this on yourself."

Yes, he had.

Ronald looked at Cleopatra, her wide milk chocolate eyes, pouty pink lips, and siren red dress. He'd verbally struck at her in retaliation for another woman's betrayal. But she'd turned his attack against him, forcing him to face the insecurity that had eaten at him for months.

The problem was, in addition to being embarrassed and annoyed, he was also captivated and aroused. He was thirty-two, but Cleopatra had him blushing like a twelve-year-old boy. The hot looks and flirtatious talk probably were retribution for his earlier criticisms. Still, they made him feel desired as he hadn't felt in many long months. He could feel the ice around his heart melting, and it scared him.

Ronald resisted the urge to drain the glass of cold water inches from his fingertips. But Cleopatra wasn't so inhibited. Her eyes were bright with defiance as they held his. She lifted her glass and took a long, slow drink. Her throat muscles contracted once, twice. Then she replaced her glass and ran her tongue over her moist lips. *Sweet heaven.*

Cleopatra took aim again. "Then why do you believe romance novels give women unrealistic expectations of relationships? Does the message of female empowerment threaten you?"

The tide was shifting in her favor. He saw his defeat in Cleopatra's eyes. Ronald spoke loudly and clearly to be heard above the audience's grumbling. "I don't have any problem with female empowerment. In fact, I support it."

"Are you disgusted by stories of healthy, loving relationships?"

He'd thought he'd been part of one. "Of course not. I—"

"Are you turned off by happy endings?"

"No, I—"

"Perhaps it's the fact that romances make up well over fifty percent of all mass-market paperback sales. Is it professional jealousy?"

Ronald laughed, surprised by his genuine amusement. "I'm very satisfied with my sales. I've been on several of the best-seller lists, and my books are being adapted into a TV series."

"Then your distaste for romance novels is baseless."

"I don't see their literary value. They're like *Playboy* for women."

The anger glowing in her eyes should have set half the room on fire. "Characters in a romance novel may not save the world like a thriller hero, but they're saving something just as valuable. Each other."

"Romances have a fantasy view of—"

"Haven't you ever been lonely? Or afraid? Or filled with self-doubt? Haven't you ever needed someone to help you through a crisis of self?"

How did she know? Could she see it in his eyes? Had he said something that gave him away? Now he was afraid to even open his mouth.

Cleopatra didn't need his answer. "Why are these stories of any less value than stories of supersecret government agencies disarming nuclear warheads?"

The panel moderator saved Ronald from having to respond.

"This is a truly fascinating debate." The frazzled woman checked her wristwatch as she hustled to the front of the room. "But I'm afraid we need to wrap up the discussion. We want to save time for at least a few audience questions."

Cleopatra arched a brow at him. Her gaze still smoldered with anger. Ronald inclined his head. The erotic romance author had earned this victory. Would she allow him to even the score?

Cleopatra's entrance into the crowded hotel cocktail lounge that evening captured Ronald's attention. She mesmerized him as she sauntered to the bar, apparently unaware of her audience. Her long, toned legs were bare from mid-thigh. And her five-alarm red dress wrapped her like a hot breath.

Ronald excused himself from a table of mystery and thriller writers to join her. In her strappy red stilettos, she was maybe three inches shorter than his six foot two. "To the victor go the spoils?"

Cleopatra turned. Her wavy raven locks swung behind her golden shoulders. Ronald wanted to run his fingers through them. With recognition came a sultry smile. "Pardon me?"

Did she know her effect on him? Was he having any on her? "Buy you a drink?"

She blinked her long-lidded eyes, bright and warm with awareness. "Thank you. I'll have a diet cola."

Ronald hesitated. That was unexpected. He'd judged Cleopatra to be a cosmopolitan or even apple martini drinker, something feminine and alcoholic.

Dismissing his surprise, Ronald ordered her soda

and asked for a beer. Her neatly clipped nails, polished bloodred, grazed his skin as she took the glass from him.

That wasn't an accident.

Cleopatra walked away. Ronald took a swig of beer before following her.

She led him through the crowded bar and past occupied tables. Cleopatra leaned against a far wall and sipped her drink. Her gaze swept the packed room, with casual curiosity. Then she turned her full focus to him.

It was hypnotic to be the recipient of someone's complete and undivided attention. Mesmerizing and, for him, rare. Ronald couldn't look away. "I'm sorry about the panel discussion."

She shrugged a slim shoulder, covered only by her dress's red spaghetti strap. "I should be used to it. People who aren't familiar with the romance genre assume it's pornography. Some of our stories are sexy, but they're *not* pornography."

"I'll take your word for it." Ronald considered her shoulder as he drank his beer. Would it feel as soft and smooth as it looked? He tightened his grip on his mug to keep from touching her.

Cleopatra shifted her attention from his eyes, allowing her scrutiny to linger on his chest before continuing down his body. He blushed. Never before had a woman checked him out so thoroughly.

When her lips moved, he realized she was talking. "Excuse me?"

"You've never read a romance?"

"No."

"You should try one. You're far too tense." She sipped more diet cola without releasing his gaze. Her warm brown eyes were casting a spell on him.

"Which would you recommend?"

"Any of mine would do you a world of good." There was blatant seduction in her voice.

Ronald propped his shoulder on the wall beside her, bringing himself closer to her soft, powdery scent. "How long have you been writing?"

"A long time, but I've only been published a few years. I haven't reached your *New York Times* best-seller status."

"Have you considered writing in another genre?"

A winged brow lifted. "Why would I do that?"

Uh-oh. He'd offended her again. "You were talking about making the lists."

"Romance authors regularly appear on the lists. Do I need to quote industry statistics? I come prepared to these conferences in case I meet people just like you."

"What do you mean?"

"Uninformed. Unaware. Unenlightened."

"I apologize. Again. I didn't mean to offend you."

"Making the lists isn't the primary reason I write. It would be nice. But I write because I have something to say."

"What's that?"

She shifted to face him, moving nearer. Her eyes were dark and mysterious in the bar's dim lighting. Her body heat warmed him. Her perfume clouded his mind. Was he starting to feel light-headed?

"What do I have to say?" She leaned closer still. Her voice was a wanton invitation. "That sex between consenting adults may be naughty, but never bad."

Ronald hunched his shoulders, coughing to keep from swallowing his tongue.

Joan was enjoying her Cleopatra persona, perhaps too much. Under the suffocating watch of her minister father, she'd never flirted so outrageously. Even though she was twenty-six years old, a business owner, and living on her own, her father's approval was still important to her.

But her home in Columbus, Ohio, was almost twenty-three hundred miles from this Los Angeles writers' conference. It was the perfect opportunity to let her hair down. And the ever-so-delicious Ronald Montgomery seemed to be the perfect man with whom to lose her inhibitions.

Ronald had stopped coughing. His reaction would have intimidated Joan. Wait. Who was she fooling? Joan wouldn't even be in this bar. She'd be hiding somewhere with her sketchbook or laptop.

But for this night—the last night of the conference— she wasn't Joan. She was Cleo, and Cleo wanted to play. "What's your position on that statement?"

Ronald cleared his throat. "It depends on the consenting adults. Is either in a relationship with someone else?"

Very clever. He was good at this game. "No."

"That's good to know."

She laughed. "Go ahead and ask me."

"What?"

Joan ran an index finger lightly over the hand Ronald used to grip his empty beer mug. The lure of his warm skin made her want to touch even more of him. His wrist. His forearm. His do-me-baby chest. "Ask me if I've ever tried the positions I've described in my books. That's what everyone wants to know."

"I haven't read them."

"I won't hold that against you later."

Ronald's eyes flared. "That's very generous of you." His voice had deepened.

Her ability to get a reaction from this man amazed her. Joan had felt an instant attraction when the moderator had introduced them. She'd shaken Ronald's hand, and she hadn't wanted to let it go.

Even as he'd angered her during the panel, she'd been aware of him. He'd been sex in a navy blue double-breasted suit. The intelligence in his coal black eyes, the clean lines of his chiseled features, the width of his shoulders, and the length of his hands had appealed to her. A man like him—successful, worldly, and hot as hell—would never notice Joan. But he'd bought Cleopatra a drink.

Joan felt empowered—and excited. "Generosity is important in all facets of life."

"I've always believed the same. If you give often and generously, the pleasures you receive in return can be greater than you've ever imagined."

He'd taken her breath away. Could she keep up? She didn't know, but she wanted to try. "More than you've ever dreamed of?"

"Much more."

"A kindred soul." Joan stroked his hand again and felt a ripple of awareness throughout her body. "I wonder how much more we have in common."

Her words were husky. Was his heart beating as fast as hers? Joan looked up and saw his Adam's apple bob. *Good.* She wasn't the only one feeling the heat from this game.

Ronald's voice was rough. "Do you think variety is the spice of life?"

"I choose my seasonings very carefully. If they don't improve the dish, I don't include them."

"Another shared preference. I like to taste the full flavor of a dish on my tongue. It enhances the experience."

If his words weren't obvious, the passion in his eyes made his message clear. Joan had never believed it possible that words alone could bring her to arousal. But her body heated, and she felt herself melt. "To the victor go the spoils?"

His slow smile made her thighs tremble. "Not spoils,

but treasure." He offered her his hand, and she followed him from the bar.

The elevator took an eternity to carry them to Ronald's hotel suite in the high-rise. It was the last night of the international writers' conference, and everyone had somewhere to go.

When they arrived at his suite, Ronald unlocked the door and allowed Joan to precede him. "Do you want a drink?" He walked past her, toward a small refrigerator.

Joan leaned against a nearby wall. "I'm not thirsty, but thank you."

Something in his voice told her he wasn't taking this night lightly, either. It was in his body language, a subtle uncertainty; in his actions, a hint of distraction.

Perhaps those were her feelings, and she was projecting them onto him? Ronald lifted a bottle of water from the fridge and downed a healthy swallow. No, she was right. He was nervous, too.

She pulled off her stilettos. Her eyes half closed with the blissful relief of taking off the high-heeled shoes. She left them in a corner and wandered farther into the suite. Her stockinged feet sank into the plush tan carpet.

Ronald's accommodations included a small kitchenette with a microwave oven, a living area with a television, and a work space with an ergonomically correct chair. Appearing on best-seller lists had its perks.

Joan joined Ronald in the kitchenette. She was eye level with his broad back. At the touch of her hand on his upper arm, he turned to face her. Joan traced his face with one finger, his high forehead, sharp cheekbones, square jaw softened by full, sensual lips. She would love to draw him.

Sliding her hands inside his suit jacket, Joan felt the warmth of his body against her bare arms. *Delicious.*

She slipped the garment free. "I don't think our hunger can be satisfied in this room."

Ronald wrapped his arms around her, leaning closer to rub his lips against her neck. "And you call yourself an erotic romance writer?"

Joan caught her breath and dropped his jacket to the floor. "What were your plans for this room?"

His laughter was warm and wicked against her ear. Heat swirled in her belly. "We'll talk about that later, after we know each other better."

"Good, because right now all I want to hear you say is, 'I have protection.'"

He molded her body against him. His erection pressed against her belly. "I have protection."

The sweetest words she'd ever heard.

Joan stood on her toes, and Ronald bent to meet her. When their lips touched, it was soft and sweet. *Heaven.* She nibbled across his mouth, enjoying his taste and texture.

Easing her hands over his shoulders, Joan pressed her fingertips into the thick, deep muscles beneath Ronald's dress shirt. All that strength and power reacting to her. She was damp with arousal.

Joan wanted to strip Ronald's shirt off and study him. But she also wanted to sink herself further into the feelings drowning her. His erection nudged her abdomen, and she chose to dive into the sensations.

She wrapped her arms around Ronald's neck, lifting herself against him. As she sighed, parting her lips, Ronald penetrated her mouth with his tongue. Her nipples puckered, seeking his touch. Joan rubbed against him, her breasts against his chest, her heat against his, hoping to soothe the ache. It wasn't enough.

She wanted the erotic attention of Ronald's tongue but needed to feel his bare skin under her palms. She leaned away and hurried to unbutton his shirt. Ronald stepped back, shrugging out of it and discarded his undershirt. He stood before her, naked to his waist.

He was a spare feast of sable brown skin and sculpted muscles—deep shoulders, sinewy arms, molded pecs, and hard abs. His chest was covered with fine hair that narrowed as it traveled to his navel, disappearing beneath the waistband of his navy pants.

Joan blinked. "I think I've seen you in a museum."

Ronald chuckled, adding boyish charm to her adult fantasy. He returned to her. Joan inhaled his scent, warm and musky. He reached behind her and, with one smooth movement, unzipped her dress. The rasping sound was final. There was no stopping now.

Good.

The bodice of Joan's dress fell forward, leaving her upper body naked but for her black strapless bra. The fire in Ronald's eyes singed her.

He unfastened her bra, drawing the undergarment from her in a slow caress. "You're so beautiful. A treasure." He whispered the words.

"So are you." She reached out, smoothing her fingers through the crisp hair on his chest, pressing her hands against his hard pectorals. "Strong and handsome. Like a sculpture."

Ronald palmed her breasts as she unbuckled his pants. Then he slipped her dress over her hips. When they were both naked, he carried her to the bedroom.

Ronald laid Cleopatra on the bed and put his wallet on his nightstand. For a moment or two, he just gazed at her. She was a fantasy, full breasts, small waist, round hips, and long legs. But beyond her physical attributes, the way she looked at him with unabashed desire warmed him. It made him feel wanted and welcomed.

He lay beside her, watching her closely, afraid that at

any moment he would lose her attention. What if she became distracted and withdrawn? He couldn't survive that. Not this night. Not this woman. He nuzzled her neck, breathing in her soft scent—soap, a fragrance, and Cleopatra. What could he do to keep this connection?

Listen to her.

The answer seemed so simple, yet said so much. He moved against her. Her soft sigh, he touched her again. Her gasp, he shifted higher. Her moan, he came closer. And when she arched into him, he knew he'd found her spot.

Ronald pressed his face into the curve of her neck. "Stay with me. Don't drift away."

"I'm here with you. I won't let go."

He followed her body's curves with his mouth. Over her breasts, along her waist, and into her navel. Her skin was silk, smooth and soft. He wanted to touch her forever. He smelled her heat, and it made him harder.

When he drove his tongue into her navel, she raised her knees, pressing her thighs against his arms. He felt her tugging at the sheets.

"Where do you want me?" His lips moved against her torso. Her stomach muscles quivered.

"Between my thighs."

"When?"

"Now."

Ronald raised himself above her, but Cleopatra pressed him back. Her voice was urgent. "Not that way."

Her gaze on his was sharp, intense. She was seeing him and nothing else. She was aware of him and no one else. That knowledge scorched him, made him want her even more.

He rolled back onto the mattress, and Cleopatra straddled his hips. "Where's your condom?"

Ronald reached for the nightstand and pulled one of the condoms from his wallet. He started to open it.

Cleopatra took his hands. "Let me."

She slid down his legs and cupped him. Her hair teased his hips. But instead of covering him with the condom, Cleopatra wrapped her lips around him. The unexpected caress, hot and moist along his shaft, drew a groan from Ronald's chest. His hips rose from the mattress, and his body stiffened. He was lost in what Cleopatra was doing to him with her tongue, lips, and fingers. It had been so long since someone had touched him like this. Had anyone ever made him feel this way?

Cleopatra moved away, and the loss of her heat made him groan again. She rolled the condom onto his rock-hard erection, then shifted over him. Her hair swung forward, brushing against his face. With one of her slender arms on either side of his head, Ronald felt caged in. It wasn't a bad feeling, he thought. In this position, her breasts were inches from his lips.

Ronald lifted his head and suckled her nipple. Cleopatra arched into him, rubbing herself against his belly. He cupped her hips with both hands and held her against him. His penis throbbed.

He switched breasts, giving the other equal devotion. Cleopatra's panting became a moan. Ronald released one hip and shifted his hand between them to touch her.

Cleopatra gasped. "Not yet. I want you inside me."

She slid down his body and positioned him at her entrance. Her touch was gentle and her movements slow, despite the pulse he saw beating double time at the base of her throat.

Seated above him, her dark hair tangled around her shoulders, her body trim, her curves full, and his penis poised to enter her, Cleopatra was an erotic image he wanted burned into his memory.

Then she moved him. His tip had slipped just inside her when she stopped. Ronald clenched his teeth and clutched the sheets. Cleopatra closed her eyes, arched her back, pushed her hips forward, and lowered the rest of the way to his hilt. Ronald lifted his hips to meet her. They stopped. The feeling was too intense. He had to catch his breath.

Cleopatra began to move, slowly finding a rhythm. Ronald helped her, his hands on her hips, guiding her. Her breasts bounced in time with their movements. He shifted his hands up her torso to hold them, loving the way her nipples grazed his skin.

She pressed her hands against his, kneading her breasts with his palms. She dragged his hands down her torso and led him to her lap. He knew what she wanted, his touch, inside and out. He traced his fingers to the juncture of her thighs. Her inner muscles clenched, tightening their hold on his shaft. He touched her with his thumbs, and Cleopatra gasped.

She bent her torso backward, her breasts pointing toward the ceiling. Ronald drove deeper inside her and harder against her. She pumped him faster, her muscles squeezing him. Ronald closed his eyes, concentrating on pleasing her and pleasuring himself in the process.

She urged him, praised him, begged him. And when Cleopatra screamed her climax, her body shuddering against him, she pulled him with her. His body drained into her, and she stayed with him, stroking him, caressing him, warming him. Melting away the cold.

Chapter 2

What had she done?

Joan opened her eyes but stayed still. She lay on Ronald's bed, on her side, in the dark. The numbers on the digital alarm clock glowed red: 3:28 A.M. Behind her, Ronald's breathing was deep and even in sleep. The tangled sheets were damp with sweat. The air was thick with sex.

What. Had. She. Done?

She, a minister's daughter, had had a one-night stand with a stranger she'd picked up in a bar. *Oh, for heaven's sake.* This wasn't the way she'd been raised. What was she supposed to do now? Joan bit back a groan.

She couldn't stay here. She needed to be long gone before Ronald woke.

Joan sent a nervous look his way before easing out of bed. Although Ronald slept the sleep of the dead—or the supremely sexually satisfied—Joan kept her movements careful and quiet.

She tiptoed, naked, out of the bedroom and used her sense of touch to navigate the rest of the suite. Joan found the kitchenette—the area in which she'd last worn clothes—but needed more light to find her belongings.

Shit. Shit. Shit.

She worked her way around to the microwave oven and held her breath as she pressed the door's release. With a snick, the appliance popped open. The noise startled her, stripping at least three years from her life.

Shit. Shit. Shit.

By the microwave's light, Joan untangled her clothes from Ronald's. Her lacy underpants and matching strapless bra, which left nothing to the imagination. Her hose, which she'd ruined in her haste to discard them.

She shook her head at the memory of her behavior. Strangely, she didn't feel shame or regret. What she felt was confusion. What had she been thinking? *Had* she been thinking?

Joan froze as another thought flashed across her mind. What if she'd suffered some sort of psychotic episode that allowed her Cleopatra Sinclair persona to take over her body?

Oh, my goodness. Had that happened? Could it happen again?

She shied away from that possibility and slipped into the little red dress she'd bought for an arm and a leg at the hotel gift shop. She'd purchased the dress—as well as the matching shoes and handbag—for Cleopatra. That should have been her first clue that something was wrong. A literal red flag.

Joan tugged on her underpants but decided she didn't need her bra for the quick elevator trip to her room. Instead, she grabbed her bra and torn hose, and snatched her handbag from the table.

Her heart stopped and she died a thousand deaths as her handbag upended, spilling the contents completely—and noisily—onto the kitchen floor.

Joan stood immobile, straining to hear whether Ronald had woken. Was there any noise whatsoever from the other room? Anything? When the silence appeared to be unbroken, Joan dropped to her knees and stuffed her belongings—including her lip balm, hand sanitizer, facial tissues, and breath mints—back into her silly, little, very expensive handbag.

She cautiously closed the microwave, then waited several seconds to see whether the snick sound had disturbed Ronald. Satisfied that it hadn't, Joan once again used her sense of touch to move across the darkened room. Her shoes stood beside the door. She grabbed them and let herself out of Ronald's suite.

As she hurried down the empty hallway toward the elevators, Joan hoped nothing like this—well, nothing quite like this—ever happened again.

Ronald stretched, reaching across the bed in search of Cleopatra's warmth. Instead, he found cold sheets. He opened his eyes and scanned the empty room.

"Cleo?" He sat up, straining to hear movements in another part of the suite. Nothing.

The alarm clock read 7:22 A.M. Ronald rose from the bed, wrapped the sheet around his naked hips, and padded into the living area. Her clothes, handbag, and shoes were gone. It was as though she'd never been here. As though he'd dreamed the whole experience. *Impossible.* He had a good imagination, but he could never have imagined last night.

Had she at least left a note?

He strode back to the bedroom and looked around. Nothing. He returned to the living area to check again. Three strikes, and he was out. Familiar ice shifted in his gut.

What did this mean? Why had she left without saying good-bye? Without saying a word? Had he left her unsatisfied? *No.* He'd heard her gasps, felt her body shiver with each orgasm. No way could she have faked that.

But a sliver of doubt remained. And the cold grew stronger with each moment the doubt lingered.

Two strides carried Ronald to the telephone. He dialed the front desk and suffered the hotel's greeting.

"Cleopatra Sinclair's room, please."

Overlapping conversations and the clacking of a computer keyboard filled the tense silence. The polite female voice returned to the line. "I'm sorry, sir. There's no guest by that name."

"Are you sure?"

"Yes, sir. Is there anything else I can help you with?"

"No, thank you." Ronald recradled the phone.

Confusion warred with frustration. He paced the width of the living area, then retraced his steps. How could she not be a guest at the hotel? She was registered for the conference.

Ronald turned toward the bedroom. A slip of yellow paper on the kitchenette's brown linoleum floor beckoned him. He changed direction to retrieve it. It was a carbonless receipt for a meal billed to one of the hotel's rooms and signed by a Joan Brown. Cleopatra's real name?

He called the front desk again. A mixture of triumph and excitement added energy to his voice. "Joan Brown's room, please."

The male receptionist sounded like a recent graduate of San Fernando Valley High. "Sorry. Ms. Brown checked out. Can I do something else for you, sir?"

He'd been given hope, only to have it taken away all

in a span of five minutes. Ronald gave in to desperation. "Do you have her address?"

A slight pause. "We can't give you that information, sir."

He hadn't thought so. "All right. Thank you." He disconnected the call.

Ronald stared at Joan Brown's very precise signature. Who was she? And who was Cleopatra Sinclair?

Her Monday morning routine eased Joan's return to normalcy. The familiarity of her morning run and her conservative Joan Brown business clothes— calf-length charcoal skirt and cap-sleeved white blouse—comforted her. After a sensible breakfast, she secured her apartment and walked the two blocks to The Artist's Haven, her art-supply store.

Columbus's trendy Short North District was the perfect location for her business. It was close to art galleries and within easy walking distance of The Ohio State University's main campus. With added pride, Joan recalled that she and her sister-cum-business partner had recently celebrated their store's second anniversary.

Joan let herself into her modest shop. She was once again in familiar territory, which made That Saturday Night in Los Angeles feel all the more like an anomaly.

Saturday night *had* only been an anomaly, hadn't it? Granted, she and Ronald had come together more than once, but they'd contained it to that one night— and the wee hours of the morning. But surely, that counted as only one really long anomaly. Didn't it?

After flipping on the light switches, she walked through the store, making sure the blond wood shelves were stocked and tidy, and the dark gray tiled aisles were free of obstructions.

Joan was loading the cash register at the customer service counter at a quarter of nine, and the bell above the entrance rang. She looked up to see her sister dash across the store's entrance. She moved gracefully despite the two oversize canvas tote bags swinging from her shoulders.

At twenty-four, Christine was the youngest of the Brown children. Looking at her sister was like watching herself. They were both tall and slender, with brown skin and shoulder-length dark hair.

With a cry of pleasure, Christine rushed forward. Her heart-shaped face brightened into a warm smile. The pleated skirt of her pale yellow dress swung around her.

Joan came around the counter to meet her sister halfway and wrapped her arms around her for a re-union hug. "You're in early."

Laughing, Christine pulled back, keeping her hands on Joan's shoulders. "I wanted to see you. How was your vacation? Did you see any movie stars?" She waggled her winged brows.

Joan's smile shook just a bit under the remembered heat of That Saturday Night. "It was great, but I missed you a lot."

Christine laughed. "You were gone only a week."

"I know. How were things here?"

"Everything went well." Her younger sister led them back behind the counter and dropped her bags. "Juanita and Kai were terrific. I couldn't have managed without them."

"I had a good feeling about those two. Have they said whether they've registered for OSU's summer quarter?"

"No, but it would be great if they could work part time this summer, too." Christine produced a folder from one of the totes and laid it on the counter. "I made a list of things we're low on."

"Thanks." Joan took the folder and flipped it open for a quick review.

"We signed up more students for the summer classes. But we'll catch up on that and your trip over lunch. I'd better get to work in the framing department." Christine glanced at her watch, then grinned at Joan. "Welcome home."

"Thanks."

Christine shrugged the bags back onto her shoulders, then turned toward the office at the back of the store.

Joan moved to the store's entrance and switched the CLOSED sign to OPEN.

She was home, where everything was familiar. Where she was Joan Brown, and Cleopatra Sinclair didn't exist.

Did she?

"Your mother's very sorry, Ron."

Worry marked George Montgomery's dark features. Looking at his father was like looking into a mirror from the future. Thick brows, dark eyes, broad nose, squared chin. Did his father look at him and see his past?

"I'm sorry, too. Sorry she didn't tell me my brother was sleeping with my fiancée."

Ronald handed his father a mug of coffee, then sat at the opposite side of his square metal-and-glass dining table. His father had come to Ronald's apartment and interrupted his morning writing—or rather, his attempts at writing—but that was fine. Perhaps talking about his brother's deception would end his writer's block.

George looked up from his coffee. "Harry asked her not to say anything. Besides, it wasn't her place to tell you."

Ronald's eyes widened in disbelief. "She's my mother."

"She wanted Harry to tell you."

"Which meant no one told me. I found out on my own."

The memory still hurt him. His fiancée, his brother, and his mother—all people he should have been able to trust—had betrayed him.

Ronald couldn't sit any longer. He picked up his mug and crossed the dining area's gray tile flooring into his living room. His bare feet sank into the plush silver carpet. Through his large picture window, Ronald studied the panoramic view of his Brooklyn neighborhood. The cluster of treetops in the distance was Prospect Park. Fifteen stories below, street vendors found a few morning stragglers to tempt with Italian ices and tropical juices on this cool May day.

But by now—nine o'clock Monday morning—most New Yorkers already were at work. Before his book sales had taken off, he'd been one of them, working at a prestigious law firm in the city. Now he worked from his apartment and had replaced his Lord & Taylor suits with much more comfortable clothes.

His Syracuse University basketball jersey and baggy terry-cloth shorts were comfortable for writing. But with his father dressed in precisely creased dark blue Dockers and a starched short-sleeved blue shirt, he felt at a distinct disadvantage.

Ronald spoke over his shoulder. "Did you know?"

"I found out after you did. When your mother told me the two of you had argued."

Ronald sipped his coffee. But now he was blind to the cityscape. "Mom protected Harry without any thought to how I would feel."

"Harry was wrong to sneak around behind your back, but what about Yasmine? She's guilty, too."

"Yasmine left the day I found Harry on top of her. I haven't heard from her since. But her guilt doesn't absolve Harry."

"Harry hasn't talked to her, either."

Anger spun Ronald around. "Harry cheated with my fiancée, then dumped her after we broke up? What kind of person does that?"

"He's asking for your forgiveness, but you're not returning his calls."

"And I won't." He could feel the chasm between his family and him widening.

George was impatient. "It's been three months, and your brother's sorry."

Two deep breaths brought Ronald a measure of control. "You always find a way to defend him."

"No. That's your mother. She's blind to Harry's faults. Besides, Harry said he and Yasmine were in love."

Ronald massaged his forehead. "What about *my* feelings, Dad?" He dropped his arm to his side. "Instead of telling me how sorry *Harry* is, why don't you ask me how *I* feel? I actually was in love with Yasmine. I wanted to marry her."

George's gaze dropped to the tiled floor beneath his feet.

Anger and hurt knotted Ronald's stomach. What was it about him that made it so easy for people to take him for granted? Harold had slept with his fiancée. His mother had protected Harold's secret. Cleopatra Sinclair—or whoever she was—had disappeared without a word. Now his parents were more concerned with his anger than with Harold's betrayal. The ice was back around his heart.

"Never mind." Ronald shoved his hands into his shorts pockets.

"Listen, Harry messed up, but he's still your brother. Don't let a woman come between you. You'll regret it for the rest of your life."

"Yasmine's not coming between Harry and me. It's Harry and his disregard of everyone but himself that's destroyed our relationship."

"Harry did you a favor by showing you that Yasmine wasn't faithful."

Ronald's hold on his temper was fraying. "Creeping around with my fiancée for months is not a favor. Maybe I could buy that if he'd told me they were attracted to each other. Maybe I could even deal with it if they'd slept together once, then told me. But they screwed each other for months while I walked around like a fool. That's not a favor."

"So this is about your pride?"

"No. It's about trust. Mom and Harry have broken my trust."

The blood drained from George's face. "How dare you accuse your mother of being untrustworthy?"

This one hurt him, too. Much more than anything else. "She lied to me about Harry."

His father's outrage grew. "She didn't lie to you."

"Lying by omission is still lying, Dad."

"She did it to protect Harry."

"You have two sons. Two." His voice was hard. He hoped hard enough to hide his pain. "If you can't understand that, then nothing I say will have any effect on you."

George stood slowly, as though feeling every one of his fifty-nine years. "All right. I guess there's nothing else to say." He paused, meeting Ronald's gaze from across the room. "We do love you, you know."

How did he respond to that?

In their way, perhaps they did love him. But their way made him feel alone. Alone and very cold. He'd never realized how cold until he met Cleopatra.

The store's bell chimed late Monday morning, breaking Joan's concentration as she reviewed product catalogs.

She glanced up with her welcoming shopkeeper's smile in place. It warmed even further when she saw her parents coming toward her. Joan hadn't realized how much she'd missed them until that moment.

If it weren't for her customers, Joan would have thrown herself into her parents' embrace, submerging herself in their touch and scent as reassurance that That Saturday Night in Los Angeles didn't mean she was going crazy.

Instead, Joan left the checkout counter and settled for restrained hugs and kisses. "I'm so happy to see you."

Tall, slender, and impeccably dressed, Caroline Brown was the perfect first lady of her church. Her hair was carefully coiffed to frame her heart-shaped face. She wore a deep rose dress with princess seams and a softly pleated skirt. Her pumps were a paler pink.

Caroline cupped Joan's shoulders and pressed her cheek to her daughter's. "Welcome back, sweetheart. Did you and your friends have a nice visit?"

At the reminder of the lie she'd told her parents, Joan tensed. Did her mother feel it? "Yes, thank you." She smiled at her father. "How was your week?"

The Reverend Kenneth Howard Brown gave her a smile full of indulgence and affection. The same smile he'd given her since childhood. "It was good. But this week is already better with you home."

Joan's heart melted. "Thank you, Daddy."

At fifty-five, her father's close cropped hair was still dark. He was almost as tall as Ronald Montgomery and broad without being fat. Joan scowled. Why did she keep thinking about Ronald Montgomery?

Caroline squeezed Joan's hands. "Is everything all right? You seem unsettled."

She didn't want to lie to her mother again, but she couldn't tell her parents she was still unnerved by the mind-blowing sex she'd had with a stranger she'd picked up in a bar.

"I'm fine, Mom. Just tired."

"You should have taken the day off so you could rest." Caroline's eyes were dark with concern.

"Chrissie's watched the store by herself long enough. But thanks for your concern."

"Well, take it slow today." Caroline reached into her spacious handbag and produced a sheet of paper. "I've made a list of tasks for your sister's wedding. Since you're an artist, I want you to be in charge of finding the perfect photographer. But you don't need to start today. Get some rest first."

"You're already planning Chrissie's wedding?" Joan hoped her parents didn't hear the horror in her voice.

Caroline handed Joan the list. "Of course. We don't have time to waste."

"But they've been engaged only two weeks. Shouldn't they enjoy the engagement a while longer?" And hopefully, during that time, her younger sister would come to her senses about the man her father had chosen for her to marry.

Kenneth chuckled. "They can enjoy being engaged while they plan the wedding."

Joan didn't see how that was possible, especially

considering the man Christine was supposed to marry. "Have they set a date?"

"Not yet." Caroline nodded toward the paper in Joan's grasp. "That's your copy. Contact as many photographers as you can by Wednesday. You can give us an update during dinner, what you've found out about their packages, pricing, and experience."

Joan scanned the list. It was very thorough. Her mother was contacting florists. Her older sister, Margaret, was in charge of caterers. Christine was shopping for her gown and the bridesmaids' dresses. Next month they were moving on to disc jockeys, reception halls, and printers. She was holding the map of a disaster in progress.

Her father rocked on his heels. "Once Chrissie's wedding's over, we can find someone for you."

Joan looked up at her father. She knew he meant well, but did she really want him to find someone for her the way he'd found someone for Christine? The thought frightened her enough to keep her awake at night.

Chapter 3

Kalinda programmed the hologram for a tropical island. Warm blue-green water gently lapped powder white beaches. Palm leaves rustled in the wind. She summoned her holographic lover. Challen's gentle obedience would assure her pleasure to ease the pain. She'd lost many galactic fighters today. Her forces had emerged victorious, but it had been a bloodbath.

She strolled the beach toward Challen. Wet sand squeezed between her toes. Sea spray dampened her nude body. Challen turned toward her. His face was shapeless silver silicon jelly and shone dimly in the sun.

Challen's featureless image didn't alarm her. Instead, she found comfort in his anonymity. He wasn't just her secret lover; he was her fantasy. There were no expectations beyond physical gratification.

Kalinda stopped in front of him. "You're the only one who can make me forget."

He cupped her cheek, his silicon hand soft and warm against her skin. "I only want to give you pleasure, Kalinda."

She moved closer, his touch already distancing her from the recent battle and bloodshed. He wrapped his arms around

*her and lowered them both to the sand. Kalinda urged him
onto his back and slid on top of him.*

*Challen tangled his fingers in her hair, massaging her
scalp. His almond-shaped coal black eyes scanned her face.
"Tell me what you want."*

Joan's fingers froze on the keyboard. When did
Challen get eyes?

Her heart thumped once, then dropped like a stone
in her chest. She'd given her heroine's lover Ronald
Montgomery's eyes. It was disconcerting—and oddly
frightening—that her one night of madness still
haunted her four days later. She had to get Ronald out
of her mind and out of her system. But how? Time and
distance were her only hopes.

The alarm on her wristwatch chimed, pulling Joan
back to reality. It was six fifteen. She had to get ready
for the weekly Wednesday dinner with her family. Her
mother expected a progress report on Christine's wedding plans. Joan pushed away from her desk. In her
opinion, the only progress would be putting the brakes
on the wedding.

"Joan, what have you found out about the photographers?"

Joan looked up from her dinner plate, sweeping her
gaze over the other diners before answering her mother's
question.

At the head of the table, her father was tense. After
almost thirty years as a minister, he was still nervous
before each sermon. His anxieties grabbed hold of him
Wednesday mornings. They built throughout the week,
until he stood before his congregation on Sunday
and delivered a successful sermon.

Margaret sat on their father's left. Her older sister was an inch or so taller than Joan. Her long dark brown hair framed her gently rounded face. A vibrant personality sparkled in her wide brown eyes and complemented her boyfriend's quieter nature.

Timothy Douglas sat between Margaret and Joan. He was a studious, thirty-year-old investment analyst with a large insurance company. He was of average height and slender build, with wire-rimmed glasses that emphasized his dark, studious appearance. Timothy and Margaret weren't even engaged yet, but Joan already considered him her brother.

Across from Margaret, on her father's right, their younger sister, Christine, seemed subdued. Perhaps Joan was biased, but Christine seemed to lose her effervescent personality whenever she was around her fiancé. She couldn't help but suspect there was a link between her sister's uncharacteristic moodiness and The Engagement from Hell.

The fiancé in question sat on Christine's right. Silas Tooner was of average height and a tad overweight. His nutmeg brown features were soft. Joan wondered whether his hair ever saw the benefit of a comb.

She reined in her musings to answer her mother's question. "I haven't heard back from some of the photographers yet. I'll follow up with them next week."

Her father reached for another dinner roll. "Why can't we use the same photographer the Tollivers used for their daughter's wedding?"

Because I need time to talk Chrissie out of this engagement. "I left a message with that photographer, too. But I want to contact several to keep the estimates competitive."

Margaret chuckled. "Always the businesswoman. Great idea."

"I'm learning from the best." Joan inclined her head

toward Christine, hoping for a smile. Her sister rewarded her with a weak one.

"We don't want to take too long." There was concern in Caroline's voice. "We don't have a lot of time."

Margaret leaned back in her chair. "Mom, you keep saying that, but, Chrissie, have you even picked a date yet?"

Silas interrupted, his voice booming with enthusiasm. "We could get married tomorrow, for all I care."

Joan almost choked on her iced tea. "How romantic." *Not.*

"I was thinking of next summer." Christine's lips smiled, but her voice was tense.

Why are you going through with this wedding when you're obviously miserable? Joan sipped more iced tea to keep from asking the question.

Caroline cut into the grilled chicken breast she'd served for the family dinner. "That's a whole year from now." Caroline seemed to shrug off her disappointment. "Still, next summer will be here before you know it."

Silas pointed his knife across the table at Joan and spoke around a mouthful of mashed potatoes. "How come I never see you with a man? Is it because you're too busy with your store?"

It was a toss-up as to which disconcerted her more, the very personal nature of the question or his lack of manners. "I . . ."

Christine came to her rescue. "I don't think I mentioned what a great job Juanita and Kai did while you were on vacation. They really helped me keep everything under control. I'll be sorry to lose them once school's out."

Joan recognized the conversational rescue and was grateful. She knew Christine recalled discussing their part-time employees three days ago. "Let's hope they take summer art classes so we can keep them during the break."

Silas's cell phone interrupted the conversation. It was the third call he'd taken during the meal. He flipped open the device. "Sly Tunes."

Joan lowered her gaze to keep from rolling her eyes. Sly Tunes didn't seem an appropriate moniker for an almost thirty-year-old gospel music producer.

Joan tuned out the conversation, knowing "Sly" would give them a full recap afterward. She sighed and sliced an asparagus spear.

"That was one of my arrangers." Silas closed his phone. "I'm putting together a Christmas album with various artists. I'm trying to get Oleta Adams, Kirk Franklin, Patti LaBelle, and a couple others."

Caroline's eyes grew wide. "That sounds wonderful."

Silas puffed with importance. "I know. Hey, maybe when I get this going, I'll let you hang around the studio for one of the tapings."

Caroline's jaw dropped. "Oh, I would love that."

From the glow in her eyes, Joan could tell her mother was mentally shopping for a new outfit.

"Do you think they'd want to sing a few of the songs at the church? You know, like a live recording?" Excitement vibrated in Kenneth's voice. "We'd be happy to put an event together."

Silas's laughter was long and boisterous. "I don't know. I don't think Holy Grace Neighborhood Church is a high-profile enough venue. But we'll talk."

Chuckles shook Silas's shoulders a while longer. Joan struggled with her temper. For a connection between their family's church and Silas's family's gospel music recording company, her parents were willing to sacrifice Christine's happiness. And Christine was allowing them. Oh, for heaven's sake.

Caroline cleared her throat. "Speaking of wedding dates, Silas, will next summer work for you?"

Food moved around Silas's mouth as he answered. "Like I said, anytime is good. The sooner the better." He winked at Timothy. "I've heard shorties are more turned on by married men. Do you think that's true, my brother?"

A snap of temper appeared in Timothy's normally calm expression. "I don't know, *brother*. The only *shorty* I'm thinking about is Margaret."

Silas responded with laughter.

Good answer, Tim. Joan wanted to applaud him.

Joan looked from Margaret to Timothy. How did they feel about her parents planning Christine's wedding to Silas, while her father withheld his permission for them to marry? That question often crossed Joan's mind—and broke her heart. At least she liked Timothy.

If anything, Christine seemed even more tense. Joan's grip tightened around her knife and fork. She couldn't allow this wedding to happen.

Plan A was to delay the preparations so she could convince Christine to change her mind. Plan B was to drug her younger sister and lock her in the attic until a month *after* the wedding day.

"Why do we always eat lunch here?" Ronald dropped onto the seat opposite Adrienne Ward. This booth must be his agent's favorite.

They went to the same dark, noisy, overcrowded restaurant and sat in the same cramped burgundy vinyl booth every time they met for lunch. Thursdays must be the noisiest day of the week for this particular eatery.

His agent glanced up from the menu. "Good to see you, too, Ron."

A server came for their drink orders. The young man committed to memory Adrienne's request for an iced tea and Ronald's for a root beer.

"Seriously. Why?"

Adrienne lowered the menu, which she should have memorized by now. It never changed. Her bright blue eyes targeted him. "It's close to my office and near your subway stop." She gestured toward his neglected menu. "Order something."

Ronald scanned the menu. He'd been right. It hadn't changed. "I'll get what I always get."

Adrienne let her menu fall to the table and caught Ronald's gaze. She ran black-tipped nails through bone-straight auburn hair. "Does your less than human disposition mean your writer's block still has you by the balls?"

This wasn't him, this "less than" human. It was the ice freezing out his feelings, shutting down his heart, that was making him so obnoxious. He'd been plenty human with Cleopatra. They'd made a connection, and the heat they'd generated had broken through his barriers.

Ronald massaged his forehead. "I'm working on something."

"Is this the same something you've been working on for the past three months? Will I ever see it?"

Their server returned with their drinks and asked for their lunch order. Adrienne requested the garden salad with light vinaigrette dressing on the side. Ronald asked for a cheeseburger with steak fries.

He tasted his root beer. "If all you wanted was a head of lettuce, you could have gone to the grocery store and saved yourself ten bucks."

Adrienne stirred sweetener into her iced tea. "Wanna see a picture of what that burger will do to your arteries?"

"I'll pass."

They talked about the industry—publishing lines opening and closing, editorial staff changes, upcoming conferences. Ronald didn't feel his usual enthusiasm for Adrienne's insider updates, though. Lately, nothing held his interest, except Cleopatra Sinclair. Who was she? Where was she? And why had she slipped away without a word?

Adrienne sipped her iced tea. "Have you given any more thought to that guest lecturer spot at Ohio State University?"

"No." Ronald drank more root beer, needing something to do.

"But they asked you to reconsider. A lot of people would be flattered by this invitation. A guest lecturer for an advanced writers' workshop."

"I'm not interested."

"Why not? It's only for the summer quarter. June to September. Three months."

"I can count, Adrienne."

"What do you have to lose? Except your grumpy disposition, which, by the way, after three months, you can stand to lose."

The server returned with their lunch, briefly halting their conversation. Ronald took a large bite of his burger, hoping to end Adrienne's interrogation. His strategy didn't work.

Adrienne poked around in her salad. "The lecturer's position may help you get over your writer's block."

"I can do that on my own." Could he break the ice holding him prisoner? Or did he need help with that?

"Ron, it's been three months. In three months, you've usually given me at least three proposals."

"I can use a break."

"Your so-called break is heading toward short-term disability." Adrienne transferred a forkful of lettuce to her mouth, chewed and swallowed. "Your next Morris Jones thriller is due out in a couple of months, but after that you don't have anything scheduled, and you can't go too long between contracts."

The pressure behind his eyes was building again. Ronald rubbed his forehead. "I know."

"Your fans will start clamoring for new stories, and your editor's already calling me every week for your next proposal."

"What are you telling him?"

Her look was pure irony. "I've been giving him the same bullshit you've been feeding me—that you're working on something—but he's not swallowing it, either."

"It's the truth."

Adrienne watched him in silence. "What are you afraid of, Ron?"

Ronald arched a brow. After seven years together, he knew her tactics. Adrienne was trying to provoke him into doing what she wanted. "I'm not afraid." *I'm cold.*

"Then you're depressed, and a change of scenery will be good for you."

"I'm not depressed, either." At least, he'd never admit to it.

"Just make sure you come back in time for the coproducers' cocktail party for your series launch."

Was she listening to him? "I can't teach a class right now."

"Why not?"

Frustration burst from him. He hadn't seen it coming, and he couldn't stop it. "How can I tell people to sit down and write when I can't do that myself? I can't write."

Adrienne's smile was pure triumph. "Then teach."

What was wrong with these plots? Ronald rubbed his forehead, straining for an inspiration just out of reach. Meanwhile, the tan walls of the spare bedroom that served as his home office moved closer.

Ronald had spent a frustrating hour after lunch with Adrienne brainstorming what-if scenarios for his next Morris Jones proposal. He had a computer page full of ideas, and they were all crap. Hostage crises. International drug rings. Nuclear weapons. They'd been done before. What made him think he could add anything new?

He stabbed the computer keys for the select all command, then deleted the text. Ronald leaned back in his chair and glared at the blank page.

When his doorbell rang, he blew out a breath. He was ready to break out of this creative prison. He strode down the stark white hall of his three-bedroom apartment and checked the peephole. Jeffrey Lane waited on the other side. Anticipation whisked away his ennui. He'd hired his childhood friend turned private investigator to find Cleopatra. The fact that Jeffrey was here must mean he'd learned something.

Ronald wrenched open his door. "I hope you've brought good news."

Jeffrey was Ronald's height, with a weight lifter's build. His full mustache made the sharp planes of his burnt sienna features appear even more menacing.

He passed Ronald, looking tough in a black jersey, dark blue jeans, and black Adidas sneakers. "Your mystery lady's in Columbus, Ohio."

Ronald froze, his hand still on the doorknob. Columbus was the main campus for The Ohio State University. Was this a coincidence or a joke?

He caught the curious look in Jeffrey's sharp ebony eyes. He shook off his surprise and led the way to his living room. "Are you sure?"

"Pretty sure." Jeffrey slouched into one of the black leather armchairs, his jeans-clad legs stretched out and crossed at the ankles.

Ronald settled into the other, knees spread and fingers steepled. It had been almost two weeks and countless billable hours, but if Jeffrey had found Cleopatra, it would have been worth the time and money. He needed answers to his questions.

Ronald steadied himself. "What's her address?"

"Want to see her photo first?"

On the glass-topped accent table between them, Jeffrey laid an $8\frac{1}{2} \times 11$ color photocopy of what looked like a driver's license picture. Staring up at him was the image of the woman Ronald knew as Cleopatra Sinclair.

Or was it?

There were subtle differences in the resemblance: the hairstyle and the lack of make-up. Jeffrey smoothed his mustache. "If she's who you're looking for, I have her address."

Ronald stared hard at the paper. Was that Cleopatra? "This could be her, but I'm not sure."

"Want me to go there and take pictures?"

Ronald shook his head, speaking almost to himself. "It's as though the woman I met is wearing a mask in this photo."

"What?"

"I can't explain it."

"Why do you want to find her if she wants to be left alone?"

Ronald pulled his attention from the copied image. Jeffrey knew about Harold's affair with Yasmine. Did his friend realize how important Joan's answers were to him, in light of his brother's betrayal? "Jeff, you've known me for twenty years. How many one-night stands have I had?"

"None."

"And I'm not starting now." Ronald tried to clear his thoughts. "I want to know why she left."

Jeffrey gave him a level look. "You're letting Harry get to you."

Ronald frowned at him. "What?"

"Harry's in competition with you, Ron. Don't let him get to you."

"Harry's not in competition with me."

Jeffrey shrugged, unconvincingly. "If you say so."

Ronald checked the photocopy. "Strange that she lives in Columbus and the university there wants me to be a guest lecturer."

"That is strange." Jeff shrugged. "Maybe you were meant to reconnect with her."

An increasingly rare smile curved Ronald's lips. "I knew it. Beneath your tough exterior beats the heart of a poet."

"So you've said. Want her address?"

Ronald took the sheet of paper on which Jeffrey had written Cleopatra's—Joan's—address. "Thanks."

His friend stood. "Talk to her. Don't stalk her. I'm not bailing you out of jail."

Ronald studied the paper. "I'll call you from Ohio."

Joan tipped her head back, draining the cool drink from her sports bottle. Her church choir had finished its Thursday night rehearsal. Its rousing rendition of "Bathed in the Waters of Life" had left her parched.

Her gaze moved over the vaulted plaster and wood ceiling of her family's church. There was a lot of history and community in this place her maternal grandfather had built.

Joan followed Margaret and Christine from the choir benches. The royal blue carpet muffled her steps as she descended the circular stairs to the main congregation area. Her sandals tapped against the oak wood flooring, which matched the pews, where the singers' purses and bags waited.

Choir rehearsals always left Joan uplifted and happier, as though there was no obstacle she couldn't handle, including an identity crisis.

It had been almost two weeks since That Saturday Night in Los Angeles, but she hadn't forgotten a single touch or taste. Neither had she felt compelled to barhop or pick up a stranger for another one-night stand. Maybe she hadn't lost her mind, just her direction for a while.

Her mother rose from her perch in the second row; a pleased smile brightened her golden brown features. "That was wonderful."

Christine laughed. "Almost as good as when you sang with the choir?"

Her mother winked. "Almost."

It was a familiar joke among the Brown women. Caroline's father had founded Holy Grace Neighborhood Church more than four decades ago, and she'd sung with the choir. However, after she'd married Kenneth, her duties as first lady didn't leave time for her singing. She didn't seem to resent that, though. Joan knew her mother loved being first lady and still attended as many choir rehearsals as she could.

A sudden commotion claimed Joan's attention from her knapsack. Silas had arrived, and he exchanged greetings with each choir member as he made his way toward them. Joan's pleasant mood fizzled and died as her sister's fiancé lingered over embraces with the young female singers. His gaze strayed where it didn't belong.

Joan looked at Christine. Tension had replaced her sister's earlier humor.

Margaret swung her purse onto her shoulder. "It's late. I'm going home." She exchanged hugs with her mother and sisters before taking her leave in the opposite direction from Silas's approach. Nice trick to avoid the budding gospel music producer. Joan was tempted to follow in Margaret's wake, but she didn't want to leave Christine. Not yet.

Caroline beamed her satisfaction. "Silas is already so popular with the congregation."

Joan frowned. "Yes, he is." *Especially the female members.*

Joan saw Christine turn her back to her fiancé. She must have seen his eyes roaming like a dog in heat. Why, then, was she still planning to marry him?

"Silas." Her mother took his hands as he approached them. "It's so nice of you to make time for our choir practice."

Silas straightened his shoulders and pushed out his chest. "I always have time for good music, Caroline." He faced Christine, giving her a quick kiss on her lips. "Hey, Shorty. Are you ready to go?"

Christine glanced at Joan and Caroline. "Are you ready?"

Joan blinked, but she was willing to play along. "Sure."

"We're giving your mother and sister a ride?" Silas sounded as surprised as Joan felt.

Christine pulled her shoulder bag into place. "It's too late for them to walk home."

Silas gestured toward the stained-glass windows. "It's still light outside."

He was right. It was late, almost eight thirty. But it was mid-May. The sun would be out for almost another hour. What was the real reason behind Christine's request for Joan and their mother to ride with her and Silas?

Joan stood beside Christine. "Thanks, Silas. We really appreciate the lift."

Caroline rested her hand on Joan's forearm. "Let's give them some privacy, Joan. When you have a man of your own, you'll understand."

Silas's laughter bounced around the sanctuary. Joan smiled despite her annoyance. "Chrissie doesn't mind, Mom. And it won't take long for them to drop us off."

"Once they've been married ten years, they won't need as much privacy. Tonight we'll walk to your house, as we usually do, and you can drive me home."

Joan sent her younger sister an apologetic look and gave her a hard hug. "We'll chat soon." *And you'll tell me why you're staying with this jerk.*

The foursome said good night in front of the church. Joan paused, watching the couple walk toward Silas's lipstick red BMW. The music producer gestured expansively as he spoke. Stray phrases floated back to her—*my fresh recordings, my mad money, my hot sales.*

Christine stared downward, her gait stiff, as she walked beside the man she was planning to spend the rest of her life with. Joan's heart clenched with concern.

She fell into step beside her mother. "Chrissie was

quiet tonight." *Especially when you implied she'd be married to that lecherous windbag for ten years,* thought Joan.

"She has a lot on her mind. She's planning a wedding, after all."

"Mrs. Tolliver's daughter was stressed when she planned her wedding, but she wasn't withdrawn. She was excited."

Caroline waved a dismissive hand. "Chrissie isn't Edith Tolliver, you know."

No, Edith married for love. "I just want to make sure Chrissie's happy."

"What's not to be happy about? She's marrying a successful young man from a prominent family."

"Yes, ma'am." *But does he love her?*

They walked the last block in silence. The warmth of the aging evening wrapped Joan like a soft sweater.

The Thursday evening pedestrian traffic was heavy, with people enjoying the extended daylight. Laughter and conversation danced out of nearby shops and restaurants. But Joan couldn't enjoy the levity with the image of Christine's troubled expression embedded in her mind.

Her mother's voice cleared her reverie. "Chrissie will be fine. You're the one your father and I worry about."

Joan stared wide-eyed at her mother. "Why?"

"You're almost thirty, but you're still single. There aren't even any prospects on the horizon."

"Mom, my life is full. I have the store, the art classes I teach, and the choir." There was no need to mention her writing.

"When was the last time you went on a date?"

Does That Saturday Night in Los Angeles count? Joan turned away, leading her mother past the row of rosebushes in her apartment building's driveway. "It hasn't been that long." *And I don't need a man to feel complete.*

"You're twenty-six years old. If you don't take more of an interest in your personal life, people will wonder what's wrong with you."

The roses added color as well as fragrance to the driveway. Joan took several deep breaths, savoring the scent as she waited for her irritation to pass.

"What about Maggie and Tim? Is Daddy going to give his permission for them to marry?" That was what her parents should be discussing. Not *her* love life—or lack thereof.

Her mother was silent for several steps. "I don't know what your father has decided."

Joan wanted to scream. She stopped beside her car, parked in the lot behind her apartment building. She unlocked the passenger door and turned to her mother. "Choosing a husband is very important. I'd rather not be influenced by other people's speculation about my personal life."

"You don't have to worry about that." Caroline's words signaled an aria of warning bells. "Your father has already spoken to several members of the church about potential prospects. Nice young men."

Joan's lips parted in surprise. Her voice was thin as she tried to catch her breath. "Mom, I wish you'd spoken to me first."

"Why?"

"Because I could have made suggestions about the man I'd like to go out with." *And you wouldn't have had to poll the church.*

Why wouldn't her parents allow her and her sisters to make their own decisions about their lives?

"Your father has everything under control." Her mother patted Joan's hand, which trembled with anger. "Really, Joan, you must be a role model for other church members. Being single without any prospects at your age sends the wrong message about the importance of family to our congregation."

"Yes, ma'am."

No way would she let her father play matchmaker. She'd seen how well he'd done with Christine. She could only imagine the prize he'd pick for her.

Chapter 4

Friday afternoon, Joan looked up as the door chimes sang. Her welcoming smile withered and died. Her heart pounded in her ears. Her body froze, then burned. Shock, then fear.

Ronald Montgomery stood at the entrance of The Artist's Haven. It was as though he'd wrenched himself from the pages of her memory to ensure she knew he was real.

Joan didn't need the reminder. She knew.

Their one night together had happened almost three weeks ago. The experience may have been distant in time, but she knew he wasn't a dream. Still, her gaze traced him as though she was hungry to refresh the sensory details of his sable brown skin, broad shoulders, and memorable thighs.

His surprised expression mirrored her own. "Cleopatra?"

"Shhh!" The bullet of fear that shot through her forced her to focus on the immediate danger—the revelation of her alter ego. Luckily, the few customers near the front shelves weren't paying attention to her or Ronald.

Dazed, deliberate steps brought him to the other

side of her counter. If she reached out, she could smooth the confusion from his forehead.

"You're Cleopatra Sinclair."

His statement sounded like a question. Should she be offended? "How did you find me?"

"It wasn't easy."

"Because I don't want to be found."

Ronald glanced around the store. "Are you in hiding?"

"We can't talk here."

Joan circled the counter. With angry strides, she led him toward the back of the store. She passed Juanita Garza, one of her part-time employees. "Could you watch the checkout counter, please? I'm going to my apartment for a moment. I'll be right back."

Juanita's gaze drifted past her to Ronald. Raunchy humor gleamed in her onyx eyes. Her Mexican accent thickened. "I'm not mad at you. Take your time."

"I'm . . ." Joan gritted her teeth.

Ronald had appeared mere minutes ago, and already he'd tarnished her reputation. This was what it felt like to be angry enough to chew nails.

Joan walked with Ronald the two blocks to her apartment. The narrow sidewalks were busy with pedestrian traffic, mainly businesspeople on their way back from lunch and students in between classes.

But all Joan could think about was the man striding beside her and the implications of his presence in her life.

How had he found her? Why had he sought her? When could she send him away?

The distance between The Artist's Haven and her apartment separated her public and private lives. She was about to breach that distance. Yet it had taken so many years and so much discipline to maintain those separate worlds, the one in which her family could approve of her and the other from which she protected them.

Joan's heart raced, almost suffocating her with the enormity of what she was doing. When she and Ronald ended their conversation, would she be able to reestablish her separate lives?

Ronald accompanied Cleopatra—Joan—from the store to her apartment. She took him to a small sitting room just off her front door. The walls were painted yellow. On the dominant wall, facing the entrance, hung plaques of the Lord's Prayer, Psalm 23, and the Serenity Prayer. The right wall bore an oil painting of the Ascension of Christ. An end table to his left held a small ceramic statue of the Virgin Mary.

Strange decor for an erotic author.

"How did you find me?" Joan's cold question returned him to his purpose.

He took in her appearance, so different from the woman in his dreams. Instead of a sexy siren's dress, this woman wore a simple pink blouse and a plain black skirt that ended mid-calf. A conservative hairstyle and minimal—if any—makeup completed the change. But was her appearance the only difference?

Ronald stepped forward and handed her a worn slip of yellow paper. "You signed your real name on a receipt you left in my hotel room."

Joan accepted the paper. "I work hard to keep my identity secret, only to be exposed by a Good Samaritan returning my credit card receipt."

"That's not the reason I'm here."

Fear and distrust—mostly distrust—hardened her gaze. "I didn't think so."

"Why did you sneak off in the middle of the night?"

"I didn't sneak off. I came home."

"After you'd gotten what you wanted?"

"What we *both* wanted."

"Do you collect a lot of sperm samples at writers' conferences?" Ronald had promised himself he wouldn't let things get nasty. He'd lied.

Blood drained from Joan's heart-shaped face, but she didn't back down. "I've never collected a deposit so easily before."

Ronald blinked. With just a look and those few words, Cleopatra Sinclair had emerged from Joan Brown's body. Joan had gone from Sunday-school teacher to Friday-night fantasy.

This was the woman with whom he needed to talk. He stepped forward, crowding her personal space. She smelled powder soft, warm, and sweet. Images from that long-ago night tumbled across his mind. Of her nude body straddling his hips, her back arched and her head thrown back. Ronald battled an instant arousal.

He took a steadying breath, regretting it when her scent stirred him again. "Do you regret what we did?"

He stared into her melting chocolate eyes and knew she remembered and maybe even relived the memories that stayed with him. Did she feel him when she closed her eyes, the way he felt her even with his eyes open?

Her throat muscles moved as she swallowed. "No, I don't regret it."

Relief made him weak, but his temper remained. "Then why did you disappear without leaving even a note?"

She turned her back to him. Her slender shoulders rose and fell. He heard her sigh. "What happened between us that night scared me."

"Why?"

"Because I'd gone too far. Cleopatra Sinclair is a role I play. She isn't me."

"Then who are you?"

She faced him, arms spread. "I'm Joan Brown. I'm no one special."

Ronald arched a brow. "So your excuse for what happened that night is the devil in the form of Cleopatra Sinclair made you do it?"

Joan lowered her fist to her hip and struck a pose reminiscent of the strong-willed seductress he'd met in Los Angeles. "What do you want? An apology? Fine. I'm sorry I hurt your feelings."

Ronald narrowed his gaze, fascinated by this very proper woman's improper attitude. There were many layers to Joan's personality. Was three months enough to discover them all? "No, I don't want an apology. I want to get to know Joan Brown."

Joan's mind went blank, and she struggled to fill it. Had this successful, worldly, and sexy-as-hell man said he wanted to get to know *her*? "Why?"

"Because you fascinate me."

She blinked once, twice. Ronald didn't disappear. Still, this couldn't be real. "You're kidding."

"I'm not." His loafers were silent against the thin tan carpeting as he paced closer to her. Close enough to touch. "I met Cleopatra. She's bold, challenging, and sexy. Joan appears to be more reserved, but I'm certain that she's just as interesting."

She scowled. "Do I look like I came down with the last rain?"

"What do you mean?"

"I can't have an affair with you." *But, have mercy, I want to.*

"I'm not asking you to sleep with me."

That's a downer. "Just so we're clear, my father is the minister of our church. That means no sleeping around."

"You're a minister's daughter?" Ronald scanned the

sitting room again. "Now the overabundance of religious objects makes sense."

"You're insulting my home?" Both brows rose.

"I'm sorry." Ronald crossed his arms over his chest, stretching his ribbed yellow polo shirt. "What does your family think of your books?"

There couldn't be a good reason for his question. "My family doesn't know about my writing."

He looked startled. "Why not?"

Joan tilted her head. He was a well-educated man. Why was this concept so hard for him to grasp? "My father's congregation wouldn't accept his daughter writing erotic romance novels."

"So you're lying to your family?"

Joan's cheeks burned. He'd put a spotlight on an issue she'd agonized over for years. "I'm not lying. I'm just not telling them about my books."

"Lying by omission is still lying."

"Why does it matter to you?"

"You shouldn't keep secrets from your family."

She struggled not to sound defensive. "My family is none of your business."

"So Cleopatra Sinclair isn't just for the public and your fans. That identity keeps your family from finding out about you, too."

"They wouldn't approve of my writing erotic romance, and our congregation wouldn't accept it."

Ronald shrugged. "It's your decision whether you tell your family the truth. And I'm willing to keep your secret."

"Provided what?" She wasn't stupid. There was a catch in there somewhere.

"Provided you let me get to know Joan Brown."

"Are you blackmailing me?" Her heart clenched

with disappointment. She'd thought he had more character than that.

"No. I just want to get to know you."

She searched his dark eyes and found the honesty and integrity she'd sensed in Los Angeles. The truth was, she wanted to get to know him, too. Who was Ronald Montgomery? What made him happy or sad? What were his likes and dislikes? Besides romance novels, that is. But how could they have a relationship without her family finding out?

Joan frowned. "What about your life in New York? Am I supposed to believe you're putting everything on hold just to spend time with me?" The idea was rather thrilling.

Ronald shoved his hands into the front pockets of his brown linen cargo pants. "I'm a guest lecturer at OSU this quarter. The temporary faculty housing is a couple of blocks from here."

His answer was slightly ego deflating. But what did she expect? This was real life, not a romance novel. The hero of her story—a handsome and successful thriller author with very expensive clothes—wasn't going to drop everything to spend the summer with her.

Joan smiled at the dramatic imagery. "Okay. I'd like to get to know you, too." Her smile faded as she led him to her front door. "But, remember, no one can find out about us. No one."

Saturday afternoon sales were always brisk. Perhaps that was a good thing. The activity didn't allow Joan time to second- and third-guess her agreement to spend time with Ronald Montgomery.

She handed her customer his change and receipt. "Thank you for your business."

The young man returned her smile as he stuffed the bills and coins into his shorts pocket.

Christine left the other cash register to join her. "It's almost closing time."

Joan glanced at her Disney wristwatch. Sleeping Beauty, Alice in Wonderland, and Mulan agreed. "We only have a few customers left."

"I've spoken with Juanita and Kai. They're both staying in Columbus this summer."

Joan shared a smile with her sister. "That's great news, especially since the store will get even busier once the art classes start at the end of June."

The entrance bell rang, and Joan's parents entered the store. Joan followed Christine from behind the checkout counter.

"How are my shopkeepers?" Kenneth hugged both daughters.

"Fine. What are you two up to?" Joan released her mother, then stepped aside so Christine could embrace Caroline as well.

"We've just come from visiting florists." Her mother sounded tired but enthused.

Christine's pleasure in their parents' company seemed to dim. Her smile was stiff. "Did you find any you liked?"

Caroline kept a hand on Christine's arm. "Several, actually, but we'll tell you all about it tomorrow, after church. We were just in the neighborhood and thought we'd drop by."

Kenneth rocked on his heels. "Next time, one of you girls can go with your mother. She dragged me to almost every florist on the list and to some that weren't. I'm beat."

Joan laughed. "I'll get you some bottled water, Daddy."

Kenneth shook his head. "We aren't staying long. We just wanted to drop in."

When the front door chimes sounded again, Joan paused to give the latecomer a welcoming smile.

Ronald crossed the threshold and smiled back. Tan pleated twill pants covered his long legs. A sapphire polo shirt hugged his broad shoulders.

Her smile froze. Raw panic hurled blocks of ice down her spine. Her worlds were colliding, and she was clueless as to how to stop the tragic accident.

Instinct had her stepping forward, right hand extended. "Ron, it's good to see you again." Her eyes pleaded with him to play along.

Did he realize he'd almost crumbled her world around her? Did he even care?

He glanced toward her family. He knew. She could tell by the gleam in his eye. The look that said, "Oh what a tangled web we weave, when first we practice to deceive."

Ronald took her hand. "It's good to see you again, too, Joan."

She held his hand, dragging him across the store to meet her family. No way could she avoid the introductions now.

"Ronald Montgomery, I'd like you to meet my parents, Kenneth and Caroline Brown."

Ronald reached forward to shake first Kenneth's hand, then Caroline's. "It's a pleasure to meet you both."

Joan gestured toward her younger sister. "And my sister Christine Brown."

Joan waited while Ronald and Christine exchanged greetings. Hopefully, she appeared poised and confident, despite the nerves tussling in her stomach. Her palms were sweating. Her heart was racing. It was an effort to keep from passing out. "Everyone, this is Ronald Montgomery. I met him on vacation. He's the friend of a friend, and he's teaching at OSU this summer."

Oh, my goodness. Would they buy that?

Christine looked impressed. "What are you teaching?"

"It's an advanced writing workshop." Ronald sounded calm and collected. Meanwhile, Joan was a bag of nerves.

"And you'll be here for three months?" Caroline's smile was pleasant despite her careful scrutiny.

"That's right. Just the summer quarter."

Caroline nodded. "Then you should join us one evening for dinner."

Oh no. Joan clenched her teeth to keep from screaming. Her panic increased when she caught her father staring at Ronald as though sifting through the younger man's mind for hints of evil intent toward his daughter.

Ronald glanced at her before returning his attention to her mother. "I don't want to impose."

Caroline waved a dismissive hand. "Not at all. We'd love to have you. Joan will bring you."

I will?

"And what about a church?" Joan's father finally spoke. "You'll want to find a church while you're here. Why don't you come to ours Sunday? Joan can bring you."

Oh no. "Of course, you're welcome to visit our church, Ron. And if tomorrow's not convenient for you—I know you're still settling in—you can join us next week."

Caroline took her husband's arm. "We'd better get home. We hadn't meant to stay this long." She smiled at Ronald again. "It was nice meeting you. Don't forget. Dinner. Monday night."

Monday night?

Ronald returned Caroline's smile. "Nice meeting you, too, ma'am."

Joan watched her mother lead her father from the store.

Christine touched Joan's arm. "Juanita and I will close up."

"Thanks. I'll see you tomorrow."

Her sister waved at Ronald. "I'll see you Monday night."

Ronald inclined his head. "I look forward to it."

As soon as Christine was out of sight, Joan turned to Ronald. The short-sleeved shirt revealed sculpted forearms. Her gaze sampled them before meeting his eyes. "Why did you come here?"

"I wanted to ask you to dinner."

She marched behind the checkout counter to close out the cash registers and collect her purse. "It's day one, and you've already reneged on our agreement."

"What agreement?"

"No one is supposed to know about us."

"Can I take you to dinner?" Ronald stepped closer to the counter.

Joan took a deep breath and caught his scent. Peppermints and musk. Just like that, her temper dissipated. *Have mercy.*

The familiar tap of sandals announced Juanita's approach. A ponytail held the young woman's pitch-black hair away from her round face. Her black T-shirt and miniskirt defied the bright May day. She smiled as she approached them. Her dark eyes sparkled with wicked humor. "Have a nice night."

The part-time employee entered a product aisle and disappeared. Joan had the distinct impression she'd been the subject of a drive-by peeking. She supposed Juanita's curiosity was understandable. It wasn't as though handsome men flocked to her. Or any men, for that matter.

Joan met Ronald's gaze. Her breathing hitched. The expression on his dark features and the message in his coal black eyes mesmerized her. *Come spend some time with me.* She wanted to do just that. An image of him naked in his hotel room slid across her mind.

Weakening, Joan closed her eyes and shook her head. "Your invitation's tempting, but we're not in Los Angeles anymore."

He grinned, a brilliant flash of white teeth, a sexy curve of full lips, and a wicked twinkle in his dark eyes. "You don't get hungry in Columbus?"

"People know me in Columbus. If they see us together, they'll have us engaged in no time."

Ronald gave her a dubious look. "All of that from one meal?"

Joan nodded in the direction in which her part-time employee had disappeared. "Do you really think Juanita needed to tour the store with those frame backers? The framing department's in the back."

"That's one person."

She tidied the area around the cash registers. Her hands shook from the strain of the battle between sensible Joan and the siren Cleopatra. "Do you want a big family right away, or can you wait for our second anniversary?"

Ronald's tone turned cajoling. "I hate eating alone."

She looked at him over her shoulder. His eyes wooed her. She was a goner. "A big family it is. Pets?"

He leaned against the checkout counter. "We're just friends sharing a meal."

Joan shook her head again. "Friends sharing a meal? I can't be the only one generating all this heat, Emeril." She rounded the checkout counter, wondering why she'd even bothered resisting him. Her parents had already met him. "I'll have dinner with you. But the meal is all we're eating."

Chapter 5

Ronald looked good in her kitchen. Joan gave him that. The few boyfriends she'd had had been more interested in the television in her family room than keeping her company in her kitchen. But Ronald seemed relaxed at her round blond-wood table.

He stood and stepped forward to examine each potted herb crowding the ledge of her bay window—thyme, rosemary, oregano, and basil. Had he never seen fresh herbs before?

The thriller author probably lived in a glamorous high-rise in the heart of New York City, with nothing around him but chrome-and-steel skyscrapers. What did he think of her modest apartment surrounded by mature trees and neighborhood parks?

Ronald looked up and caught her watching him. "Are you sure you don't want me to take you to dinner?"

Joan set the ingredients for their spaghetti meal beside the stove and glanced at her Disney watch. It was after six o'clock. "Are you afraid I can't cook? Scared I'll make you sick?"

One corner of Ronald's mouth curved in a smile.

"I feel guilty that you're going to all this trouble, especially since you've been on your feet all day."

"Good. You can make the salad." She jerked her head in the direction of the refrigerator. "The vegetables are in the bottom right crisper. The salad bowl is in the far right cupboard."

He crossed the cream patterned kitchen flooring with long, fluid strides. Ronald carried lettuce, carrots, celery, and tomatoes to the kitchen sink, washed them, then brought them to the center island.

Joan put a pot of water to boil. The stove's heat was in front of her. Ronald's heat was at her back. They worked in comfortable silence for several moments, but every inch of her was aware of him standing near.

"I read one of your books."

Joan jumped at the sound of his voice. "Oh? Which one?" She continued cutting the onions and tomatoes for the sauce.

"Your first one, *Pleasure Quest*." Ronald kept an even rhythm as he chopped vegetables into the salad bowl. He must be used to cooking.

Joan braced herself to hear that this author she'd admired for years hated her book. He didn't connect with her characters. Her story was flat. He wanted to know how she'd ever gotten her first contract, much less a second one. Joan put the brakes on her insecurity before a lack of oxygen rendered her unconscious.

"You must have enjoyed it, otherwise you wouldn't tell me this while I'm holding a knife." She used the sharp edge to nudge the chopped onions and tomatoes into the pan, ready to be sautéed.

"I did enjoy it."

"But?"

"I don't understand why her lover is faceless."

"He doesn't exist."

Ronald put the prepared salad in the refrigerator. "I know he's a hologram, but what's the significance of his not having a face?"

The water boiled. Joan broke the spaghetti as she dropped it into the pot. She then turned to cook the ground turkey in the same pan with the tomatoes and onions. "Her lover doesn't have a face, because the man she needs doesn't exist."

"What kind of man does she need?" Ronald's question seemed too urgent for idle curiosity.

Joan channeled the heroine of her erotic fantasy series as she cooked the ground turkey. "One who doesn't judge her or try to make her conform to the person he thinks she should be. One who sees who she is and understands who she wants to be. Someone who respects her enough to allow her to make her own decisions even if he doesn't agree with her."

"What makes you think that man doesn't exist?"

Joan arched a brow. "What makes you think I can't separate myself from my characters? Have I asked if you've saved the world today, Secret Agent Man?"

"Point taken. What makes *Kalinda* think that man doesn't exist?"

"Because she hasn't found him." Joan continued to brown the ground turkey.

"Then why don't you create a Mr. Right for her?"

"That's not what Kalinda is about. She's a strong woman in her professional life, but she has private insecurities."

In the silence that followed her response, Joan tested the spaghetti to make sure it was cooked before draining the pot. She added tomato paste to the ground turkey, then covered the mixture so it could simmer.

Ronald helped her set the table. "The sex scenes were very well written."

Joan chuckled. "But . . ."

Ronald filled the bowls Joan had given him with the salad he'd prepared. "Between the faceless lover and Kalinda calling all the shots, it read as though you were using sex as power."

"Kalinda already has power. She's the captain of a space station. She has sex for pleasure. It's female empowerment, the right of every woman to express herself and what she wants as well as what she can give, whether in the boardroom, the baby's room, or the bedroom."

"Female empowerment through sex?"

Joan carried the plates of pasta to the table. "I didn't hear you complaining about it that night in Los Angeles."

He didn't remember complaining, either. There wasn't anything he'd change about that night. But, if given a chance, he'd rewrite the script for the next morning.

"No, I wasn't complaining." Ronald collected the filled salad bowls and followed Joan to the table.

Joan's kitchen served a warm welcome. Oak cabinets lined one wall above green-veined marble countertops. Pale green walls made a cool backdrop for gleaming silver appliances. The large bay window hung behind the kitchen table and framed a view of the back garden, with evening shadows weaving between blooming rosebushes.

Joan accepted her salad bowl as she sat. "May I say grace?"

Ronald bowed his head and listened as she said a brief blessing over their meal.

She ended the grace and reached for her salad. "Even in the twenty-first century, society sends a subtle message that nice women don't enjoy sex. I want my stories to free us from those restraints. When Kalinda launches the hologram program, she sets the time, place, and position."

The imagery was erotic. Ronald sipped his lemonade to cool his body temperature. "How did a minister's daughter come to this realization?"

Joan ate more salad. "I don't kiss and tell, Ron. But it's a long and often challenging road to self-discovery, and I haven't reached my destination yet."

"It's ironic that your self-discovery is taking place under a false name."

Joan saluted him with a forkful of lettuce. "It's not ironic. It's deliberate."

"Explain to me again how lying protects your family."

"If my family needed to know about my writing, I'd tell them."

"You say you're not ashamed of what you write, but you act as though you are."

Joan set down her fork. "I don't have anything to be ashamed of, but not everyone shares my enlightened view of literature. Take the comments you made at the writers' conference, for example."

Ronald set aside his salad bowl. "Point taken. But how do you know your family would have the same reaction I had? You should give them a chance."

Joan sipped her lemonade. "It's not just my family. My father's congregation wouldn't approve, either. I don't want people leaving his church because of me."

"Then ask your family to help you keep your secret, but don't lie to them."

Joan laughed dryly. "You're not part of a church community, are you? It's very hard to keep secrets in a congregation. Once you tell one person, there's no stopping the leak."

Ronald swallowed a forkful of spaghetti. "If you're

so anxious to keep your identity a secret, why did you go to the conference?"

Joan shrugged a shoulder and looked at her as yet untouched pasta. "The conference was in Los Angeles, three time zones away."

"And you look very different as Cleopatra Sinclair."

She laughed, swirling her fork around the noodles. "You should have seen your expression when you walked into my store. You looked as though you'd just fitted the glass slipper on a pumpkin instead of a princess."

"I'm not going to inflate your ego by telling you how beautiful you are as either Joan or Cleopatra—"

Surprise blinked across Joan's features. "Oh, risk it."

"But Cleopatra does look very different from Joan."

Joan tipped her head to the side. "I bet your family is proud of your work."

Ronald picked up his fork and looked at his spaghetti. "Yes, they're very proud."

"Have your parents read all of your books?" Her voice sounded wistful.

"I honestly don't know."

"Haven't you ever asked them?"

"No. I know they're proud of me, and that's all that matters." If he repeated it often enough, he'd begin to believe it.

Joan returned her attention to her dinner. She gathered more spaghetti. "Well, I'm proud of my work, and that's all that matters to me."

"Your family should be a part of something as important as your publishing career."

Joan's gaze locked with his. Suspicion built in her brown eyes. "You've really got a one-track mind, don't you? I'm beginning to wonder if there's more to this than your concern about my family."

"Honesty is very important, especially in relationships as close as your family."

Joan was silent. Ronald could feel her watching him as he ate, but he wouldn't look up.

Finally she spoke. "Who are we talking about, really, Ron? You or me?"

He looked up. "We're talking about you."

Joan didn't seem to believe him. That made two of them. He didn't believe himself, either.

Sunday morning Ronald's cell phone rang as he peeled off his sweat-soaked running jersey. He let the garment drop heavily into the white combination shower-bathtub before striding across the hall to the beige and brown bedroom. He grabbed the phone from his nightstand.

Jeffrey's name appeared on his caller identification. As usual, his longtime friend didn't waste time with greetings. "Call your mother."

Willpower kept Ronald upright and his thoughts from fracturing in panicked directions. "Is she okay? What happened? When did you talk to her?"

"She's fine." Metal collided with porcelain. Jeffrey had poured his first cup of coffee.

Ronald slumped against the wall beside the queen-size bed. The wallpaper was scratchy against his damp, bare back. "Then why do I need to call her?"

"She's called me twice since your sojourn to Ohio."

"I've given my parents my cell phone number. Why won't they use it?"

"Couldn't tell you."

"What does she want?"

"To talk to you."

Other kitchen sounds carried over the phone,

cupboards opening and closing, more metal on metal. Jeffrey was cooking breakfast.

Ronald's stomach growled. "Did you give her the number?"

"She has it."

His mother was going to drive him crazy. Ronald massaged his forehead. "I'm sorry she keeps calling you—"

"Not a problem."

"I'll call her later and remind her to use my cell phone."

"You usually tell them where you're going."

"I'm surprised they noticed I was gone." Ronald pushed off the wall and paced the bedroom's worn brown Berber carpeting.

"Okay."

The starkness of that word chided Ronald. "I'm not sulking."

"Good."

Ronald snorted. "It's no wonder your relationships don't last. You suck as a communicator. People need more than okay and good."

"I didn't realize we had a 'relationship.' Was Ms. Brown happy to see you again?"

Ronald stopped pacing. "She didn't have me arrested for stalking her. That's a plus."

Still restless, he turned and strolled down the hall. Whoever had decorated the faculty apartments lacked imagination. All the furnishings were beige and brown. The apartment itself was tiny. And he really missed his fifty-eight-inch plasma screen television. He should have made his own living arrangements for his three-month stay. It wasn't as though he couldn't afford it.

His laptop sat open on the linoleum-and-metal kitchen table. He'd written seven pages before going for an hour-long run across campus. Adrienne had been right. The change of scenery had ended his writer's block. He now felt confident enough to submit a new proposal.

The sound of pans sizzling continued in the background. Metal struck metal as Jeffrey cooked. "You get your answers?"

"Not all of them." More sweat rolled down Ronald's forehead and chest. He needed a shower. And breakfast.

"You've been there three days."

"And every day I get answers, but they lead to more questions."

"That's a lot of work for one woman."

"Maybe. But it's interesting." *And exciting and stimulating.* Something—*someone*—was holding his attention again. "I can think of worse ways to spend the next three months." Ronald swiped sweat from his brow. "I've got to go. I just got back from my run and need to clean up."

"What is it about this woman that has you so caught up?"

What was it about Joan that *didn't* have him "so caught up"? She was strong when they were alone, but vulnerable with her family. What was most important was her interest in him as a person and the way that made him feel.

He walked back to the bedroom. "It's not one thing. There are many facets to Joan Brown, and I want to learn all of them."

Ronald climbed the five front steps to Joan's apartment. He rang her doorbell and waited, his back to her door. He'd enjoyed the almost two-mile walk from his apartment on the university's campus, past the shops and diners on High Street, to her home.

The sun was still out, but the neighborhood was much quieter this Sunday afternoon than it had been when Joan had returned him to his apartment Saturday night. A row of tall, old trees lined the block. Their leaves rustled in a gentle late-afternoon breeze.

Ronald turned and rang Joan's bell a second time. As he started to knock on the door, he saw a movement at the curtains in her front windows. Seconds later, Joan answered the door.

He'd met sexy Joan at the conference and conservative Joan at her store. Now casual Joan appeared, wearing blue denim knee-length shorts and a loose white T-shirt.

His gaze made it back to her eyes. "Feel like some company?"

Her smile was warm as she stepped aside to let him in. "I suppose I can make the time."

"How did you spend your day?"

Joan's dark winged eyebrows took flight above the teasing light in her eyes. "It's Sunday. All roads lead to church."

"I would have gone with you."

Joan closed her front door. "Next Sunday, then. And how did you spend your day?"

Ronald turned and looked at her upturned face. His breath stopped. His body heated. Joan's wide chocolate eyes glowed with humor. Her moist, pouty lips trembled as she struggled with a smile. He might not be able to satisfy every woman's fantasy, but he wanted to become this woman's. An invisible lure as undeniable as a sunrise drew him forward, pulling his head and shoulders closer to her warmth and laughter.

Joan's eyes widened. Surprise? Rejection? Her almost

imperceptible withdrawal stopped him cold. The sudden fall to reality wrenched his heart. Ronald raised his right hand to rub the ache in his chest.

"My day?" A short backward step cleared his head. "Writing. I spent most of it writing."

Joan blinked. She stared at him a moment longer, then turned to lead him past her sitting room to her living room. "That's wonderful. You must have had a very productive day."

The room smelled comfortingly of the vase of yellow roses standing on a corner table and the vanilla-scented candle burning before it.

She offered him the love seat. "Would you like some lemonade?"

"Please."

His gaze fell on a sketchbook folded open on the coffee table in front of him. Penciled images covered the top page. Ronald picked it up for a closer look.

A variety of images flowed across the first few pages—people in action, silhouettes in prayer, religious symbols. Each stroke and curve conveyed motion and emotion. Ronald was fascinated.

He looked at another page. Disney images lived on the page. Sleeping Beauty rose toward her prince. Alice in Wonderland spiraled down the rabbit hole. Mulan charged into battle.

Captivated by her talent, Ronald turned to another entry. This subject rendered him speechless. A pencil drawing of himself stared up at him. It filled the twenty-by-twenty-eight-inch page. In the drawing, he lay faceup, supported by his elbows—and completely naked. "You're a very talented artist."

Joan hesitated on her return from the kitchen. She stared at the back of Ronald's head. His tone was strange. What was wrong?

She carried the glasses of lemonade to the living room—and froze when she saw what he held. "Oh. My. Word."

Ronald smiled at her over his shoulder. "I'm very flattered."

Joan was mortified. Her skin was hot with embarrassment. Since the ground didn't open up and swallow her, she thought humor was her next best defense. "I was going to send your mother a thank-you card, but I don't have her address."

She handed Ronald his glass, hoping he didn't notice its slight shaking. Joan circled the coffee table and took a seat on the sofa. She'd probably left a trail of smoke back to her kitchen.

"Remind me, and I'll give you her address before I leave." Ronald's words were cocky, but a wash of color highlighted his sharp cheekbones, and his head and upper shoulders seemed stiff.

"Ha! You're embarrassed, too." Joan grinned, jabbing a finger in his direction. "Serves you right for snooping around in other people's belongings."

"I wasn't snooping." He had the nerve to mumble the denial with the evidence still in his lap. "You're very good. Did you study art?"

Joan held out her hand for the sketchbook. "I'm mostly self taught. I took some classes, but my parents were less than enthusiastic over the nude models. So I switched my major to business and opened an art store with my sister."

"Did she want to be an artist, too?"

Joan felt a burst of pride when talking about her sister. "Chrissie's art is business. I've always imagined her making a name for herself on Wall Street. But my parents aren't ready to let her leave the nest, so she's settled for High Street."

"What are those first sketches? Are they for your family's church?"

Joan flipped to the silhouette images in prayer. "They're ideas for a flyer promoting our church's fall festival. I've been working on them all week, but none of the drawings seem right."

Ronald rose from the love seat to sit beside her on the sofa. He touched her, shoulder to shoulder and thigh to thigh. "They're all great."

She wanted to lean into his long, hard muscles. But this was Columbus, not Los Angeles. Here she was Joan, and Joan didn't lean into men she hardly knew. "I'm running out of time and ideas."

"You need a break." Ronald closed the sketchbook and put it back on the coffee table. He stood and tugged Joan from her seat. "Why don't you take me sightseeing?"

She loved the way he made her laugh, at him and at herself. "How self-sacrificing of you to take me sightseeing for my own good."

She also loved the way he made her feel. Feminine and desirable. His touch alone made her want to throw caution in the trash. A dangerous temptation indeed. Still, she couldn't release him.

Ronald led her back toward her front door. "You can even pick the place. Anywhere you'd like to go."

Chapter 6

Forty-five minutes later, Ronald hiked beside Joan on a steadily rising dirt path. Each breath carried the scent of warm earth and lush foliage. On their right was a sheer drop into a valley bisected by a shallow rock creek. On their left was a steep hill covered with trees and bramble.

Ronald felt the pull in his glutes and hamstrings. If he weren't a dedicated runner, this unexpected exercise would wipe him out. He glanced again at Joan, striding easily beside him. If her long, toned legs and firm butt weren't evidence of regular workouts, her stamina on this hike was.

Ronald tipped back his head, taking in the sight of climbing vines and straining treetops. "Highbanks Metro Park is beautiful."

"It's one of my favorite places."

The path leveled and changed from dirt to a layer of pebbles and broken stones. "Why?"

Joan directed his attention around them. Her expression reflected satisfaction and peace. "It's wild and rugged, vast and beautiful. I can spend hours here."

"I hadn't expected you to take me someplace like this."

"What were you expecting?"

Ronald shrugged. "A mall or a museum."

He sensed a subtle shift in the dynamic between them. A brief silence ended with Joan's tense words. "You mean, as Cleopatra, you thought I'd take you to Victoria's Secret to pick out naughty lingerie. Or as Joan, we'd do something more staid."

Ronald caught her upper arm and brought them both to a stop. Her peace had been shattered. He felt the tension running up and down her slender muscles. "I didn't mean to offend you."

"Cleopatra doesn't exist, Ron. I'm just Joan. Sorry to disappoint you."

"You haven't disappointed me." The words were too important. She had to hear them. He took her other arm and looked into her eyes. "*You* haven't disappointed me."

Her gaze sharpened, zeroing in on him. He had the sense that she saw more of him than anyone ever had, more of him than he wanted her to see this time.

Joan took a step toward him. "Then who did?"

Ronald released her and stepped back as though she'd threatened him. "No one."

Joan followed him. She cupped her small, slender fingers along his cheek. Her warmth seeped into his skin, working away at the ice stubbornly clinging to him. "Yes, someone did. Who was it?"

Ronald swallowed to keep his throat from closing. His reluctance to tell his story was that great. But there was caring rather than curiosity in her eyes. Her gaze held him and wouldn't let him look away.

"My family. They disappointed me."

Joan's eyes widened. Her lips parted. In her world, he knew a family member's betrayal was unimaginable. "How?"

He needed to walk. Ronald pulled away from her touch. Despite his sudden chill, he turned to continue on the path. He heard Joan's sneakered footsteps keeping pace beside him.

"My brother had an affair with my fiancée. My mother knew about it but didn't tell me."

Ronald advanced three more paces before he realized Joan wasn't with him. He turned to find her staring at the path in disbelief.

She met his gaze. "I'm so sorry."

Ronald shrugged. He couldn't let it matter. "It happened three months ago."

"How did you find out?"

He took a deep breath, releasing the emotion to speak dispassionately. "I walked in on them in my bed."

Joan pressed her hand against her chest. "Oh, for heaven's sake. I'm so sorry."

"It happened three months ago." He repeated the words as though they could remove his bitterness.

Joan put a hand on his arm. "That's why you're so intent on my telling my family about my writing. 'Lying by omission is still lying.' You said that because your mother didn't tell you about your brother and fiancée."

He met her gaze. "You should be able to count on your family to be honest with you no matter what."

Joan looked away first. "Even if telling them the truth could do more harm than good?"

"Sometimes the truth hurts, but we get over it in the end."

"Have you?"

He shrugged. The truth was, he couldn't let the hurt his family had caused matter because there was nothing he could do about it.

* * *

"We timed it just right." Joan watched the Monday lunch crowd file into the sandwich shop just as she and Christine snagged a corner table.

Joan bowed her head while she and Christine silently said grace.

"You always make weekday lunches sound like a competitive sport." Christine shook her head in amusement.

"And to the victor go the spoils." Joan paused as the heat from the familiar words brushed over her. "How are you today?"

Christine gave her a strange look. "You've seen me all day. I'm fine. How are you?" A teasing sparkle appeared in her eyes. "Are you looking forward to dinner with Ron tonight?"

"Ron's just a friend. Actually, he's more the friend of a friend." Joan hurried to change the subject. "But I am excited about the art classes starting next month. You signed up a lot of new students."

Christine winked. "Just enough to keep you busy."

"The whole store will be busy." Joan spooned up some of her chicken noodle soup. "It's going to be a hectic summer, especially for you."

"Why especially for me?"

Joan shrugged, trying to appear innocent. "You're the one planning a wedding."

Christine's expression turned somber. She was suddenly absorbed in the soup and sandwich on her tray. "I'll be fine. Everything will be fine. I'll have a lot of help with you, Maggie, and Mom." Her sister's smile was weak. "Or are you planning to desert me?"

Joan took the question seriously. "You know me better than that. I would never desert you."

Christine's smile brightened. "Then everything will be fine."

They ate in silence for a while, ignoring the activity around them. The sandwich shop was full almost to capacity with diners deep in serious conversation or abandoned to carefree laughter. The air was fragrant with the scent of fresh bread.

Joan tuned all of that out as she searched for another avenue down which to take their discussion. "Are you feeling any pressure at all? If we're going too fast, you should let us know. We can give you more time. After all, you're the bride."

Christine broke her crackers into the soup bowl. "I'm not feeling pressured. We don't need to slow down."

Joan noted her sister's hesitation. She took a deep breath and prepared for a more direct approach. "Chrissie, do you love Silas?"

There was a longer hesitation, with a sense of near panic. "I like and admire Silas. He's a hard worker and has a lot of ambition."

"But how does he make you feel?" Joan hated to push, but this was too important, and they were running out of time.

Christine's giggle was more bitter than amused. "Real life isn't a romance novel, Joan. You don't find Mr. Perfect and live happily ever after. Silas cares for me. Mom and Daddy like him and his family. That's enough."

Translation: No, she doesn't love Silas. "Have you noticed Silas looking at other women?"

"He's a man. Men look at other women. Besides, we're not married yet."

Now Joan was the one panicking. How could she convince her sister not to sacrifice her happiness? "If you don't love Silas, you don't have to marry him. Mom and Daddy will understand."

Christine plucked at her whole-grain roll. "Mom and Daddy said he'll make me happy. That the love will come."

"He'll make Mom and Daddy happy. That doesn't mean he'll make you happy."

Christine gave her a puzzled look. "I've never heard you talk like this before."

"This situation is too important to beat around the bush."

"I don't want to disappoint them." Panic built in Christine's voice.

"They'll get over it." Exasperation pulled at Joan. "Don't sacrifice your happiness just to avoid disappointing Mom and Daddy."

Christine's expression hardened. "It's fine for you to tell me to call off the wedding, but when have *you* ever gone against Mom and Daddy? When have you ever told them no?"

Joan started to speak but changed her mind. Christine was right. She'd never told her parents no. She'd gone to the schools they'd wanted her to attend and given up her art classes for a business major. She'd even joined the choir, although it took time away from her writing.

Her writing was the only thing she'd done that her parents wouldn't approve of. But that wasn't quite the same thing, was it? Her parents didn't know about her life as an erotic romance author. That made the difference. Her parents wouldn't approve of her writing, and Joan hadn't felt the need or found the courage to tell them. Yet.

"The answer would be never. You're right. I've never said no to Mom and Daddy."

Christine sat back in her chair. "You might get that chance. They're looking for a husband for you now."

"I know."

"What are you going to do?"

Joan finished her diet soda, then collected the remains of her lunch. "If they don't do a better job than they did for you with Silas, I guess I'll have to put my money where my mouth is."

He was starving. Ronald saved the word processing file of his thriller proposal. He shut down his computer and rose from the kitchen table where he'd set up his laptop. With a few twists and stretches, he worked the kinks and stiffness from his muscles.

The kitchen in the faculty apartment made Joan's seem palatial. His was a tight fit, impersonal and cold. What Joan's kitchen lacked in size, it more than made up for in personality. The space had an abundance of energy and warmth, just like its owner.

Ronald's stomach growled again.

A few steps carried him across the kitchen's yellow linoleum flooring. He pulled soda, bread, cheese, and cold cuts from the refrigerator. With those ingredients, he had the makings of a simple but filling lunch. For good measure, he took a bag of chips from the cupboard and shook some out beside the sandwich on the plate. He popped a couple of chips into his mouth, then carried the dish and soda to the living room.

Punching a couple of buttons on his remote control, Ronald tuned the television to the Cable News Network. The anchors gave him a recap of the past weekend, then brought him up to date with Monday's events.

He'd finished half of his sandwich when his cell phone rang. Caller identification warned him his mother had caught up with him.

"Hi, Mom. Is everything all right?"

"That's what I'm calling to ask you. What are you doing in Ohio?"

His manner cooled in response to her accusatory tone. She sounded as though he'd deliberately withheld information from her. *How ironic.* "I'm working."

"Why did you get a job in Ohio?"

Ronald put his plate on the coffee table and picked up his soda. "You didn't call to ask that. What's on your mind, Mom?"

She sighed, part frustration, part regret. "You know, it wasn't so long ago that you'd tell me everything."

"It wasn't so long ago that I thought you'd do the same."

His mother hesitated. "I see you still haven't forgiven me for what Harry did."

"You're not to blame for Harry's behavior."

"Then why are you punishing me? You don't call anymore. I have to find out from your friends where you are."

Ronald held on to his patience, though it was hard. "Even when I did call, you and Dad weren't interested in what I was doing. It was all about Harry's newest crisis."

"We were interested." Her indignation lifted her voice several octaves. "Just because we weren't screaming and jumping up and down doesn't mean we weren't interested."

"You never came to any of my events."

"That's because Harry . . ." His mother's voice trailed off.

"Needed you." He didn't care whether his mother heard the bitterness in his tone. She had two sons. "It's not easy to forget that you chose to protect Harry's deceit at the expense of my happiness."

"My hands were tied. What would you have had me do, Ronnie?"

"I wish you'd told me the truth."

"I never lied to you." Anger joined the desperation in her voice.

Ronald massaged his forehead. He'd grown tired of this debate, first with Joan, now his mother. "Lying by omission is still lying."

"Harry told me he was going to tell you himself."

Ronald clenched his teeth. "But he didn't. I found out on my own." An awkward silence moved in.

"So what can I do to regain your trust?" His mother sounded tired.

Ronald couldn't believe he was having this conversation with the woman who'd given birth to him. The woman who'd nursed him when he was sick and helped him become the man he was today. "It'll take time, Mom."

"Well, we're not going to have that time with you in Ohio." Her tone was frustrated. "When are you coming home?"

Ronald leaned forward, his elbows on his knees. "I'm teaching a class through the summer quarter. The quarter ends in September, but I may stay longer."

"Why would you stay? What's in Ohio?"

"There are some things I need to take care of."

"What?"

"Just a few things." He hated referring to Joan as a thing, but he wasn't ready to discuss her with his family. Not yet.

"Why are you being so mysterious? You won't tell me what you're doing or how long you're staying. If I want to reach you, I have to use your cell phone. What's the big secret?"

Ronald stood. "It's complicated, Mom." In the silence, he sensed his mother's disappointment.

"All right, Ronnie. I guess you'll tell me when you're ready."

It would have been so easy to just tell her everything. About his fascination with Joan. About her secret life and the way she was helping him see things about himself he'd never realized before. But his sense of betrayal was still too fresh.

"Thanks for calling, Mom."

"You don't sound grateful that I called."

Ronald didn't react to her attempt to make him feel guilty. "I am grateful. This conversation was a step in the right direction, but we've got a long way to go."

"Do you ever miss being a corporate lawyer?" Margaret speared a roasted green bean while waiting for Ronald's answer.

Ronald lowered his forkful of turkey. At this rate, he'd starve. "I liked practicing law. But I prefer writing fiction."

Monday's Brown family dinner was a lively event. There was just as much—if not more—talking as eating. But oddly enough, Ronald enjoyed it. The abrupt change of subjects. The interest in each other's welfare. The spontaneous laughter and good-natured teasing. It was a meal that fed more than the body, and he'd be a liar if he didn't admit he was a bit jealous of Joan and her family.

Silas Tooner, whom Joan had introduced in less than enthusiastic tones as Christine's fiancé, waved a forkful of stuffing dripping with gravy. "But which one gets more shorties? The writing gig or the law thing?"

Ronald began to understand Joan's reluctance to

welcome Silas into her family. He looked at the others around the table for their reactions. Seated beside him, Joan ignored Silas's question and picked up her iced tea. Margaret also didn't appear to have heard him. Christine played with her green beans. Caroline gave Silas an indulgent look, but Kenneth's attention remained on Ronald.

Joan touched his wrist. "Ron is a wonderful story-teller. He's made the best-seller lists."

Her words had an intimate feel to them, as though she'd touched him in a place no one had ever taken the time to find. "Thank you."

Kenneth interrupted the moment. "How long have you known my daughter?"

Ronald sensed Joan become tense. He didn't want to lie to her father, but what did she want him to say?

Apparently, Joan didn't want to risk it. She answered for him. "I thought I'd mentioned, Daddy, that I met Ron in Los Angeles. He's the friend of a friend."

Friend of a friend? Did she mean Cleopatra? Ronald wondered.

Kenneth had a follow-up question. "Did Joan tell you about the family's church?"

Again, Joan responded first. "Ron and I didn't have much time to talk."

Kenneth gave her a curious smile. "Aren't you going to let him speak for himself?"

"That's right." Silas lowered his half-empty glass of soda. "Joan's always speaking for other people."

From across the table, Joan gave Silas a hard look before turning away. There didn't seem to be a lot of regard between the two. What did Christine think about her sister's dislike of her fiancé? What did Joan's parents think? Were they at all concerned?

Ronald left that thought to respond to Kenneth.

"Joan and I met the last day of her vacation." It was the truth. There was no need to elaborate. Ronald glanced at Silas. He had the feeling they'd never grilled Christine's fiancé this way. The younger man seemed to think he had a lot of latitude.

On the other hand, Kenneth seemed more interested in grilling him than eating his dinner. "Do you belong to a church in New York?"

Ronald met Kenneth's probing stare and dared to tell the truth. "No."

Caroline called to him from the other end of the table. Her eyes, twinkling with warmth, reminded him of Joan's. "You're welcome to join our church family while you're here."

"Thank you." With one meal, Joan's family made him feel more welcome than his family had in months. "How old is your church?"

The question seemed to please Caroline. "My father founded Holy Grace Neighborhood Church in nineteen sixty-three. My husband became the pastor in nineteen eighty-one."

Kenneth inclined his head. "That was a proud moment for me. I've been trying to build on the legacy Caroline's father entrusted to me."

"Daddy would be proud of everything you've done." Caroline gazed the length of the table at her husband, love and pride in her eyes.

Kenneth addressed Ronald. "But it's not just *my* duty to continue my father-in-law's legacy. It's the whole family's responsibility. We're aware of appearances and the fact that everything we do reflects on our church."

Ronald read the translation. *Are you worthy to be seen with my daughter?*

Ronald inclined his head. "Yes, sir." Your message was received and understood.

Caroline swallowed more turkey and gravy. "Your parents must be so proud of you. Achieving your goal and being so successful."

"Thank you." Ronald glanced at Joan.

What did she think of her mother's comment? Did it encourage her to share with her family that she'd achieved her goal as well? Judging by the way her gaze was glued to her half-eaten dinner, he didn't think so.

A little more than an hour later, Joan breathed a sigh of relief as she drove Ronald away from her parents' house. "I'm sorry about my father's questions."

"It wasn't so bad. Besides, you'd warned me."

Joan could hear the shrug in his voice. It made her more uncomfortable. They drove for a few blocks in silence. Finally, she glanced at him. He seemed deep in thought, staring out the passenger-side window as they drew closer to his apartment complex.

She pulled her subcompact up to a red light. "I'm sorry also that you were put in a position to lie to him."

"When?"

She heard rustling as Ronald shifted toward her in the passenger seat. "When he asked if I'd told you about our church."

"I didn't lie to him. I told him we didn't have much time to talk." He sounded surprised.

Joan was amused. She pulled into his parking lot and found a spot for her trusty Toyota beside his Lexus SUV. "Isn't that skirting the truth?"

His laughter was warm and wicked. "Would you rather I'd admitted we didn't have much time to talk because we spent the night making love?"

Heat flashed through her veins, and images of his nude body filled her night vision. "No, I wouldn't."

"I didn't think so." His deep voice reverberated in her chest. Joan struggled to control her breathing.

Ronald released his seat belt and laid his hand on her headrest. "I don't mind your father's questions. He wants to get to know me because he cares about you. He doesn't want me to hurt you. I'm not going to."

The look in his eyes, hot and heavy, said, "*I want you.*" Desire and a heady sense of feminine power rushed over her. With a will of its own, her hand reached out to cup his strong jaw. "I know. I won't hurt you, either."

Ronald turned his head to kiss the inside of her wrist. The sensation radiated up her arm and pooled in her abdomen. Joan leaned closer to him. Perhaps that was the signal he'd waited for. He unfastened her seat belt and drew her to him.

His lips were warm and firm on hers. He took his time with the caress before parting his lips and sliding his tongue against the seam of her mouth. With a sigh, Joan let him in. Ronald covered her mouth with his. He stroked her tongue and the roof of her mouth. And his hands. His large hands were everywhere, stirring her, arousing her. She was lost in his touch, his taste, and his scent. She moaned into his mouth, wanting more of this feeling. Wanting more of him.

Then he cupped her breast, kneading her. The heat of his hand rose through her cotton blouse. His fingers plucked her nipple. She felt it through her blouse, even through her bra. Her feminine core pulsed with each teasing touch.

Joan moaned. She tried to slide closer to his heat, but the edge of the bucket seat pushed her back. She stilled. Realization sliced through the passion-induced haze in her mind. No, not in a car. The Brown daughters didn't make out in automobiles.

Joan grabbed Ronald's wrist, tugging his large hand away as she put distance between herself and temptation. "Ron, I can't."

He lifted his head. By the parking lot's security lights, she met his unfocused gaze. "What's wrong?"

"This." She made a vague gesture between them. "This is wrong. I can't do this."

"Why not?"

"For one thing, we're in a car parked under a light. I'm really not interested in providing your neighbors with tonight's X-rated entertainment."

He stroked her arm, his gesture persuasive. "Come inside with me."

She smiled, shaking her head. "You're very tempting, but no. I told you I can't have another one-night stand or even a summer fling. I'm sorry."

Ronald turned away. He exhaled a heavy breath. Joan waited, tense, although she knew she had nothing to worry about.

He met her gaze again. "I'm sorry, too." He leaned forward, giving her a quick, hard kiss before climbing from her car.

Joan watched his long, strong legs close the distance to his apartment. That last taste of him had only made her hungrier. She felt like Eve straining to resist a very appealing apple.

Chapter 7

Neither of her parents could be labeled subtle. Ever. Take as an example tonight's Brown family dinner.

This Wednesday her parents had invited the Reverend Dr. Wendell T. Hines. Joan thanked the associate pastor as he handed her the broccoli and carrots. The reverend was attractive, pleasant, intelligent—and obviously meant to be her love connection. Joan waffled between amazement and embarrassment.

If Christine's fiancé was her family's entrée to the gospel music industry, Joan's prospective suitor was her father's attempt to carry on the family business. In addition to being Joan's future husband, Wendell was Kenneth's chosen successor. How romantic. *Not.*

Caroline prodded the dinner conversation as she accepted the plate of vegetables from Joan. "Girls, your father invited Dr. Hines to be our guest pastor this Sunday."

Joan assumed an expression of interest. "What topic will you speak on?"

"Duty." Wendell offered Joan the basket of her mother's home-baked rolls. They were still warm. "Your duty to your community, your family, and God."

"And what do you see as our duty?" Joan selected a roll, then passed the basket to her mother.

The reverend shrugged. "Actually, the question is what do *you* see as your duty?"

Joan frowned. "What do you mean?"

"What are your talents? How are you using them? *Are* you using them? God has given us our talents for a reason, and it's our duty to use them, wouldn't you agree?"

He'd piqued her interest. "Yes, I would."

The young pastor pushed his glasses back into place. "That's as far as I've gotten. I don't usually write my sermons until the night before. Procrastination is one of my many failings."

His self-deprecating smile charmed her and brightened his boyish features.

Joan returned his smile. "Talk about deadline pressure. Daddy starts making notes the week before. But everyone's different."

Wendell's warm brown gaze bounced from Joan to the friends and family members gathered around the table—her father, Silas, Christine, Margaret, her mother, and Timothy.

"I do have some notes." Wendell spoke faster as his enthusiasm built. "For example, the gifts you bring to your family. How do they compare to the gifts you bring to your church, your workplace, and your friendships? Are you being true to yourself and sharing your gifts, or are you hiding your gifts in a misguided attempt to please the people around you at that moment in time?"

Joan blinked. He was reading her mind. How could he know her so well? "That's fascinating."

"How long have you been preaching, Dr. Hines?" Christine passed the basket of rolls to Margaret.

Joan looked at Christine. Her sister sat between Silas and Margaret. Her expression was as dazed as Joan felt. Were Wendell's words resonating with her as well?

The pastor's shy smile reappeared. "Please call me Wendell. I haven't been preaching long. Only three years. But I always knew I wanted to be a pastor. I'm honored by the opportunity to deliver a sermon at your family's church."

Joan felt herself being watched. She turned and caught the quiet look of approval Caroline gave her before her mother engaged Margaret in a side conversation.

Christine gave Joan an encouraging look, which said, "Maybe this one's not so bad."

Joan poked at the steamed vegetable medley. No, this one wasn't so bad. And he was her parents' choice.

"Joan." Her mother's voice interrupted her musings. "Help me bring out the dessert, will you?"

Inwardly Joan groaned. Christine and Margaret gave her sympathetic looks as she rose to follow Caroline to the kitchen for her mother's interrogation.

Joan paused beside the kitchen counter and watched Caroline lift the cover from the peach cobbler. The cobbler's warm, fragrant scent mocked her lack of appetite.

Caroline cut modest slices of the dessert. "There's ice cream in the freezer."

Joan brought the vanilla ice cream back to her mother, then lifted bowls from a cupboard.

Caroline added a slice of cobbler to each bowl. "What do you think of Wendell?"

"He seems nice. Friendly, well spoken, and smart." *You and Daddy will be very happy with him.*

Joan crowned each slice of cobbler with ice cream. The silence went on a beat too long. She tightened her lips to keep from filling the void with pointless chatter.

Caroline pinned her with a chiding gaze. "Is that it?"

She squared her shoulders and tried to assert herself. "I appreciate that you and Daddy are trying to help me, Mom. Wendell seems like a very nice man, but I don't think he's the one for me."

"Then who is the one for you?"

She closed her eyes, hoping to banish Ronald's image. But his presence was so strong. Joan felt as though he stood beside her. "I'll know when I meet him."

Skepticism tightened her mother's lips. "How?"

"I don't know. But shouldn't I feel something special?" *Like when I met Ronald?*

Shaking her head, Caroline put the empty baking pan in the sink. "Life isn't a fairy tale. You're not one of the princesses on your Disney watch."

"Didn't you feel something special when you met Daddy?"

Her mother pulled down two trays from a cupboard above the refrigerator. "My father picked your father for me. The love came later."

Why hadn't she known that? "You and Daddy were lucky."

"No, not lucky. My father knew what was best for me." Caroline transferred the dessert bowls to the trays.

"I'm happy. Isn't that the most important thing?"

"I'm glad you're happy, but it's time to get serious." Caroline lifted one tray from the counter. "Give Wendell a chance."

"Mom, I don't—"

Caroline straightened to give Joan a firm stare. "Your father likes him. Give him a chance."

"Yes, ma'am." Joan cursed her lack of spine and lifted the second tray.

This was how they were getting Christine to the altar. If she weren't careful, she'd be marching down the aisle right beside her sister, the other dutiful daughter.

Ronald rose from Joan's front steps and watched her pull her Toyota Tercel into her apartment complex's driveway.

She stopped and lowered her passenger-side window as he approached her car. "Why are you sitting on my steps?"

Ronald leaned down to meet her gaze. Her car's air-conditioning cooled his face and neck. "I wanted to see you."

Joan's features were in shadow. Still, there was enough daylight to see fatigue and frustration in her eyes. Apparently, she'd had a bad evening.

She pressed the control to release the car locks. "Get in."

Ronald folded his body into her Tercel to ride the short distance up the driveway to the complex's parking lot.

After securing her car, she let him into her apartment. "Would you like some lemonade?"

Her subdued tone worried him. What had happened? Would she tell him? Did he matter enough? He followed her to her kitchen. "Lemonade would be great. Thanks."

Joan plucked glasses from her cupboard and filled them with the refreshment. Ronald took his drink and joined her at the kitchen table.

She sipped her lemonade. "How was your evening?"

No more small talk. "What's bothering you?"

Joan stared at her glass and the clouded liquid

within it. "My parents want me to marry an associate pastor from another church."

Ronald fought the urge to yell no. When did he get so possessive toward her? They hadn't even known each other a week. But did anyone know him better? "Have you met him?"

"My parents invited him for dinner tonight."

He pictured the pastor sitting in the same chair he'd had when he'd joined the Browns for their family dinner. He'd sat beside Joan, his arm brushing against hers as they ate. "What do you think of him?"

"He's very nice, intelligent, charming. But I'm not attracted to him."

Yes. Relief made him weak. "Then tell your parents no. I don't see the problem."

"My parents have already decided this is the man who'll take over for my father when he retires. I can tell. And, if he marries me, the church my grandfather founded will stay in the family."

His mood soured again. "This is the twenty-first century. No one in this country arranges marriages anymore."

"Apparently, my family does."

"You're going along with this?"

"No." Joan stood, crossing to the refrigerator. "I don't know."

"Assert yourself. Tell them to stop trying to control you. And, while you're at it, tell them you write erotic romance."

Joan tossed him an amused look from over her shoulder. "Assert myself? That's kind of funny coming from you."

"Why?"

She carried the pitcher of lemonade to the table and topped off both of their glasses. "Ron, I love your

Morris Jones series. But your hero's girlfriend, Tanya Smith, is spineless."

Ronald worked to process the compliment within her complaint. "You've read my books?"

"Every one of them. You already know this, but you're a great writer."

Her pronouncement—delivered with a brilliant smile—meant more than making the best-seller lists or having a television production company pick up his series. But what had she said about his hero's girlfriend? "Morris's girlfriend isn't spineless."

"She's a doormat. How can you criticize me when your heroine—your ideal woman—is a spineless ninny?"

Ronald took offense on his female protagonist's behalf. "Tanya is smart, supportive, and strong."

"But she can't make a move without checking with Morris. I understand that Morris needs to feel needed, but women want to be independent. She sets us back eighty years."

He stared at Joan in disbelief. She couldn't be right. But that sickly feeling coming over him suggested she was. What did that say about him? "There's a difference between having others protect you and standing on the sidelines while your parents arrange your marriage."

Joan inclined her head, which Ronald took as an indication of agreement. "So Tanya's role is to be protected?"

He sensed a trap. "Yes."

"Women bring so much more to a relationship than as an object of adoration. We want more control."

"Like your heroine. She's the captain of a space station. That's a very powerful role."

"Exactly."

"And her lover is a faceless hologram. What does that say about the role of men in your books?"

Joan paused, the glass against her lips. Her eyes widened, and a blush warmed her golden skin. "Good point." She chuckled. "I wonder what our books say about the way we each view the opposite sex?"

"I'm more interested in what you're going to do about the prospective husband your parents have chosen for you."

"So am I."

Chapter 8

The doorbell broke his concentration. Although, even if someone held a gun to his head, Ronald wasn't sure he'd be able to say where he wanted to go with this scene. He saved the document before crossing to the front door.

His mind was still on the scene he was writing, but habit made him check the peephole. He was glad he did.

His mother, father, and Harold waited on the other side of the door, in the apartment's courtyard. *Unbelievable.* It was hard to get their attention when he was home in New York. Now that he'd come to Ohio for distance and answers, they'd found the time and means to bridge the gap. What was it? A ten-hour drive from Brooklyn to Columbus? But they rarely made the thirty-minute drive from their house to his Brooklyn apartment.

It was almost too tempting to return to his manuscript. But that seemed cowardly, and he could still hear Jeffrey's sarcasm the last time he insisted he wasn't running from his family.

Ronald unlocked the door and pulled it open, but

he didn't step aside. He nodded to his parents and ignored his younger brother altogether.

George Montgomery stood straight and stiff in his gray short-sleeved shirt and dark blue khaki pants. A blue blazer hung over his forearm. The resignation in his expression told Ronald his father was only there to support his mother.

Ronald looked into his mother's soft, round face, framed by a conservative flip. "What are you doing here?"

Hope dimmed in Darlene Montgomery's smile. "We're here to see you."

"What couldn't wait until I got home?"

Darlene smoothed her slender, cream and brown striped cotton dress. She looked small and vulnerable standing between his father and Harold. Ronald cursed himself for hurting her and cursed himself for caring.

She sent an uncertain look toward her husband before facing him again. "Well, Ronnie, we didn't know when you'd be coming home."

George wrapped an arm around his wife's trim waist. "Let us in."

Ronald wanted to refuse the command. But his father's tone recalled unpleasant childhood memories. He stepped aside.

His mother's cheer restored, she led the other two men into Ronald's living room. His father gave him a firm but empathetic look as he walked past. Harold tried to catch his gaze. Ronald congratulated himself on not closing the door in his brother's face.

Darlene looked around. "This is nice. Do you have to pay rent?"

With careless steps to mask his tension, Ronald moved closer to his family. "It's part of the compensation package."

He took his mother's arm, feeling the tension her casual conversation attempted to mask. She sent him a searching look. She was trying to judge his mood and the best way to approach him. Ronald didn't want to be approached. He wanted to be left alone.

He escorted his mother to the sofa. His father sat beside her. Ronald sat in one armchair. His brother took the chair opposite him, closest to the door.

Darlene crossed her ankles and settled her purse on her lap. She split her attention between her two sons. "Well, I think it's time you boys put your differences aside. I don't like the way this whole incident is tearing our family apart."

If he hadn't been sitting, Ronald would have fallen. He glanced toward the door. He wouldn't show his parents out, but Harold was a different case. The image of throwing his brother out was extremely satisfying.

The silence stretched. George scowled. "Answer your mother."

Ronald felt like a child again. "What do you want me to say?"

Harold finally spoke. "I don't know what *they* want you to say, but *I* want you to say that you forgive me."

Ronald looked at his brother for the first time in almost four months—and found a stranger. "Forgive you for lying to me? For breaking my trust? Well, that's not asking too much."

Darlene stretched a pleading arm toward him. "Ronnie, he's your brother."

George took her hand and tucked it between them. "Darling, let them talk."

Harold sat taller in the chair. "I didn't mean to fall in love with Yasmine. It just kind of happened."

Anger stirred in Ronald's veins, eating at his

self-restraint. "Then why did you leave her a month after we broke up?"

"I couldn't stay with her. I felt too guilty after hurting you."

His heart was beating too fast. His vision was turning red. Ronald took a couple of deep breaths and hoped his head didn't explode. "Guilt should have kept you out of her bed, the bed *I* shared with her."

"Ron, you're my brother. I never meant to hurt you. It just happened."

"Those words would mean something if you'd slept with her once, but you repeatedly deceived me."

"I've said I was sorry. What else can I do to get you to forgive me? Just tell me what to do, and I'll do it."

Ronald let his gaze reveal all the anger and disgust he felt toward his brother. "Turn back time."

"You know I can't do that. But I can earn back your trust."

"How would you do that?"

"I can convince Yasmine to go back to you."

Harry's in competition with you, Ron. Jeffrey's words played loud and clear in his mind, confirming his ugliest suspicions and chilling his blood. "Get out."

Harold looked surprised. "What?"

Ronald stood but didn't approach him. He was afraid to touch him, afraid he'd lose control. "Get out."

Harold looked at their mother, silently expecting her help.

Darlene stood, too. "Ronnie, calm down."

"Once he leaves."

How could he make his mother understand the sense of betrayal he felt? This wasn't young Harold destroying a toy he hadn't asked to play with. It wasn't teenage Harold totaling a car he didn't have permission to drive.

George stood beside his wife. "Harold, wait for us by the car. We'll be out soon."

Darlene turned to her husband. "George—"

George gave Darlene a quick hug. "That's enough for today, Darling."

With a sulky expression, Harold left the room. Some of the tension eased from Ronald's muscles.

"Ronnie, you shouldn't be so unforgiving. Harry's trying to make amends. Of course, he can't turn back time, but what do you want him to do?"

Ronald rolled his shoulder. The movement eased the knots there and in his neck. Then he turned to face his mother. "Imagine you'd walked into your bedroom and found Aunt Dorothy—your sister—in your bed, naked, on top of Dad. How would you feel?"

His mother glanced at his father, then hurriedly away. "All I'm saying is that he's your brother."

"She's your sister. How would you feel?" At the scandalized look on his mother's face, Ronald wondered if he'd gone too far. He shouldn't speak to her that way. A few more deep breaths and his temper was back under control. "Never mind."

Ronald was just tired and disgusted. And his family was in town.

Her parents' family room hummed with curiosity. Joan studied their expressions and those of her sisters as they sat watching her. Her mother and father shared the puffy plum love seat. Margaret and Christine sat beside her on the sofa. They'd all just returned from Thursday night choir practice.

As late as it was—going on 9:00 P.M.—her family patiently waited for her announcement. They didn't realize she was about to flip their reality upside down and inside out. Joan was nervous, but her only regret was not having had the courage to face this moment sooner. Then she wouldn't be facing it now.

She stood and dug the paperback from her purse. With quaking knees, she walked away from her sisters and handed her mother a copy of *Pleasure Quest*. Joan stood to the side to divide her attention between her sisters on her right and her parents on her left.

Caroline took the novel. She stared in confusion at the smoky image of a nearly naked couple kissing on the cover. "What is this?"

Here was her last chance to back out. Joan could say she'd found the book and didn't know where it had come from. She could claim to be as shocked as they were.

But Ronald was right. What she was doing was wrong. Why was she denying her identity? If she couldn't be true to herself, how could she be true to anyone else? It was time to own up to those gifts Wendell Hines had talked about during last night's dinner.

A deep breath stretched Joan's shoulders and eased the clutch of fear in her chest. "That's my first published novel. I wrote that."

Margaret and Christine sat straighter, trying to see the book's cover.

Her mother looked as though Joan had told her she was marrying a merman and moving to a castle under the sea. "You wrote a trashy novel?"

And so it begins. "It's not trash, Mom. It's a story about looking for love and female empowerment."

Her father snatched the book from Caroline's hands and shoved the cover toward Joan. "They're naked. This isn't love. It's pornography."

Joan locked her knocking knees and stood her ground.

"Sex is one way to express love. That expression of love gave you three daughters."

Her father's face flamed purple. Joan started to respond, but Caroline interrupted her.

Her mother pointed at the novel in her father's fists. "You didn't write that. The cover says Cleopatra Sinclair. You're not Cleopatra Sinclair."

"Yes, I am, Mom. I write under a pseudonym."

"Why didn't you tell us?"

Joan heard the shock in her older sister's voice. She looked at Margaret. "I thought it was best to keep my writing a secret. I didn't want to cause a problem with Daddy's church."

"So you lied to us." Her father's judgment echoed Ronald's feelings.

"I didn't mean to deceive you, Daddy, but I knew you wouldn't understand."

"You're right. I don't understand why my daughter would choose to write pornography. Your mother and I didn't raise you in a gutter. We raised you in the church."

It was getting harder to hide the pain her family's barbs were causing. "I'm your daughter. You must know I wouldn't write pornography."

Christine's voice was hard. "Until two minutes ago, we didn't know you wrote at all, and I'm with you every day."

Shame and regret heated Joan's cheeks. "I'm sorry for that."

Her younger sister didn't acknowledge Joan's apology. "Who have you told about your writing?"

"When I'm discussing my books, I use my pseudonym. Very few people know me as Joan Brown."

Christine gave her a narrow-eyed stare. "Does Ronald Montgomery know you're Cleopatra Sinclair?"

"Yes."

Christine gestured toward *Pleasure Quest*. "And you don't think the fact that you write about sex is the reason he's with you?"

"No, I don't." The implication hurt—as Christine probably intended it to.

Joan glanced at Margaret's dazed expression. It seemed her older sister didn't have anything to add after her initial question.

Her father redirected the discussion. "How many books have you written?"

"I've had two published. Another one will be released in a few months, and I'm working on a fourth."

Kenneth waved Joan's book again. "Are they all as disgusting as this?"

Joan heard the blood swoosh in her ears. "How can you judge what you haven't read?"

Her father's brows lifted. "What are we supposed to think when we see this cover?"

Christine added to her father's concerns. "Suppose someone from the church finds out what you're doing?"

Joan desperately wanted to sit but was afraid she'd shatter into a million pieces if she even moved. "They won't. That's the reason I use a pseudonym."

Christine waved her hand angrily. "Your pseudonym isn't a guarantee that people won't learn who you really are."

Joan tossed another look at Margaret. She didn't understand why her older sister remained silent, but she was grateful for it. One less verbal minefield to navigate.

Her mother's sigh was long and deep. The sorrow weighed on Joan's heart. "Ever since you were little girls, your father and I have told you to be good examples for our congregation." She nodded toward the copy of Joan's book still gripped in Kenneth's hands.

"By bringing this into our church, you've corrupted everything we've built."

Joan's guilt turned to ashes under her rising temper. "How can a love story corrupt our congregation?"

Impatience snapped in her father's dark eyes. "How can you write about sex and call it love?"

Joan struggled to maintain her control and not lash out in her disappointment. "The two aren't mutually exclusive."

"Sex outside of marriage is a sin."

"Sex as an expression of love between consenting adults should be celebrated, not censured."

Kenneth stood. "If you insist on writing your scandalous stories, keep our family out of it."

Fear paralyzed her. "What are you saying?"

Her father's features were rigid, as though carved from stone. "If we stand with you, the congregation will think we condone pornography."

Joan turned cold and numb with shock. She glanced at her mother, who stared wide-eyed at her father. "I don't write pornography. I write romance."

Kenneth crossed his arms. "There are far more virtuous stories you could write."

Joan stepped forward, her outstretched hand shaking. "Daddy, please don't ask me to change who I am."

"I'm not going to argue with you. Either stop writing those stories or stay away from the family. Those are your choices."

Joan dropped her arm and blinked rapidly. Her tears fell anyway. "Give up my family or give up my writing? Why can't I have both?"

Caroline's eyes were bright with concern. "Asking you to give up your writing may seem unfair now, Joan. But in the end, you'll thank us."

Joan scrubbed away her tears. She looked at her

sisters, who seemed to be holding their breaths. Their wide-eyed expressions reflected shock. Margaret stood but remained silent.

She thought of all the years she'd spent polishing her writing and studying the publishing industry. The roller-coaster ride of manuscript requests and rejections. The day she received her editor's phone call offering a contract. The culmination of years of daydreams and hard work.

The lump in her throat burned like a vise. Her voice was husky as she forced the words out. "I can't, Mom. I just can't give up my writing. But I'm sorrier than I can say that you don't approve."

Her father's expression tightened. "Then you've made your choice. If you change your mind, we'll be happy to welcome you back."

Joan couldn't think of anything else to say that would persuade her father to give her and her writing a chance. She stared at him, willing him to change his mind. He didn't seem open to further discussion. She looked at her mother, whose eyes were red and wet. In Joan's gaze, her sisters were blurry images.

Her tears fell faster as she faced her father. "Whether you ever let me through your doors again, I'll always be a part of this family. I won't let you turn your back on me."

Joan secured her purse on her shoulder, crushing its strap in her fist, and left.

Chapter 9

The lump in her throat cut off her oxygen. Her heart hurt like it would explode out of her chest and splatter against the windshield of her twelve-year-old Toyota.

Joan turned her car's cassette player to near deafening levels and cranked up the bass. The music helped shut out the pain. Gloria Gaynor insisted she'd survive, but how could Joan survive this pain?

Her parents didn't want her or her sisters to be independent women. Her mother and father wanted them to remain children, doing exactly as they were told. The Stepford Daughters.

It was coming up on 9:30 P.M. She'd lost the early summer daylight and could barely see through her tears. Joan clutched the steering wheel and drove her orange subcompact carefully down High Street.

She made an impulse turn into a grocery store parking lot midway between her apartment and her family's house. Joan turned on her car's interior lights and found several fast-food restaurant napkins scrunched toward the bottom of her glove compartment. She scrubbed her cheeks, dried her eyes, and blew her nose. Unfortunately, she still looked as though she'd been bawling for hours. Her cheeks were pale, her nose was red, and her eyes were swollen and puffy. *Oh, for heaven's sake.* She tugged on her purse, crawled out of her car, and entered the store.

Twenty minutes later, Joan returned to her car, carrying her guilt, misery, and a box of fat-free, sugar-high double chocolate cookies. Sitting in the now dark parking lot, she ripped open the box but couldn't bring herself to eat. The lump in her throat made it hard to breathe, much less swallow. And it was growing and starting to burn.

Joan dropped her head into her hands, bent into her steering wheel, and released the misery from the bottom of her soul. Her parents said she'd brought shame on the family. They never wanted to see her again. Even her sisters had turned against her.

She should never have told them about her writing. Who needed this kind of condemnation and scorn, especially from family? Who wanted their parents to so completely reject them?

Joan knuckled tears from her eyes and cheeks and struggled for composure. It wasn't a good idea to fall apart in a public parking lot. She'd rather finish this at home. She started her car and checked her rearview mirror.

Why had she ever thought this would be a good idea? Her gasp became a hiccup. Because Ronald had told her she shouldn't keep secrets from her family. Joan sat, glaring blindly through her windshield. This had been Ronald's bright idea. And now he had to make it right.

Steadier now that she had a plan, Joan put her car in gear and headed for Ronald's apartment. She wasn't going through this pain, guilt—and, yes, anger—alone.

The summons of his doorbell was angry, insistent, and annoying. The liquid crystal display clock on the cable box read 10:10. Ronald didn't know anyone in Columbus who would lean on his doorbell like that, especially not this late at night. He was tempted to ignore the interruption, but he really wanted the noise to stop.

He laid the newsmagazine facedown on the coffee table and swung his bare feet over the side of the sofa on which he'd stretched out. He strode to the door and checked the peephole. Surprise washed away his irritation when he saw Joan standing on the other side, revealed in the courtyard lights.

He opened the door and stepped aside to let her in. Joan's anger hit him like a furnace blast, but the despair in her eyes stopped him cold.

"I told my parents about my books. They disowned me." Her voice broke on her final words, and her face twisted in pain.

Her misery made Ronald desperate. He shoved the door closed and wrapped his arms around her. His palms stroked over her slender figure, trying to soothe her pain. Joan's sobs were terrifying in their silence. Each tremor that racked her body ripped his heart. Ronald drew her even closer, offering his body as a sanctuary from anything and anyone who'd harm her. He would give all of himself and more, if she wanted him to.

Ronald lost track of time but didn't care. Her fragrance drifted over him, powder soft and feminine, clouding his thoughts. Joan's warm skin and firm body brought to the surface a dizzying memory of tender caresses and fierce satisfaction. She turned her face into his neck, her breath hot against him. Ronald's muscles tightened in response.

Joan pulled away. Had he held her too tightly? Ronald gave her the distance, feeling a part of himself tearing away with her. Her head bowed, Joan reached into her purse and pulled out a tissue. She dabbed her eyes and blew her nose.

Ronald watched her walk to his kitchen. "Do you want to talk about it?"

Joan dumped the tissue in the trash can beside his sink. "No."

Ronald tracked her movements as she walked past him—and into his bedroom. He followed.

Joan tossed her purse onto his nightstand. She closed the distance between them and rested her palm against his chest. "I don't want to fight this anymore just to be the daughter my parents want. I realized tonight, I can't ever be that perfect person. I can only be me."

Ronald covered her hand with his own. "Who wants perfection?"

Joan gave him a weak smile. He stopped worrying about her and let himself want her even more. Her strength when she challenged his opinions. Her vulnerability when she came to him for comfort. Her fire when she shared herself with him. Ronald wanted all of her.

She rose up on her toes and pressed her lips to his. When she sighed, he opened his mouth and let her in. Slow and gentle. Soft and sweet. He molded her body against him and lost himself in the feel of her. The taste of her.

Her tongue stroked against the roof of his mouth,

then withdrew. Wanting more, he followed, sucking it back. Joan pressed against him, moaning her pleasure. Ronald captured her tongue so he could hear that sound again.

Her fingernails pierced his cotton T-shirt and dug into his shoulders. Ronald's body shook, responding to her abandon. He pulled his mouth away from hers and buried his face in her hair. He breathed deeply, trying to regain his control. It had been so long since he'd touched her this way, held her this way. He didn't want to come after her like the cold and hungry man he was.

"You won't hurt me." Her voice was soft.

"What?" Had he spoken out loud?

Joan leaned back to see him. Her cheeks were flushed; her eyes bright; lips swollen. "You didn't hurt me our first time. What makes you think you'll hurt me now?"

Ronald relaxed, letting his desire for this woman lead him, instead of allowing past insecurities to control him.

He unhooked the clip holding her hair at the nape of her neck and ran his fingers through the thick black tresses until they flowed over her shoulders like silk on satin.

She pulled his dark green T-shirt from the waistband of his shorts and pushed her hands up his torso. Ronald's stomach muscles trembled.

He removed her tank top. In her flesh-toned bra, she looked like a Victoria's Secret advertisement. He held her gaze as he reached behind her to unclasp the lingerie and free her breasts. They were full, firm, and round. Perfect.

With his help, Joan stripped off his T-shirt, then

pressed herself against him. The feel of her soft, warm skin rubbing against his torso made his body burn.

Joan felt Ronald's rising erection against her stomach. Her pulse quickened in anticipation. With one hand, she traced his spine down his smooth, hard back. Her other hand unfastened his shorts before she drew them down, along with his underwear.

Because of her upbringing, Joan had denied herself this freedom. Instead, she'd expressed her desires in her books. But now she'd met a man who made her want to experience those fantasies personally.

Dropping to her knees in front of him, Joan braced her hands on Ronald's muscular thighs. He had long, straight legs. Powerful legs. She remembered the way they felt entangled with her own. Her body moistened.

Joan reached up and stroked Ronald's thickening member. He was hot and silky smooth moving against her palm. He moaned, and his pleasure emboldened her. Joan braced both hands on his hard thighs and leaned closer to draw him deep into her mouth. The muscles in his legs shook. Joan pulled back, then moved forward again and again, stroking him with her tongue. His harsh breaths praised her.

"Wait." Ronald grasped her arms with unsteady hands to help her up.

In the blink of an eye, he removed her shorts, and Joan kicked off her sandals. Ronald laid her on the side of the bed, her feet flat on the old carpeting. He knelt in front of her, spread her knees, and moved in. His naked torso pressed against her heat. Excitement made her heart beat faster. Joan clenched her knees against his sides.

Ronald reached out and curved his hands around her breasts. His large, rough palms smoothed one and kneaded the other. He pulled at one nipple, rolling it between his thumb and forefinger. Moisture pooled inside her as her excitement built.

Ronald's fingertips scored a path down her abdomen. Her stomach muscles quivered at his touch. He paused at her navel. One finger trailed inside, exploring the dip with feather touches. His head lowered to her body to plant wet kisses in her belly button. His breath against the damp made her squirm even more.

Then his hand moved on, lower, to brush her nest of curls. His fingers played tauntingly in her hair. So close to where she needed him. Just an inch away. Joan lifted her hips, trying to close that distance. She ground her teeth as he pressed the heel of his palm to her.

Joan whimpered.

Ronald touched more wet kisses to her navel. "What do you want?" He breathed the words against the moisture. She writhed against his palm.

"You inside of me." Her voice was weak and breathless.

"Like this?" He slipped first one, then a second finger inside her.

Joan's eyelids dropped, and her hips sprang from the mattress. Her moisture flowed.

"Open your eyes and look at me, sweetheart." Ronald continued to slide his fingers in and out of her while his other hand played with one nipple, then the other.

He was magic, casting a spell over her with his rhythm. Joan's hips moved as he wanted her to move, following where the pleasure led her. These were the feelings she'd fantasized about and written about in her books. Now her fantasy lover had come to life to fulfill her very real desires.

Joan raised her arms and pressed her fingertips into Ronald's taut shoulders. "Come inside of me."

He drew his right fingertips down her torso even as

he continued to move his other hand. "Is that what you want?" He lowered his head and stroked in and around her navel with his tongue.

Joan panted at the intensity of his caresses inside and outside her body. She squeezed her eyes shut as the sweet pressure built. "Yes. Now."

Joan gasped as Ronald withdrew his fingers.

He looked at her with raw desire. "This won't take long, sweetheart."

He reached inside his nightstand and removed an unopened box of condoms. He pulled one from its package. She helped him roll it onto his erection, now even more eager to feel him inside her.

Ronald wrapped his right arm around her waist, half lifting her from the bed. Her head dropped back as his mouth closed around her breast, hot and wet. His lips suckled her nipple. His tongue twirled its peak.

It was too much.

Joan moaned low and long as her orgasm broke over her. Ronald covered her lips with his and kissed her deeply. He held her tighter as her body shook, and Joan screamed her pleasure into his mouth.

She screamed again as he entered her with a strong, deep thrust.

Ronald felt hard as a pipe. He left Joan's lips and clenched his teeth as he pushed himself all the way inside her. She was soft and tight, wet and hot, burning him inside and out.

He'd ached to be with her again. That first night they'd spent together, he'd felt more than a physical release. She'd reached a part of him that had been cold and alone. And now she was touching him there again. He was no longer cold, and he wasn't alone.

His eyes locked with hers, Ronald moved with Joan farther onto the mattress. He began to move again, working his hips against her, pressing and stroking her spot. He could feel her fire building, ready to consume him.

With each thrust, her breasts trembled, caressing his chest with a light touch. Joan arched, pressing her head against the pillow and bringing her breasts closer to his lips. Ronald bent his head to suckle them, first one and then the other. They pebbled quickly, straining up to him. He kissed them, and Joan twisted beneath him. Her inner muscles pulled at him. Clenched and released him, holding him tight, letting him go, then gripping him again.

Ronald moved deeper. Joan wrapped her arms and legs around him, drawing him into her. He moved faster. He kissed her, sliding his tongue into her mouth the way he worked his body into hers. He pressed into her, and she rose to meet him, her lips moist and parted.

Joan kissed him again, running her hands over his shoulders, down his back, to his hips. Her fingertips drilled into his glutes, pressing him even deeper into her. Ronald tightened his hold on her. Her body stiffened, and he covered her mouth with his. She screamed, and he felt her orgasm rush through her, pulling him along. He tensed on top of her. His hips thrust deep once, twice, and then again. He relaxed above her, joined, sated, and warmed.

"I came here to give you a piece of my mind and ended up giving you something else entirely." Joan lay under the covers, spooned into Ronald. She loved the feel of his warm, hairy chest against her bare back.

"What saved me?" He sounded sleepy. Come to think of it, she was tired, too. Pleasantly so.

"When you held me, I didn't feel rejected or alone anymore."

He shifted and kissed the nape of her neck. "What happened?"

She heard concern in his voice. But knowing he was tired, she gave him only the highlights. She'd rather not relive the experience, anyway. He listened without interrupting.

"Afterward, I decided to come here. I wanted someone else to blame. Initially, I chose you because you pushed me to tell them the truth."

Ronald stroked her arm under the covers. "It's natural to want to blame someone else."

"Yes, but I would have been wrong to blame you. I did the right thing by telling them the truth. I feel freer now that I don't have this big secret hanging over me. But I won't feel completely free until my family accepts me and my writing."

"Your family loves you. I can see that. Right now they're surprised, but with time, they'll come around."

Recalling the scene in her parents' family room, Joan felt less confident. "I hope so. I hate being at odds with them. Thank goodness this doesn't happen often."

"Of course it doesn't. You and your sisters usually agree with everything your father says."

Joan wanted to pout, but Ronald was right. "I wonder how long they're going to stay angry."

Ronald stroked her arm again. The gesture soothed her. "They may surprise you."

Joan snorted. "Perhaps you haven't noticed, but my family doesn't like surprises."

Friday morning Ronald surfaced from sleep to the sound of someone ringing his doorbell. It was déjà vu all over again. But instead of an angry, insistent summons, this was a hesitant interruption.

Beside him, Joan pulled one naked arm out from under the covers to swat at the air. He grinned. She was probably trying to turn off her alarm, not realizing, first, that the alarm clock was on the nightstand beside *him* and, second, she wasn't in her own bed.

Ronald leaned in to kiss her hair. "Go back to sleep."

Joan sighed and brought her arm back under the covers. *Ah, the power of suggestion.*

His doorbell rang again. Ronald eased free of the covers and pulled on the shorts and jersey he'd discarded last night. He strode down the narrow hallway, through his living room, to the door. He ducked his head and peered through the peephole.

Damn. His mother stared intently back at him. His father scowled at his watch.

Ronald unlocked his door and pulled it open. "Good morning, Mom, Dad."

His mother frowned at him as she led his father across the threshold. "What took you so long to answer the door?"

"It's not quite six thirty. I was sleeping. My class isn't until later this morning." Ronald gestured for his parents to make themselves comfortable in his living room.

Darlene sat on the sofa, looking from Ronald's creased jersey to his wrinkled shorts. "Oh, I'm sorry. We thought you'd be up."

His father sat beside her. "No, *we* didn't."

Ronald strained to hear any sound from Joan that signaled she was waking. "It's okay. What's the matter?"

"We're going to have breakfast as a family." Darlene made the announcement as though this was something he'd enjoy.

Ronald raised his eyebrows. "Harry's awake?"

"Your mother called him when we got up."

Ronald took a calming breath. "I'm sorry, but I have other—"

His father stood, then reached for his mother's hand to help her from the sofa. "We'll meet you at the car in twenty minutes. There's a restaurant that serves breakfast two blocks from here. I'm hungry."

Ronald stood, speaking firmly. "I have other plans."

Darlene pulled her husband to a stop halfway to the front door. "But we're all here. We might as well have breakfast together."

Ronald looked down into his mother's eyes and spoke as gently as he could. "I came to Columbus to get away from the family."

George shoved his hands into the front pockets of his brown denim shorts. "I thought you were here for a woman."

Ronald frowned. "What made you think that?"

His father shrugged. "That's what Harry told us."

Ronald folded his arms across his chest, trying to ward off another disappointment. "And you believed him?" He looked at Darlene. "I told you I was teaching a class."

Darlene spread her arms. "I thought you were just saying that. Why would you come to Ohio to teach when there are so many good schools in New York?"

So his parents thought *he* was lying and *Harold* was telling the truth. After years of Harold's antics, that was hard to take.

Ronald opened his front door. "I have to get ready for work."

Darlene pouted. "You can't take a break from your class to have a meal with us?"

"I'm sorry, Mom. I can't." Ronald's tone was cool. He couldn't help it and didn't care. His anger was justified.

There was real regret on Darlene's face. Ronald almost gave in to the urge to please his mother. But if he continued to pander to his parents, they'd continue to take him for granted. He couldn't accept that any longer.

George broke the silence with quiet authority. "Ron, your mother wants the family to have breakfast together."

Ronald met his father's glare with calm resistance. "I'm sorry, Dad. Maybe I'll see you both later."

He wished his parents a good day as they walked out. Remembering Joan asleep in his bed down the hall, he softly closed and locked the door.

Ronald heaved a sigh and massaged his forehead. He wanted to see Joan. He needed to see her. With just a look or a touch, she made him feel like he mattered. When he was with her, he wasn't the invisible man.

Ronald rounded the bed to sit beside her. He reached down to rub her shoulder until she woke.

Joan gave a sleepy groan and slowly rolled over. She smiled at him, soft and dreamy, as she touched her palm to the side of his face. Then she shot up in the bed, causing Ronald to rear back out of harm's way. Zero to sixty in 9.2 seconds.

She looked wildly around the room. "What time is it?"

Ronald glanced at the alarm clock sitting on the opposite nightstand. "It's almost ten to seven."

"Oh no. I've got to open the store." She shot across the mattress, grabbing her clothes as she raced naked toward the bathroom.

So much for waking her gently. "Your store doesn't open until nine."

Joan's voice carried from behind the locked bathroom door. "There are things I have to do before opening the store. I hadn't meant to spend the night."

Ronald moved closer to the bathroom and waited for the water to stop running before he responded. "I'm glad you did."

Her voice warmed. "So am I. But now I'm completely disoriented. I've usually finished my morning run by now."

"You jog?"

Joan came out of the bathroom and gave him a smile. "Six mornings a week."

"So do I. Maybe we can go for a run together sometime."

"I'd like that." She slipped past him and looked around for her shoes. "And now that my parents think I'm a woman of loose morals, it won't matter that you're not a member of our church."

"See, some good has come from your telling them the truth." Ronald dropped to his knees and rescued her sandals from under his bed. He held them out to her. "We don't have to hide our relationship anymore."

Joan took her sandals from him. "My prince."

Ronald stood, smiling briefly at her reference to Cinderella. "Let's not get carried away."

She sat on the edge of the bed and looked up at him. "But you are a prince. You woke me up and made me realize I had to tell my family the truth. It wasn't easy, but you were right."

She made him feel valued. She made him feel a part of something, a part of her life. Ronald leaned down and kissed her lips. "And your family will get over being upset soon."

Joan gave him a quizzical look. "I hope you're right, but I don't think it will be that easy." She slid on her sandals. "Now it's my turn to ask. What's wrong?"

Ronald sat beside her on the bed and stared at the carpeting. "My parents are here."

"In Columbus? When did they get in?"

"Yesterday. And they brought my brother."

Her eyes were wide with amazement. "How did the reunion go?"

Ronald shrugged. It didn't ease his restlessness. He stood to pace. "Not great. My mother wants me to forgive Harry so we can go back to being one big, fake happy family. She wanted to start with breakfast this morning."

"Can you try to forgive him? For your mother's sake?"

Ronald turned to face her, frustration making him tense. "No, not even for my mother. I'm not going to pretend nothing happened."

"Forgiving Harry doesn't mean you forget what he did."

He resumed his pacing. "What about me?"

"What about you, Ron?"

"Sorry isn't cutting it anymore."

"Then what do you want? What do you need?"

Her quiet questions stopped him. "I want my parents to realize they can't keep saving Harry. For God's sake, he's thirty years old. He has to accept responsibility for himself."

"What else?"

The words didn't come easily for him. "I want my parents to realize they have two sons."

He sensed her coming toward him before he felt her hands on his shoulders, her cheek against his back. "Then that's where you start."

Ronald snorted. "That should be great breakfast conversation."

He felt her smile. "Maybe you can save that for coffee."

Ronald turned and kissed her lingeringly. "As long as we can meet for dessert."

Chapter 10

"What else don't we know about you?" Christine crossed the threshold of The Artist's Haven as she hurled the words at Joan.

Joan laid her hands flat beside the cash register. She hoped she was the picture of calm on the outside because inside, she shook like Jell-O. "That was my only secret. I'm sorry I upset you."

Christine strode to the checkout counter, her tan sandals clapping against the gray tile. In her calf-length, pleated pastel peach skirt and white cotton blouse buttoned to her throat, she looked twelve years old. "If you really cared about us, you wouldn't have written those books."

Joan held her temper in the face of her fire-breathing younger sister. "That's what you said last night. I still disagree."

"I don't care what you think." Christine even sounded twelve years old.

"I can see that." Joan flicked her gaze toward the store's entrance. Hopefully, they wouldn't get any customers until they were past this argument.

"I'm the one who had to listen to Mom and Daddy

fret about your books all night and worry about what the congregation will think when they find out about them."

"*If* they find out."

"Be honest with me for a change." Christine flipped her raven hair behind her shoulder. Tortoiseshell hair clips kept most of the thick tresses off her face. "Did you want me to tell Mom and Daddy I don't want to marry Silas just to distract them from your writing?"

Joan frowned at her younger sister, her business partner, her friend since birth. Her heart hurt knowing there was more than this checkout counter between them. "No. I wanted you to tell them you don't want to marry Silas because you *don't* want to marry him."

Christine set her hands on her slender hips. "What makes you think that?"

"Because no one in her right mind would want to marry him. He's selfish, self-centered, and untrustworthy."

"That description sounds a lot like you."

Joan flinched. Bitter satisfaction hardened Christine's gaze.

She struggled to keep her voice steady. "I'm your sister, and I love you. I don't want you making a mistake you'll spend the rest of your life paying for."

The ice in Christine's eyes melted, leaving behind uncertainty. "Silas is a good man. I won't regret spending the rest of my life with him. Can you say the same about having your name on those books?"

Christine needled her the same way she'd tried to get under her skin when they were children. Joan reminded herself she wasn't a kid anymore. "I'm proud of my work."

"And I'll be proud to be Mrs. Silas Tooner."

"Who are you trying to convince, Chrissie? Me or you?"

Her sister blinked in surprise.

The bell above the entrance chimed. Joan smiled at

the young men who entered their store. With her welcoming expression firmly in place, she waited until their two customers disappeared down a product aisle.

Turning back to Christine, Joan noted the fear and frustration in her sister's eyes. "Will he make you happy?"

"With Silas's connections, we'll bring even more prestige to our church. The more prestige we have, the more members we'll attract."

"So you're marrying Silas to bring more members to our church? How very philanthropic of you."

Christine's eyes widened with alarm. "What's happened to you? You've never spoken like this before."

Joan scrubbed her hands against her face. Her temper was on the rise. "How do you want me to speak? You just told me you're marrying some loser to help build our congregation."

"Stop twisting my words."

"I'm not twisting your words. You really do sound that crazy."

Christine brushed away tears. "Why are you being so mean?"

Her sister's misery drained Joan's anger. "Just tell me if you truly believe he'll make you happy."

Christine stood mute. Defiance and uncertainty warred in her brown eyes. She scowled at Joan before spinning on her heels and striding away.

Joan had her answer.

"How much longer are you staying?"

Ronald raised his eyes at his mother's question and lowered his coffee mug to the table. "As I said before, the quarter is over in September. I'll be here at least until then."

It hadn't taken Ronald long to find his family. There

was only one restaurant within a two-block radius of his apartment that served a breakfast his father would consider acceptable.

His gaze ventured around the interior, taking in the checkered tablecloths, the cherrywood chairs, and the other Friday morning diners. He looked at everything except his brother's face, directly across the table.

Beside Harold, Darlene spread more orange marmalade on her wheat toast. "We're leaving tomorrow. Your father and I have to get back to work Monday, and it's a long drive."

"Harry doesn't work. He can drive while you and Dad rest."

To Ronald's left, George dug into his eggs and hash browns as though he hadn't had a real meal since leaving New York. If only he could also tune out the tension around them and enjoy his pancakes. Instead, he drank more coffee and let his breakfast grow cold.

Darlene set aside her knife. "We'll split the drive between the three of us. That's easier than making one person drive the whole way."

Even though that person doesn't have any other responsibility. "Whatever you prefer," said Ronald.

He looked up as their server appeared with the coffeepot. The young man topped off Ronald's mug. "Is your meal all right, sir?"

Ronald nodded. "Yes, thanks."

The server looked dubiously at the untouched pancakes. He poured more coffee for George before moving away.

"Why did you choose now to take this teaching position in Ohio?" Darlene sounded hurt. "Don't you think healing the relationship with your family should be your first priority?"

Ronald gripped his mug. "It takes communication

and trust to keep a family together, Mom. We don't have either."

George broke his silence. "This incident's in the past. Let it go."

Ronald watched as his father sipped from his fresh mug of coffee. "The past has a way of repeating itself. And, since we ignore it each time it rears its head, we've never dealt with the problem."

Darlene frowned again. "What problem?"

Ronald looked directly at his brother for the first time since he'd arrived at the restaurant. "Harry's irresponsibility."

Harold remained silent, but his eyes narrowed with hatred. A muscle pulsed in his jaw.

Darlene's eyes widened at Ronald's accusation. "What are you talking about?"

Ronald's words were for his parents, but he kept his eyes on Harold. "He's never kept a job longer than three months. How long are you going to let him bleed you dry?"

Darlene sent an uncertain look toward her husband. When George continued to sip his coffee, she returned her attention to her son. "Ronnie, Harry is doing his best."

"Are you, Harry? Is living off parents who're getting ready to retire the *best* you can do?"

Harold shrugged and swallowed the last of his home fries. His plate clean, he met Ronald's gaze without a hint of shame or remorse. "Things don't come as easily for everyone."

Ronald rocked back in his seat. That was far from the expected response. "What're you talking about?"

Harold's tone was just short of a sneer. "Right out of law school, you're given a job with one of the biggest firms in New York. You decide to write a book, and publishers trip all over themselves for it."

Ronald's laughter was more amazement than amusement. "I've worked hard for everything I've ever had. How hard are you working?"

"I don't have to explain myself to you." Harold propped his elbows on the table and leaned forward. "But I'm curious. You think our folks aren't giving you enough attention. Does the great Ronald Montgomery need more praise?"

Anger heated Ronald's skin. He stood and collected the bill. "I'll pay for the meal." He looked at Harold. "Do you have money for a tip?"

Ronald walked away, ignoring his mother's plea to come back.

"Your mother's pretty upset." Four hours later, his father stood on the threshold of Ronald's campus office.

He looked up, not bothering to ask how his father had found him. George Montgomery was a resourceful man. Besides, hunger was making him testy. Ronald glanced at his watch. It was almost half past noon. He should have choked down those pancakes when he'd had the chance, tension or no tension.

That was when he noticed the bags cradled in his father's arms. They were from a neighborhood deli, one Joan had taken him to last week. "Is that for me?"

"It's for us, if you'll let me in."

Ronald had had enough of his family to last him the rest of the summer. But since he hadn't eaten breakfast, he was starving. He stood and gestured his father into his office.

George walked to the small conversation table in a

corner of the room. "Your mother always gets upset when someone criticizes Harry." He ripped open the bags and set out the sandwiches and sodas.

"Who else criticizes Harry?"

"I do."

Ronald pulled out one of the two chairs at the table before he fell down. "I've never heard you complain about him."

His father sat. "And Harry's never heard me complain about you."

"Fair enough." Ronald opened his sandwich and plucked out the onions. You'd think after thirty-two years, his father would know he didn't like them. Joan didn't like onions, either. "Why does Mom keep rescuing him?"

"If he were your son, what would you do? Let him live on the streets because he can't pay rent?" George took a bite of his sandwich and washed it down with a swig of raspberry cola.

Though he agreed with his father's point, it didn't lessen Ronald's frustration. "But she's let him get away with a lot over the years."

"I share that blame, but that's in the past. We have to deal with Harry today."

"How are you going to do that?"

"I don't know. But your punishing your mother for trying to help Harry isn't making the situation any easier."

"I'm not punishing Mom. But I'm tired of being the invisible family member."

"The invisible family member?" George looked as though he doubted Ronald's mental stability. "Act your age, Ron. The world doesn't have time to coddle you."

Ronald arched a brow at his father. "Have you given Harry that lecture?"

"You can't keep whining about your brother sleeping with your girlfriend. It's been three months. Let it go."

Ronald gritted his teeth. "I am letting go. You're the ones who followed me."

"What are you doing here?"

"I told you. Teaching."

"Are you sure you didn't come to Columbus because of a woman?"

Ronald spread his arms. "You're sitting in my office."

George shrugged. "Harry said you'd probably met some woman and followed her to Columbus."

Ronald frowned. "This isn't a romance novel. I'm not going to relocate to some town halfway across the country for a woman I don't even know, regardless of what Harry tells you."

His father gave him a skeptical look. "But I'm supposed to accept that you came to Columbus to teach a class?"

Ronald stilled. "The real question is, who are you going to believe? Harry or me?"

"Will your father really stop helping Harry?" Joan sank onto the love seat with Ronald.

They'd just finished dinner at her apartment again. Ronald found it interesting that Joan preferred to cook. Yasmine had always wanted to go out, to see and be seen. It hadn't bothered him at the time. But, looking back, it was as though she'd been dining with everyone at the restaurant except him. Cooking with Joan made a much more relaxing transition from his day.

And now that the meal was over, Joan sat close beside him. He breathed her scent and felt the heat from her right palm soaking into his thigh. Ronald tried not to let that distract him. "If he was going to, he would've done it before."

Joan squeezed his thigh before scooting back against the thick love-seat cushions. "What do you want to happen now?"

She wasn't making idle conversation. She really wanted to know. Her interest in his thoughts and feelings continued to warm him. But they also challenged him. "I don't know."

She bent her right knee onto the cushion to better face him. "You said Harry needs a job."

"At least then my parents wouldn't have to pay for all his bills." He wanted her hand back on his thigh.

"Could you get him a job?"

Talking about his brother always made Ronald restless. He stood to pace. "I've gotten him jobs in the past. He hasn't been able to *keep* them."

"Don't give up on Harry. For your parents' sake. They can't help him alone."

Ronald massaged his forehead. "I know. But it's frustrating that the only way they acknowledge me is through Harry. I want them to see me for who I am rather than as a foil for my brother."

Joan rose from the love seat. She kneaded his shoulders, easing his tension. "It can't be easy when your role in your family isn't what you think it should be."

He turned to face her, and Joan's arms dropped. "Did you speak with your parents today?"

"I'm giving them some time before talking with them again." Joan returned to the love seat, tucking one leg under her. "Chrissie cursed me out, though. And Maggie's still not speaking to me."

"Your older sister's giving you the silent treatment?"

Joan shrugged. "She hasn't returned my calls."

"I'm sorry."

"You don't have anything to be sorry for. I guess we've both rejected the roles our families chose for us. I'm no longer the dutiful daughter. And you're no longer the invisible son."

Ronald joined her on the love seat and twined his fingers with hers. "Don't pretend this is your first rebellion. You've been rebelling against your family's rules for years."

She looked surprised. "What do you mean?"

"You no longer study art, but you opened an art-supply store, and you still draw. You knew they wouldn't want you to write erotic romance, but you did it anyway, under a pseudonym."

Joan frowned. "I've never looked at it that way. I guess I've been giving them what they wanted, but on my terms, all along."

"That was your way of protecting who you are, but still showing them who they want you to be."

Joan's gaze lowered to their joined hands. She was quiet for a long time. Ronald respected her contemplation, sitting silently beside her.

Finally, she looked up, looked at him. "Will you spend the night?"

Ronald blinked away the heated images and focused on Joan. This wasn't a simple invitation. She might be Cleopatra Sinclair, but she was also Joan Brown, a woman who'd spent the last twenty-six years accommodating her parents' every command. If she took this next step, she might never be able to return to her family.

He ignored his growing arousal. "What about your parents?"

Her slight shrug didn't mask her unease. "If they ask me if we're having a relationship, I'll tell them the truth. I'm not going to volunteer that we're sleeping together. Some things are private. But I'm not going to lie."

Ronald shook his head. "That probably won't help you reconcile with your family."

"I want them to accept me for who I am. And the woman I am very much wants to have a relationship with you."

Ronald's breath caught. He stood and offered his hand. Joan accepted, and he helped her to her feet. "I'd very much like to have a relationship with you, too."

Joan smiled, relief and an answering desire in her eyes. They'd taken only a few steps toward her bedroom when she stopped and turned to him. "I'd like to try some of the things from my books."

Ronald's grin was slow satisfaction. "So would I."

Her secretive smile made him harder. "Do you think you can keep up?"

"Maybe I'd better pace myself. Why don't we start with *Pleasure Quest* and work our way up to *Double Dipper?*"

He heard music, a fast, sexy song. A radio alarm clock? Whatever. He ignored it. It was too early. Besides, wasn't today Saturday? He didn't teach on Saturdays. Ronald groaned and tried to fall back to sleep.

But now that he was awake, he was more conscious of his surroundings. Like the warm, silky skin beneath his palm and the powdery, soft scent of woman. His erection stirred.

The music stopped.

"Wake up, lazybones." The sleepy voice sounded amused.

He groaned again. With his eyes closed, he scooted even closer to her warmth. "What time is it?"

"Five thirty. Time for our morning run."

He tightened his hold around her waist. "Let's jog later. Much later."

"This is the best time of the day for a run."

He opened his eyes and looked into her amused ones. "Are you sure about that?"

The light in her eyes shifted as she caught his meaning. She was tempted. He could see that, but she took a deep breath, and the moment was gone.

"Come on, slacker." She kissed him before slipping out from under his arm. The soft, sweet caress wasn't nearly long enough.

Ronald turned his head to look at the time. Five thirty on a Saturday morning. He groaned again.

Twenty minutes later, they jogged down her block and across the street to Goodale Park. The neighborhood park was a modest size, about two city blocks.

Ronald ran beside Joan. It felt strange jogging in the clothes he'd worn last night. When he stayed over again, he'd have to remember to bring his jogging shoes and shorts in addition to his toothbrush.

He took in the rolling lawns, old trees, and manmade ponds as they circled the park's perimeter. "I hadn't expected to see so many people running this early."

"Um." Joan led him around the corner, past the tennis court, then fell back into step beside him.

"It's a beautiful park. I can see why you like it."

"If you want me. . ." She drew in a deep breath and let it out slowly—"to talk and jog with you at the same time—" She sucked in another breath. ". . . slow down."

Amused, Ronald slowed his pace. "Sorry. I usually run alone."

"I can tell." Joan blew out a deep breath. "I usually

jog with Maggie on the weekend, but I had a feeling she wouldn't be joining me today."

"I'm sorry." He heard the disappointment in Joan's voice. For her sake, he hoped her family got over their surprise soon. "It's nice to have company. I hadn't realized how much time I spent alone until this week."

They settled into an easy pace around the park. A flock of birds provided theme music as they continued their first lap. A gentle breeze brushed morning dew along his skin. Ronald enjoyed the jogging tour of Joan's neighborhood. He felt its quiet dignity in the maturity of its trees and its proper Victorian architecture.

They turned another corner. About a block away, half hidden by a tangle of vines and trees, Ronald could see a freeway. To his left, in the distance, was the city's skyline.

Joan broke the pensive silence. "Our families are very different. Yours doesn't spend much time together. My family gets together several times each week."

Ronald envied them. "My family couldn't handle that much bonding time. It would be torture."

"Will you see your family before they drive back to New York today?"

His gaze swept the park, noting a middle-aged woman walking a pack of dogs, a young couple pushing a baby stroller, an older man feeding ducks near the pond. "I don't know."

Silence settled between them again as comfortable as their conversation. Almost forty minutes later, Joan led them back to her apartment. She slowed when they reached her steps, and Ronald joined her as she walked to the opposite street corner to cool off.

He touched her arm. "You know I leave Wednesday for the cocktail party celebrating the TV series' launch."

Joan wiped the sweat from her eyes. "Oh yeah. That's Thursday night, isn't it?"

"Yes. I'll be back by Saturday."

Joan didn't look at him as she turned and walked back to her apartment. "I hope you have a nice time."

Disconcerted, Ronald followed her. "You could come with me. We still have time to get a plane ticket for you."

Joan stopped at the foot of her front steps. She looked startled. "Four days? The ticket would cost the earth."

"I'll pay for it."

Joan slanted him a you've-got-to-be-kidding look. "I couldn't accept that. Besides, I can't leave my store again so soon. But thanks for the invitation."

Ronald followed her through the front doors. "If you change your mind, let me know. It would give you a chance to see your editor again."

He tried to sound casual, but he was desperate to have someone with him to endure the spotlight for once. He was desperate to have Joan with him. How had he come to rely on her so much in just a week?

Chapter 11

Margaret's home phone rang four times before tossing Joan into her older sister's answering machine.

"Hi, Maggie. It's me." She hesitated. *Now what? Keep it brief.* Her other messages had been long enough. "Could you call me? I'm at work. Thanks."

She exhaled an impatient breath and dropped the phone receiver back into its cradle. Where would her sister be at nine on a Saturday morning? It wasn't like Margaret to give someone the silent treatment, but that was exactly what she was doing. *For heaven's sake.*

Joan sipped her diet cola and stared at her partially open office door. She wasn't hiding. Not exactly. Disappearing into her office to catch up on bookkeeping, rather than spending the morning in the store as she usually did with Christine, Kai, and Juanita wasn't hiding. It was a healthy change of pattern. It proved she wasn't a creature of habit. Besides, Christine's sulks and glares were making it hard to digest the cereal and orange juice she'd had for breakfast.

Joan launched the inventory database on the office computer and stared at the columns, trying to analyze stock movements. A shadow in her doorway startled her.

Wendell T. Hines stood in the threshold. "Chrissie said it was all right to come back here to see you."

Since Joan had managed to avoid her younger sister's sulks, Christine had found another way to get back at her. But in fairness, Joan liked the associate pastor—in a platonic way.

"Hi, Wendell. How nice to see you. Please have a seat." She gestured toward the only other chair in the cramped office.

"I hope I'm not interrupting." Before sitting, the pastor shifted the seat sideways to accommodate his long legs.

"Not at all. I can use a break. What brings you to the Short North?"

"I was in the neighborhood and thought I'd stop by to see your store. It's very nice."

Joan tilted her head and considered him. He seemed a little uncomfortable and had trouble holding her gaze. "Why, Dr. Hines, I don't think you're being completely honest with me. Is there something you'd like to confess?"

Nervous laughter in such a big man—tall and fit—was oddly charming. "You're very direct. I like that. The truth is, I wanted to see you again, Joan."

She was flattered. What red-blooded, breathing woman wouldn't be flattered when a handsome, intelligent man told her he was attracted to her? But she also was annoyed.

Her parents had put her in this position. To them, she was a tool to keep the church in their family with Wendell as their son-in-law and, after her father retired, pastor. Maybe she would have gone along with their plan if she hadn't met Ronald and realized she'd outgrown the part in which her family had cast her. Now the only role she wanted to play was herself.

"Wendell, I don't know what my parents told you. You seem like a nice person. I'd be honored to have your friendship, but that's all."

His smile was crooked. "I know I don't seem very interesting or exciting. But you may be surprised once you get to know me."

Joan didn't know about that. In his cream jersey and blue jeans, he seemed plenty interesting and exciting to her. He was markedly different from the Wendell who'd worn slacks, sports coat, shirt, and tie for dinner with her parents. There obviously was more to the associate pastor than met the eye.

Joan smiled to soften her words. "You'll make some lucky woman very happy. But I'm involved with someone else."

His disappointment was evident as the light in his dark eyes dimmed. "Your parents told me you weren't seeing anyone."

They could have asked first. But would it have made any difference to them? "I hadn't told them about him at the time."

"He's a lucky man."

"Thank you. I'm serious about our being friends."

"I'd like that." Wendell rose. "I guess I'll see you Sunday."

Joan stood as well. "I'm looking forward to your sermon. It sounds very inspiring."

He gave her his self-deprecating smile. "I hope so." With a nod, he turned and left her office.

Well, that had been difficult.

It took Joan a few moments to shift gears and refocus on the store's inventory trends. She got caught up in the stock movements, customer item requests, and product catalogs. Time sped past before another interruption claimed her attention.

"Joan, you have visitors." Christine's voice was only a little less stiff than it had been earlier that morning.

Maybe their audience had something to do with that. Her sister had led Ronald, an older couple, and a young man to her office.

Joan stood, feeling crowded. The little shoe box of a room wasn't designed to accommodate so many people. "Thanks, Chrissie."

Ronald squeezed forward. "Sorry to interrupt you. I wanted you to meet my parents before they drove home." He gestured from Joan to the older couple. "Joan Brown, my parents, George and Darlene Montgomery."

Joan smiled her delight. Did Ronald realize what he was admitting with this act? He hadn't given up on his family.

"It's a pleasure to meet you." Joan stepped forward to shake their hands.

"It's nice to meet you." Darlene looked hungry for answers.

Her husband gave Joan a businesslike handshake.

Joan felt Christine's gaze boring into the side of her head. Her younger sister seemed to scrutinize Joan's every action as though cataloging how her behavior fit into Christine's revised opinion of her.

The young man leaned forward, offering his hand. "I'm Ron's brother, Harry. You must be the reason he's in Columbus."

"I don't think I'd say that." Joan looked at Ronald as she took Harold's hand, noting his taut facial muscles and lowered brows.

Harold still held her hand. "What other reason would there be?"

"I'll need that hand back." Joan wouldn't have any part of whatever game Ronald's brother was playing.

Harold released her, and she returned her attention to Ronald's parents. "How did you like Columbus?"

George shoved his hands into his front pockets. "We didn't get to see much of it, just the downtown."

Darlene looped her arm around George's, but her gaze was glued to Joan. "Ronnie was busy, George. He couldn't take us around."

George frowned down at his wife. "This is Ron's first trip to Columbus, too."

Darlene ignored George to smile at Joan. "How did you two meet?"

Joan exchanged a look with Ronald. Despite Christine's presence, she decided to tell the truth. "We met at a writers' conference in Los Angeles."

Darlene gazed at her with inquisitive eyes. "Are you a writer, too?"

"Yes. I write romance."

Christine's voice was sharp. "When did you go to this writers' conference?"

Joan straightened and turned to her sister. "At the beginning of May."

"You told us you got together with school friends."

"I'm sorry." Joan braced herself for Christine's reaction. Her sister nodded once, then left the office without another word.

"What was that all about?" Harold sounded amused.

"Mind your business." Ronald stepped closer to Joan, putting his hand on her arm. "Are you okay?"

No, and she might never be. But she nodded anyway.

Joan woke with dread Sunday morning. It was an unusual feeling. She'd always looked forward to church, and she'd particularly looked forward to Wendell's sermon. But between Christine's glares, Margaret's silent treatment, and her parents' anger, church wouldn't be the usual Brown family bonding experience.

She rolled over to sit on the edge of the bed, mentally preparing herself for whatever the day might hold.

"I'll come with you."

She looked over her shoulder at Ronald's words. "When was the last time you went to church?"

"I think I was twelve."

Joan smiled at her mental image of a solemn twelve-year-old Ronald in his Sunday finest. "You don't have to come. I'll be all right."

The sheet pooled around his hips as Ronald shifted closer to caress her bare back. "Your faith is important to you. I'd like to join you for the service."

She wouldn't read too much into his words. Joan blinked to ease the sting of tears. "I won't be able to sit with you. I'm singing with the choir."

"I know. I'm looking forward to hearing you."

Her laughter came as a surprise, considering she woke almost sick with nerves. Joan leaned forward and kissed his lips. "Thank you."

Ronald's company made the morning a little easier, but Joan's nervousness had returned by the time she pulled into Holy Grace Neighborhood Church's parking lot. She collected her choir robe from her Toyota's rear seat, locked her little sedan, then walked beside Ronald toward the front doors.

"I'll make sure you get a good seat in the pews." Did her smile look as fake as it felt?

"I'll be fine." Ronald settled his hand in the small of her back as he escorted her up the front steps.

Joan paused inside the church's front doors and glanced around the lobby. She loved greeting church members, the majority of whom she'd known most of her life.

Her attention landed on a small, full-figured older woman who was worrying the strap of a cream and brown handbag.

Joan approached her with a cheerful expression. "How are you today, Miss Alice?"

The older woman's wide brown eyes gave Ronald a thorough examination before smiling up at Joan. "It's my granddaughter I'm worried about, Joan. They have to remove her tonsils tomorrow. She's just a little thing and so scared."

She knew the granddaughter in question. Joan squeezed Alice's soft cinnamon hands. "I'll keep her in my prayers."

Alice glanced at Ronald again. Her interest was clear.

Joan gestured toward Ronald. "Ronald Montgomery, I'd like you to meet Alice Crumb. Miss Alice, this is my friend Ron."

Ronald extended his hand. "It's a pleasure to meet you, ma'am."

Alice beamed as though presented with a gift. "It's nice to meet you, too."

Joan touched the older woman's arm. "Enjoy the sermon, Miss Alice."

She moved on to a stick-thin woman in a red paisley print dress. Here was her greatest Sunday challenge of all. Joan gave the other woman a warm smile, even though the elder's expression could form ice cubes in the desert. "How are you today, Miss Lettie?"

Lettie Quints glared at her. "I'll be much better once my grandson returns home to his parents. That boy will be the death of me. I don't know whose bright idea it was for him to stay with me for an extended visit."

Joan frowned. "I thought it was your idea, Miss Lettie." Ronald's coughing distracted her. "Are you all right?"

At his nod, Joan made their excuses and moved on.

Ronald coughed once more. "I thought people were supposed to be happy when they came to church."

"They are. Lettie Quints is happiest when she's complaining about something." She paused beside an older woman with a cane. "How's your arthritis this morning, Miss Gayle?"

"It's paining me a bit." Gayle Sharpe's voice was weak and unsteady.

"Would you like some help to your pew?"

"Yes, please."

Ronald stepped forward, cupping the woman's free arm at the elbow. "Allow me."

Joan's heart swelled with gratitude. She followed her tall, fit suitor as he slowly assisted the frail woman half his size down the sanctuary aisle.

Joan watched Ronald help Gayle into a pew. "Enjoy the sermon, Miss Gayle."

Joan led Ronald to a familiar figure sitting near the front of the sanctuary. She kissed her soon-to-be brother-in-law's cheek. "Hi, Tim. Could Ron join you for the service?"

She watched Timothy closely. He didn't appear to know anything was amiss within the Brown family.

Timothy stood to shake Ronald's hand. "Of course." He moved down the pew, giving Ronald room on the bench.

With a smile, Joan left the two men and continued down the aisle toward the three-tiered riser where the choir sat. As she shrugged into her robe, she watched Christine and Margaret sitting silently together. Neither sister looked her way. But her father must have been waiting for her.

Kenneth descended from the riser and blocked Joan's path. "No, Joan." Her father's voice was low but firm.

Joan halted. "What do you mean?" But she knew the answer.

"You can't sing in God's house if you're writing filth."

Joan felt cold. She looked up at the singers. Her sisters still avoided her gaze. The other women and men of the choir watched the exchange between her and their pastor with open interest.

"Won't you at least read one of my books before you pass judgment?" Her entire family had forgotten the biblical verse about not judging others.

"I'm not stupid. I know what you write about in those books. It's immoral."

Joan glanced back at Ronald. His concern gave her strength. He'd been a stranger less than two months ago, but he'd come to her church because of its importance to her. On the other hand, her father had chosen to condemn her without reading her book. "My characters don't have indiscriminate sex."

Her father hissed her to silence. "Sit in a pew with the rest of the congregation, Joan. When you're ready to stop writing sin, you can rejoin the choir."

A few choir members avoided her gaze, but some continued to show their interest. Margaret and Christine ignored her.

She didn't want to give in. She belonged on that riser with the rest of the choir. But a house of worship wasn't the place for this argument. Joan swallowed the burning lump in her throat and turned to join Ronald and Timothy in the pews.

At the worry on Ronald's face, Joan blinked faster to keep the tears from falling.

He stepped out of the pew to let her in. "What happened?"

Joan shook her head. She stepped past him and sat down. "I'll tell you later."

"Do you want to leave?" Ronald shifted closer to her on the bench and took her hand.

Joan held on tightly. "No, I'm not leaving. This is where I belong."

Almost three hours later, Joan rang Margaret's doorbell. She knew her older sister's schedule. Right about now, Margaret and Timothy were preparing lunch. There was no place for her sister to run, nowhere to hide.

Timothy let her in. "Hi, Joan."

It was hard to face him after what had happened in church today. Did he know why her father had barred her from the choir? If so, what did he think? "Hi, Tim. It's been a while."

The lame joke only embarrassed her more. But Timothy smiled and kissed her forehead.

"Too long. Maggie's in the kitchen." He turned to lead the way, but Joan touched his arm.

He was like an older brother. His rejection would hurt her just as much as the rest of the family's. "Has Maggie told you what's going on?"

It helped that he didn't pretend not to understand her meaning. He covered her hand with his large, warm palm. Through his thin-rimmed glasses, his dark brown eyes showed compassion. "Have faith, Joan. The tide will turn soon enough."

He deserved a smile for his kindness. The one she gave him was forced but sincere. "Is that what's kept you going the past three months? The hope that the tide will turn and my father will give his blessing for you to marry Maggie?"

Timothy's eyebrows shot upward, the only indication

her question disconcerted him. "I love your sister. That's what keeps me going."

"Thanks for not taking offense to my question."

He adjusted his glasses. "I'm not used to your being so blunt."

"I've found that I like the direct approach." She squeezed his hand before drawing away. "For what it's worth, regardless of whether my father comes to his senses, I consider you part of my family."

His hug was brief but hard. "I know, and that's worth a lot."

"My father may not stay angry for long if you show him how much money you could save if you and Maggie got married."

Timothy laughed. "Your father's a very cost-conscious person. But you're right. Keeping two apartments is expensive, and I'm always over here anyway."

He led her to the kitchen. At their approach, Margaret turned from the stove. Her brown eyes flashed surprise and then exasperation. "What are you doing here?"

Joan gripped the back of a dark wood chair. "Thanks, sis. I feel so welcome."

Margaret blinked, startled. She shifted her gaze to Timothy, and a silent message passed between them. They'd done that before with a private joke or a shared memory. But instead of envy, this time Joan was annoyed. What were they thinking, and why couldn't they tell her?

"See you later, Joan." Timothy squeezed her shoulder on his way out of the room.

Alone with her sister, Joan steadied her breathing to prepare for the confrontation. "You haven't returned my calls."

Margaret lowered the gas flames on the chrome stove

top and stirred the contents of her soup pot. "I don't know what to say."

The kitchen was filled with the scent of vegetables, an explosion of carrots, onions, potatoes, and celery. A bag of bagels, a pack of cold cuts, and some cheese lay on the green tile counter beside her older sister.

"Why don't you start with what you're thinking?"

Her back still toward Joan, Margaret lifted her wavy dark hair from her neck. "I don't know what to think. That's the problem."

"Then how do you feel?"

Margaret put down the metal spoon and washed her hands. Yellow curtains a shade darker than the painted walls fluttered in the open window above the sink.

Her sister dried her hands, then turned and crossed her arms. "I feel betrayed."

The words were hard to hear, but Joan listened, for herself as well as for Margaret. "I'm sorry."

"I've known you all of your life. I thought we were friends as well as sisters."

Joan breathed through the pain. "We are."

Margaret's eyes widened. "How can you say that? I don't even know you, Joan. You've lied to me— apparently for years."

How could she make her sister understand? "It was either lie to you or ask you to lie to Mom and Daddy. I couldn't do that."

Margaret pulled a chair out from under the table and sat. "I would've understood."

Joan paced the length of the kitchen, pausing across the room from Margaret. "I was also afraid you wouldn't approve of what I was doing."

Margaret arched a winged brow. "You should've let me decide that for myself."

"It was too risky, Maggie. Your approval means a lot to me."

"Well, I definitely don't approve of your lying to me."

Joan tensed like a windup toy ready to break. "I've wanted to write for so long. Maybe it was a mistake to write sexy books, but these are the stories I'm drawn to write, and these are the characters who speak to me."

Margaret looked at her as though looking at a stranger. "I can understand wanting to write sexy books. I can even understand not wanting to tell Mom and Daddy. What I don't understand is why you felt you had to hide that side of yourself from Chrissie and me. I thought we've always been close to each other. We know each other better than anyone else knows us."

Propelled by frustration, Joan paced back across the room. "You know me in the role I play in our family."

"What does that mean?"

Joan took the chair across from Margaret, undaunted by her sister's impatience. "Everyone in our family plays a role. Daddy's the dictator. Mom's the enforcer. You're the competent daughter. I'm the dutiful daughter. And Chrissie, poor thing, is the eternal baby daughter. I feel sorriest for her."

"Why?" Margaret sounded more than baffled. Perhaps Joan's theory was too much for her sister to absorb at once.

"Because no matter how old she gets, she'll always be the baby, which means Mom and Daddy will never stop telling her what to do."

"You mean like picking a husband for her?" When Joan nodded, Margaret continued. "They did the same thing to you."

"That's because I'm the dutiful daughter, and they thought I'd go along with their plans."

"Will you?"

"I'm tired of playing a role to please other people at the expense of losing myself. It's time I was accepted or rejected for who I am, not who you want me to be."

Margaret watched her for a long, silent moment. A lot rested on what she saw. Her sister's stare was hard, almost piercing. But Joan held her gaze. It felt good to speak out. It felt empowering.

"I don't know what to say, Joan. It's odd imagining my little sister writing sexy romances."

Joan angled her head, her gaze direct and challenging. "But that's my point. Your little sister's a grown woman."

Margaret looked away. "I guess I'm not ready to accept that."

Chapter 12

How could he just sit there and write? Joan squinted across the kitchen table at Ronald. He stared at his laptop, eyes tracking the movement of his words as they seemed to fly across the screen.

They both were experiencing a tense time with their families. But whereas he'd been writing steadily for almost an hour, Joan had yet to type a page.

"How do you do that?" She winced at her sharp tone.

Ronald unglued his eyes from his computer screen and raised them to Joan. "You say something?" His attention was unfocused. He must still be in the story.

"How do you shut out your emotional turmoil and concentrate on the story?"

"What emotional turmoil?"

Joan's lips parted. Was he kidding? "The argument you're having with your family."

He actually shrugged. "That's nothing new. It's just out in the open now."

"But doesn't it bother you?"

"Why should it?"

Again, he left her with her mouth hanging open. "They're your foundation. That's why it should bother you."

Ronald leaned back in the oak chair and studied her features. Seconds went by. "That's your family, Joan. Not mine."

She looked away. Her attention dropped to her laptop. Joan hit the space bar, and the screen-saver message, "Writers write," disappeared. The blank page mocked her.

"That *was* my family." She pushed away from the table and wandered to the sink to stare out of the window. The linoleum was cool against her bare feet.

It was after nine o'clock. The sun was just setting. Through the sheer curtains, she studied the narrow walkway between her apartment and the parking lot. The weeds were taking over real estate in the tiny side garden.

Joan kept her back to Ronald. "We were so close. Weekly dinners, working together, singing together, attending church together. You don't really value what you have until it's gone, do you?"

"I envied your relationship with your family. I wish my family got along that well." Ronald sounded suddenly tired.

"It turns out there was nothing to envy, though." Joan turned away from the view outside and hugged herself. "You were right."

His gaze was puzzled. "About what?"

Joan shrugged a shoulder, feigning an acceptance she didn't feel. "How real was my family's togetherness if they could so easily turn away from me?"

"They haven't turned away. They're just surprised."

"This is more than surprise. They're angry. I'm not a carbon copy of my mother. I'm not obeying my father, so they're punishing me." Her anger stirred. "I'm twenty-six years old. I think I can make my own decisions about the way I live my life."

Ronald rose and approached her. "They're as upset as you are."

"What do you mean?" Joan stepped back. She needed room for the storm inside her.

Ronald halted. "Your family is too much a part of each other's lives for this argument to be easy for anyone."

"That's part of the problem. My parents think they can control every facet of my life and my sisters' lives."

"You mean like deciding who you'll marry?"

Joan heard the amusement in his tone. "It's not funny. They crossed every imaginable line with that."

"They care about you."

Joan laughed without humor. "You're upset with your family because they don't care enough. I'm upset with my parents because they care too much. What does that say about either of us?"

Ronald's lips curved in a smile, but his ebony eyes remained somber. "We always want what the other person seems to have."

"I'd settle for a happy balance." Joan filled the kettle. She put the water to boil, then stood staring at the stove. "I feel lost. At times like this, I usually turn to my family. But this time, they're the reason I feel this way."

His large hands settled gently at her waist. He pulled her back against him, resting his cheek against the top of her head. "Then turn to me."

She faced him, accepting his embrace. Her arms wrapped around his shoulders. They were firm and broad, and felt capable of bearing a great deal of weight. She rested her cheek against his chest. His cotton shirt was soft and smooth against her skin. She inhaled deeply, enjoying his scent. Warmth. Musk. Comfort.

He surrounded her. His body heat seeped into her blouse and shorts, warming her until she melted against his hard muscles.

His fingertips traced her spine. "Let me be the one you turn to."

Joan's body and her heart responded to the yearning in Ronald's command.

Ronald needed this. He needed Joan to lean on him and to let him lean on her. He wanted to express physically the emotional connection he felt with her. He had to have her warmth.

Ronald tightened his hold on Joan's slender waist. He tucked his face into the elegant curve of her neck and inhaled the scent of roses and powder. It was like a drug, shooting through his system and heating his blood. He took another hit, then pulled her closer, nibbling his way to her ear. Joan tipped her head back, lengthening his journey.

He traced the outer shell of her ear with his tongue and enjoyed the feel of her body shivering against him. Her pleasure added to his. Her need turned up his temperature.

Joan's hands eased up from the waistband of his shorts and stroked his spine. Her fingers pressed into the muscles along his back and upper arms, then dug into his shoulders. As she touched him, he enjoyed every expression that flitted across her features—satisfaction, pleasure, hunger.

Ronald brushed his mouth against hers. Her full, pouty lips were soft and responsive. His tongue brushed the seam of her mouth, seeking entrance. Joan parted her lips, then moaned when he suckled her tongue.

Ronald looked into her upturned face. Her thick

lashes lay against her golden skin. "Joan, open your eyes. Open your eyes and see me."

Joan lifted her eyelids. Her melted chocolate eyes met his gaze. She pressed her lips against his, and a bell rang in his ears. No. Not a bell. A whistle. The water had boiled.

Ronald took a steadying breath, then released Joan. He reached around her to turn off the stove. "Are you thirsty?"

She smiled into his eyes and stroked her hand down the front of his body. She cupped his thickening groin. "For you."

It was a wonder his eyes didn't cross.

"The sofa's closer than the bed." Joan rested her hands against Ronald's pectorals. Beneath her palms, his chest flexed and tensed.

She applied just a bit of pressure to direct him out of her tiny kitchen and backward to her living room. She reveled in the feel of his excitement, the heat of his arousal; she'd done that to him. It gave her a heady sense of power, of control.

Her feet sank into the thick sapphire carpet as she stopped him in front of her sofa. Holding his gaze, Joan cupped a hand behind Ronald's head and drew him down for a soul kiss. With her mouth pressed to his, she used her tongue to lure his lips apart. Her free hand worked his cargo shorts open.

"Wait." His breath fanned her lips as he eased back.

Ronald pulled off his T-shirt. Joan followed his movements, her mouth watering as the motion stretched the well-defined muscles in his chest and abdomen.

She helped remove his shorts and underpants so he stood bare before her. He was long, dark, and lean. She dampened just watching him.

Joan kneaded her palm over his sculpted chest and

ran her fingers through his short, soft chest hairs. "This is my kind of foreplay."

Tension edged Ronald's chuckle. He took a condom from his wallet and handed it to her. "We'll have to get serious soon."

Joan dragged her nails down his torso, thrilled that her touch made his stomach muscles tremble. "Just a little longer. I want to feel every inch of you." She circled her index finger inside his navel. Then she warmed her hand with his heat.

Ronald pulsed in her palm. Joan stepped closer, not yet ready to sheath his erection with the condom. Rising on her toes, she fit her body into his, pressing her breasts against him. She exposed her hunger with a deeply ravenous kiss. Her tongue stroked him, suckled him, coaxed him. He groaned into her mouth and pressed himself deeper into her fist. Without breaking the kiss, Joan reached around and cupped his buttocks. Those muscles contracted and relaxed as he pumped into her hand.

"I need to feel your hands on me." Joan unbuttoned her blouse.

She let Ronald ease himself from her hold. He helped her strip off her clothing; then he pulled her hips to his and rubbed himself tight against her. Joan's head fell back. Her passion pooled between her thighs. She bit her lower lip to keep from crying out. Joan pressed Ronald onto the sofa and followed him, straddling his lap. She took his penis in her hand and positioned him at her entrance. "Playtime is over."

"Thank God."

Joan chuckled into the warmth of his neck. The laughter helped ease her almost painful arousal. Until she breathed in his scent. So warm, so erotic. He was her hearth when she was alone. Joan closed her eyes and slid onto him, letting Ronald in a little way at a time.

Bit by bit, his flesh pressed into her, drawing out her desire. Ronald's fingers tightened on her waist as he seemed to strain for control. Joan clenched her teeth as pleasure, passion, and a thrilling sense of power washed over her. She exhaled as she finally claimed all of him.

Here she was welcomed. Wanted. Maybe even needed? Ronald accepted who she was and who she wanted to be. Gratitude joined the whirlpool of emotions and feelings churning through her.

Joan moved her hips side to side and front to back, rubbing herself against him. Ronald cupped her buttocks, lifting and lowering her on his length. Her pulse quickened as he worked her, moving with her and sometimes against her. He gave her all of him. Still, she wanted more of him. His fingers danced down the cleft of her derriere. She squirmed against him.

Who was in control? Was she playing his body? Or was he directing hers?

Ronald leaned forward and suckled her breast into his mouth. Liquid flowed from her. He grazed her nipple with his teeth, stroked his tongue around her peak.

Joan pumped her hips faster and heard his groan. His body shook as he pressed her tighter against him. Who was in control? Maybe they both were.

With a final kiss on her left nipple, Ronald moved to her right breast. Joan dug her fingertips into his shoulders and arched her back, giving him more. She rode him, squeezing and releasing him inside her. Ronald drew his hand from her hip and slipped it between them. He touched her, rubbing his thumb against her tip, stroking her intimately. Coaxing her to the edge. It was too much sensation. She was losing control. But with him, it was okay. Joan knew he would give it back. She tipped back her head and screamed her release.

Ronald blinked until the yellow digits on Joan's radio alarm clock came into focus. It was 5:17 a.m. The music would play in thirteen minutes. He hated waking before the alarm, especially when there wasn't enough time to go back to sleep.

He was spooned around Joan's bare back. She was soft and warm against him, and the reason he wasn't anxious to leave her bed. He kissed the curve of her neck, then tightened his arm around her waist.

In a few minutes she'd wake and drag him out for their morning jog. It had only been a few mornings, but they'd settled into the routine. It gave him a sense of togetherness he'd never felt with anyone else. He enjoyed it, even though it meant waking up at the butt crack of dawn.

Joan stretched her long, slender body against him. She turned to face him, laying her head on his chest.

Ronald kissed the top of her head. "I'm sorry."

"For what?" Her lips caressed his skin as she whispered back. He tried to ignore his body's response.

"That I've caused a rift between you and your family."

Joan leaned back to frown up at him. Cool air came between them. "How are you responsible?"

Accepting blame was hard enough without her pretending not to know what he was talking about. "I convinced you to tell them about your writing."

"It was my decision to tell them. You could have talked until you were blue in the face. If I hadn't wanted to tell them, I wouldn't have."

Was that true? "If I hadn't interfered in your life, you wouldn't have had to make that decision."

"You're giving yourself a lot of credit."

"I'm trying to apologize." Frustration and guilt made a bitter cocktail.

Joan rolled onto her back and stared at the ceiling. "There's no need. It was time to tell them."

"Maybe not. If I hadn't pushed you, you could have eased your family into accepting your writing."

Joan met his gaze. Even with the sunrise straining through her venetian blinds, he couldn't read her eyes. But he sensed her impatience.

"You didn't push me, Ron. And it doesn't matter when I told them. They still would have been angry. It's better to get it over with sooner rather than later."

Her words might absolve him of guilt, but he needed to know if she blamed him. "Come with me to New York Wednesday."

"We've talked about this. I'm tempted, but that's only two days away."

"So?" That was why he'd purchased her ticket. They were running out of time, but he'd held on to hope.

"I just got back from vacation. I can't leave Chrissie to manage the store alone again so soon." She flipped off the sheet and slid out of bed.

Joan's golden brown body was tight—taut waist, flat stomach, slender hips. Her long legs were toned. The muscles flowed smoothly as she strode toward her closet. Her full breasts bounced lightly with each step.

Ronald envied Joan's consideration for her sister. How did it feel to have someone think of your happiness before their own?

"What about your needs?" He sat up, adjusting the pillow behind him.

Joan paused at her closet, glancing over her shoulder.

She looked like a *Maxim* magazine model. "What I don't need is Chrissie to be even angrier with me if I leave her to manage the store alone again. That's a lot of work, Ron."

Say you'll come with me to New York. "We wouldn't be gone long. We'd leave Wednesday. The studio's cocktail party is Thursday. We'll return Saturday, or even Friday."

"Four days is a long time." Joan shrugged into her robe and tightened its belt. After last night's passion, this morning's modesty seemed strange. Was she Cleopatra at night and Joan in the morning?

Ronald refocused. "Think of it this way. You'll be out of the cross fire while your family gets used to the idea of what you write."

"What makes you think they'll ever get used to that idea?"

"Your family loves you. They're your foundation, just as you're theirs."

She shook her head. "That foundation was built on trust. They don't trust me anymore."

Say you'll come with me. "They need time, Joan. And getting away from Columbus would do you good. It'll help put things in perspective."

Joan tipped her head to one side. "Why are you so anxious for me to go to New York with you?"

"I need a date for the launch party."

She arched a brow. "Try again."

"It's the truth." Ronald climbed out of bed, naked in more ways than one. "Having a TV production company serialize my novel is a milestone. I want someone I give a damn about and who gives a damn about me to be there."

He didn't want the sympathy that softened her gaze. He didn't want the concern that knitted her brows. He

just wanted her company during the launch party—
and forever.

Joan slipped her hands into her robe's pockets.
"Have you invited your parents?"

"I always do."

When she looked away, he knew she'd realized that, although he always invited them, they had yet to show up.

Joan returned her attention to him. "I'd really like
to go with you."

That was something, wasn't it? "I understand. Family
first." His yearning to have that family first role was
like a physical pain.

"I'll talk to Chrissie." Joan smiled, but he could see
the concern in her eyes. "I don't know whether I want
her to tell me to stay or ask me to leave."

Ronald knew his preference, and he tried not to feel
guilty.

Chapter 13

She was through with hiding in the back office. Joan leaned against the checkout counter as she worked on the lesson plans for the store's summer art classes. If Christine didn't want to see her, *she* could go to the office.

The bell above the entrance pealed. It was just a little after the store's nine o'clock start time. Joan looked up with a smile, ready to greet their first customer of the day.

Her expression soured as Silas walked toward her. "I'm surprised to see you up this early."

He didn't look as though he'd slept in the dark blue jeans shorts and black T-shirt.

Silas gave her the cocky smile that made her grind her back teeth. "You're bitchier than usual, Joan."

"I've always been pleasant to you, Silas, but I can easily change that."

Silas rested his bare forearms beside one of the cash registers and leaned toward her. Male mockery gleamed in his dark eyes. "A man knows when a woman doesn't like him."

"Maybe *some* men." He obviously hadn't caught that

vibe from Christine. Her sister wasn't that good of an actress.

"Or are you just jealous because your sister's getting some and you aren't?"

His mendacity didn't surprise her. "Don't you think it's too early to show your baser side?"

"Don't hate a brother. I can give you what you need."

And his father was a gospel music producer. This apple had fallen far, far, far from the tree and had rotted in the sun.

Joan straightened, crossed her arms over her chest, and pasted a sugary smile on her lips. "Can you, Sly? What I need is for you to be faithful to my sister and make her happy. Can you give me that?"

His cocksure smile faded, and his face tightened. "You don't think I can make Chrissie happy?"

He'd skipped that whole faithful thing altogether. "I don't know. That's why I'm asking. How do you define making my sister happy?"

"That's none of your business, bitch."

Hmm. Two "bitches" in one conversation. "My name is Joan. Feel free to use it."

Silas straightened from the counter. "I'll call you whatever I want."

What exactly made her parents think Silas Tooner was a good match for any of their children?

Joan kept her voice calm despite Silas's increased volume. "It's a simple enough question, Silas. You're planning to marry Chrissie. How do you define making my sister happy?"

Silas narrowed his eyes and stuck out his jaw. "I can make any woman happy."

The sexual innuendo in that statement didn't bode well, especially since she was fairly certain Silas had slept with several women in the congregation, and none of them was Christine.

"You're becoming a member of my family." She almost choked on those words. "This means you'll be a member of Holy Grace Neighborhood Church's first family. Have my parents told you what that means?"

"What *what* means?"

"The first family is held to very high standards."

His eyes widened with disbelief. His voice grew louder. "Are you lecturing me?"

Joan struggled to keep her voice calm, grateful there weren't any customers to hear this exchange. "I'm telling you what you need to know."

"*You* need to know to mind your own business."

"I've seen you flirting with women in the congregation. I know they're flirting back. But once you join my family, that behavior has to stop."

"That behavior has to stop? Who are you talking to like that?"

"I can't allow you to embarrass my family. I have a responsibility to protect my family's name and reputation."

Christine's voice carried from behind her. The tone was heavy with disgust. "You have some nerve talking about protecting the family's name and reputation."

Joan turned at the sound of her sister's flat heels tapping against the gray tile as she approached. "I have every right to be concerned about those things."

Her sister stopped beside Silas. Her finger trembled as she pointed at Joan. "After what you've done, you have no right."

"What's she done?"

Joan ignored Silas's question. She smothered the urge to argue Christine's point further. "Have you talked to Silas about respecting our family's reputation, then? If you have, your lecture didn't take. He's still trolling our church like it's a singles bar."

"Silas is right. You should mind your business."

Knowing Christine's phrasing was meant to hurt didn't stop the sting. Joan ignored the verbal slap and Silas's smirk. She ignored his presence completely. "He doesn't respect you. He flirts right in front of you, and you know he's slept with several women in the congregation. Do you want that to continue even after you're married?"

Silas's glare was pure hatred. "Shut up."

Joan disregarded Silas's warning and instead willed her sister to open her eyes and see the truth.

Christine fisted her hands on the counter. "*You* don't respect yourself. If you did, you wouldn't write those dirty books."

"What dirty books?" Silas continued his attempts to join the conversation.

"Daddy chose Silas for you, Chrissie. But we're adults. We run our own business. We pay our own bills. We have the right to make our own choices. Is Silas your choice? Or are you going to play Daddy's little girl for the rest of your life?"

"Don't listen to her, Chrissie." Silas's words rang like a command.

The silence lengthened, and Joan began to nurture hope. She watched the expressions shift across her sister's features. Anger, confusion, resolve.

Silas softened his tone. "Come on, shorty. Don't listen to her."

Joan heard panic in Silas's voice. Still, she remained silent, praying Christine would reject him.

Her sister angled her chin and squared her shoulders. "I'm not going to add to the damage you've already done to our family."

Christine's response punched the breath right out of Joan's lungs. After a moment, Joan found the strength to nod. "If that's your choice, good luck to you. I hope you'll both be happy."

Joan stared at her lesson plans, but her mind was blank. She listened as Christine and Silas crossed to the back of the store. Tears of frustration stung her eyes. She blinked quickly before they could fall.

Ronald was right. She needed a break from all this drama. Once she stopped shaking, she'd call and accept his invitation to join him in New York.

"Lose my number?" Jeffrey's cell phone greeting still needed work.

"Have you ever considered starting a call with 'Hello. How are you?'" Ronald set down the pen he was using to grade student essay assignments in his campus office.

"This is as warm and fuzzy as I get."

"I've noticed."

"You think I'll know through osmosis when your flight lands Wednesday?"

Ronald turned to his computer and logged on to his e-mail account to forward his online travel information to his friend. "Sorry. I've been busy."

"Remember that when I'm not waiting for you at La-Guardia."

"I don't leave for another two days."

"I still have to put you on my calendar. Not everyone flies by the seat of their pants like you do."

Ronald grunted at his friend's accusation, tapping the commands to send his travel itinerary. "The information's on its way."

He pictured Jeffrey hunched over his desk, entering

Wednesday's flight itinerary into his BlackBerry. The man needed to relax.

"You don't sound interested in the studio's homage to you."

Ronald pushed away from his desk and stood to stretch. The office wasn't big, but he didn't need much room to pace. "Between the writing course and this manuscript, I've got a lot on my mind."

"Saved any young minds with that cushy teaching gig?"

"It's too soon to tell."

Ronald considered the blank beige walls surrounding him. A couple of pictures or posters would be a good idea. At least they'd keep his voice from echoing around the office.

"Meet any interesting coeds?"

"I'm seeing Joan." Ronald heard the concern in Jeffrey's silence.

"Two weeks. That's quick."

"I knew Yasmine for almost a year before I asked her to marry me." He could talk about it now without pain. In fact, he didn't feel anything.

"How's the erotic writer?"

"Erotic romance. She's fine. Her family's giving her a hard time about her books, but they'll come around."

"That's what happens when your family cares too much. They tell you what to do."

Ronald shook his head, pacing back toward his desk. He knew the comparison Jeffrey was making. "I just want my family to care a little. I don't think I'm asking a lot for them to help celebrate my successes and be there for my defeats."

"That's not the family you have. Get over it."

He took a deep breath as impatience and irritation constricted his chest. "Celebrating alone isn't much of a celebration."

"I'd go to this studio thing, but I don't want people thinking I'm your date."

"I appreciate the thought."

"What about Joan?"

Ronald tasted the bitter wash of disappointment again. "She has family commitments."

"You two getting serious?"

Why was he hesitant to answer his friend's question? His feelings for Joan had been growing stronger. Was he in love with her? Maybe not yet, but he easily could be. Soon.

Ronald sat at his desk. "We've been spending a lot of time together."

"You tried the positions from her books?"

Ronald chuckled with Jeffrey. He knew his friend didn't want an answer to that question. He was trying to lighten the mood. It worked. "Keep your mind out of my bedroom, Lane. See you Wednesday."

"Are you going to spend the night here?"

At the sound of Joan's voice, Ronald looked up from his notes for tomorrow's lecture and found her smiling in his office doorway. She looked vital and warm in a peach blouse and blue skirt. The fatigue he'd felt building within him abruptly disappeared. He checked his Movado wristwatch. It was almost six o'clock. He hadn't known it was so late. Then he realized Joan must have left work early. "Do you have a better offer for me?"

"Actually, I'm here to take you up on your offer, if it's still available."

He was afraid to hope. Afraid to ask. "What are you saying?"

She moved farther into his office. Her hips swayed gently beneath the calf-length skirt. "Your invitation to go to New York with you. I'd like to be your date for the cocktail party."

The warmth started in the pit of his stomach and built. This time he wouldn't celebrate alone. "What made you change your mind?"

Joan stopped behind one of his visitors chairs. "Chrissie doesn't mind if I leave her again so soon after coming back from Los Angeles. In fact, I think she's looking forward to my absence."

She spoke with nonchalance, but saying the words must have hurt her. "I'm sorry." Then a frown tightened his forehead. "Does she know who you'll be with?"

Joan gripped the back of his visitor's chair. "I told her the truth, that you invited me to your TV series launch party."

Another reason for her to blame him for the rift between her and her family. "What did she say?"

Joan shrugged, her gaze sliding away from him. "I'm sure she's added that to my list of transgressions. She'll probably tell my parents tonight."

Now he felt torn between being happy that she was going to be with him and sad that her family continued to make her feel like an outsider. Added to that guilt was fear that maybe, like Yasmine, Joan wasn't going to be with Ronald Montgomery the man but with the best-selling author.

He pushed out of his chair and stood behind his desk. "I'm glad you changed your mind and decided to come with me."

Her smile lacked its usual brilliance, a sign of the toll her family's silence was taking on her. "I'm grateful for your invitation."

"Why?"

She looked confused. "That's a strange question.

You invited me repeatedly to come with you. Are you regretting asking me?"

"I want to know what makes you happy, Joan. Is it meeting studio and publishing executives?"

"I'm looking forward to the cocktail party tomorrow evening. You did promise me a good time." She sounded annoyed.

"It also gets you away from your family."

"That's true. And things are getting pretty tense."

She wasn't telling him what he needed to know.

Ronald faced her, finding the courage to learn the truth. "Are you coming with me because you want to spend time with me, or are you coming to escape your family?"

Joan sighed. As tension seemed to drain from her, his wound even tighter. "If I'd wanted to escape from my family, I could just stay in my apartment. It would be a lot cheaper and less hassle."

"I'll pay for your airline ticket." He wouldn't tell her that her ticket was in his nightstand.

The look she gave him was pure disgust. "Meeting studio executives and your publisher will be nice, but they're not priorities for me. I'm happy with my publisher."

"It's always good to keep your options open."

"That may be. But, since I'm not going to network with industry bigwigs or to hide from my family, I must be going to spend time with you, see where you live and some of your favorite places. You're spending the summer getting to know Joan Brown. I'd like to know Ron Montgomery."

It was the oddest feeling, like receiving a standing ovation, to know that someone was putting him first. It felt incredible. "That's good to know."

She was shaking her head even as he spoke. "Silly man. How could you not realize that?"

"It's the questions you don't ask that get you into trouble."

"But you didn't need to ask that question. I'm going to New York because I want to spend time with you."

Ronald looked into her eyes and smiled. For the first time in a long time, New York sounded like home.

"She's different from the women you usually date." Jeffrey settled into one of the twin armchairs in Ronald's living room.

As promised, his friend had met Joan and him at the airport that afternoon and had driven them back to Ronald's apartment.

Ronald sank onto the sofa and glanced at his bedroom door. He didn't want Joan to walk into his living room to find them talking about her behind her back.

"I have a type?" That was news to him.

Jeffrey took a long drink from his can of root beer. "Yeah. Women who need saving."

Ronald squinted as a relatively small parade of females marched through his memory. "That's not true."

Jeffrey snorted. "Even Yasmine needed saving."

"From what?"

"Self-destructive behavior."

His laughter tasted bitter. "Then I should turn in my superhero cape because hooking up with my brother is one of the most self-destructive things a woman could do."

"No doubt." Jeffrey drank again. "Harry's sibling jealousy is self-destructive."

"I still don't get why you think Harry's jealous of me."

Jeffrey made a show of looking at the black and chrome

modern furnishings of Ronald's spacious three-bedroom apartment. "Harry lives with his parents."

"By choice."

Jeffrey drank his soda. "Joan doesn't need saving."

Ronald was amused. "You can tell that in less than an hour?"

"She waited less than ten minutes before telling me to change the radio station." His friend balanced his soda can on a coaster on the accent table in front of him. "That woman can take care of herself."

Ronald swallowed a laugh before taking a drink of root beer. As long as he lived, he'd never forget Joan telling Jeffrey he'd lost his mind because he was listening to a shock jock on his car radio. "I've told you for years to stop listening to that crap. It's rotting your brain."

Jeffrey grunted. "Your other girlfriends never said anything. Neither have mine."

"You intimidate people. That's why they don't comment on your dubious entertainment choices."

"I don't intimidate you or Joan."

"She's got a lot of heart." Hopefully, with enough room for him.

"That's why this one's going to save *you*."

Ronald scowled his confusion. "From what?"

"You'll see."

"As I said before, you have the heart of a poet beneath that tough exterior."

Joan entered the living room. "Are you gentlemen done talking about me?"

Ronald had been so caught up in his conversation with Jeffrey that he'd forgotten to watch the bedroom door. Now he couldn't take his eyes off Joan as she strutted past Jeffrey's armchair. She sat beside him on the sofa, crossing her long, long legs.

Cleopatra Sinclair had taken center stage.

Jeffrey smiled at Joan. "Just about."

Ronald shook his head, exasperated. "I think Jeff's decided to forgive you for making him change radio stations."

Joan arched a winged brow. "I was doing him a favor." She scanned his apartment. "Our decorating styles are very different. How did you keep from losing your mind when you came to my apartment?"

His dark furniture and somber accents were the flip side to her more vivid decor. He was the night to her day.

Ronald entwined their fingers. "Your brighter colors take getting used to."

Joan squeezed his hand in return. "What's on the agenda for today?"

"I'm going to show you New York." Ronald chuckled at the twinkle of excitement in her eyes.

Joan's expression dimmed. "Do your parents know you're in for the weekend?"

Ronald's smile stiffened. "It doesn't make sense to call them. We're not here for that long."

"We can make time, Ron. Their house could be part of our New York tour."

Jeffrey grabbed his empty root beer can and stood. He nodded at Joan. "Nice to meet you."

Joan rose to shake Jeffrey's hand. "It was a pleasure."

Ronald started to stand, but Jeffrey gestured him back. "I can find the door. Make your plans."

Ronald read the sorry-for-your-luck message in Jeffrey's eyes. The other man thought he was leaving Ronald to a confrontation with Joan. There wasn't anything to argue about. Ronald wanted to enjoy their long weekend, which meant his family's house wasn't going to be a stop on their sightseeing agenda.

He listened to the sounds of Jeffrey leaving. When they were alone, Ronald stood and circled the sofa, stopping in front of the big picture window. He stared down at the Matchbox cars creeping along the boulevard, the busy street vendors hawking their wares, the lush greenery of nearby Prospect Park.

"This one will save you," Jeffrey had said. Was he a project to her?

Ronald turned back to Joan. The concern in her eyes was genuine. She didn't see a project when she looked at him. She saw him. He smiled and she relaxed.

Ronald reached for her. "Let me show you New York."

Chapter 14

"You're wearing the red dress."

Joan halted in Ronald's bedroom doorway, suddenly uncertain. "You said I didn't have to wear black."

"You're beautiful."

His expression said even more. Dazed. Mesmerized. Hungry. She wasn't the only one remembering the night Cleopatra Sinclair first wore this dress. Power and confidence replaced nerves and self-doubt.

Joan straightened her spine and ran her gaze over Ronald, head to toe. "Thank you. You look pretty delicious yourself."

Any more mouthwatering and she'd need a bib. His simple black double-breasted suit looked custom tailored to trace his broad shoulders, taut waist, narrow hips, and very long legs.

Ronald took Joan's shimmery silver wrap from her arms. "If you're good, tonight I'll let you taste me."

"How much of a taste?"

"As much as you want." His voice was deep, full, stirring. His personal brand of foreplay.

"There's no doubt I can be good, but can you handle my tasting you, or will you need to be restrained?"

He slipped the wrap around her and pulled her close. "If you think it would be best, tie me up or hold me down."

The picture his words drew singed the edges of her imagination. Joan needed a moment to catch her breath. She cleared her throat, but her voice still came out in a hoarse croak. "You know my weaknesses, don't you?"

His lips curved in a slow expression of satisfaction and triumph, which made her toes curl in her strappy red stilettos. "I know you."

Ronald stepped back, settling his palm on the small of Joan's back, and escorted her from his apartment to the elevator.

Joan fought the urge to fan herself. The cocktail party hadn't even begun. Still, it couldn't end fast enough for her.

The food smelled wonderful. Servers dressed in white shirts with black vests and pants offered hot hors d'oeuvres, soups, fruit, vegetables and dips. Joan inhaled deeply, then sighed.

"Would you like a drink?" Ronald raised his voice to be heard above the live music from the jazz trio.

"Yes, please." She wasn't thirsty, but holding the glass would keep her from fidgeting. Hundreds of important-looking people mingled in the hotel's ballroom. What was she doing here?

Ronald offered her a glass of red wine and a toothpick topped by a Swedish meatball. "It's going to take a lot of this finger food to constitute a meal."

Joan studied the delicacy. "We should have stopped for a burger on our way into the city."

A tall older man with a thick gray ponytail stopped in front of Ronald. He was a monochromatic wonder in a fashionably cut gray suit and matching tie. "You made it."

Ronald accepted the newcomer's proffered hand. "I wouldn't miss my own party. Thanks for arranging it."

"We're very excited. And the gods must be, too. For once, everything's running on time and on budget. Knock on wood." He tapped his head with his free hand. The other held a glass of red wine.

"That's great news." Ronald took Joan's elbow, drawing her closer. "Scott Bishop, I'd like you to meet Cleopatra Sinclair. Scott is the executive producer of the Morris Jones television series. Cleo is a close friend and an author."

Joan felt a shiver of excitement to have Ronald use her pen name for the introduction to the producer. She watched Scott's cornflower blue eyes brighten with interest.

The older man shook her hand. "Co-executive producer. My sister and partner in crime, Gillian Landoff, is around here somewhere."

"Nice to meet you, Mr. Bishop." Joan gave the older man's bony hand a firm shake.

Scott looked at her with theatrical dismay. "Please call me Scott. And may I call you Cleo?"

"Of course," replied Joan.

Ronald's hand remained on her back, reminding her of how thin her dress was. His palm was hot; his fingers were long.

Scott's voice pulled her back from the bedroom scene in her mind. "What do you write?"

Joan tapped into her alter ego's confidence and took a sip of her wine. "Romance."

Scott's eyes widened, deepening the wrinkles across his high forehead. He looked from Joan to Ronald and back again. "Really?"

Ronald wrapped an arm around Joan's waist and brought her close. "Really."

The older man narrowed his eyes. "Do I know your work?"

"*Pleasure Quest* and *Double Dipper*." The pride in Ronald's voice warmed her. "Her series's heroine is the captain of a space station."

Scott's eyebrows rose. He gestured hugely with his glass. "Ooh. Sounds interesting. I'll be sure to look for them. So, Cleo, how excited are you over the television series?"

Joan took a moment to catch up with the conversation. A television executive had not dismissed her writing. She was breathless. *Calm down. He is probably just making conversation.*

"I'm very excited. I've read all of Ron's books, and I'm looking forward to the show."

A short, plump matron in a bedazzling evening gown approached, with arms wide open. She wrapped them around Ronald. "How's our man of the hour?"

Scott glared at the back of her raven head. "Where have you been?"

The woman stepped out of Ronald's embrace, and her smooth features brightened with a serene smile. "I'm not your appendage, Scotty. I am an independent entity with my own space and time. Do try to remember, hmm?" Her twinkling cornflower blue eyes widened when she noticed Joan. "And who have we here?"

Scott grumbled the introductions. "Cleopatra Sinclair. Gillian Landoff."

Gillian tipped her head back to give Scott a narrow-eyed stare. Then she took Joan's hand. "Cleopatra Sinclair. Such a dramatic name. Are you an actress, darling?"

"No, I'm an author," said Joan. A thrill went up and

down her spine as she realized she could say that in this New York crowd. She wanted to say it again.

"You would have known that if you hadn't wandered off." Scott's grumbling continued behind Gillian's back.

Gillian stepped closer to Joan. "Younger brothers can be quite tedious. Although I suppose older brothers could be, too."

Joan gave Gillian's hand a sympathetic squeeze. "I have two sisters."

The older woman tilted her head to one side, and her blue eyes, so like her brother's, became pensive. "That would be ideal." She looked up at Ronald. "Where have you been hiding this young woman, Ron? Very poor of you. Very poor indeed."

"She lives in Ohio."

Gillian contemplated Joan. "Ohio. He hid you well." With a wink and final pat on the hand, she released Joan and gave Ronald her full attention. "Did Scotty give you a production status?"

Scott sighed long and loudly. "This is a cocktail party, Gilly. I try not to mix business with pleasure."

Gillian arched a brow at her younger brother. "Our business is pleasure, Scotty." She met Ronald's gaze as he towered almost a foot above her. "Let's go find your editor. I think he's over there." She gestured across the room. "Your agent's here, too. I saw her during my walkabout. Scotty, bring young Cleopatra along. It's time to work the room."

Gillian first led them to Ronald's agent, an auburn-haired tour de force who looked ready for the catwalk. "Good evening, Adrienne. Have you met Ron's friend, the authoress Cleopatra Sinclair?"

Joan bit back a smile at the elaborate introduction. "It's a pleasure to meet you, Ms. Ward."

Adrienne's electric blue eyes scanned Joan as they

shook hands. Her gaze wasn't warm, but neither was it unkind. "Adrienne. Ms. Ward is my mother." She turned to the stunning blonde beside her. "This is my partner, Shelley Brackett."

"Good to meet you, Cleo." Shelley's voice was as angelic as her features. "So, Ron, when will you let me paint you?"

Ronald gave a lopsided grin. "Probably never, Shelley."

Shelley wagged a finger, her gray eyes tracing Ronald's features as though drawing him in her mind. "Never say never."

Joan watched with amusement as the thriller author blushed. She arched her brows at Shelley. "Are you an artist?"

Shelley dragged her gaze from Ronald. Her blond curls bounced as she turned to Joan. "Yes."

Joan smiled. "What medium do you use?"

Interest sparked in Shelley's eyes, and she gave Joan her full attention. "Mostly oils, but I use charcoals for more stark, dramatic images. Are you an artist?"

Joan shrugged, remembering when art had been her goal. She'd let go of that dream, so glad she'd kept her writing. "It's more of a hobby."

Ronald slipped an arm around her waist. "I've seen her work. She's very talented."

Gillian touched Joan's shoulder. "So good to see you again, Adrienne, Shelley. We must move on. Enjoy the rest of your evening."

A little more than an hour later, Joan dropped into a chair on the edge of the room. She felt light-headed, and her feet were on fire. That was what happened when you wore I-can-rock-your-world stilettos to a distance race masquerading as a cocktail party.

Gillian leaned against the wall beside her chair. "A little overwhelmed, darling?"

The older woman reminded her of the Energizer bunny. She checked the executive producer's shoes. Much more appropriate footwear. Still, Joan stood to offer her the chair.

Gillian waved her down. "I'm fine, darling, but thank you."

Joan sank into the chair. "This event is a little overpowering."

"It should be. It wasn't easy getting published, was it?"

Joan chuckled wryly. "No, it wasn't."

"Nothing worth having comes easily, and keeping it is even harder."

"Once you've built a name for yourself in the television industry—or in my case, the publishing industry—it should get easier. Shouldn't it?"

"No." The word was flat and final. "If you get comfortable in either industry, people will get comfortable with you. They'll know what to expect from you, and then they'll take you for granted."

Gillian wasn't just talking about their industries, was she? Had she seen through Cleopatra Sinclair and recognized that Joan Brown was trying—and failing—to fit in?

Joan felt the chill of sudden exposure. "How do you keep people from taking you for granted?"

"Don't allow other people to define you. You must define yourself. Establish your own boundaries and expectations. But, even as you do that, remember to be true to who you are."

Good advice and she would take it. Once she figured out who she was.

* * *

"You see the *News* article about the cocktail party?"
Adrienne Ward greeted Joan and Ronald as they
joined her Saturday afternoon.

Their cozy booth was toward the front of the tony
Times Square restaurant. Joan had been surprised to
be included in the agent's let's-do-lunch invitation.
She felt like Alice slipping down different rabbit holes,
each leading to yet another world. What was their destination today?

Ronald slid into the booth, beside Joan. "We read
the *Times* this morning."

Adrienne plucked the newspaper's Gossip section
from her large black leather purse and passed it across
the table to Ronald. She addressed Joan. "The reporter mentioned you."

"Me?" Joan blinked. "What did he say?"

Ronald gave Joan's forearm a bracing squeeze as he
skimmed the article. "Nothing to be nervous about.
He wrote, 'The usually solo Ronald Montgomery was
accompanied by the lovely romance author Cleopatra
Sinclair. Is this a romance on paper only, or are these
two an item?'"

Adrienne nodded toward the *News*. "Publicity is
good. You want your name out there."

Did she really? Publicity was a double-edged sword.
She needed it to build her name recognition and grow
her career. But too much attention could cause a
problem for her family.

Ronald gave her arm another bracing squeeze.

Adrienne continued. "It's good you showed up with
someone, Ron. You go to too many of these things
solo. The loner image is fine, but after a while, you get
a creep factor."

"Thanks, Adrienne."

His agent shrugged. "I'm just saying." She sipped

her water. "So, the studio's feted you. Your name's in the Gossip section. How are we going to capitalize on this? I've got some ideas."

Ronald leaned back in the booth. "You usually do."

Joan was eager to hear his agent's thoughts as well. This lunch would be a great learning experience for her. They were interrupted when a server asked for their orders.

Once the young man left with their drink requests—pink lemonade, root beer, ginger ale—Adrienne returned to their discussion. "Let's look at only the next two years, which will take us to another contract."

She gave them her thoughts on co-op promotion with the publisher, contractual performance bonuses, and book tours. Ronald had ideas of his own, which Joan never would have considered approaching her editor with. But then, Ronald was a *New York Times* best-selling author with a television series deal. He could dare a lot more with his contracts than she could with hers.

Their orders arrived. Adrienne cut into her grilled salmon salad. "So, Cleo, how much longer are you in New York?"

"We fly back to Ohio tomorrow afternoon." Joan tested her French onion soup.

"That's right." Adrienne turned to Ronald. "How's the teaching thing?"

Ronald chewed and swallowed a steak fry. "It's good. Better than I thought it would be."

"Make sure you're getting your writing done." Adrienne swallowed a forkful of salmon and lettuce.

Ronald smiled. "I am. I think this story is even stronger than the last one."

"Great." Adrienne addressed Joan again. "So, what do you think of New York?"

"It's been really exciting. I've had a wonderful time." Joan spooned up more of her soup.

Adrienne stabbed a lettuce leaf. "Think you could live here?"

Joan's expression sobered. Where had this question come from? "I haven't thought about it."

"You should. It's a great city. There's a lot going on. And the publishing industry is right here." Adrienne nodded toward the window. "You can walk down one street and knock on the doors of three publishing houses."

Joan poked at her soup with her spoon. "I would love to be this close to publishers. I'm sure it would help me to feel more a part of it. But I can contact editors with e-mail and phone calls, too."

Adrienne shook her head. "Nothing beats face time, especially when you're starting out."

Ronald sipped his iced tea. "I doubt editors want authors knocking on their doors unannounced and uninvited."

Adrienne shrugged. "I'm just saying." She gave Ronald a sly look. "Besides, I'm sure you wouldn't mind if she moved to New York."

Joan looked at Ronald. He caught and held her gaze.

"No, I wouldn't mind if Cleo moved to New York. But it's up to her."

Joan tried not to look as shocked as she felt. Was he saying that to be polite, or did he really want her to become a part of his world? How did she feel about that?

She stared at the remains of her French onion soup. Did she want to explore the rabbit hole and leave her family's world behind? Who did she want to be, Cleopatra Sinclair or Joan Brown?

* * *

Ronald unlocked his front door and let Joan precede him into his apartment. He almost sighed with relief at the cool temperature of his air-conditioned home. "This evening, when it's not as hot, we'll go back to the city."

"Okay." Joan leaned her hips against the entryway wall and slipped off her sandals.

Ronald locked the door. Joan didn't sound very enthusiastic about his plan. "What do you want to do now?"

Joan placed her sandals side by side in a corner beside the front door. "Let's look at your family photo albums."

"I don't have any."

Confusion clouded her eyes. "Everyone has family photo albums."

Ronald shrugged. "I don't."

"How about loose pictures? I can help you put an album together."

Ronald was shaking his head before Joan finished her thoughts. "I don't have any pictures." The look she gave him made him feel as though he'd just stepped off the spaceship at the end of *Close Encounters of the Third Kind.*

"Now that's just sad."

He strained against a ridiculous sense of defensiveness. It wasn't a national crisis that his family wasn't big on taking photos. Just because her family was snap happy didn't mean his family had to be. So why was she making a big deal out of this?

Ronald slipped his hands into the front pockets of his khaki pants and rocked back on his heels. "Sorry."

"There's no need to be. This is a problem we can easily fix." Joan led the way into his living room. "When we go back out tonight, we'll buy a disposable camera."

"What are we going to take pictures of?"

Joan hesitated. "Each other, to start." She lowered herself onto his cloth-covered sofa. "Once you've bought a digital camera, you can start on your family photo album."

Time to change the subject. "Do you want to watch a DVD?"

"What are my choices?"

Ronald pulled the large DVD album from his entertainment center, then sat beside Joan on the sofa. He rested an arm on the back of the sofa, behind her shoulders and slid closer to her. His thigh touched hers as he enjoyed her warmth and fragrance.

They spent the next few minutes evaluating Ronald's movie library. He was proud of his extensive list. The titles showed his preference for action/adventure and science fiction films.

Joan raised her eyes to his. "Where are the romance movies?" At Ronald's blank look, Joan sighed and started flipping through the binder backwards. "Which DVD would you recommend?"

He'd opened his mouth to respond when the doorbell cut him off. He glanced at his watch. "Who could that be?"

Joan lifted the DVD binder from his lap. "The only way to find out is to answer the door."

Ronald rose from the sofa. "Smart aleck."

"I'm just saying."

He laughed at Joan's impersonation of his agent as he padded barefoot to the door. His humor ended abruptly when he checked his peephole.

Ronald released his security locks and jerked open his door. "Mom?"

Darlene's smile was hopeful. "Hello, Ronnie. May I come in?"

Ronald recovered from his surprise. He stepped back from the door. "Yes. Sure."

His mother crossed his threshold. Her low-heeled sandals tapped against the hardwood flooring of his entryway.

She stopped and turned to him. "You didn't call to let us know you were home."

Ronald closed and locked his door. "Then how did you know I was here?"

"I called her."

Joan appeared behind his mother, in the archway between the entryway and his living room. Her expression was determined, but she grasped the hem of her red short-sleeved blouse in both fists.

The betrayal cut deep. "Why?"

Joan's shoulders rose and fell on a long sigh. "You're home for several days. You can spare a couple of hours to see your parents. It may be months before you get another opportunity."

Her tone was reasonable, almost cajoling. But Ronald's temper grew. Yasmine, his mother, and now Joan. It didn't matter why she'd decided to go behind his back and then keep secrets from him. All that mattered was she'd just joined the growing club of women who'd lied to him.

Ronald caught his mother's wide-eyed, darting glances and her stiff posture. She was obviously uncomfortable standing literally and figuratively in the middle of their tense exchange. He'd let go of the argument. For now.

"Come on in, Mom. Can I get you something to drink?"

Darlene's expression relaxed. "Some iced tea would be lovely, if you have it."

Ronald walked the few steps from the entryway to

the kitchen. Time and distance from Joan and Darlene would help calm him. He took his time assembling a tray with a pitcher of iced tea, sweetener, and three tall glasses filled with ice. He rolled his neck along his shoulders, releasing the tension from his muscles.

Finally, he carried the tray to his living room and served the drinks, pretending not to feel Joan's searching gaze.

Darlene accepted a glass from him. "Your father would have come with me, but he's busy with some chores."

His father found more satisfaction in his tomatoes, corn, and lettuce than in his sons.

Ronald returned to the sofa, this time leaving almost the full width of it between him and Joan. "How's his garden?"

Darlene's lips pursed with disapproval. "He wants to see you—"

"But he'd prefer to weed his garden. I guess his need to see me wasn't urgent, after all." Ronald couldn't resist the comment.

Joan frowned at him. "That's not fair, Ron."

Darlene's polite mask slipped, briefly revealing her temper before she composed herself. "I'm not sure where Harry is. He's probably looking for work. He's always looking for work."

"And never finding any," Ronald noted.

His mother's mask wavered again. "He's trying. That's what matters."

"How hard is he trying if he never finds anything?" Ronald asked.

"You're always tearing him down," Darlene replied.

"And you're always making excuses for him. You're not doing him any favors."

Joan leaned across the sofa, resting her hand on

Ronald's thigh. "You're only here for another day. Don't spend it arguing."

Ronald reined in his temper. "You wanted to spend family time with the Montgomerys. Well, this is it. Enjoy."

Darlene set her untouched drink on the tray balanced on the coffee table. "Believe it or not, Ronnie, I didn't come here to argue with you. I came to invite you and Joan to dinner."

"Thanks, Mom, but I was going to show Joan more of the city."

Darlene spoke over him, smoothing her floral-print skirt as she stood. "Your father's expecting you. Dinner's at seven. That gives you plenty of time to show Joan the city before we eat."

"Mom, I'm sorry, but we're—"

Joan popped off the sofa like a jack-in-the-box. "We'd love to accept your invitation. Thank you."

Darlene smiled, morphing from army general to lady of the manor. "You're welcome. We're looking forward to having you there." His mother looked at him. "Both of you."

Ronald followed his mother across his living room to the front entrance. He reached around her to unlock and open the door.

Darlene grasped his arm. "She's very special. I'm happy for you."

Right now, he wasn't.

Ronald kissed his mother's cheek, then closed and locked the door after her.

"How angry are you?"

Ronald turned. "Pretty damn angry. You lied to me."

"I want you to give your family another chance. Tell them what you want. How you feel. You started to before, and then you just gave up."

He crossed his arms. "That's almost funny coming from you. You're not exactly a shining example of open communication. You've spent the past twenty-six years hiding the real Joan Brown from your family."

Joan inclined her head. "You're right. It's often easier to give advice than to take it. I took your advice and told my family the truth. Now they're trying to cut me out of their lives. But, Ron, I'm not giving them up without a fight. That's all I'm asking of you. Don't give up on your family without a fight."

Ronald uncrossed his arms and strode past her. "What makes you think they're worth fighting for?"

Chapter 15

The dining room was soaked in tension. It seeped into Joan, making it hard to swallow the cheese sandwich. She stared at her plate of fruit salad, green salad, and various finger sandwiches: cheese, tuna, and ham. *What a waste of food.*

She glanced at Ronald. He ate without making eye contact with anyone. Instead, he sat beside her and stared into the distance, the same way he did when he was working out a scene in his manuscript. Was that what he was doing? Pretending he was home writing instead of with his relatives? It seemed sad to waste family time wishing you were somewhere else.

The other Montgomerys weren't reacting to the strain, either. They didn't even seem aware of it. Maybe they'd learned to function under these dysfunctional conditions. But much more of this deafening silence would give her indigestion.

Joan took a fortifying gulp of lemonade before breaking the almost ten-minute silence. "Ron and I had a wonderful time at the TV series launch party last night. We talked to the executive producers."

Silence returned, and Joan confronted three blank stares. Ronald continued to ponder the far wall.

"Oh, was that last night? How exciting," Darlene finally said, then returned to her finger sandwich.

Joan glanced at Ronald, then tried again. "I also met his editor."

"That's nice." Darlene turned to Harold. "Where were you this afternoon?"

Harold finished chewing before he answered. "I put in some job applications."

Darlene beamed. "Where?"

"A couple of department stores in the city," Harold informed his mother.

Joan caught Ronald's gaze. He tapped his chin with his index finger, then pointed at her. Joan closed her mouth, embarrassed that it had been hanging open. But Ronald's parents hadn't noticed. Their attention was on Harold.

George looked disgusted. "I didn't pay four years' worth of college tuition for you to work in retail."

Irritation brightened Darlene's dark eyes. "It's an honest job, George."

George snorted. "If an honest job was all he wanted, I wish he'd figured that out thirty thousand dollars ago."

Joan couldn't listen anymore. "Excuse me." All four Montgomerys turned to her. "I don't understand why you're so disinterested in what Ron's doing. But you're completely attentive to Harry's job search, even though it sounds like you've had this same discussion several times before."

George glanced at both sons before giving Joan his attention. His high forehead and wide-set eyes were familiar. If she knew Ronald in another thirty years, this was what he'd look like. "We're not worried about Ron. He has a job. Harry needs one."

Joan was still confused. "We're here with you for the entire evening. There's time to share Ron's good news as well as discuss how to help Harry."

Darlene grew more agitated. "We weren't able to attend the party." She turned to Ronald. "We would have liked to, but we weren't able to."

Suspicions tickled the back of Joan's mind. "You've said that before. What do you mean? Why weren't you able to attend?"

"We were busy." George stabbed a grape. "But we're glad you had a good time."

"I wish you'd been there," Joan said, then looked to Ronald. Why wasn't he saying anything? "His agent asked about you."

Finally, interest lit Harold's dark brown eyes. "Oh? What did he want to know?"

Joan frowned. "She. His agent's a woman." Why didn't his brother know that?

Harold smirked at Ronald. "Is that how you get your contracts? By turning on the charm?"

Ronald wasn't amused. "No. I earn my contracts with hard work."

Darlene scowled. "There's no need to brag, Ronnie. It's very unpleasant."

Shock rolled down Joan's spine. "Is that why you don't care about what Ron's doing? Because you think he's bragging?"

Darlene turned her frown on Joan. "While his brother is struggling is not the time to rub his success in Harry's face."

This family was a constant source of confusion. "You criticize Harry because he hasn't done anything with the thirty thousand dollars you spent on his college tuition. Then you criticize Ronald because he has," Joan pointed out. "I wonder, is there any pleasing you?"

Ronald looked surprised. Well, he could just save it. He'd spent the entire evening staring at a wall. Now that she'd lost her patience with his dysfunctional family, he'd decided to look at her.

George straightened in his chair. "You're going to sit at my table and insult me?"

Joan considered the Montgomery patriarch. He seemed more curious than angry. "I don't think it's considered an insult when what you're saying is the truth. I think it's called an observation."

Ronald laughed. "She's right. I've spent my life trying to earn your approval, but I don't know how. That's not my fault. You don't know what you want. It took someone from the outside looking in to show me that."

Harold grinned. "Maybe you should try being a major screwup like me. Then you could have Mom's attention and Dad's disapproval twenty-four-seven, too."

George put down his fork. "You're grown men. You shouldn't need our approval. All that matters is whether you're doing what's right."

Ronald leaned forward, drawing his father's attention. "Why is it so hard for you to give your approval when it's so easy for you to hand out disapproval?"

George rested his forearms on the table. "Bad behavior needs correcting."

"And good behavior deserves disinterest?" Ronald retorted.

Darlene spoke up. "It's not that we're not interested in what you're doing. It's just that you don't need our support."

Ronald sighed. "That's where you're wrong, Mom. Whether the news is good or bad, it's always nice to have your family's support."

The meal ended shortly after that exchange. Ronald

was impressed but not surprised when Joan helped his mother clear the table. He carried platters back to the kitchen while his brother and father escaped to the living room.

The livery car Ronald had arranged to pick them up after dinner arrived on time. Ronald hugged his mother, waved good-bye to his father and brother, then followed Joan down the front steps to the curb where the car waited.

What had Joan thought of the cold farewells? In contrast, it probably took the Brown family an hour to say good-bye. He remembered because he'd been a part of that ritual. The good nights were as long as the meals.

Joan slipped into the backseat. "I still think I was right."

"Of course you do." Ronald climbed in beside her, closed the door, and fastened his seat belt.

The driver pulled away from the curb and merged into the traffic. Ronald loved everything about living in Brooklyn—except the traffic.

He stared at the passing scenery. It was after nine at night, yet friends still conversed in front of houses and on steps, reluctant to end the day. At the bodegas, older men would gossip and younger ones would listen to music well into the night. These city scenes were different from the quieter streets of Columbus.

Joan adjusted her seat belt. "You were right, too, though."

"You're throwing me a bone?"

Joan's laughter poured over him. He smiled. Truth be told, he wasn't angry anymore, but he'd wait awhile before admitting that. She'd lied. That part still bothered him.

"You were right that dinner with the Montgomerys isn't a pleasant experience."

Ronald snorted at the understatement. "It's torture."

There was a rustling sound as Joan turned to face him. "Why doesn't your family talk during meals?"

He recalled the sights, sounds, and feel of the Brown family dinner. Especially the sounds. It was no wonder Joan found the Montgomerys' silent meal an alien experience.

Ronald looked at her. "I've said before, our families are different. In your family, a meal is an excuse for a social gathering. In my family, eating is survival, in more ways than one. Conversations are arguments, and no one has ever survived an argument with either of my parents."

Joan shook her head. "I was always taught not to argue during meals. You're supposed to wait until after you've eaten."

"I tune out the arguments."

Joan quirked a brow. "I noticed you fixedly staring at the wall. Were you pretending to be somewhere else?"

Ronald shrugged. "It helps get me through these meals."

Joan hummed noncommittally, turning to look out the window.

Ronald studied the back of her head. Her raven hair flowed over her shoulders, capturing the glow from intermittent streetlights. "Thank you."

Frowning, she met his gaze. "For what?"

Ronald heard surprise in Joan's voice. "For standing up for me when I'd given up on myself. For helping my family see that helping Harold doesn't mean shutting me out."

"Oh." A moment of silence. "You're welcome."

Ronald smiled to have thrown her off guard. She'd taken him off guard often enough, between the different aspects of her personalities and her strong sense of family, whether for the Browns or the Montgomerys.

The livery car pulled up to the curb outside Ronald's apartment building. He tipped the driver, then escorted Joan to his fifteenth-floor apartment. His cell phone rang almost the moment he unlocked his door and stepped back for Joan to enter first.

The display read NO CALLER ID. With a mental shrug, Ronald took the call, anyway. "Hello."

A beat of silence. A stream of static. And then a voice. "Ron, it's Yasmine."

Ronald watched Joan walk farther away from him, into the living room. Perhaps she wanted to give him privacy for his call. Still, he wasn't comfortable speaking to his ex-girlfriend while his current girlfriend was nearby.

He rubbed his forehead and stepped into his office. "What do you want?"

"I saw in the paper that you were in town. How are you?"

"I'm fine. Thanks for calling." He started to hang up, but some inexplicable instinct made him pause when she called out.

"Wait, Ron. I just want to talk."

"You slept with my brother—in my bed. That's an automatic end to any conversation between us."

"I'd hoped we could still be friends."

Had she taken notes from some sappy 1930s romance movie? "How would that be possible?"

"Can't we at least try?"

"No. Please stop calling me."

Ronald was starting to disconnect the call again when Yasmine's voice, soft and pleading, reached him.

"Ron, I need help."

He didn't owe her anything, much less help. His

feelings for her had withered and died after he'd found her under his brother. But she sounded desperate.

"What is it?" His self-disgust grew as the silence lengthened. Why did he care? He was halfway to ending the call when she spoke.

"I'm pregnant."

Shock sucked the air from the room. Ronald's mind was blank of everything but the words *she's pregnant.* They played a discordant drumbeat in his ears.

An image of Joan came to mind, and he found the courage to ask the obvious. "Whose is it?"

"Don't worry. The baby's not yours. It's Harry's. I'm almost three months pregnant."

Sweet relief made him weak. "Does he know?"

"Yes." On a sob, her answer broke into two syllables. "I told him I love him, and that I want him to be a part of his baby's life."

Ronald shook his head. Yasmine was naive to believe Harry would go easily—if ever—into fatherhood. "What did he say?"

"I've left him messages for the past two weeks, but he won't return any of my calls. That's why I need your help."

Harold had claimed to love Yasmine. Now that she was pregnant, both Harold and his love had disappeared.

"What do you expect me to do?" Disgust made Ronald's voice flat.

"I just want you to talk to him. Get him to call me. You're my last hope."

Ronald leaned against the front of his desk and rubbed his forehead. A headache was threatening. "He won't listen to me."

Yasmine sobbed again. "I don't know who else to call."

"Call my parents."

"They won't help. They won't make Harry grow up. Instead, they let him get away with everything. I love him, but it's time he stopped being a boy and started acting like a man."

Shame weighed on Ronald that Yasmine was a victim of his brother's spiteful games. Anger that another generation would suffer because of Harold's irresponsibility burned him. It was time for his Peter Pan brother to grow up.

Ronald straightened from his desk. "I'll talk to him. But I don't know if it will do any good."

Yasmine gave a tremulous sigh. "Thank you, Ron. I know I'm asking a lot. And I'm sorry if it's hard for you to hear that I love your brother."

"It's harder to hear that my thirty-year-old brother needs to grow up, even though I know it's true."

He ended the call and went in search of Joan. She was sitting on the sofa, reading a magazine. Her green, red, and gold floral-print sundress was a vivid splash of color against his black and gray room. She looked up at his approach.

Ronald stopped in the archway. "I have to go back to my parent's house. I may be a while."

He'd grown used to the welcoming warmth of her chocolate eyes. But this time her eyes were cautious, almost distant.

"Do you want me to come with you?"

"No. I'll come back as fast as I can."

Joan laid the magazine in her lap. "Does this have anything to do with your phone call?"

Ronald folded his arms. "Were you listening to my call?"

Joan stood and walked toward him. She stopped an arm's length away. "I wasn't eavesdropping. The words 'you slept with my brother' were hard to miss. What did Yasmine want?"

"I'm sorry, but that's not your business."

A small smile tipped her lips without reaching her eyes. "I'm the one in your bed now, Ron. That makes it my business. What did your ex-lover want?"

Ronald turned away. "I have to go."

She reached out and took a firm hold of his elbow. He turned to look down at her.

"I care about you. What hurts you hurts me. Tell me what's wrong," she said.

He wanted that to be true. He wanted her to care about him even half as much as he'd come to care for her. But if he shared his pain and anger with her now, he'd never leave. And this was a matter that had to be dealt with tonight.

With a gentle touch, he pushed her hand away. "Not now, Joan."

The hurt in her eyes almost made him change his mind. But this was for his family. They ignored him. They'd deceived him. They made him feel like an outsider in their lives. Still, they were his family. Gathering his resolve, Ronald left the apartment and locked the door.

A block from his apartment, he caught a bus that, almost half an hour later, left him two blocks from his parents' house. Ronald could have used his house key, but it was after ten o'clock, and his parents weren't expecting him.

His father came to the door. "Did you forget something?" George let Ronald in.

"I need to speak with Harry."

George frowned, possibly sensing Ronald's agitation. He gestured toward the living room. "He's watching TV."

Ronald climbed the entrance steps and nodded a greeting to his mother before turning toward the living room. The television screen gave him a glimpse of scantily clad women screaming at each other before he turned to confront his younger brother. "I have to talk to you."

Harold looked at him in annoyance. "I can't see the TV through you."

Ronald turned and hit the power button on the sixty-three-inch plasma-screen television set. How Harold had convinced his parents to buy it was beyond him. Did they ever watch it?

Ronald returned his attention to his brother. "I have to talk to you *now.*"

Behind him, Ronald sensed his parents enter the nearby dining room. He felt them watching the exchange between their sons.

Harold's annoyance shifted toward aggravation. "What's so damn important that you have to interrupt my show?"

Ronald lowered his voice. "Yasmine." He saw the understanding in Harold's expression.

Despite the fact that Ronald had whispered her name, his father overheard him. "When are you going to let that go? It's over," called George.

Ronald smile humorlessly. "But it's not over, is it, Harry? Far from it."

Harold popped off the sofa. "Let's talk in my room." Hostility hardened his brother's features.

Ronald was angry, too. Angry with Harold for not accepting responsibility for the life he and Yasmine were creating. Angry with himself for possessing a sense of duty that compelled him to try to reason with Harold. Angry with his parents for letting Harold get away with everything.

He followed Harold to his room and shut the door behind them. "Why haven't you returned Yasmine's calls?"

Harold flopped down on his bed, folding his hands behind his head and crossing his ankles. "What's there to say?"

Ronald's muscles were stiff with anger. "How about, 'Yasmine, I accept my responsibility. What do you want to do?'"

"It's up to her whether she keeps the baby. That's not my deal."

"You're the baby's father. That makes it your deal."

Harold gestured around his room. "I live with my parents. How am I supposed to care for a baby?"

Ronald worked to control his temper. "I thought you loved her."

Harold folded his hands behind his head again. "I had a change of heart. I mean, any woman who'd sleep with her fiancé's brother can't be very trustworthy. What do you think?"

Ronald's vision narrowed to Harold, casting everything around him in a red haze. "You're thirty years old. Get a job, and take responsibility for yourself and your actions."

Harold smirked. "Easy for you to say, Mr. Perfect. But I'm not you."

Ronald's heart was drilling a hole through his chest. "I'm sick of your feeling sorry for yourself. You have a child coming into this world. Stop thinking of yourself, and think of your child."

"I'm not going to ruin my life over some woman's stupid mistake. Besides, that child would be better off without me."

"Or that child could give you a reason to grow up. It's your choice, Harry. But you're running out of time."

Harold's expression hardened. "Are you done?"

Ronald rubbed his forehead. "Yes. I'm done with you."

Chapter 16

Ronald entered his apartment and followed the sound of rapid typing to the dining room. Joan sat at the table, seemingly oblivious to everything but her laptop.

He watched her for a few seconds before interrupting. "I'm back."

She stopped typing. Ronald could tell the moment she returned from her story world to his dining room.

"So I see." She tapped a couple of commands into her laptop, then stood and shut it.

Ronald regretted the chill building between them. With forced optimism, he went in search of her warmth. "How's your writing going?"

"That's none of your business."

"I deserve that."

"I know. But I'm not as angry as I was when you first left. My heroine killed three people and had great sex. I feel much better now."

Ronald arched a brow, unable to hold back his smile. "Did you start without me?"

Joan crossed the room, her robe swinging around

her bare legs. She paused beside him. "I'm going to finish without you, too." She glided from the dining room.

If she'd meant for her response to arouse him, it had worked. Ronald bit his tongue to keep from asking if he could watch. Instead, he followed her to his bedroom.

Ronald watched her from the doorway as she stood before his dressing table, brushing her hair. "I didn't mean to upset you."

"Oh? Then what did you mean for me to feel when you threw my concern back in my face?"

"I wasn't ready to talk then about what was going on. If you're still interested, I'd like to tell you now."

Joan was silent for a moment. Finally, she turned to face him. The frost melted from her tone, and her concern wrapped around him. "What happened with Yasmine that upset you?"

He walked toward her, took her hand, and led her to sit beside him on the edge of the bed. "Yasmine asked me to talk to Harry. She's pregnant with his child."

Her shock was a tangible thing. Ronald could feel it radiating from her. He could see it in her widened eyes and parted lips.

She spoke hesitantly. "Are you sure it's Harry's baby?"

"Very. Yasmine and I broke up more than four months ago, and she's three months pregnant." Ronald's tension drained as Joan's shoulders relaxed.

"Is Harry going to help her?"

"No, but that doesn't surprise me. Even though he said he loved her, a part of me often wondered whether Harry slept with Yasmine to get at me."

"Do you still love her?" Joan's voice was small, the words reluctant.

"No." Ronald answered without hesitation. "I don't hate her anymore, but I don't love her, either. She betrayed my trust in one of the worst ways possible."

Joan shifted to face him. Her knee pressed into his thigh. "What did your parents say?"

"I didn't tell them."

"Why not?"

"This is between Harry and Yasmine. It's up to them to tell my parents."

"Do you think they will?"

"No." Ronald gripped the edge of the mattress to keep his anger in place. "But I've done my part. It's up to them to decide what to do now."

Joan pried his left hand from the bed. She held it between her palms. "You're a good person, Ron."

He frowned. "Why do you say that?"

"Because even though Harry and Yasmine hurt you very badly, you answered her call, and you tried to get Harry to do the right thing."

"I don't want Harry's mistakes to affect another generation of Montgomerys."

Joan cupped Ronald's cheek, tilting his head up to meet her gaze. "That's out of your control. As you said, it's up to Harry and Yasmine."

Ronald covered the back of Joan's hand with his. "I like the way you make me feel."

She looked quizzical. "How's that?"

"Like I matter to you. Like you're proud of me."

Joan stroked her thumb across his cheekbone. "You do matter to me. I am proud of you."

"It meant a lot to me when you told me you cared for me. I'm sorry I walked away from you and from those words."

Joan turned her hand so they were holding on to

each other. "You needed time. Yasmine dropped a bomb on you. I understand that now."

Ronald kissed her hand. "I care for you, too."

She gave him a soft, lingering kiss that heated his blood and healed his heart. "Prove it."

Ronald traced her cheekbone. "Is Cleo ready to come out and play?"

Joan's smile faded slightly. "I don't know about Cleo, but Joan's ready."

"They know my name." Her vision blurred over the article in the Saturday *New York Daily News*'s Gossip section.

Ronald looked up from *The New York Times* Sports section. "Who?"

"The newspaper." Joan's grip was unsteady as she held the paper so Ronald could see the headline, SAINT OR SINNER? BEST-SELLING AUTHOR'S NEW THRILLS WITH PASTOR'S EROTIC DAUGHTER.

Ronald took the pages from her. "What the hell?"

The short article was stuffed with information about the cocktail party, Joan's erotic romance novels written as Cleopatra Sinclair—and her father, a pastor in Columbus, Ohio.

Blood drained from Joan's head. Shock made her dizzy. "How did they know who I was?" She struggled but failed to control her strident tone, brought on by threatening hysteria.

"Don't worry. This will blow over by tomorrow. Neither of us is interesting enough to make the national news."

"*I* may not be, but *you* are. If the congregation finds out about this, it will ruin my father." She stood and strode toward his bedroom. "I've got to warn my family."

Ronald followed her. She snatched her purse from his chest of drawers and dug through it for her cell phone. Hysteria made a sharp left turn toward icy fear. "I can't believe this. How did they find out? Why do they even care?"

Ronald watched from the doorway. "Are you sure you want to call your family now? You could be worrying them for nothing. We're not going to make the national news."

"I can't afford to take that risk."

Joan pressed the speed-dial command to call her parents. She listened as her call connected, praying her mother would answer the phone. After four rings, she heard her father's voice.

She swallowed her panic and took a deep breath. "Hi, Daddy. It's Joan."

Kenneth's tone hardened. "Is it true you're in New York with a man?"

Joan looked at the man her father believed was leading her down the path to hell. "Yes, Daddy. I'm visiting with Ron."

"I'd thought I raised you better, but I was wrong. All you've done lately is disappoint me." His voice was low, almost as though he spoke to himself.

Joan gripped her right forearm with her left hand, trying to steady her cell phone. Delivering her news had just gotten that much harder. She restrained the temptation to ask to speak with her mother. As much as she might have wanted to, she wouldn't take the coward's way out of this.

"Daddy, there's a story about us in the *New York Daily News*."

"You and Ron?"

Joan flinched as Kenneth spat Ronald's nickname. "And you."

"Me? Why would I be in the paper?"

She was shaking all over—her head, arms, and voice. "Because the newspaper learned my real identity."

Silence, long and loud. "What do you mean?"

"They know my real name is Joan Brown and that you're a pastor."

The full weight of her father's anger bore down on the satellite connection. "How did they find out?"

"I don't know." Her response was little more than a whisper.

"They printed that in their paper? If that story is picked up by our local paper, I'll be ruined."

"I know, Daddy. I'm sorry."

"I'll be humiliated in front of the entire congregation."

"I'm sorry, Daddy."

"I'll lose credibility for my sermons and my counseling. The congregation will never listen to another word I say."

"I'm so sorry." Her tears flowed freely, her words choking with them.

Ronald was beside her in two long, rapid strides. But as his arms reached for her, Joan shook her head violently and stepped back. She didn't deserve comfort. She'd brought shame upon her family and their church, and deserved every word her father lashed at her.

"All your life, I've told you your one obligation was to serve as a role model for the congregation. The congregation is our main concern."

"Daddy, I'm sorry."

"How can I stand behind the pulpit and preach the word of God when my daughter is standing against me, condoning the sins of the flesh?"

"But, Daddy, that's not—"

"And everyone knows it." He spoke over her, as though her words had no value.

"Please forgive me, Daddy. I didn't mean for any of this to happen."

His voice grew louder with his anger, overpowering even her thoughts. "Sorry? You're willfully writing filth. You've taken up with an atheist. And you're having sex outside of the sanctity of marriage. Little girl, it's not me whom you should tell you're sorry. Ask God to forgive you."

The call exploded as he dropped the phone. Joan crumpled to her knees, folded at her waist, and sobbed her misery. She was too shattered to stand, too ashamed to open her eyes, too weak to reject Ronald's embrace. Her father's judgment was an icy blade carving her flesh down to the bone and even to her soul.

Ronald pulled her closer, soothing her back and crooning words she couldn't recognize into her ear. But nothing could ease her pain. This was the end result of the choices she'd made, choices that had repercussions for her family as well as for herself. How could she have chosen so wrongly?

Hours later, Ronald's temper had settled to a simmer. He wanted to confront Joan's father over his harsh and hurtful words. But his main concern was Joan's reaction to the condemnation. Her eyes were dim. Her skin was pale. She moved around the apartment like an automaton.

Ronald glanced at his watch, then looked at Jeffrey.

"It's almost noon. Let's load your car, then get lunch before going to the airport."

Jeffrey lifted Joan's suitcases from the bedroom floor. "Lead on."

Ronald hefted his own suitcases, then led his friend down the hall to the front door. He paused beside the kitchen entrance. Joan's back was to him as she stirred chicken stew over the simmering stove.

She hadn't met his gaze even once since that morning. Was he losing her? He called her name twice before she answered.

"Jeff and I are going to the garage to load his car. We'll be right back."

"Okay. Lunch is almost ready."

Her voice was painfully polite. It only increased his worry.

The pealing doorbell redirected his thoughts. Ronald set down his suitcases and checked the peephole. With resignation, he opened the door for his parents.

Darlene gripped the strap of her navy shoulder bag, the same color as the stripes in her loose-fitting summer dress.

His mother stopped just inside the entrance, his father close beside her. She smiled at Jeffrey. "How are your parents?"

"Fine, thanks, Ms. Montgomery. And both of you?"

"We're managing. Some days are easier than others," replied Darlene. She glanced at Ronald, then away.

George faced his son. "We need to talk to you. Now. In private."

Ronald checked on Joan. After greeting his parents, she returned to the stew, preoccupied.

Ronald caught Jeffrey's attention and inclined his head toward the suitcases. "Wait for me."

"Sure." Jeffrey dropped Joan's suitcases and meandered into the living room, presumably to wait for Ronald's return.

Ronald led his parents to his office. He turned on the overhead light and closed the door before moving behind his desk. He rested his hands lightly on the back of the chair. "Why do I have the sense you're not here to wish me a safe trip?"

George stood in the middle of the room beside his wife. He stood stiffly in a lightweight tan shirt and brown pants. "We're here to try to talk some sense into you."

Ronald knitted his eyebrows. "About what?"

Darlene's eyes widened as though in disbelief. "About Yasmine having your baby. You're going to be a father."

Ronald reeled. He tightened his grip on the chair's back. "Who told you the baby was mine?" As though he didn't know.

George glared at him. "Harry told us about Yasmine's pregnancy after you left the house last night."

Ronald's reaction ran the gamut. Disappointment, sorrow, anger. "And you believed him?"

George blinked, and Ronald knew his father was remembering the last time Ronald had challenged him about taking Harold's word over his.

Darlene took a step toward Ronald, her confusion plain. "Yasmine called Harry last night. She told him the baby was yours."

Fact and fiction spun in front of him. Ronald rubbed his eyes with his thumb and two fingers. "Did Harry tell you that?"

Darlene nodded. His brother had weaved quite a story for their parents.

"I seriously doubt Harry spoke with Yasmine last night," Ronald told them.

George scowled. "Are you calling Harry a liar?"

Frustration burned Ronald from the inside out. *Stay calm.* "One of your sons isn't telling you the truth. The question is, do you know which one?"

Darlene looked from Ronald to George and back again. "Why would Harry lie to us?"

Ronald stared at his mother. "Why would I?"

George jammed his fists into his pants pockets and rocked on his heels. "Harry's concerned for you, Yasmine, and the baby. He asked us to talk to you."

Darlene's smile was shaky. "Do you see how much your brother cares about you? Isn't that wonderful?"

The depth of Harold's mendacity took Ronald's breath away. His temper threatened to fray. "Did Harry tell you how I took Yasmine's news?"

George's frown turned from anger to confusion. "Why do you need us to tell you what you said?"

"Because apparently I don't know." Ronald saw that his snapped response added to his father's confusion.

"He said you were angry. That you weren't going to let Yasmine's mistake—your words—mess up your life," George revealed.

Ronald gritted his teeth and paced the small office. Had he entered *The Twilight Zone*?

He wanted to roar, break something, punch a wall. If his brother had been anywhere near him, Ronald would have punched his teeth out.

Darlene continued Harry's lies. "You told Harry you weren't going to leave Joan to marry Yasmine just because she's pregnant. But, Ronnie, Yasmine needs you more."

George pulled his hands from his pockets and waved dismissively. "Joan seems like a nice person, even though she likes to argue. But she can get along without you. Yasmine can't. Be a man and accept your responsibilities."

Ronald stopped pacing. His vision was blurred with anger. "I never said any of those things, and I can't believe you'd think I would. Don't you know me, the son you raised?" His eyes narrowed with fury as he watched his mother. "Don't you know your *Ronnie*, Mom?"

Darlene extended her arms toward him beseechingly. "But Harry said you did say those things."

In his mind, Ronald saw himself knocking everything off his desk—lamp, phone, reference books. Instead, he forced himself to remain still. He didn't want his parents to think he'd lost his mind. That wouldn't help his position. "Why are you so quick to assume the worst of me? What have I ever done to make you question my integrity?"

His parents exchanged a look in silence. He couldn't tell what they were thinking.

George met his son's gaze. "We wouldn't have believed you capable of denying your child if Harry hadn't told us what you said."

Ronald's mind went blank with shock. "Why are you so eager to believe Harry is telling you the truth?"

"You slept with Yasmine." His father's tone was blunt.

Well, if they are going to go there . . . "So did Harry, as you both know. I was the one who was going to marry her, until I found out my brother was sleeping with her. Don't you remember that?"

Darlene flinched. "If Yasmine is pregnant with our grandchild, we want to make sure they're both taken care of."

"With Harry as the father? Good luck with that." Ronald's mental lightbulb went off. "Is that why you decided I was the baby's father? Because you know Harry won't accept his responsibilities?"

George took exception to Ronald's words. "*We* didn't decide you were the father. Yasmine did."

Ronald arched a brow. "Did you ask Yasmine?"

Darlene shook her head. "It's not our place to talk to Yasmine."

Ronald sighed. They couldn't talk to Yasmine, but

they could falsely accuse him, the *other* son. Someone they should know better than they apparently did.

"I'm not cleaning up Harry's messes anymore. This isn't a broken toy, a wrecked car, or a ruined engagement. This is a baby. And it's Harry's." Ronald glanced at his watch as he walked toward his office door. "Please excuse me. I have a plane to catch."

His mother followed him. "You're not going to talk to Yasmine?"

Ronald held the door open for his parents to precede him. "You're the ones who should talk with Yasmine."

Chapter 17

"Miss Brown, this is Stacy Smalls. I'm with Channel Twelve news here in Columbus." The voice on Joan's answering machine was both assertive and salacious. Her skin crawled. "Call me so we can talk about how you, as a minister's daughter, could write, much less publish, a pornographic novel. My number is—"

Joan erased the message before it ended. "I'm getting tired of telling people I don't write porn."

"The other four messages are probably the same as the first three." Ronald's voice came from behind her. They'd gotten back from Port Columbus International Airport about half an hour earlier, and he sounded tired.

Joan pressed the heels of her hands against her eyes. "I can't believe this is happening. Are they calling my parents, too?"

"Probably. They're calling either the church or your parents' home. Maybe even both."

"You're not helping." She looked at him over her shoulder. Seeing him slouched on the arm of her sofa broke her heart. "You look like you've been up for twenty-four hours. Why don't you take a nap?"

"I'm fine."

He was lying.

Joan turned to him, lightly resting both hands on his shoulders. "No, you're not. You couldn't be, after the argument you had with your parents this morning. It hurt me, and they aren't even my parents."

He squeezed her hands before standing to wander her living room. "I don't know why I'm letting it bother me."

"How could you not? Your brother lied to them, and they believed *him*."

"Why don't they trust me? What have I done?"

"This isn't your fault, so stop thinking that." Joan sighed, taking his seat on the sofa's arm. "I'm so sorry. I'd hoped this weekend would help make things better between you and your family. Instead, it made things worse."

"No one could have guessed this would happen."

"Something's been bothering me about Yasmine's pregnancy. Wasn't she using birth control?"

"I asked her about that when I gave her Harry's answer. She was on an antibiotic at the time. Harry wouldn't use a condom."

Joan crossed her arms. "Humph. No birth control, no sex."

Ronald gave her a tired smile. "Spoken like a responsible romance author."

"Not a porn writer." Her answering smile faded. "What was Yasmine's reaction to Harry's response?"

Ronald's shoulders rose and fell with a deep sigh. "She was disappointed but not surprised. Everyone but my parents realizes Harry's irresponsible."

The silence was heavy with contemplation. Ronald returned to sit on the sofa. She leaned against his shoulder.

He wrapped an arm around her. "I'm sorry the media's harassing you."

"So am I."

"Are you going to talk to any of those reporters?"

Joan straightened to face him. "For heaven's sake, no. That would only bring more attention to my family, and they would hate that."

"Do you blame me for all this?"

"I don't blame you for any of this. I've told you before, it was my choice to tell my family."

"But I pushed you to make that choice."

It was Joan's turn to wander the living room. The thick sapphire carpet was soft against the soles of her feet. "I have no one to blame but myself. I made the choice, but maybe I didn't have the right to."

"What do you mean?"

"Everything I do reflects on my family. My father's been telling me that my entire life, but I never really understood what he meant."

"Until now?"

Joan nodded. "The choice I made has put my entire family under the spotlight. Maybe the best thing—the only thing—for me to do is to stop writing."

Ronald stood. "That would be the worst thing for you to do. Your family loves you. Just give them time."

She threw up her arms in frustration. "The longer I wait, the worse the situation gets. I'm running out of time."

Joan pulled into a space in the church parking lot and turned off the ignition. There were more cars than usual in the lot. She was almost twenty minutes early for Sunday's first sermon. She hadn't noticed until now how tense her neck and shoulders were. She tried stretching them.

Ronald reached over to rub her neck. "You're here

to pray. It doesn't matter what other people think."
His touch and words brought comfort.

Joan forced a laugh. Perhaps if she pretended to be
courageous, the courage would come. "It's not their
thoughts that I'm concerned about. It's their reactions. I've known some of these people all of my life. I
don't want them to look at me with contempt—or
avoid looking at me, for that matter."

"You won't be alone. I haven't known you all your
life, but I'm here with you now."

Joan swallowed a lump of emotion and sought
Ronald's eyes. "That means a lot."

"We'll sit here until you're ready to go in."

This time the laughter wasn't forced. "Why aren't
you suggesting we just go home?"

"Cleopatra has too much courage to run."

Joan's smile faded. "What about Joan? Do you think
she'd go home?"

"No. She and Cleo are the same."

His answer puzzled her, but this wasn't the time to
worry about it. Joan pulled the key from the ignition,
unfastened her seat belt, and climbed from the car.
Nerves or no nerves, she was done cowering in the
parking lot.

She walked into the church, grateful for Ronald's
supportive hand on the small of her back. The first
people she saw were three of the elder church ladies,
chatting in the hall in front of the sanctuary doors.
Joan's smile was reflexive, warm, and welcoming. The
three ladies looked right through her, then away.

She'd been expecting the slight. Still, it hurt. "It's already started."

Ronald took her hand. "We'll get through this."

Joan slowed her step and greeted each woman by
name, reminding them of their last conversation.

"Miss Gayle, how are you managing with your arthritis this morning?"

"Fine." Gayle Sharpe gripped her cane and turned her back to Joan. Apparently, the small, frail woman had forgotten that last Sunday Joan and Ronald had helped her to her pew.

Joan gently tugged Ronald to a stop. "Miss Alice, is your granddaughter feeling better?"

Alice Crumb tugged at the bodice of her royal blue dress. She lowered her gaze and nodded without a word.

"I'll continue to pray for her." Joan switched her attention to a stick-thin woman in an overly busy floral-print skirt and matching blouse. "Miss Lettie, is your grandson still living with you?"

Lettie Quints stared at Joan in wide-eyed censure. "Yes."

Joan's smile was again warm and welcoming, a gracious salutation from the minister's daughter that strained the muscles in her jaw. "Enjoy the sermon, ladies."

Joan accompanied Ronald into the sanctuary, head high, shoulders back, and eyes straight ahead.

The pews were crowded, although more than ten minutes remained before the start of the service. Seating hadn't been a concern when she sang with the choir.

She looked up toward the pulpit, where the choir sat in flowing blue robes. They were an impressive sight, and she'd return to them soon.

Joan looked around at a crowd of new faces. They all stared at her. Some were pointing. "Oh, for heaven's sake. They're here because of the newspaper."

"What do you mean?" Ronald frowned at her.

"The people staring at me. They're here because of the story the local paper picked up from the *Daily News*."

Ronald looked around. "Don't pay any attention to them. We'll get through this."

He used those words as a mantra, and Joan picked it up. With knocking knees, she walked with him to the front pews, their shoes tapping against the hardwood flooring and blending with murmured conversations and hushed giggles.

Timothy stood as Joan stopped beside him. "I'm glad you came. I've saved room for you."

Joan tilted her head. Her smile shook around the edges. "Everyone else has stopped speaking to me. Why haven't you?"

Timothy shrugged. "I like you."

"I like you, too." She kissed his cheek. "Maggie had better hurry up and grab you."

Timothy hugged her back. "Maybe you should speak to her."

"I will, as soon as she's speaking to me again. Thanks for saving seats for us."

"You're welcome." He shook Ronald's hand. "It's good to see you again."

Timothy moved farther down the bench, giving Joan and Ronald room to join him. Joan sat between the two men. "Really, Tim, why aren't you pressuring me to stop writing?"

Timothy put his arm around Joan's shoulders. "It's much ado about nothing, princess. Your family's upset that you didn't tell them you were a published author. They know now. You apologized. It's time to move on."

"They aren't the only ones having trouble with my books." Joan glanced around at the congregation. She caught some parishioners staring at her before looking away.

Timothy released her. "This will all blow over."

Ronald leaned forward. "In the meantime, you've

brought more people into your family's church. Some may even become members."

Joan shivered. "I feel like the star of a freak show."

Timothy winked at Joan. "The next Brangelina sighting. The next time Britney Spears leaves her house without her underwear, you'll be old news."

Joan chuckled. She lifted her eyes to the pulpit and the seats behind it. Her mother and sisters were already seated—and studiously ignoring her. Her smile faded.

Sitting behind Christine, an older woman—Vivian Barnes—smiled at Joan. The greeting was so cordial and unexpected, at first Joan just stared. Vivian added a small wave to the smile. Joan waved back, still disconcerted. Vivian's smile brightened before she sobered and looked away.

Joan gritted her teeth to keep her smile in place. "Maggie is lucky to have you."

Timothy winked. "Don't I know it?"

A real smile replaced her fake one. Joan reached over to squeeze Ronald's hand. "And I'm lucky to have you."

"I'm the lucky one," said Ronald. He stroked a finger down her cheek. "But, in the end, you have to decide who you are and what you want."

"Why do I have to choose?" Joan stared at the choir members. "Why can't I have both? My family and my writing?"

Shortly after Joan opened The Artist's Haven Monday morning, Juanita entered the store, squealing and clapping her hands. Alarmed, Joan stared at the college student, trying to determine what was wrong. Kai stood beside her, a wide grin splitting her face.

Juanita practically bounced on her toes. "Why didn't you tell us you're a published author?"

Kai grinned. "We work for a published author. How cool is that?"

Relieved, Joan started to laugh. "Don't get too excited. If it weren't for this place, I'd probably starve to death."

Kai's grin never faltered. "It's still a great accomplishment. Congratulations." She walked past the checkout counter, where Joan stood, on her way toward the back aisles.

"I can't wait to read your book." Juanita hurried after Kai.

Joan shook her head, amused and touched by the young women's excitement. She was still smiling when, moments later, the chimes above the entrance stirred. She looked up—and found a video camera and a microphone shoved in her face.

"Joan Brown? Stacy Smalls from local Channel Twelve news. I'd like a comment from you on the pornography you write."

Shock took Joan's breath away and left her numb. Too many thoughts and reactions overwhelmed her. Her mind went blank except for one thought. "I don't write porn."

A red light glowed on the camera. Were they rolling tape?

Joan looked down at the mic inches from her face. She followed its handle to the bony television reporter on the other side of her checkout counter. Her plastic blond hair framed a rounded face subtly made up for a peaches-and-cream complexion. There was a feral glow in her wide, glass green eyes.

The reporter shifted the microphone to her own mouth. "If you don't call it pornography, what *would* you call it?"

The mic tipped back to Joan. She eyed it and the

television reporter in bemusement. Who was this woman, and what made her think Joan would answer any of her questions?

Her thoughts cleared. Joan gave the cocky reporter a hard stare. "This is private property. You can't bring a camera in here."

"This will take only a few minutes. I only have a few questions."

Joan's arm shook as she pointed toward the front door. "Get out of my store."

"Right after you answer a few more questions," Stacy insisted.

Joan's voice grew strident. "Turn off that camera, and get out of my store now."

"What does your father think of your writing? He's a minister, right? A man of God?"

The microphone swung back to Joan. She unclenched her teeth. "I'm not answering any of your questions, so pack up your toys and get out of my store."

The entrance bell chimed, and two college-age male customers walked in. They did a double take when they saw the cameraman and the reporter. Joan gave them a polite smile, inclining her head before turning her attention to the camera crew.

Stacy spoke into the mic. "Speaking of toys, I understand you use several of them in your books. Are these scenes written from personal experience?"

There weren't any toys in her books. The reporter hadn't read her work, but she was prepared to condemn it. Why was everyone so quick to judge without the benefit of knowledge?

Joan's entire body shook with anger. "I'm not discussing my personal life with you."

"Are there any sexual aids you can recommend to our viewers?" asked Stacy.

Joan's heart was beating so fast. Too fast. She couldn't catch her breath. "Are you deaf or just dumb?"

Anger flashed across Stacy's heavily made-up features. "Come now, Ms. Brown. Haven't you heard any publicity is good publicity? How many men have you slept with?"

An image of herself leaping over the counter and smashing the camera into Stacy Smalls's face played like a movie preview before Joan's eyes. Instead, she opened her mouth to verbally blast the twentysomething fake Barbara Walters, but Christine spoke first.

"You have five minutes to step your scrawny behind out of our store. Otherwise, the first call we make will be to the police." Her sister came to stand beside Joan. "The second will be to one of your rival stations, promising them an exclusive, while you won't even get a quote."

Christine's presence beside her helped Joan breathe again. She no longer felt as though the world were spinning around her. For this moment at least, she wasn't standing alone.

Stacy gave Christine a considering look. Her sister didn't appear imposing. She wore a powder pink cap-sleeved blouse, buttoned to her neck. Hot pink hair clips held shoulder-length raven locks from her face. But Christine's words had been tough, and looks could be deceiving.

The reporter smirked. "Haven't you heard of freedom of the press? I'm here to do my job."

Christine put her hand on the telephone receiver. "Four minutes, fifteen seconds, and counting."

Joan worked hard to conceal her amazement. She'd no idea her baby sister had this tough-as-nails crisis negotiator side. Sweat rolled down Joan's spine. She had no doubt that in her commando role, Christine would call the police. She just really hoped it wouldn't come to that.

Stacy turned the microphone to Christine. "You'd get rid of me faster if you gave me a quote."

"Three minutes, fifty seconds, and counting."

Joan almost shivered at the climbing frost in Christine's voice and the cold look in her eyes.

Stacy paused, but just briefly. "All right." She turned to her cameraman. "Come on. Let's show these *ladies* we won't outstay our welcome."

"One moment." Christine held out one slim arm. "The tape, please."

Stacy's mouth formed a wide O. "You can't have our tape."

"We didn't give our permission for you to record here." Christine wrapped her palm around the counter's edge and gave the reporter a challenging stare. "Unless you want me to push the panic button to lock you in here with us, you'll hand over the tape."

"Give me the tape," Stacy demanded. Her glare squelched the mutiny on the cameraman's face. She flounced back to Christine, tossed the tape on the counter, then marched away.

The knot of anger in Joan's chest loosened with each step Stacy and her cameraman took toward the door.

Once they'd left, Joan's shoulders relaxed, and she faced her sister. "A panic button?"

Christine shrugged. "The lie worked, didn't it?"

Joan exhaled heavily. "Thank you."

The younger woman didn't look at her. "Thank Kai and Juanita. They told me what was happening. I couldn't have a scene in the store. This is a place of business, not some daytime soap opera stage."

Joan took a deep breath, hoping to ease the sting

from her sister's comment. "Why couldn't *I* get her to leave?"

"She was playing on your emotions. I didn't show her mine. But, believe me, I wanted to clean her clock."

Joan released a startled chuckle. "So did I."

Christine grinned. "That was obvious."

Joan surveyed the store. Several customers looked away when she caught them watching her. Her skin burned with embarrassment. She was tired of people staring at her. "Thanks for referring to us as 'we.' That felt really good."

Her sister's grin disappeared. "Mom and Daddy's phone's been ringing off the hook since Saturday with newspaper reporters and TV newscasters pressuring them for interviews."

"I'm very sorry."

"So are we. Some of these calls are from outside of Columbus. It's ridiculous. They're calling night and day."

"I hate that this is happening." Joan glanced toward the front displays. Two women lingering at the shelves looked away.

"We're going to hate it for a while. At least until the media gets distracted by another story."

Joan watched Christine scrutinize the store. "Do you think we'll get more surprise visits from TV news crews?"

"You can bet your boots we will."

Joan's eyebrows jumped. "Bet my boots? What's gotten into you?"

"Nothing." Christine glanced at her, then returned to studying the store. "But until this garbage goes away, stay in the office." She nodded toward the women spending an inordinate amount of time before a counter display. "I think some of these customers might be more interested in the local pornographer than in our inventory."

"I don't write pornography." The response was automatic. Joan tossed a look at the young women and men peeking at her from the aisles. Christine probably had a point, though. "I'm sorry this is happening." She'd said it before, but it was worth repeating.

"So am I."

Joan turned toward the back office. She agreed with Christine that she should stay away from news crews and avoid the stares of curiosity seekers. But her main purpose in retreating was to run from the hostility in her sister's eyes.

Chapter 18

"The only thing that will help me now is a time machine, something to make it so this never happened." Joan stood at the kitchen counter, peeling a potato for dinner.

In the background, the evening broadcast news discussed local events. To her right, the water began to jump in the pot.

Ronald stood at the island behind her, cutting broccoli. "Besides, Cleopatra Sinclair doesn't run from confrontations."

Joan slashed the potato in half. *Why* did he keep calling her that?

"I'm not Cleopatra Sinclair. I'm Joan Brown." She cut the potato into fourths and lowered the pieces into the boiling water.

"You're both."

She snorted. "In your fantasies maybe. And while you're hanging out in your imaginary world, I'm trying to keep mine from falling apart."

Ronald's hands settled on her shoulders, using the leverage to turn her to face him. "I don't have to fantasize about your strength. It's very real."

"If I'd been strong, none of this would have happened. I'd have told my family about my books from the beginning."

Ronald dropped his arms. "You had your reasons for keeping them secret."

"Now you're making excuses for me?" Joan bent to check the chicken broiling in the oven. "Today's Wednesday. I've had dinner with my parents every Wednesday since I moved out of their house years ago."

"Tonight you'll have dinner with me."

Joan looked into Ronald's eyes and found a measure of peace. "That sounds nice." She straightened and closed the oven door. "I do miss greeting my customers at the store, though. I've been hiding in my office since Monday."

Ronald dropped the knife he'd used to cut the broccoli and pulled her into his arms again. "It's probably better that way. You can't risk another media attack."

She leaned into him. "That's what Chrissie said, too. I know you're both right. I still don't like it, though."

Her attention shifted to the television. Shock numbed her. Her lips parted. It took a couple of attempts before the words came. "What is Stacy Smalls doing in front of my family's church?"

Ronald turned, his hands sliding away from her. Joan stepped around him, grabbed the television's remote control, and punched up the volume.

Stacy struck a pose for the camera, a cross between serious news reporter and wannabe lingerie model. "I'm standing here in front of Holy Grace Neighborhood Church, where K. Howard Brown is the pastor. It's recently come to light that the Reverend Brown's daughter Joan Brown is the infamous erotic novelist Cleopatra Sinclair."

Waves of nausea made her weak. Was this her worst

nightmare? It probably came close. Ronald wrapped his arm around her waist and guided her to a kitchen chair. Joan dropped into the seat, her attention fixed on the television.

Stacy shifted to her right. The camera pulled out, widening the shot. Joan gasped. Her father now stood beside the broadcast reporter.

"Reverend Brown, how do you feel knowing your daughter is a pornographer?"

Joan gasped. She was cold with shock and sick with fear. Ronald's large hands cupped her shoulders. She reached up and clutched one, an anchor in the storm.

Kenneth glanced at the camera. Pain and shame tightened his dark features. Joan's eyes burned with threatening tears.

"It's been hard on the family." Kenneth cleared his throat. "Her mother and I don't know where we went wrong. This isn't the way we raised our children."

"So you think there was a problem with your parenting?"

"No, that's not what I'm saying. We raised our children in the church. But even if you give your children a solid moral foundation, outside forces can still distract them."

Outside forces? Joan's shattered thoughts shifted together as she focused on that phrase.

"What outside forces are responsible for your daughter's behavior?"

"The media, for one. There's plenty of sex and violence on TV, in the movies, and, of course, in books."

Stacy sighed, setting a hand on her hip. She shifted the microphone from Joan's father back to herself. "Reverend, your daughter is a grown woman. Do you believe she can't tell the difference between sex and violence on television, and sex and violence in real life?"

Kenneth shrugged, a jerky, uneasy motion, and glanced again at the camera. "She knows the difference between television and real life. But she's lost her moral compass to know what's right and what's wrong."

"Why do you think that is?"

"She's taken up with a man who doesn't have her best interests at heart. He doesn't know her or share her values."

Joan's heart stopped, then raced to make up time. She hadn't expected this attack, not from family. She tightened her grip on Ronald's hand.

A look of vicious triumph flashed across Stacy's features. "You mean Ronald Montgomery, the thriller author." The reporter made it a statement of fact.

"Yes. She went to New York with him. We believe he had something to do with Joan's decision to write these books."

"How could he think that?" Joan's voice was weak and shaky.

Ronald released her hand and folded his arms across his chest. "Your father is searching for someone to blame, and he's settled on me."

She regretted the cynicism in Ronald's voice. He was probably adding her father's false accusation to those his parents and brother had leveled against him. Who could blame him for being upset? She was upset on his behalf.

Stacy pointed the microphone back to herself. "What are you going to do about that?"

"As you said, my daughter is a grown woman. My wife and I told her how disappointed we were that she'd chosen to write these sinful stories." Kenneth looked into the camera. "If the decision were her own, we're positive she wouldn't write them anymore. But obviously, she's under a less than honorable influence."

Joan stared at the television even after Stacy wrapped up the interview. She couldn't believe what her father had said. She couldn't believe what he'd done.

Ronald's voice broke her trance. "Your father's using that interview to make his ultimatum public. Your family or your writing. Choose."

Joan spun to face him. Anger warmed her muscles. "Why the heck are you being so darn calm about this?" She stabbed a finger toward her TV. "My father just slandered you on the news."

He stared at her. "So?"

Her eyes stretched. "Aren't you afraid of what that negative publicity will do to your career?"

"Your father's tirade won't affect my career. He was using the interview to vent."

"No. He was using that interview to assert his control." Her temper spiking, Joan grabbed her purse and car keys from the hall cabinet. "He condemned you because he thinks you're a threat to his control."

Ronald followed her to the front door. "How?"

"Don't wait on me for dinner."

"Where are you going?"

Joan paused, looking over her shoulder. "I'm going to tell my father he can't use you to control me."

Joan let herself into her parents' house. Her tan low-heeled sandals clicked against the tiled floor, drowning out the conversation drifting from the dining room. She stood in the threshold between the entryway and the dining room, studying the group seated at the table.

As though sensing her presence, her family looked up from their dinner plates. Her sisters tensed. Her mother looked concerned. Silas ignored her. Tim welcomed her with a smile.

Joan took a steadying breath. "Did you enjoy your fifteen minutes of fame, Daddy?"

Kenneth's gaze was cool as he chewed his food. "Don't come to my house with a disrespectful tongue, little girl."

"Don't insult my friends," Joan replied.

Her mother dropped her fork. "Do you have to do this over dinner?"

Joan's gaze locked with her father's. "Daddy picked the time. The six o'clock news. You must have known I'd come to speak with you, Daddy. I hope you weren't expecting an apology."

"If you haven't come to apologize or to agree to stop writing, give me your keys to this house and leave." Kenneth extended his hand, palm up.

Joan pressed her fists against her thighs, bare beneath the hem of her burgundy shorts. "Ron had nothing to do with my decision to write erotic romance. You had no right to bring him into this."

Kenneth pressed forward, into the table. His voice was gritty. "He brought himself into this when he took you to New York."

"No one *took* me anywhere. I went of my own free will. The only person trying to control me is you."

"Joan." Her mother's voice shot like a bullet across the room. "Give your father respect."

Kenneth sat tall in his chair at the head of the table. "You can have all the free will you want. But when your decisions cause harm to this family, I'm going to exert my authority."

Joan locked her knees to keep her legs from collapsing. "We aren't little girls anymore, Daddy. We don't need your approval of our decisions. We don't even have to ask your opinion."

Kenneth lunged to his feet. Dishes clattered. Drinks jumped. Nervous gasps spun around her.

"That's where you're wrong, little girl." Her father jabbed a finger toward her. "Nothing happens in this family without my approval."

Margaret lifted a shaky hand toward her sister. "Joan, stop now." She turned toward their father. "Daddy's the head of the household. We all know that. Let's all calm down."

Joan stood her ground. "I respect you, Daddy. But when you brought Ron into this, you crossed the line."

"Stay away from him, Joan." Her father barked the order. "He's not good enough for you."

"How do you know that?" Joan swung her arm toward the dining table. "Do you know that the same way you know Silas is good enough for Chrissie? Silas's family may be good for the church, but *he's* not good for Chrissie."

"Silas will be a good husband to Chrissie," Kenneth declared.

"No, he won't. But Tim's perfect for Maggie. The only reason you disagree is that you didn't choose him," Joan asserted.

Kenneth was visibly shaking. "I'm your father. I know what's best for you."

"No, Daddy. You know what's best for you," Joan retorted.

Kenneth held out his hand again. "Give me your key and get out, little girl."

Joan lifted her chin. "I'll leave, but I'll never return my key. I'm a member of this family, whether you like it or not."

* * *

Ronald stared at Joan's bent head. Did she know he knew she was pretending? She might be moving her food around the plate, but she wasn't eating.

She'd told him to have dinner without her, but he'd waited, anyway. Mashing potatoes, steaming broccoli, and broiling chicken had partially distracted him from whatever was happening at her parents' house.

Ronald swallowed a bite of chicken. "Your father tells you what to write and Chrissie who to marry. Why does Maggie get a pass?"

"Actually, he's controlling Maggie *and* Tim." Joan shifted some mashed potatoes to another section of her plate. "Maggie won't marry Tim without my father's approval, and Daddy won't give it."

"What does he have against Tim?"

"Who knows?" Joan spoke on a sigh. "But Maggie picked Tim, and Daddy picked Silas. Whose instincts do you trust?"

Ronald speared a broccoli crown. "If it were you, you'd have married Tim regardless of your father's approval."

Joan frowned at him. "What makes you think that?"

Ronald answered her question with a question. "What happened to the pastor your father picked for you? Dr. Wendell Hines?"

She went back to playing with her food. "Maggie doesn't want to put Tim in an awkward position with my father. That's why she's still waiting almost three months later for his approval."

"But all Tim wants is Maggie."

"Maggie may be right about waiting for Daddy's approval."

"Why?"

"Apparently, Maggie realized the extremes my father's willing to go to get his own way. I didn't." Her gaze met his. "I don't want him to damage your reputation or your career."

"I appreciate your concern, but your father can't hurt me professionally."

Joan sliced another piece of chicken. "How do you know that?"

Ronald drank his root beer. "The national media isn't going to run with a story about a father feuding with his daughter's lover."

No, Kenneth couldn't hurt him professionally. Personally? Perhaps. Ronald considered her father's ultimatum: family or writing. What would happen to him if she chose her family?

Joan forced a humorless laugh. "I didn't think the press would care about two people dating. Then my father appeared on the local news to tell neighbors and complete strangers that my lover has corrupted my moral compass. Imagine my surprise."

"There's no reason to worry about me."

"If you say so." Joan looked as unconvinced as she sounded.

Ronald thought about Margaret and Timothy. He couldn't imagine Joan letting a situation like that remain in limbo for so long. Not the woman who'd stormed out of her apartment on a mission to confront her father about him.

"When will you get tired of defending me?"

Joan looked up from her still-full dinner plate. "What are you talking about?"

Ronald sliced into his chicken so he wouldn't have to meet her eyes. "First, you defend me to my family, and now you've defended me to yours."

"My father never should have involved you, especially not on TV."

Her voice shook with an anger that still confounded

him. She cared about his feelings. She was taking his side over her father's. Why?

Ronald held her gaze. "You haven't answered my question."

"Your question doesn't make sense." Joan stopped playing with her food. She pushed away from the table and collected her dishes.

"It does to me." Ronald stood, blocking Joan's path to the counter. He took her plate—still heavy with food—and her silverware and put them back on the table. "Why would you go out of your way to defend me? Why do you care what other people say about me?"

The question seemed to stop her cold. "Why wouldn't I care?"

"That's what I need to know." The words weren't coming easily, and her reaction made it harder. He gritted his teeth and tried again. "I'm not used to someone rushing to my defense. Why do you? Because you think I can help you with your career? What's the catch?"

Her sudden stillness and the storm in her eyes told Ronald he'd gone too far.

Joan stepped closer and drilled a finger into his chest. "How many times do I have to tell you that I don't care how many best-seller lists you've appeared on?"

"Then why—"

"And a *catch*? What's the *catch*?" Her tone rose with her incredulous anger. "There is no *catch*, Ron." Joan snatched the plate from the table, spilling broccoli to the floor, and stalked to the kitchen counter.

"Joan, I'm—"

"I don't want a damn thing from you, Ronald 'Aren't I Full of Myself' Montgomery." She flung open a cupboard door and grabbed a box of aluminum foil. "It mattered to me what my father said about you because you're my friend. Or at least you *used* to be." She wrapped her plate in the foil.

"I'm sorry. I didn't mean that the way it sounded."

Could he call for a "do-over"? He needed the last three minutes of his life back.

Joan marched to the refrigerator and yanked open the door. "You didn't mean to call me an opportunistic slut? You're a best-selling author, Ron. You should be able to do a better job expressing yourself."

She deposited her plate in the fridge, slammed the door, and started to leave the kitchen. With quick strides, Ronald caught her from behind. He turned her to face him, gripping her rigid shoulders. The hurt and disappointment in her eyes scalded him. He'd been a fool to question her friendship just because he was beginning to want so much more.

Ronald eased his hold on her slender shoulders. "Please listen to me. Is it surprising that I'd wonder why you'd jeopardize reconciling with your family when my own family's so quick to condemn me?"

"Yes." The short, sharp word burst from her. Joan tried to shrug out of his hold, but Ronald wouldn't let her go. "You should know me better than that."

Fear and regret bore down on his chest, making it hard for him to breathe. "Your family's important to you."

Joan took a deep breath. Beneath his hands, Ronald felt her relax slightly.

"So are you, Ron." Reproach seasoned her words. "I always fight for the people I care about, and I care about you."

Ronald closed his eyes, feeling the pressure ease from his chest. "I guess I was stupid, but I wanted to hear you say that."

Joan arched a winged brow. "You made me angry,

hoping to hear me tell you I care about you? That's beyond stupid, Ron."

"I'm sorry. Is there any way I can make it up to you?" The warmth of Joan's smile washed over him. "I have a few suggestions. But how hard do you want me to make it for you?"

He grinned at her deliberate innuendo. "The harder the better."

Chapter 19

Was there a special circle of hell for men who slept with ministers' daughters? Judging by the expression on Joan's father's face, the answer was yes.

Ronald watched Joan's parents and sisters emerge from the sanctuary after Thursday's choir practice. He'd stood in the hallway for almost half an hour, listening to the rehearsal. The choir was good. He understood why Joan missed performing with them.

He straightened from the wall and met Joan's family halfway. He nodded to Caroline, Margaret, and Christine. They returned his greeting warily.

Then Ronald looked Joan's father in the eye. "Reverend Brown, may I speak with you, sir?"

"You have a lot of nerve approaching me and, even more, coming here, to my place of worship." Contempt coated Kenneth's words.

Ronald kept his voice level, his expression calm, despite the anger building in him. Kenneth was playing an emotional game with his daughter because she wanted to live her own life. Ronald cared too much for Joan to sit by and allow that. "My feelings for your daughter give me the nerve to be here, sir."

Sudden coughing drew his attention. Christine gave him a self-conscious smile. Ronald returned his attention to Kenneth, waiting for the older man's decision.

Kenneth's features twisted with resentment. He pivoted on his heel and called to his family over his shoulder. "Wait for me here. This won't take long."

The reverend's shoes beat a staccato rhythm as he marched across the tiled floor. Ronald followed in his wake. He also hoped their meeting wouldn't take long, but he wouldn't bet money on it.

Kenneth opened a door at the end of the hallway. His office was a ruthlessly well-organized space. Two short, wide file cabinets stood against the right wall, beneath a black lacquered cross. A tall, broad bookcase on the left housed various research and spiritual texts.

The walls were bright white. The furniture was black upholstery. Ronald caught the subtle message. Things were either black or white. There were no gray areas in Kenneth Brown's world.

Kenneth crossed the ebony carpeting and sat behind a wide black lacquered desk, bare except for a telephone, an in-box, a desk organizer, and a laptop.

The reverend hadn't offered him a seat, but Ronald had never stood on ceremony. He claimed one of the three guest chairs facing Kenneth's desk. "Reverend, I've read Joan's books. She's an excellent writer. She has a gift."

Kenneth didn't appear impressed. "If you're here to convince me to accept that my daughter writes filth, you're wasting my time and yours."

Ronald ignored a jab of temper. "What's really bothering you about Joan's work?"

"How is that any of your business?"

"You made it my business when you blamed me for Joan's fall from your grace."

Kenneth's narrowed stare confirmed he'd caught Ronald's insinuation that, in his family, the pastor considered himself God. "Joan was a good girl before she met you."

"Joan is the same woman she's always been. Nothing has changed."

"Of course she's changed. She doesn't share our values anymore."

"She knows the importance of family, friendship, loyalty, and love. Are those the values you're talking about?"

"Sex outside of marriage is a sin."

As Kenneth's voice rose in volume, Ronald struggled to keep his level. "What's really bothering you about your daughter's writing? Are you upset she kept it a secret from you? Should she have asked permission first?"

"She writes filth."

The pastor was a broken record. Did he realize he was using repetition in place of a valid argument?

Ronald leaned back and took stock of the Reverend K. Howard Brown. The older man sat stiffly in his chair, emanating waves of impotent anger. He was an aging patriarch who sensed himself running out of power. His dark eyes were wary, as though evaluating a threat.

Ronald made himself relax. He didn't want to present a challenge. "I'm not a threat to you. We both care for your daughter. We both want her to be happy, but your rejection is hurting her."

"I won't condone anyone whose work is peddling sin. Not even my own daughter."

Ronald's body tensed as he came up against the wall of Kenneth's intolerance. "You know she didn't mean to hurt you. That's why she didn't tell you sooner."

"She didn't tell me sooner because she's ashamed, and she should be."

Ronald stared hard at Joan's father, hoping to get through to him. "Don't make your daughter choose between her writing and her family. Joan loves you very much, but she also loves to write."

"Don't tell me how to treat my family." Kenneth's voice rose in outrage.

"Suppose someone you loved asked you to choose between them and the church. How would you feel?"

Kenneth's anger simmered between them. "I can manage my family without your help."

"Reverend, have you considered that your daughters don't need you to manage them anymore?"

Ronald stood. He hadn't waited for an invitation to enter Kenneth's office. He wouldn't wait to be asked to leave. Without another word or even a glance, he crossed the room, let himself out, and closed the door behind him.

"Leave my daughter alone."

Startled, Ronald looked up. Caroline watched him from across the hall. She looked tidy and cool in a light purple summer dress. She stood alone. Joan's sisters must have gone home. He wondered cynically how they'd found the courage to leave after their father had ordered them to stay.

Caroline stepped closer, her sandals slapped against the tile. "You're tearing my family apart."

Ronald moved away from Kenneth's office. "*I* am?"

"Yes, you are." But she didn't sound as certain this time. "My daughter belongs in the church. She can't stand with one foot in the secular society and one foot in the church community."

Ronald slid his hands into the front pockets of his slacks. "Do you think Joan woke up one day and published three books? She's been writing for years—while she sang in the choir and attended Sunday services."

Caroline's eyes narrowed and her lips thinned. "We don't approve of content like that."

"Have you read the psalms? The greatest story ever told isn't only an inspirational. It has elements of suspense, paranormal, mystery, and—yes—romance. Your husband preaches from it every Sunday."

"Don't twist my words. I only want what's best for my daughter."

Ronald stepped closer to Joan's mother. "Haven't you ever had a dream, Mrs. Brown? Something you wanted so badly and worked so hard to achieve? Now imagine you're living your dream, but someone who loves you wants you to give it up. What would you do?"

He didn't wait for her answer. Ronald doubted anything he said would make a difference to this family. They'd already passed judgment. But he'd had to try. For Joan.

She didn't want to make this call, but Joan didn't have a choice. She'd closed herself in her small office in the back of The Artist's Haven for privacy. Friday morning store traffic was usually slow, so she'd have plenty of time to talk with her agent.

The line clicked as the call connected; then her agent's phone rang. Once. Twice.

"Good morning. This is Heather Gibson."

Joan closed her eyes and swallowed the saliva pooling in her mouth. "It's Joan."

"What's wrong?"

She heard the concern in Heather's voice as clearly as her agent must have heard her reluctance. "I wanted to tell you . . . I think you should know . . ."

"Joan, you're scaring me. Just spit it out."

She wiped her damp palm on her pale cotton skirt. "After I complete this contract, I'm not going to write anymore." Joan exhaled a heavy breath, but the weight of regret remained on her shoulders. If anything, her tension increased as she waited through several beats of Heather's silence.

"Are you looking for other literary representation?"

Joan's jaw went slack. How could Heather have misinterpreted her so badly? "That's not it at all."

"Then talk to me. What do you want me to fix?"

My father. "There's nothing for you to fix. I've given this a lot of thought, and I've decided it would be best for me to give up my writing."

"Best for whom?" Confusion replaced Heather's concern.

"My family." Joan took a deep breath, but she still felt like crying. Instead, she told Heather about the media outing her as Cleopatra Sinclair. "My family was already opposed to my writing erotic romances. The media just made it worse."

Heather's sigh filled a long silence. "Joan, do you want to write?"

"Yes." The depth of feeling packed into that small word surprised even her. Bitterness at feeling forced into this decision struggled against regret.

"Then why does it matter what your family thinks?"

Joan pressed into her gray faux leather chair, staring blindly at the cluttered corkboard hanging on the scarred beige wall opposite her. "I love my family. I don't want them to be ashamed of me, and I don't want to alienate them."

"Joan, don't quit on me now. Your sales are increasing with each book. We can negotiate an even better contract next time. Don't give up now."

She was tempted to say yes. She really wanted to say yes. But the memory of her father on the evening news forced Joan to say no. "I can't keep writing when my family disapproves."

They sat in silence for several moments. Joan sensed that Heather was trying to find a solution to their problem. There wasn't one.

"Do you want to write something else? Try another genre?" Heather seemed hesitant.

Joan rubbed her temple, her eyes squinting again at the cluttered corkboard. "Erotic romance is what I write. I don't want to try anything else."

Heather sighed. "I thought you'd say that."

"Thanks for everything you've done for me, Heather. You helped make my dream come true."

"I wish I could convince you not to give up on that dream."

Joan winced as she swallowed the lump of regret in her throat. "Don't make this harder than it already is." Her voice was husky.

"All right. But if you ever change your mind and want to get back into the business, call me."

"I'm not going to change my mind." Her voice was subdued. "Writing is important to me, but my family means more."

Heather sighed. "I hope they appreciate what you're giving up for them."

Joan imagined her father's satisfaction at realizing he'd won. "They will. In their own way."

At the knock on his university office door Friday afternoon, Ronald looked up from his students' papers. He must be hallucinating. His parents stood beside each other in the threshold of his campus office. He blinked, but they didn't disappear.

His father spoke as though in answer to an unasked question. "We need to talk with you."

Not this again. Ronald laid his pen among the papers scattered across his desk and leaned back into the support of his chair's dark blue cushioning. "There's nothing more to say."

His mother held on to George's hand. "Please, Ronnie, just hear us out."

Ronald swallowed a sigh of resignation and gestured for his parents to enter his office. "Why didn't you call? You didn't need to fly here."

"We drove again." Darlene led George to the matching guest chairs in front of Ronald's modular desk. "It took ten hours, but it was worth it."

Ronald noted his parents' nervous expressions, their subtle fidgeting. "Why?"

Darlene twined her fingers with George's. "What we need to say we have to say in person."

He looked first at his father, then at his mother. "What's on your mind?"

Darlene blinked rapidly. "We want to apologize for not believing you when you said you weren't the father of Yasmine's baby. We were wrong, and we're sorry."

Tears pooled in his mother's dark eyes. His father looked both contrite and defiant.

His parents' apology should have removed a burden from his back. Instead, it only increased his tension. Ronald didn't think he'd like the reason for their regret.

He picked up his pen and rolled it between the fingers of his right hand. "Why did you change your mind?"

Darlene's free hand trembled as she pressed it against her chest. "We spoke with Yasmine."

Why was he surprised? He shouldn't be disappointed.

Ronald kept these feelings out of his voice. "She told you the baby's Harry's. Why didn't you believe *me* when I told you the same thing?"

George leaned forward, gripping his knees beneath his green Bermuda shorts. His voice was gruff. "Harry said you told him Yasmine was having your baby."

"Why is Harry more trustworthy than me?" Ronald asked.

George sat back in the tan chair. "It's not that Harry's more trustworthy. You're more responsible."

Ronald nodded with realization. "It's as I thought. You wanted me to be the father, even though I told you I wasn't."

"Harry's not father material." George's voice was tight with impatience. "He's not even an adult."

"George." Darlene scowled at her husband.

"Stop kidding yourself, Darling. Harry's criminally irresponsible. The idea of his becoming a father chills my blood. It'll be like a child raising a child."

"George." Darlene snapped at him.

"You know he's right, Mom. As harsh as it sounds, denying it won't change the truth."

His father heaved a sigh. "It's not that we believed Harry. It's that we *didn't* want to believe you. You're better situated to take responsibility for a child. You'd make a good father."

Ronald's mind went blank with surprise; then a picture of Joan flashed across it. He blinked and the picture was gone, but the warmth of his father's praise remained. He couldn't remember the last time his parents had had a good word to say to him.

Darlene nodded. "We realize we hurt you by not believing you, and we're sorry."

As much as Ronald appreciated their apology, it

wasn't enough. "Harry isn't completely to blame for his immaturity. You're both partly responsible."

Darlene turned her scowl on him. "You can't force someone to grow up."

George turned to his wife. "Yes, we can, Darling. We can stop doing his laundry, cooking his meals, cleaning up after him."

Darlene's eyes widened. "So this is all *my* fault? What about *you?*"

"I know I'm not perfect, but I'm going to fix that."

Ronald was skeptical. This seemed like a case of too little too late. "How?"

"I'm going to start charging him rent."

Ronald swallowed a laugh. What was his father thinking? "There's one problem with that plan, Dad. Harry doesn't have a job."

George stood firm. "He'd better get one, because I'm also going to tell Yasmine to have his salary garnished for child support."

"George, he's our son. Whose side are you on?"

"I'm on my grandchild's side."

Darlene flinched, as though George's quiet answer set her back a step or two.

Ronald remained skeptical. "When are you going to talk to Harry?"

"Now," George said, then stood and helped Darlene from her chair. "We'll talk about it over lunch."

"Harry came with you?" Ronald waited for Darlene's nod. "Why?"

Darlene stepped closer to Ronald's desk. "This family has a lot of healing to do. I know we're asking a great deal, but will you join us for lunch?"

Ronald stared at Darlene, shaking his head. "I won't sit with Harry and pretend bygones are bygones after what he's done."

Darlene looked distressed. "It will be easier for Harry to apologize if he knows you're willing to forgive him."

Ronald's pulse beat faster as his anger rose. "Can you imagine how I felt to have my brother tell one of the ugliest lies about me to my parents? And to have you believe him? I'm not willing to forgive him. That's something he'll have to work for."

"You've won, Mom." Joan clenched the telephone receiver in one hand and bounced a pencil against her desk, eraser end down, with the other. The quick, hard push echoed the blow to her heart.

"Won what?" Caroline's voice came through the telephone line thick with confusion. That might have been funny if Joan's heart weren't breaking.

She dropped the pencil again, harder, letting it slip between the thumb and forefinger of her right hand. "I'll stop writing. You and Dad have got what you wanted."

The silence on her mother's end was disconcerting. Joan scanned the office, feeling trapped. She hoped to crawl out of this cave and into the sunshine next week, after the local media cooled off. Just two more days. She glanced at her Disney watch. It was almost noon.

Caroline's tone was pensive. "I don't know if that's true."

That wasn't the response Joan had expected. "Excuse me?"

"Have you spoken with Ron?"

Joan straightened in her chair and tightened her grip on the phone. "About what? What's going on, Mom?"

"Ron spoke with your father after choir practice last night. Didn't he tell you?"

It was a toss-up as to which reaction was stronger:

anger or anxiety. Joan dropped the pencil onto her desk. "No, he didn't. I thought he met with a student last night."

He'd lied to her. Mr. Lying-by-Omission-Is-Still-Lying had been deliberately dishonest. Joan couldn't wait to hear him explain that one.

Caroline continued. "He probably knew you wouldn't want him to confront your father that way."

"What way?" Joan balanced her right elbow on her desk and braced her forehead on the heel of her palm. What had Ronald done?

"Never mind that. I'm glad he spoke to your father."

"Why?"

"Whatever Ron said left an impression on him. He's been subdued since last night."

Joan's head was spinning. She needed to get off this ride. "How's that a good thing, Mom?"

"It means Ron gave your father something to think about." Her mother sounded satisfied. "He gave me a lot to think about, too."

Her father wouldn't listen to her, but he'd listened to Ronald. For heaven's sake, how annoying. "What did Ron say?"

"Your father won't tell me. I was hoping you knew."

"Not yet, but I'll be sure to tell you whatever I find out."

Chapter 20

"Looks like I got here just in time."

Ronald turned in resignation at the sound of his brother's voice. Harold leaned against the office door-jamb, cool and relaxed in tan khaki shorts and a brown cotton T-shirt.

Ronald straightened from his bookcase. "Why are you here at all?"

"The folks wanted me to come and apologize, but it looks like you're on your way out."

Harold's smile contradicted the temper in his eyes. His younger brother had always been a study in contrasts. Thoughtful words but thoughtless deeds. The best of intentions resulting in disastrous acts. The character of a child in the body of a man.

"Do *you* think you should apologize?" Ronald watched his spoiled younger brother struggle to find a noncommittal response.

"Of course, I'm sorry. I mean, first, I take your girl from you, and then I get her pregnant." Harold cocked his head. "You weren't able to get her pregnant, were you?"

"We didn't *try* to get pregnant. We used birth control."

"So did we."

Harold shrugged. It was a careless gesture, but Ronald sensed his tension. Harold didn't want to be there any more than Ronald wanted him near. So why didn't he send his brother away?

"The pill isn't effective when used with antibiotics. Yasmine explained that to you."

Resentment masked Harold's features. He pushed off the door frame and marched into the office. "Do you think you know everything?"

"We're too old for sibling rivalries."

"I'm not competing against you." Harold's sudden stillness signaled his lie.

"Yes, you are, and it's time the competition ended."

"You're so full of yourself." His brother's voice rose several decibels. "You think everyone's always thinking of you, that everyone wants to be like you or be in your presence. You're so full of yourself."

For the second time in as many days, Ronald faced a very upset man. Harold's face was flushed. The muscles of his neck stood taut. His hands were clenched into fists. Luckily, Ronald's legal experience had taught him how to diffuse angry adversaries.

He lowered his voice. "I don't think any of those things."

"Good, because no one cares about you. No one cares what you're doing. No one cares what you think."

A month or so ago, those words would have hurt him, but not anymore. Thanks to Joan, Ronald knew they weren't true. She cared about him—what he was doing and what he thought—even if no one else did. That knowledge helped him deflect Harold's attack.

"Harry, you're a thirty-year-old man, not an eight-year-old boy. Grow up."

"You think everyone wants to be like you. Who would want what you have, anyway?"

"You would." Ronald stepped forward. "But you aren't willing to work for anything. You want it all handed to you."

"I've worked for what I have."

Shock almost made him stutter. "What do you have? Mom and Dad give you money, so you don't have a job. You live with them, so you don't have any bills. What do you have?"

Shame and fury burned in Harold's eyes. "You talk about having to work for what you have. But what do you know about struggling? Everything always comes so easily for you." Harold spat the words in disgust.

With whom was he disgusted? Ronald couldn't tell, but either way, he was nearing the end of his rope.

"That's bullshit." Ronald spoke through clenched teeth. "The difference between us is that I make an effort to succeed. And I've tried to help you. But you don't want help. You'd rather someone do everything for you."

"I've always given my best effort. I've never shirked my responsibilities or looked for the easy way out."

"What?" Ronald wanted to grab his brother and shake him until he got some sense. Not trusting his restraint, he moved to stand behind his desk. "What about Yasmine? You told Mom and Dad that I was the father. What do you call that if not shirking your responsibilities?"

Harold wiped sweat from his upper lip. With the spotlight on his actions—or inactions—he no longer looked cool and relaxed. "You have a job and a place of your own. You're in a better position to take care of Yasmine and her baby."

"It's your baby, too. And just as I said, you want someone else to do your job for you."

Harold crossed his arms. "I need more time to get myself together."

Ronald shook his head. "You're running out of time. Your baby will be here in about six months. You need to get yourself together now."

"Where did you go last night?" Joan stood behind Ronald, holding her dirty dinner dishes. Would he tell her the truth?

Ronald straightened from the dishwasher and met her gaze. By the look in his eyes, Joan could tell he knew she already had her answer. She arched a brow, a silent prompt for his response.

He took her dishes and stacked them in the machine. "Who turned me in? Your parents or your sisters?"

"Why didn't you tell me?"

"I was trying to avoid an argument."

She laughed. "Nice try, but all you did was postpone it."

Ronald closed the dishwasher and leaned against the counter. "Okay. Go ahead. But I warn you. I've been getting a lot of practice arguing the past two days."

He'd told her about his parents' visit and his argument with his brother. It seemed family confrontations were becoming regular events for them.

Joan stepped close enough to breathe his warm, masculine scent. She reached up to massage the knotted muscles in his broad shoulders.

Ronald moaned his pleasure. His head tipped forward to land gently against hers. "If this is your idea of an argument, bring it on."

Joan chuckled. Her searching fingertips found and

concentrated on easing one particularly tense muscle near Ronald's nape. "I'm sorry about what happened with your brother this afternoon. He has a different reality, doesn't he? But the argument you had with my father yesterday, you brought on yourself."

"Your father has a different reality, too."

"Yes, he does. If you'd talked to me first, I could have told you that."

Ronald lifted his head and settled his hands on her waist. "If I'd told you I wanted to speak to your father, what would you have said?"

"That it wouldn't do any good."

He kissed her forehead. "There you have it, then."

Startled laughter flew from her lips. Joan stopped massaging his neck. She stepped back, far enough to see him better without losing his embrace. "What does that mean?"

"I didn't tell you I was going to see your father because you would have talked me out of it."

Joan tightened her hold on his forearms. "You thought you were helping, but you did more harm than good. My father's been very moody since you spoke with him."

"Good. Maybe he's thinking over what we talked about."

Joan frowned. "What did you say to him?"

"I told him his daughters were old enough to make their own decisions."

She closed her eyes and shook her head. "Trust me, he didn't even hear that." Joan pulled out of his embrace, although she knew she'd miss the warmth of his touch. "It's more likely that he's planning his next attack. He wants to win this argument, and he doesn't care who he hurts in the process. I don't want that person to be you."

Ronald straightened from the counter and folded his arms across his chest. "I appreciate your concern, but I won't hide behind you."

Joan gave his lean frame a slow once-over, from the obstinate angle of his squared jaw to his well-muscled torso and long, strong legs. Ronald looked invincible, but her father's battle would be waged with words. Often they caused far more damage.

She turned and let a few strides carry her from him. Telling him about her conversation with her agent was one of the hardest things she'd ever have to do. She'd made that call in part to protect him. Still, she knew it would change his perception of her, and she really liked the way she looked in his eyes.

"Ron, I called my agent this morning. I told her I wasn't going to write anymore."

He stared at her in shocked silence. "Are you giving up your writing because of me?"

"I don't want you in the middle of this argument between my father and me. My writing doesn't have anything to do with you, but my father won't believe that."

He stepped closer to her. "I told you I can take care of myself."

"That's not the point. This argument isn't about you. It's about my relationship with my father and who's in control. I guess he is." Joan turned and started to walk away, not wanting Ronald to see the tears in her eyes.

But Ronald captured her forearm to stop her. "Cleopatra Sinclair wouldn't give up so easily."

That caused the tears to fall. "Cleopatra Sinclair doesn't exist. There's only Joan, and I guess she's not as strong as you'd believed her to be."

Ronald frowned. "Joan is as strong as you want her to be."

"Not strong enough to stand by while someone attacks your character, and not strong enough to walk away from my family."

"Why do I put myself through this?" Ronald stopped his Lexus SUV at a red light and checked his rearview mirror. His father's car was still right behind them, following them to the designated restaurant for lunch.

Joan reached over to squeeze his thigh. Her touch was firm but far too brief. "Because they're your family. They infuriate and annoy you, hurt and sadden you, but you still love them."

He snorted. "I do?" He studied her profile, so delicate, yet so strong. More strength than even she realized. He could stare at her forever. "How are you feeling? You didn't sleep much last night."

Joan folded her hands in her lap. "I'm fine."

No, she wasn't, but he didn't push. She hadn't wanted to talk about her writing career last night, nor had she wanted to talk this morning. But somehow he had to convince her not to give up her writing. Not to give up on them.

"Thank you for coming with me. I know your first Montgomery family meal wasn't a great experience."

"It's the least I could do. You've been coming to church with me the past three weeks while I've been a Brown family outcast." She tossed him a forced smile. "Besides, you should know there's at least one person in the room who's on your side."

"I appreciate that."

The light turned green. Ronald crossed the intersection and pulled into the restaurant parking lot. It was crowded with Saturday afternoon guests. Ronald helped Joan out of the car before surrendering his keys to a valet attendant.

He and Joan waited for his father to park and join them on the sidewalk outside of the restaurant. His feeling of dread returned. Joan stepped closer to him, wrapping her arm around one of his and staying close to his side. Her right breast pressed into his left arm. Her ability to distract him was phenomenal.

They'd both changed clothes for the gathering. He'd chosen a pair of gray pleated linen pants with a matching sport coat over a blue short-sleeved shirt. Joan's yellow sleeveless dress was deceptively modest. It skimmed her slender figure and showed off her long, shapely legs.

His parents and Harold finally joined them in front of the restaurant.

"I hate valet parking." George's announcement didn't bode well.

His mother forced a brilliant smile. "This looks like a nice place."

Ronald couldn't think of a response.

Joan came to his rescue. "It is. I've eaten here before. We hope you like it."

Ronald led the small party into the restaurant. Their hostess found their reservations, and they were shown to their table.

Joan had been unsure of eating here. The menu was a bit expensive, especially for a party of five. But Ronald had declined her offer to cook, assuring her that he could afford the bill and pointing out that neither of their apartments could accommodate five diners.

Joan slid into the booth ahead of Ronald. His mother sat across the table from her. Harold sat between his parents. Ronald sat beside Joan, gritting his teeth at the prospect of having to see his brother's face each time he looked up from his meal. That was going to be hard on his digestion.

The hostess, a young brunette, presented each of them with a menu. "Enjoy your meal," she said and, with minimal fuss, disappeared.

"So, Joan, you said you've eaten here before. What's good?" His mother scanned the menu, a determined smile frozen in place.

Ronald tuned out Joan's response and selected a seafood pasta entrée. Very few places could go wrong with pasta.

Their server showed up, a thin young man with pale features and a shock of dark glossy curls. "Good afternoon, ladies and gentlemen. My name is Bryce, and I'll be helping you today. May I take your drink orders?"

He took their requests for iced teas and lemonades, then promised to return for their entrée orders.

With Joan's help, his family made their food selections, then closed their menus.

Darlene tried to get the conversation rolling. "So, what plans do you have for the rest of the weekend?"

Ronald leaned back in his seat, trying to ignore Harold. "Joan and I are going to church tomorrow morning."

"Oh." Darlene blinked, glanced quickly at Joan, and blinked again.

Ronald swallowed a laugh. He sensed his mother scanning her memory for blasphemous comments the family might have made in Joan's presence. Ronald was touched that she cared enough to want to make a good impression on someone who meant so much to him. "Joan's maternal grandfather founded Holy Grace Neighborhood Church."

"Dude, you're going to church?" Harold chuckled. "This must be serious."

Ronald didn't like the speculation in Harold's eyes as he stared at Joan. "Joan sings in the choir."

Their server returned with their drinks, took their entrée orders, then retrieved their menus before leaving.

"Are you trying to convert my son?" George's tone was accusatory.

If Joan experienced the same defensiveness Ronald felt in response to his father's tone and question, she didn't show it. She gave George a negligent shrug. "I like your son the way he is. I don't see any reason for him to change. None at all."

Harold's smile widened. "I thought you wrote those romance books. How can you go to church and still write that stuff?"

Ronald felt Joan stiffen, but her voice remained calm. "Writing romance isn't a sin."

His brother's smile never wavered. "You write books, run a store, and sing in the choir. You're a woman of many talents."

Ronald wasn't imagining the innuendo in Harold's words. The mental warning bells were almost deafening. Ronald held Harold's gaze while he sent his silent message: *I'm not losing this one.*

Harold's expression turned cocky. Ronald could almost hear his brother's response: *We'll see.*

Ronald's anger ignited, a fast and furious burn. His skin heated, and blood drummed in his ears. But he was trapped beneath his brother's mocking gaze. There was no way to release the pressure while they sat in the restaurant.

Conversation was stilted as they waited for their meals to arrive. Through the pounding in his head, Ronald could only half hear his mother's description of how his family had spent their morning. He hoped Joan's attention masked his distraction.

Their server mercifully brought a temporary reprieve from his family's discussion when he arrived to distribute their orders. After checking whether they needed anything else, the young man left.

Ronald looked at his seafood and fettuccine in Alfredo sauce. It might as well have been a bowl of porridge. He sliced the pasta into smaller pieces, more for something to do. "Have you spoken with Yasmine yet, Harry?"

Conversation stopped, leaving only the sound of his pulse pounding in his ears.

Venom replaced mockery in Harold's eyes. "No, I haven't."

Ronald stuck his fork into the mountain of fettuccine. "Have you found a job?"

Harold stabbed his salmon fillet. "You need to mind your own business."

"I'm trying to get you to mind yours."

Darlene gasped. "Ronnie, do we have to do this now? Here?"

George looked up from his steak and loaded baked potato. "Your mother and I will help Harold get on his feet."

Ronald glanced at Joan. She was applying her knife and fork to her summer vegetable salad as though she planned to make coleslaw.

Ronald leaned forward to better emphasize the urgency. "We've gone beyond helping Harold get on his feet. In less than six months, he's got to be able to walk on his own."

Harold swallowed a mouthful of salmon. "Oh, now the great Ronald Montgomery is not only a *New York Times* best-selling author but advisor to the world?"

Exasperation edged Ronald's words. "I don't know everything that having a baby entails. But even I know six months isn't a lot of time to prepare. Why haven't you started?"

Harold gave him a parody of a smile. "You have all the answers. Why don't you tell me?"

Darlene reached over to rub Harold's upper arm. "These things take time, Ronnie."

Ronald shook his head in exasperation. "Nothing has changed. You're still making excuses for him."

"Try to understand, Ronnie. Things come more easily for you. It's not as easy for Harry."

Joan finally stopped shredding her salad. She spoke without inflection. "Ron didn't breeze into an Ivy League college or happen into one of the top law schools in the country. That requires a lot of hard work. The same hard work he used to get hired by a top law firm and make the *Times* list."

Once again she was defending him. Keeping the ice at bay.

George pinned her with a stare. "What do you know about my family?"

Joan held his father's gaze. "Only what I see, Mr. Montgomery."

Why couldn't she see how strong she was? Why was she able to stare down his father but unable to stand up to her own? Now that she'd given in to her father's demands to stop writing, how much time did he have until her father ordered her to stop seeing him? Would she agree to that, too? He couldn't lose her.

George grunted. He switched his attention to Ronald. "Don't worry about Harry. He isn't your problem."

Ronald looked at his brother. "I hope you're right."

Chapter 21

Joan mounted the steps of Holy Grace Neighborhood Church. Ronald was beside her. A cool breeze teased her hair and flirted with her deep gold dress. But the sun was high, promising hot temperatures later in the day.

She looked up in time to see her mother emerge from the church to monitor her progress from the top of the stairs. The breeze never touched her mother's perfectly coiffed curls or her warm cream dress with matching cropped jacket.

She gave her mother a tentative smile, which Caroline returned with warmth. Joan's heart lifted.

She stopped on the top step beside her mother, and kissed Caroline's cheek. "Good morning, Mom."

"Good morning, sweetheart." Caroline offered Ronald her hand. "We'll discuss your dreams next time."

Ronald's answering smile piqued Joan's curiosity. What was this secret code her mother had shared with her lover?

Caroline released Ronald's hand and turned to Joan. "Do you have your choir robes with you?"

"They're in the backseat of my car."

"Good. Put them on." Her mother reentered the church without waiting for a reply.

Joan didn't need to be told twice to get her robes. She grabbed Ronald's hand and practically raced back to her car.

Minutes later Joan left Ronald with Timothy and continued toward the pulpit and the choir benches beyond. The spring in her step caused the royal blue robes to dance around her. She heard the murmurings from church members as she traveled the aisle. She didn't pause. She never faltered. *Let them stare.*

Joan watched Margaret and Christine, hoping for a reaction. Hoping she would reconnect with them the way she appeared to have reconnected with her mother. But her sisters refused to meet her eyes. *Patience*, Joan chided herself. After all, it was a virtue.

"Joan." Her father's sharp tone stopped her as she reached the pulpit. "Where are you going?"

Hadn't her mother spoken with him? She had a bad feeling about this. "Good morning, Daddy. I'm rejoining the choir."

"With whose permission?" He stopped within arm's length of her.

"Mine." Caroline's voice was calm.

Kenneth's expression went blank with disbelief. "Why?"

Caroline put an arm around Joan's shoulders and pitched her voice low. "She's our daughter, and this is our church. She has every right to sing in the choir."

Caroline turned with Joan toward the riser.

Kenneth blocked their path. "Caroline, we should have discussed this."

Her mother smiled. "You didn't discuss your decision to remove our daughter from the choir. But, if you'd like to discuss her rejoining it, we can do so now.

In front of the entire congregation. Including the new members."

Joan glanced around in discomfort, wondering if others could overhear their disagreement. "Mom, I don't think this is such a good idea."

Caroline gave her a bolstering squeeze. "Hush. This is between your father and me."

Joan felt twelve years old again. "But we don't want our parishioners to see us fighting."

Caroline ignored her. "Do you want to discuss this now, Ken? Or would you rather Joan sang with the choir, and we'll discuss this matter later?"

A muscle worked in her father's jaw. He wasn't used to anyone challenging his decisions, not even his wife. It didn't seem a comfortable concept for him. Joan knew it wasn't comfortable for her. Why did they have to put her in the middle?

Kenneth's lips tightened with anger, but he nodded once. "We'll discuss it later."

With another reassuring smile and bolstering hug, Caroline stepped aside so Joan could join the rest of the choir. Joan nodded to Margaret and Christine as she walked past them to a space on the opposite side of their bench.

At a tap on her shoulder, Joan looked behind her at Vivian Barnes, the choir member who'd waved at her last week.

After greeting Joan, the older woman whispered her request. "I want you to sign my books after the service."

Joan's eyes widened. What surprised her more? That someone in the choir had read her books, or that Vivian had admitted to reading them and had asked for her autograph? Joan managed to return the other woman's smile, then faced the congregational pews.

How very surreal.

* * *

Ronald climbed out of his father's car. Joan had driven him to his family's motel right after church. He'd gone to the gas station with George, Darlene, and Harold, and paid to fill the fuel tank before his family drove back to New York.

"I thought your books were doing well."

Bemused, Ronald glanced at his father. "They are. Why?"

George waved disdainfully toward the faculty apartment building. "This is the best you could do?"

It amused Ronald that his father and he had the same reaction to the building. "It's what the university offered. I didn't have time to check around." He scanned the parking lot. "Joan's already here. Do you want something to drink before you leave?"

Harold laughed. "Sure. Besides, if the outside's this ugly, I've got to see inside."

His brother's cackling annoyed him. Ronald didn't want Harold in his apartment. He didn't want him in his life. But it was a package deal. The invitation to take care of his parents automatically extended to his brother.

Darlene gripped Ronald's arm to keep him by her side. "You go ahead, Harry. Your father and I want to have a private word with Ronnie first."

"Suit yourself." Harold shrugged and walked away.

"Good morning, gorgeous."

Joan scowled at Harold's greeting. She stepped back to let him into Ronald's apartment. Spying Ronald talking to his parents in the parking lot, she closed but didn't lock the door.

She turned to face Harold, taking in his white tennis shoes, midnight blue denim shorts, and crimson tank top. He stripped off a pair of Ray-Ban sunglasses. How did an employment-challenged individual come by such an expensive accessory?

Joan returned to Ronald's kitchen, where she'd been making fresh lemonade. "Will Ron and your parents be much longer?"

Harold followed her. "They're coming. But for now, it's just you and me, sunshine."

Startled, she glanced back at Harold. "What's that supposed to mean?" She saw the invitation in his eyes. *Oh, heck, no.*

He leaned his right hip against the counter, crowding her. "What do you want it to mean, sweetheart?"

"Let's start with you backing away from the counter and giving me some room."

Harold stepped back, laughing as though she'd given him the punch line to a very naughty joke. The sound made her skin crawl.

"Does that *feel* better to you?"

His sexual innuendos were too heavy-handed to be taken seriously. Was this how he'd wormed his way into Yasmine's bed? And they said ministers' daughters were naive.

"What game are you playing, Harry?"

"It's no game. I'd like to get to know you better. You're a very sexy woman, Joan."

She wanted to tell him what he could do with his fulsome compliments. She wanted to tell him liars and cheats didn't appeal to her. But she wasn't up for an argument with Ronald's family. Been there, done that. Instead, Joan strained to measure her words. "You have an amazing attraction to your brother's girlfriends. Why is that?"

Temper sparked in Harold's eyes before he lowered his gaze. "I see you as your own woman, Joan. Not as an extension of my brother."

"Nice try, Harry. But that's the wrong answer." She was fairly certain the confusion in his eyes was feigned.

"What do you mean?"

"You should have said I'm both. I'm an independent woman who's very happy to be with your brother."

"Oh yeah? What does he have that I don't have?"

"Don't compare yourself to Ron. You'll only get your feelings hurt."

Without releasing her hold on his arm, Darlene moved to stand in front of Ronald. Her expression was earnest as she studied his face. "Joan seems like a very nice woman, Ronnie. The kind of woman who takes care of the people she loves."

He thought of Joan's love for her family and her willingness to defend him to anyone and everyone, including her father. "She is."

"I'm glad." Darlene looked to George, then back to Ronald. "You deserve someone like that in your life."

Ronald glanced between his parents. "I thought that would be my family."

George grunted. "When haven't we taken care of you? We raised you."

Ronald arched his brow. "Thanks for that."

Darlene released Ronald. "What your father means is we did our best. We realize that may not have been enough, but it was all we could do."

George gave another grunt. "Raising two kids is tough. Wait until you have some of your own. Hopefully, your kids will be easier."

Ronald cocked his head. "How did I make things hard on you?"

Father and son stared at each other. George broke the silence. "You'll see what I mean when you have kids of your own."

Ronald turned toward his apartment. "I hope not."

Harold gave Joan a narrowed, mean stare. "Talking about getting your feelings hurt, you do know Ron's only using you for sex?"

Joan wouldn't let Harold see how the accusation stung. "I know better than to believe anything that comes out of your mouth."

Harold chuckled. "You don't think he's with you for your prayers, do you? He's with you because you write porn."

"I don't write pornography."

"Mr. Responsibility wants to walk on the wild side. But he doesn't care about you. Once he's had his thrills, he'll pack his bags and step."

"Ron knows the difference between the person I am and the books that I write."

His smile taunted her. "Are you sure about that?"

Joan clenched her fists to keep from smacking the smile from Harold's face. Her short nails bit into her palms. She knew she shouldn't listen to him. She knew this was another trick to try to turn her from Ronald. "This from the man who stole his brother's fiancée. What makes you think your opinion means anything to me?"

Harold gave her a hard look. "Tell me something. How does someone steal someone else's fiancée?"

"You can't justify your actions."

"I didn't force Yasmine to leave Ron. She came to me willingly."

"You betrayed your brother. And now you're trying to deceive him again with me. Why do you hate him so much?"

Harold laughed. "Oh, Ron's a great guy. Love him to death. But I don't care what he thinks or says. He's not better than me. He needs to know that the things he comes by so easily can be just as easily taken from him."

Before Joan could move or even say a word, Harold grabbed her shoulders, hauled her against him and pressed his lips to hers.

Joan's mind went blank, and then anger shot through her like a flare. Harold's tongue pressed against her lips, grinding them against her teeth when she kept her mouth shut tight.

With a strained effort, Joan wrested herself from Harold's grasp, pushing back from him. She dragged the back of her hand across her mouth, fury making her body shake. "How dare you put your hands on me!"

"Harold!" A woman's voice flung his name across the room as though hurling it through a storm. "What have you done?"

Joan spun toward the front door. Ronald and his parents stood just inside his apartment, staring toward the kitchen. George's face was creased with disgust. Darlene's expression was stunned dismay. And Ronald appeared as the embodiment of rage.

Fury crashed over Ronald like an inferno. With his heart thudding like sprinting footsteps, he couldn't catch his breath. His pulse thundered like a subway train in his ears, blocking out any other sound. And all he could see was Harold through a red haze.

He took a blind step forward. Immediately, hands restrained him, pulling him back. Ronald came out of his temper-induced stupor and looked around. His parents stood on either side of him. Joan watched him from across the room, concern in her eyes.

"Harold, what have you done?" Darlene's voice cracked like a whip as she repeated her question.

"I haven't done anything." Harold responded to his mother, but his wary gaze was riveted to Ronald.

Ronald fought his baser instinct to shrug off his parents' restraining hold so he could rip Harold's head from his shoulders and kick it across the room. When Harold had betrayed him with Yasmine, he'd reined in his desire to pummel his younger brother. This time, he didn't want to exert that much control. He shouldn't have to.

Darlene slashed a trembling arm through the air. "Don't. Lie. To me." She delivered the command even before Harold finished speaking. "You've already torn this family apart once. Now you're trying to do it again."

"Mom, that just happened." Harold's voice cajoled. "Yasmine and I thought we were in love. We were wrong, and I've said I'm sorry."

"Then what were you doing with Joan?"

"We were just talking, Mom."

George snorted. "With your tongue in her mouth? How stupid do you think we are?"

Ronald glared across the room at his brother. He wanted a few minutes—one or two minutes—alone with Harold, during which he needed his brother to experience the same pain he was feeling. He tugged against his parents' grasp. They both held fast. His anger and frustration grew. Why were they still protecting Harold?

"Even after your affair with Ronnie's fiancée, I believed in you. I defended you. But you were lying to me, too. Weren't you?" Darlene's voice shook with disillusionment.

The sound touched Ronald's heart. He blinked to clear the images of him battering his brother and saw the real hurt in his mother's eyes. He wanted to comfort her, but his parents wouldn't release him.

Harold extended one hand beseechingly. "No, Mom. I didn't lie to you."

Darlene went on. "You had no intention of telling Ronnie about you and Yasmine, did you? You said you did, but you didn't. Instead, you asked me to keep your secret."

"I *did* intend to tell Ron, but I was afraid to."

Harold looked the picture of sincerity. Ronald wanted to rip the mask from his face.

Temper thickened Darlene's voice. "You used me to hurt my own son."

Surprise jolted Ronald's system. Did his mother now understand why he felt isolated from his family? Did she finally see the wedge Harold continued to drive between them?

Ronald looked into his father's eyes and saw regret. Both parents understood, and that understanding doused his anger. He stopped straining against their grasp. Now, instead of Joan defending him to his family, his parents were taking his side.

Ronald's gaze sought Joan—he wanted to share his happiness—but she watched him with a wary expression. Did she think he blamed her for Harold's pass? Ronald shook his head and saw Joan relax. She smiled as she crossed the room to join him and his parents.

"Mom, I've never used you," Harold seemed surprised by the accusation.

Ronald snorted. "Are you kidding? You use both of our parents every day for free room and board, and spending money. With them around, you've never had to grow up."

George interrupted. "He'll have to grow up now. I'm not going to bankroll a liar."

"Why, Harry?" Darlene sounded tired. "Why did you trick me into lying to Ronnie?"

Harold's gaze shifted from his mother to his brother and father, then returned to Ronald. "Because good ol' Ronnie doesn't appreciate what he has."

Ronald narrowed his eyes. "What?"

Harold scowled back. "You don't know what it's like to fail. You had a high-paying job, a fancy apartment, and a beautiful fiancée, but you took them all for granted."

"No, Ronnie doesn't take anything for granted." Darlene turned away from Harold and spoke to Ronald. "We're the ones who've taken you for granted. You've always been able to take care of yourself. You did your homework, got to school on time."

George released Ronald's arm. "Harry's a different story. He couldn't have gotten to class on time if he'd slept at the school. And homework was a foreign concept to him. That should've been a clue that he'd have trouble later on in life."

Darlene still looked only at Ronald. "Harry's always needed more attention. But that has meant short-changing you. It took almost losing you to realize how much we've hurt you. I'm sorry, Ronnie."

George cleared his throat. "I'm sorry, too, son."

Ronald couldn't speak. So much emotion burdened his words, but not their sincerity. He blinked, hoping to clear his vision. "Thank you."

Darlene turned back to her younger son. "Harry, I'm not sure what to do with you. You used me. I don't know if I can ever trust you again."

"Of course, we can't trust him anymore." Anger and disgust deepened George's voice. "You're on your own now. The free ride is over."

Harold's eyes widened. "But I still need your help."

Darlene shook her head. "You don't want us to help you. You want us to take care of you."

George scowled. "You're stuck on being jealous of your brother when you should start learning how to take care of yourself."

Ronald leveled a cool gaze at his brother. "It's time *you* stopped taking for granted the things you have and the people who care for you."

Ronald leaned back against his locked front door. How long would the understanding he'd found with his parents last? How long before they'd go back to making excuses for Harold? For today, he wanted to believe his family had made a positive, permanent change.

He looked at Joan. She'd helped him get to this point. She wouldn't let him give up on his family. And she'd been right. "Thank you."

Her expression was somber. "For what?"

"Convincing me to tell my family how I felt and what I wanted. I didn't think it would work, but you were right."

"When are you going to ask me about your brother's kiss?"

Ronald noted the tension in the taut curves of her body. He didn't want to hear about his brother's kiss, but she obviously thought it was important to address the incident before putting it behind them. That must be a woman thing. "What do you want to tell me?"

She took a nervous step forward. "I didn't invite or

encourage him to touch me. He grabbed me and wouldn't let go. I had to shove him away."

He flinched. The details were as bad as Ronald had imagined. He closed the gap between himself and Joan. Could he touch her, or was it too soon after she'd pushed someone else off?

Ronald stood with his arms at his sides. "I know you didn't invite Harry's . . . attention. I'm sorry for what he did."

Joan seemed to relax. "I'm glad you believe me."

A smile raised a corner of his mouth. "I saw you push him away. I also heard what you said. But even if I hadn't, I know how loyal you are. You'd never betray someone you cared about."

Joan stepped closer to him, close enough for Ronald to feel her heat and smell her powder-soft scent. "What a beautiful thing to say."

He brushed her raven tresses behind her shoulder. "I've said before that you're a strong woman. It's just one of your very attractive qualities."

Instead of returning his smile, Joan frowned. Concern flashed in her chocolate eyes. "I'm not strong."

Ronald gripped Joan's shoulders, loosening his hold when she winced. "Yes, you are. You have to believe that. I need you to believe that."

Because if she went back to being Pastor Brown's dutiful daughter, he was lost.

Chapter 22

"Who are you sleeping with?"

Ronald paused with the iced-tea glass pressed to his lips. Joan watched his eyes widen as he lowered the drink. The day had been long, even for a Monday. Maybe now wasn't the best time to have this conversation. But later wouldn't be any better.

He set the glass on a coaster on the coffee table. "Excuse me?"

Joan squeezed her hands together, gathering her nerve. She shifted on the love seat to better face Ronald, who sat on the sofa. "You're sleeping with me. But who are you having a relationship with? Cleopatra Sinclair or Joan Brown?"

Ronald's gaze bounced around her living room as though he expected a hidden camera to pop out from behind the television, stereo, or coffee table.

Okay. Maybe it sounded like a stupid question. Joan certainly felt like an idiot for asking. But it wasn't stupid. In fact, it might be one of the most important things she'd ever ask him.

Ronald gave her a baffled smile. "Is this a trick question?"

"No."

His smile faded. "I'm making love with you."

She swallowed. How she wished that were true. "Me, who? Joan or Cleo?"

"Both."

Joan heard confusion in his voice, but she didn't know how to make the question any clearer. "Cleo doesn't exist."

"She's a part of you."

He still didn't understand, and she really needed him to. *Tell me you know who I am. I'm Joan.*

She waved a hand, encompassing her hair, tied at the nape of her neck; her white T-shirt; and her gray gym shorts. "Cleo is an image that I project. She's confident, glamorous, and exciting. But I'm not. I'm insecure, plain, and boring."

"People aren't confident, glamorous, and exciting all the time. It's not possible. But that doesn't mean you aren't ever those things."

Joan's palms were sweating, but her throat was dry. Her heart was racing, but her thoughts were slow. She could hear Harold's mocking words. *He's with you because you write porn.* Joan crossed the room, needing to put distance between herself and that ugly memory.

She stood with her back to Ronald. "My sisters and I always knew that everything we said or did, even our clothes, reflected on our family and our church." She turned and arched a brow at Ronald. "That put a real damper on spontaneity."

"I can imagine."

"Then imagine how I felt when I met you. I thought I'd found someone who saw the real me and liked me, anyway. I didn't have to weigh my words or measure my actions or preplan my wardrobe."

"You don't have to do any of those things for me. Just be yourself."

"And who would that be, Ron? Joan or Cleo?"

Ronald's head dropped onto the back of the sofa. Joan could tell he was struggling to hold on to his patience. She was struggling to hold on to hope. This conversation was far too important not to see it through.

He raised his head and pinned her with his gaze. "Why are we having this conversation?"

"Because I don't want to pretend to be someone I'm not anymore. Not with you."

"You aren't pretending with me."

She felt a piece of her heart break. "You don't understand."

Ronald stood and paced in the opposite direction from her. "You're not wearing that slinky red dress now, and I haven't left your apartment. We've been together night and day for weeks. Have I complained about your being insecure, plain, or boring?"

Joan watched Ronald's agitated movements. She just needed him to know her the way she really was. *How can I make you understand that I need you to see Joan?* "Who have you been spending those nights and days with? The minister's daughter or the erotic romance author?"

His sigh was thick with masculine impatience. "I'm sleeping with you, Joan."

"Then why do you ask for Cleo before we make love?"

Is Cleo ready to come out and play? Joan saw the flash of memory in Ronald's eyes.

He rubbed his forehead. "I don't know."

Another piece of her heart broke off. "I think the answer's obvious."

"How do you think you were able to create Cleo? She came from you."

Joan shook her head. "She's a role I play. And,

apparently, I play it especially well when I'm in bed with you."

"You're the same person." Ronald's voice rose with frustration.

Joan's voice shook with disappointment. "How many times do I have to show you who I am before you see me?"

"I've always seen you. But obviously, you can't see yourself."

She stared at Ronald, speechless. *He'll never understand.* Her heart crumbled to dust. Joan didn't want it to come to this, but she couldn't accept the alternative. Was there any point in prolonging a pretense? She could never be the woman he thought she was.

How had she come to care so much for him in such a short span of time? "If you want a strong, exciting, confident woman, I'm not the one for you." She watched Ronald's expression shift from impatience to fear.

He stood. "You're exactly the woman for me." His voice was a husky whisper.

"Cleo wouldn't let her father dictate whether she would write or not."

"Neither would Joan."

She shook her head. "You have your family back, and I'm happy for you. It's time I worked things out with my family. If I have to be someone I'm not, I might as well play a role for them. It would destroy me if I had to pretend with you."

Ronald looked away before returning his attention to her. Fury and frustration swirled in his coal black eyes. "I knew this would happen. You've gone back to being the dutiful daughter. Your father told you to stop writing, so you did. Now, anticipating he'll tell you to stop seeing me, you're ending our relationship."

"This isn't about my father. It's about you and me, and whether you really know who I am."

"I know who you are. I've always seen you as clear as day. You're the one who doesn't know the real Joan Brown."

Joan shook her head, unable to continue the conversation. She turned her back to him, hoping he would understand what she couldn't bring herself to say. *Please. Leave now, before I fall apart.*

He did. In a few moments, she heard his muffled footfalls carry him out of the living room and across the kitchen. Her eyes stung as his footsteps faded down the hall. The front door's closing felt like a gunshot to her heart.

A guttural cry ripped from her lungs. Joan collapsed to her knees and dropped her head into her hands. She sobbed until her throat ached, until her eyes swelled. She would have wept until her heart burst— but Ronald had taken that with him.

"When I was in my teens, I wanted to be the next Dorothy Dandridge. I thought, If I can have leading men like Harry Belafonte, sign me up."

Joan blinked at her mother's revelation.

It had been a long and tiring Tuesday. She'd rushed home so she wouldn't keep her mother waiting. Now, as they shared the settee in her apartment's small sitting room, Caroline spoke of a crush she'd had on Harry Belafonte. How should she respond to that? "Okay."

Caroline tipped back her head and laughed. Joan heard amusement, delight, and a heavy dose of affection in the sound. "Have I shocked you?"

Memories of her childhood dreams seemed to have

added a glow to her mother's delicate features and a twinkle to her chocolate eyes.

"You're a beautiful woman, Mom. And you have a lovely singing voice. I think you could have been a movie star."

Caroline sobered. "But I'll never *know*."

Joan's eyes flared with surprise. Her mother was serious about being Dorothy Dandridge. "What happened?"

"I wanted to be an actress. It might not have been a realistic goal, but it was mine. My father—your grandfather—convinced me that our family's future was in our church. So I gave up my dream to continue his legacy."

An uncomfortable foreboding touched Joan. Where was this conversation going? She looked around the sitting room at the religious objects, which had appeared to have so disconcerted Ronald the day he found her in Columbus—the plaques, the paintings, the statues.

She brought her attention back to her mother. "Is that why you married Daddy?"

"Your grandfather introduced me to your father." A small smile played with Caroline's lips. "I was so disheartened. First, my father told me to give up my dreams. Then he introduced me to an associate pastor who seemed to have all the personality of a wet rag."

Joan's hand flew to her mouth, and she stared at her mother in horror. "We thought you loved Daddy."

Caroline chuckled. "I do. I said he *seemed* boring. When I got to know him, I realized he was everything *but* boring."

Her mother winked at her. She actually winked as though they were two girlfriends exchanging wicked secrets.

Joan returned the conversation to her comfort zone. "So everything worked out for the best."

"Yes, but I had my doubts at first. I thought that it was all so unfair, that when I became a parent, I'd do things differently. I'd let my children make their own decisions, follow their dreams, and marry whomever they wanted to marry."

Joan held her mother's gaze and knew they both realized the same truth. "That's not what you're doing, though."

"A parent's natural instinct is to protect her child at any cost. You don't want her hurt. You don't want her to experience pain or disappointment. You're so sure that you know what's best for her. And who's best for her. Parents often forget that sometimes the best lessons are those you learn on your own."

There was wisdom as well as regret in Caroline's words. But what should she make of her mother's message? "Why are you telling me this?"

Caroline reached across the settee and cupped Joan's hand as it rested on her lap. "I'm not completely comfortable with what you're writing, but I'm so very proud of you for pursuing your dream. If this is what you truly want, don't ever give it up."

Joan dashed the tears from her cheeks. "That means the world to me, Mom. Thank you. But what about Daddy? He won't ever accept what I'm doing."

"You're not doing it for him. You're writing for yourself. I don't regret marrying your father or raising you and your sisters. But I have always wondered whether I could have been a star." Caroline's smile was self-deprecating.

"Did you ever tell Daddy you wanted to act?"

"My father told me to put that behind me, and I did." Caroline squeezed Joan's hand. "Don't make the same mistake I made. Follow your dreams."

"It's not just about me anymore. What about our

church? Stacy Smalls made sure her viewing public, if not the entire metropolitan area, knew I was the minister's daughter who writes erotic romance."

"And because of that publicity, we lost a few members. But we also gained a few. We'll get through this as a family." Carolyn smiled. "I saw you signing Vivian Barnes's copies of your books."

"I'm glad to have your support, Mom. But Daddy's going to be a bigger hurdle. And Maggie and Chrissie aren't exactly supportive, either."

"Don't worry about your sisters. They're just surprised. I'll deal with your father. But keep in mind, he'll probably never accept Ron. He isn't the man your father picked for you, and he doesn't belong to our church."

Joan looked down at her lap. "Ron and I aren't together anymore." *Even saying the words hurt.*

Her mother seemed speechless. "What happened? He really cared about you."

She stared at her hand joined with her mother's. How did she explain to her mother that her lover was sleeping with the woman she wanted to be?

"I don't think I'm the right woman for him."

"Why not?"

"He's looking for a confident, exciting woman, and I'm just . . . not."

Caroline's shocked expression was flattering. "Of course, you are. You know what you want, and you fight for it. What's more exciting or confident than that?" She squeezed Joan's hand. "Now, if you give up the fight because you'd rather coddle your man than love him, I understand why he'd have second thoughts. I mean, any man worth his salt would."

"Mom!" Her mother had never spoken so frankly to her before.

Caroline continued, undaunted. "And what about you? Could you be happy trying to be who someone else thinks you should be?"

Joan glanced up at the plaque of the Serenity Prayer, the one that asked for the wisdom to know the difference between what you could and couldn't change.

"I told my agent I've given up my writing." Joan mumbled the admission.

Caroline sighed, as though tired of dealing with a particularly dense student. "Then tell your agent you've changed your mind. That's your prerogative."

Caroline and Joan were silent for a moment. Joan had a lot to absorb. "What made you change your mind about my writing, Mom?"

Caroline released her hand and smoothed back Joan's hair. "I guess I finally realized my baby's a woman now." Her laughter was a little shaky. "I haven't decided whether I like that or not."

"What about you? Perhaps you could try community theater or something."

Caroline waved a dismissive hand. "Oh, Joan. I'm fifty-three years old. That ship has sailed."

Joan gave her a chastising look. "As long as you're alive, it's never too late to chase your dreams."

"Maybe you're right. Maybe it's not too late. I'll think about it." Caroline turned to her purse and pulled out a book. "In the meantime, I need you to autograph this." She handed Joan a copy of *Pleasure Quest*.

Joan stared at the book, lips parted in surprise. She was pleased and mortified at the same time. "You're going to read it?"

"Of course. You gave it to me. Who knows? Maybe I'll pick up some suggestions. Not that your father needs any help in that area." Her mother winked at her again.

Joan held up a hand, palm out. "Mom, that's a mental image I don't need."

Caroline tipped back her head and laughed.

Joan smiled, too, as she autographed her debut novel for her newest fan.

"She asked who I was sleeping with." Ronald growled into his cell phone as he paced his living room. He'd made several futile attempts to reason with Joan since Monday night. It was now Tuesday evening.

"You're creeping on her?" Jeffrey sounded disbelieving. That was small comfort.

"No, but she thinks I am." And he'd spent most of Tuesday trying to figure out how an otherwise rational woman could have such irrational ideas.

"With who?"

"With her."

A satisfying pause came over the satellite connection. *Good*. He wasn't the only one who thought that sounded crazy. He'd started to wonder.

Ronald paced as he waited for Jeffrey to catch up after that verbal hard left turn. But now his strides were far less agitated. He imagined his friend sitting on his sofa, his feet stacked on his coffee table, watching the Yankees on television with the sound off. Ronald was too restless to watch the game.

"Excuse me?"

Ronald collapsed into an armchair. "You heard me. She thinks I'm cheating on her—with her."

"How?"

"She thinks I'm sleeping with Cleopatra Sinclair."

Ronald stared across the beige and brown furnished apartment into its faded, cold kitchen, and imagined instead Joan's warm and vibrant room. Strange that he didn't think of the kitchen in his New York apartment instead.

Again Jeffrey hesitated. "Cleopatra Sinclair doesn't exist."

"Yes, she does. She's a combination of some aspects of Joan's personality. But they're traits Joan doesn't recognize in herself."

"Whatever."

Ronald imagined his friend rolling his eyes. "*You* don't have to understand it, but I have to get *her* to understand it."

"So you called *me*—during the game—because . . . ?"

Ronald stopped pacing. He shoved his left hand into his shorts pocket and rocked once on his heels. "I don't have Dr. Phil's phone number."

"Here's a better question."

"Okay?" Ronald prompted when his friend remained silent.

"You live in New York. She lives in Ohio. You're only there for the summer. Why put this much effort into a summer fling?"

Was it a summer fling? Had he begun to hope for more?

"She helped me establish a better relationship with my family. Regardless of what happens in September, I want to help her realize everything she has to offer."

This time Jeffrey's pause seemed contemplative. "This isn't a fling?"

"I don't know yet." Ronald massaged his forehead. "I don't want it to be."

"You worry me."

Whatever Jeffrey was about to say would undoubtedly annoy him. "Why's that?"

"You almost married Yasmine, who's now pregnant with your brother's baby. The woman you're seeing now thinks you're sleeping with her alter ego."

"Joan's not crazy." Ronald felt guilty because for a moment yesterday, he'd worried that she might be. He was sure he would be forgiven for that momentary lapse. "Her idea may *sound* crazy, but she's not crazy."

"I'm worried about you."

"You don't need to be. I'm fine and so is Joan."

"Your track record stinks."

"I made a mistake with Yasmine, but Joan's not Yasmine."

"If you say so."

"I'm serious. She's definitely not a cheater, and she's definitely not crazy."

"You know her better."

Ronald released a heavy sigh. "I wish I knew how to convince her that I know the real Joan and that she's just as confident and exciting as she imagines Cleopatra Sinclair to be."

Jeffrey snorted. "Have you considered getting the two of them in a room together and introducing them?"

Ronald paused. "Jeff, sometimes you're brilliant."

Chapter 23

If you give up the fight because you'd rather coddle your man than love him, I understand why he'd have second thoughts.

Joan watched the cursor flash on her office computer. Her mother's words still haunted her a day later. She wished the problem between her and Ronald was as simple as her being overprotective toward him. But there was a much bigger issue. Who was doing the coddling? Was it her or Cleo? Apparently, Ronald couldn't answer that.

The knock on her door startled her. Joan angled her body away from the entrance and wiped her eyes before facing her visitors. She stiffened when she saw her sisters.

Margaret lifted a take-out bag from one of Joan's favorite coffee shops. "We've brought your lunch."

The smell of chicken noodle soup and fresh-baked rolls escaped the bags they each held. The scents were tempting, but Joan was wary. Was this an olive branch or an ambush?

Her sisters looked sincere, maybe a little anxious. Joan mentally shrugged. Repairing her relationship with her sisters was worth the risk. She glanced at her Disney watch. It was after noon on Wednesday. The week was flying by. "It'll be a little crowded in here."

Margaret crossed the threshold, glancing over her shoulder at Christine. "We'll make it work."

Christine carried in an extra chair, and they sat around Joan's desk. Margaret handed Joan a cup of soup and a salad before starting on her own lunch.

Joan poked at her salad with the plastic fork. "If you've come here to tell me how angry you are at me and how disappointed you are in me, I already know."

Margaret stared at her sandwich. "We aren't here for that."

Joan glanced at her older sister, sensing Margaret's discomfort. "Then why are you here?"

Margaret reached into her purse. Silently, she pulled out a copy of *Double Dipper,* Joan's second book.

Joan's gaze dropped to the cover. She blinked, trying to correct her vision. "Where did you get that?"

Margaret was embarrassed but direct. "I bought it when it came out last year. I have *Pleasure Quest,* too."

Not only was Joan's vision playing tricks on her, but her hearing was on the fritz as well. "You bought my books?"

Joan looked from Margaret to Christine and back. Was this a joke? Her gaze shifted to the book in Margaret's hands. It looked as though it had been read, perhaps more than once.

Margaret laid the paperback on her lap. Her hands covered it in an almost protective gesture. "I didn't know you were Cleopatra Sinclair."

That comment shouldn't bother her. "Would it have made a difference?"

Margaret paused. "Yes, it would have." She gave Joan an apologetic look. "I know my little sister is a grown woman. But"—she tapped *Double Dipper*—"this aspect of your growth is something I needed to ease into. I had no idea you could write something like that."

Disbelief mingled with amusement. "But it's all right for you to *read* something like that?" Another thought occurred to Joan. "Does Tim know your reading preferences?"

Margaret's smile was secret pleasure. "He's benefited from it. He sends his regards, by the way."

Beside Margaret, Christine shook her head. "This I don't need to hear."

Joan scowled. "I think you've given me writer's block."

The image of Timothy and her sister wrapped in some of the intimate positions described in her books was a mental vision she had to get rid of. Quickly.

Margaret laughed, the bubbly sound reminding Joan of their mother. "Mom and Daddy have done it, and I think more than three times."

Christine cupped her hands over her ears. "I *really* don't need to hear this."

Joan groaned. "Neither do I." *Curse Maggie.* Would she ever be able to look at her parents again?

Christine lowered her hands. "I haven't read your smut books yet, but I'm looking forward to them."

Joan's laughter startled her. "Well, when you put it that way, I hope you enjoy them. I think." She studied her sisters, who were sitting with her and joking as though nothing had happened. "What made you change your mind about my writing?"

Margaret and Christine exchanged looks before her older sister finally answered. "We were jealous."

Her answer wasn't anywhere on Joan's list of possibilities. "Of my writing?"

Margaret shook her head. "No, although I do enjoy your books."

Christine looked earnest. "You said no to Mom and Daddy."

Joan waited, but neither sister added anything else. "So?"

Margaret sighed. "We weren't able to do that. Ever. It made us angry, and we took it out on you." She met Joan's eyes. "We're sorry."

Christine nodded. "Very sorry."

Joan studied the two women, who returned her gaze anxiously. All that pain and anger because she'd wanted to make her own decisions? "I thought you were disgusted with me because of what I wrote."

Christine worried her fingers. "It was easier to blame you than it was to admit that we were really angry with ourselves."

Joan was amazed. What would Ronald say if he could hear this conversation? What would he think? She clenched her teeth. *Stop thinking about Ronald. He's not a part of your life anymore.*

Margaret stared at her sandwich. "When Daddy said he didn't want me to marry Tim, I should have said, 'I'm marrying him, anyway.'"

Christine spooned up her vegetable soup. "You know, you're lucky Tim has stuck around as long as he has. If I were him, I'd have moved on three months ago."

Margaret's chuckle was full of surprise. "Thanks a lot."

Christine swallowed more soup. "You're welcome."

Margaret rolled her eyes. "What about you and Silas?"

"That's not going to happen. It's like Joan said. If Mom and Daddy think he's such a great catch, they can marry him."

Joan had fallen down the rabbit hole with Alice. On Tuesday her mother had confessed that she'd wanted to be Dorothy Dandridge. Today Joan was presiding over a mutiny of Reverend Brown's dutiful daughters. She was having trouble adjusting to this new reality.

Christine continued. "I don't want to be called Chrissie anymore. I want to be called Chris."

That was the final straw. Joan stared at her younger sister. "You're telling us now, after twenty-four years of calling you Chrissie?"

Christine raised an eyebrow. "This from the woman who's lived a double life for five years?"

Joan chose not to mention the nine years she'd been writing before she was offered her first publishing contract.

Margaret patted Christine's knee. "Better late than never."

Joan glanced at her cooling soup. "So now that you've decided you aren't angry with me, what are you going to do?"

Margaret looked determined. "I'm going to marry Tim."

Christine crossed her arms. "And I'm *not* going to marry Silas."

Pleased, Joan nodded. She'd had no idea that admitting she'd written a couple of books would cause such an upheaval in her family. One wedding off, another wedding on, and maybe a second career for her mother.

She smiled at her sisters. The transition from dutiful daughters to independent women was almost complete. "Now, who's going to tell Daddy?"

Hours later Joan had moved back to the store's checkout counter, but she still couldn't concentrate. She tried to draft lesson plans for her beginner, intermediate, and advanced art classes, but her mind was on her breakup with Ronald. Harold's words played on a loop in her mind. *He's with you because you write porn.*

Why was she giving Harold's accusation so much of her time? Joan expelled her confusion on a short, sharp breath.

Consider the source, Joan. The man has made a career out of lying to and cheating his family. Not exactly a stellar character. You can't believe what he says.

But when she considered Harold's words in conjunction with Ronald's—*Is Cleo ready to come out and play?*—Harold's comments gained credibility.

She kept coming back to that one critical question: Who was Ronald having a relationship with? Joan or Cleopatra?

The chimes rang merrily above The Artist's Haven's entrance. Joan slipped on her welcome-to-my-store smile. Her expression iced over and shattered when Christine's soon-to-be ex-fiancé entered.

"Silas." She added a nod to her greeting. "I'll let Chris know you're here."

"That's okay, Joan." Christine's voice carried to her.

Joan turned to watch her sister approach them. She looked cool and confident in her lemon yellow cap-sleeved blouse and mint green linen pants. Her wavy raven hair bounced around her shoulders in time to the clacking of her sandals against the gray tiled floor.

Christine stopped beside the checkout counter. "Hi, Silas. Thanks for coming."

Joan blinked. "You invited him here?"

Silas sneered. "What's wrong with that?"

Joan cocked an eyebrow. "Would you like a list?"

"Joan." Christine gave her a pointed look. "Silas and I have a wedding to discuss, and the sooner the better."

Joan met her sister's eyes. *Are you sure you want to talk to him alone?*

Christine responded to the look. *I'll be fine.* She led Silas to the back of the store.

Joan glanced at the lesson plans. She certainly wouldn't be able to concentrate now. Her gaze followed Silas and her sister until they disappeared behind the shelves that kept the office door just out of sight.

During lunch, Christine had considered telling Silas privately that their wedding was off. Joan had thought she and Margaret had talked their younger sister out of that. They'd recommended ending her engagement during the Brown family dinner tonight. The family would be nearby in case Silas became difficult.

Apparently, Chris wasn't as compliant as Chrissie had been.

Joan could see Christine's point. Telling him while they were alone was a much more sensitive way of handling a broken engagement. Although Silas was volatile, Joan was sure he wasn't dangerous. Still, she'd feel better if Christine weren't confronting him alone.

Joan left the checkout counter, her attention on the back of the store. She stopped at a product aisle in which Kai was stocking inventory on the shelves.

"Kai, could you watch the service counter for a few minutes, please?"

Kai stood and brushed off her pants. "Sure, Joan. Are you going out?"

Joan watched Kai nudge the paint containers closer to the shelves, out of the way of potential customer traffic. "No. I'll just be in the back if you need me."

Kai grinned. "Okay." She passed Joan on her way to the counter, her purple-tipped, spiky raven hair unmoving.

"Thanks, Kai." Joan turned, hastening her pace.

As she drew closer to the office, she stepped with much more care. It would be awkward if she was detected. Christine's and Silas's voices carried, albeit muffled, through the closed door. Joan strained to make out Silas's words.

"What do you mean you're not going to marry me? Then who are you going to marry?"

Joan barely heard Christine's response. "No one."

"Then why not marry me?"

There was a pause. Joan leaned her head closer to the door. "I don't love you, Silas. And you don't love me, either."

"I *do* love you."

Joan clamped both hands against her mouth to muffle a disbelieving snort.

"Do you really, Silas?"

"Why else would I ask you to marry me?"

"Because your father told you to."

"What? Are you questioning my manhood now? You don't think I can think for myself?"

Joan mouthed the word *no*.

"If you loved me, you wouldn't flirt with other women, especially not in front of me." Joan heard the exasperation in Christine's voice.

"I'm a man. Men notice pretty women."

Joan closed her eyes and shook her head. If Silas put as much effort into his family's production company as he put into defending his manhood, Joan predicted the company would grace the cover of *Fortune* magazine within five years.

Christine's reply was cool. "The man I'm going to marry will notice them with a little less enthusiasm."

Joan sent a silent cheer for her sister's response.

"Your bitch sister put you up to this, didn't she?"

Joan's jaw dropped in outrage.

"Neither one of my sisters is a bitch. Don't call them that." Christine's words were hard, her tone harder.

"I'm not talking about Maggie. You know that. I'm talking about Joan. She made you do this. All right. That's fine. What do you think your parents are going to say?"

"It's my decision who I marry, no one else's."

Yes. Joan threw a mental fist punch.

"Okay, bitch. You made your decision. Now I'll make mine. Don't come crawling your ass back to me when your parents tell you you're a fool for letting me go. No one breaks up with me. Do you hear me? No one."

Joan took that as her cue to disappear. She hustled to the front of the store as quickly—yet quietly—as possible.

She stood to one side as Kai finished with a customer's transaction.

Kai smiled as she gave the customer his change and bag. "Thank you."

The older man mumbled a reply, then turned from the counter. The next customer stepped up.

Joan interrupted. "Thank you, Kai. I'll take over now."

Kai gave a relieved sigh. "Thanks, Joan. I can handle paints. The cash register makes me nervous."

Joan squeezed Kai's shoulder. "I was nervous at first, too."

Joan heard as well as sensed Silas stomp his way to the checkout counter.

"I need to speak with you." His voice shook with temper.

"Just a moment, please." Joan waited on the last customer in her line. She handed the frazzled middle-aged woman her change and her purchases. "Thank you and have a nice day."

The woman tossed her a distracted smile before wandering out of the store.

Joan turned to Silas. "Now, what can I do for you?"

He jabbed a rigid finger in her direction. His burgundy T-shirt almost matched the angry color in his face. "You think you've won by getting Chrissie to break up with me."

"I didn't talk Chris into doing anything. It's her life and her choice."

Silas dropped his hand. "Well, congratulations. She chose to be a bitter old maid with you."

Joan ignored the insult. "Chris probably did both of you a favor by calling off the wedding."

"You'd better do her a favor and get her to change her mind."

Joan shook her head. "If *you* couldn't get her to change her mind, what makes you think *I* could?"

"Because for some stupid reason she listens to you."

She arched a brow. "If Chris loved you, she'd listen to *you*."

"Why do you keep calling her Chris?"

"Because she asked me to."

"I don't like it."

Joan shrugged. "It's not your choice."

"It makes her sound like a man."

"That's a really stupid thing to say, and yet another example of why you and Chris wouldn't have been happy together."

Joan caught a movement in her peripheral vision. Christine came to them, her steps slow but confident.

"Silas, leave Joan out of this. This is between you and me."

Silas divided his glare between the two sisters. His nostrils flared with his heavy breaths. "No, it's not. It's her fault you're not going to marry me."

Christine's lips firmed. "I'm sorry that I've hurt you, but this argument won't change my mind."

"You haven't hurt me. But when you realize you've made a mistake and decide you want another chance, give me a call—so I can laugh in your face." Silas stomped to the entrance and out of the store.

Joan studied her sister's pensive profile. "How do you feel?"

Christine smiled. "Good. Really good." She looked at Joan. "I should have listened to you a long time ago."

"You made your decision when the time was right."

"Maybe." Christine arched a brow at Joan. "So, did you eavesdrop?"

Caught off guard, Joan opened her mouth, closed it, then opened it again. Her cheeks heated, and she gave her sister an embarrassed smile. "How did you know?"

Christine laughed. "Because I would have."

Joan sobered as she looked again at the front door. This wasn't the last they'd heard from Sly Tunes. "You know he's going to call Mom and Daddy."

"I know. I left a message for Mom to call me."

Joan sighed. "Tonight's dinner with the Brown family's going to be pretty interesting."

Chapter 24

Joan mounted the steps to her parents' house Wednesday evening. The banister bore most of her weight since her leg muscles were shaky. Yes, she had her mother's support, and Margaret's and Christine's, too. But unless she changed her father's heart, her family would remain fractured. No wonder she didn't have an appetite.

She used her key to let herself into her family home. Why was she going through this stress? What was the point? Ronald wasn't even in her life anymore. What did she have to prove?

What a stupid question. Of course she wasn't doing this for a man. She'd long ago earned the right to be her own woman. She was done with letting her father—or anyone else—dictate who she should be. And she didn't need Ronald waiting in the wings for her declaration of independence to have meaning.

Joan entered her parents' dining room just as everyone else—Kenneth, Caroline, Margaret, Christine, and Timothy—was sitting to eat. Her mother gave her an encouraging smile. Margaret looked sympathetic. Timothy regarded her with brotherly affection. Christine's expression said, "Don't chicken out and mess this up for the rest of us."

Nothing like sibling support to put her at ease. *Not.*

Joan clenched her courage with both fists and faced her father. "Hello, Daddy."

"What are you doing here?"

"Eating dinner with my family." Joan slipped into the seat beside her mother, aware that her father was tracking her movements. She leaned back into the chair, grateful for its support.

"Have you stopped writing that filth?"

Joan heard her father's words—just barely—over her thudding heart. Her hands shook as she plucked the napkin from the extra place setting. She spread it over her lap. "I've never written filth."

"You aren't welcome in this house until you stop writing those books."

Joan bled a little from his words. She opened her mouth to respond, but Caroline spoke first.

"*Our* child *is* welcome in *our* home." Caroline raised her chin and dared her husband.

Kenneth's expression blanched with surprise. "We've always taught them that actions have consequences."

Caroline braced her hands on the table. "It's time we both realized our daughters aren't little girls anymore. We wanted them to be strong, independent women. But now that they're grown, we're the ones holding them back."

Kenneth shook his head. "We're not holding them back. But there's too much at stake for them to think only of themselves."

Joan interrupted Caroline. A strong, independent woman wouldn't let her mother fight her battles. "What's at stake?"

Kenneth directed his impatience at her. "The church.

You know that you're supposed to be a role model for the congregation."

"Daddy, if you're asking me to choose between being a role model and being myself, I choose being myself."

Her father's scowl grew darker. "You're being irresponsible."

Margaret reached over and squeezed Timothy's forearm, drawing her boyfriend's attention. "Then I'm going to be irresponsible, too. If my choices are to be a role model or Tim's wife, then I choose being Tim's wife." She gave her soon-to-be fiancé a tremulous smile.

Timothy's silverware clattered to the table as though his fingers had gone numb from shock. He stared at Margaret, eyes wide and lips parted. Slowly, his surprise changed to joy, and a warm smile brightened his round face. Timothy cupped Margaret's cheek. "I promise that's a choice you'll never regret."

It was a scene from a romance novel come to life. Joan blinked away tears.

Christine cleared her throat and claimed her family's attention. "I'm irresponsible, too." She looked first at her mother and then her father. Her slender shoulders rose and fell with a deep, fortifying breath. "I've broken my engagement to Silas."

Kenneth pointed toward his youngest daughter. "Silas called me. We're going to talk, little girl."

Christine nodded. "All right, Daddy. But I'm not going to change my mind."

Kenneth gave her a disapproving look, but Christine's eyes never wavered. He shifted his attention to Margaret and then to Joan. "This is all your fault. You've turned them against our family and against our church."

Joan straightened in her seat and stared. "No, sir. I had nothing to do with this. My sisters made their own decisions. They're grown women. That's their right."

Caroline broke the impasse. "I know what you're doing, Ken. If our daughters don't marry men you think could somehow advance our church, you'll feel as though you've failed."

Joan's brows met in a frown. "Failed who?"

Kenneth spoke over Joan, as though she weren't part of this discussion. "It's not about me. It's about making sure our daughters are safe and happy."

Caroline had started shaking her head even before Kenneth answered. "If that were true, Maggie and Tim would already be married or at least engaged. And we never would have pressured Chrissie into marrying Silas."

"This family's future is tied to our church. The decisions I make are meant to secure that future." Kenneth's voice was strained.

Her mother's heart-shaped face softened with understanding. "But you've gone too far, Ken. You've put more importance on a building than your children's happiness."

Kenneth rose to his feet, his movements jerky with frustration. He turned his back to the room. "Your father expected me to grow his congregation."

Joan was disconcerted to see her father so agitated. She'd always seen him in strong roles—pastor of their church, head of their household. But now she was witnessing an insecurity in him she'd never suspected existed.

Caroline's gaze followed her husband's movements. "It's your congregation, Ken. It's been yours for more than fifteen years, and you *have* grown it. My father would have been very proud of you and the work you've done."

"The church is your father's legacy. I wanted to make it one of the premier churches in the community."

Caroline sighed her impatience. "You don't have to do things bigger and better than my father. You don't have anything to prove, to us or your congregation."

Kenneth rubbed his hands over his hair, turning back to face his family. "Even after all these years, I still don't feel as though it's my church. I don't think I've earned it."

"You have earned it, Daddy." Joan shifted in her seat to face her father. "But you have to figure out where the church ends and your family begins. When are you Pastor Brown, and when are you . . . Daddy?"

"Chris, what have you done to your hair?"

Joan turned at Margaret's shocked exclamation. Christine strutted down the church's center aisle. Her jewel green tank top set off her golden skin. The matching pleated skirt twirled around her knees and showcased her long, slender legs.

Christine stopped beside the pews near where Joan, Margaret, and Timothy stood waiting for the Thursday night choir practice to begin. She struck a pose, left hand on her hip, while she fluffed her shortened locks. "You like?"

The long, wavy tresses that had swung past Christine's shoulders just that morning had been sheared. Now bouncy locks framed her heart-shaped face and kissed the nape of her neck. Gone was the Goody Two-shoes, little-girl-lost look. In her place was a strong, sassy woman.

Joan stepped forward and circled her younger sister. "I love it."

Margaret grinned. "You're really going all out with the new you. You look great."

Christine laughed. "I feel like I've been asleep for a really long time, and now, finally, I've woken up."

Joan blinked. That was exactly how she'd felt when Ronald convinced her to tell her family about her writing. Like she was Sleeping Beauty waking up to an Alice-in-Wonderland adventure. But who was she now?

She glanced at her wristwatch. Sleeping Beauty, Alice, and Mulan stared back at her. Joan pursed her lips. At the end of the story, Mulan's identity was revealed. She'd saved China and scored the oh-so-sexy captain.

Joan took a deep breath, trying to ease the pain in her gut. It didn't work. But Christine's sudden scream managed to distract her.

"Oh, my goodness! Oh, my goodness!" Christine grabbed Margaret's left hand. She continued to squeal as she stared at her sister's three-carat, emerald-cut diamond engagement ring. "When did you get this?"

Margaret gave her fiancé a radiant smile. "Tim gave it to me last night when we got home from dinner. He bought it months ago. He said he'd just been waiting until I was ready to put it on my finger."

Christine swiped away her tears, then threw her arms around her older sister. "I'm so happy for you." She released Margaret to smile up at Timothy. "You are one brother who knows how to invest wisely."

Timothy grinned in the easy, natural manner of a man in love. "I have to. This account is too valuable to risk."

Joan smiled, watching the exchange in silence. She'd done more than her share of screaming, laughing, and crying when Margaret and Timothy had shown her the ring earlier. Timothy was right. The love he and Margaret shared had been well worth waiting for. It was like a fairy tale.

Familiar footsteps announced new arrivals. Joan turned in time to see the surprise on her mother's face.

"Chrissie, what have you done to your hair?" Her mother's words parroted Margaret's amazement.

Joan tensed at her father's unsmiling expression.

Margaret stepped closer to Joan. Her whisper echoed Joan's concern. "Do you think Daddy's going to kick us out of the choir?"

Caroline stopped in front of Christine. She held her daughter's shoulders, turning her left, then right, to examine the new hairstyle. "Chrissie, you cut all your pretty hair." She drew her fingers through the shortened strands.

Christine's lips curled downward. "Well, I think it still looks pretty, Mom."

Caroline stepped back. "It looks beautiful."

Joan grinned as Christine's spirits were restored. Her baby sister's face glowed like a lamp. But Joan's expression sobered as her father remained silent.

Caroline turned to her husband. "What do you think, Ken?"

Joan could almost hear her sisters holding their breath. She exhaled before she passed out.

Kenneth looked over Christine's face. "I liked it long. But it's pretty this way, too, honey."

He turned his attention to Joan and Margaret. Joan shifted under the close scrutiny. From the corners of her eyes, she noticed Christine and Margaret fidgeting as well. Timothy pried Margaret's clenched hands apart to claim one. For one weak moment, Joan wished Ronald were with her to do the same. She shoved away the thought, unclasped her hands, and let her arms drop to her sides.

"The three of you look happier than you've looked in months." Kenneth's chuckle sounded forced and uncertain. He sobered, and his tone took on a soul-deep sincerity. "I'm sorry. I never meant to cause you so much unhappiness."

He approached Timothy and extended his right hand. "Welcome to the family."

Timothy recovered from the surprise much more quickly tonight. He grasped Kenneth's hand. "Thank you, sir. I'll make your daughter happy."

"You already have." Kenneth kissed Margaret's cheek before turning to Christine. "I'm sorry I pushed you to marry Silas. I guess I got carried away."

Christine's smile was radiant and relieved. "I should have spoken up sooner." She kissed her father's cheek, and he cupped the side of her face.

Finally, Kenneth turned to Joan. Her nerves were brittle with tension. *Breathe in. Breathe out.*

"I understand that writing is something you feel you have to do. I don't understand why you've chosen to write those kinds of books, though."

"I don't write filth, Daddy."

"You may not consider it to be, but I don't think I could read one of them."

Filth or not, Joan wasn't certain she wanted him to read her books, either. "I understand."

"But I've accepted your decision to continue writing. Your mother told me not to take away your dreams."

Joan caught her mother's eye. Caroline winked at her. She hoped her mother could read the gratitude in her gaze. She turned her attention back to her father. "Thank you, Daddy."

If he accepted her decision, why did she still sense a distance between them? And where were her hug and kiss on the cheek?

The director called the choir members together. After

a last uncertain look toward her father, Joan followed her sisters to the benches behind the pulpit.

On the altar steps, Christine paused and turned to Joan. "What do you think? Would now be a good time to tell Mom and Daddy that I want to get my own apartment?"

Joan shook her head. "You have a lot of issues, Chris. We get that. But let's take them one at a time."

"Heather, I'm going to keep writing." Joan turned away from her office computer and gave her telephone conversation with her agent her full attention.

Unlike most Fridays, this one had been hectic. Joan was glad of that. The pace had protected her from her own thoughts. But she couldn't keep the lonely weekend at bay for much longer.

What was Ronald doing this weekend?

Stop it. That's none of your business anymore.

"Joan, that's wonderful." Her agent's enthusiasm carried clearly over the phone line. "What changed your mind?"

"I got my father to change his."

The line went silent for a beat. "What aren't you telling me?"

Heather's question caught Joan off guard. "What do you mean?"

"You're calling with great news, but you sound as though you've lost your best friend."

Joan's breath caught in her throat. Her agent's words came too close to the truth. She *had* lost her best friend, her lover, and her champion. Joan tried but couldn't shrug off the grief cloaking her.

"I'm just a little tired, I guess. I feel emotionally

drained after dealing with my family these past couple of weeks."

"I understand." Heather didn't sound as though she did. "But now you can concentrate on your writing again. Are you going to continue with erotic romances?"

"Yes." Joan nodded definitely, although she sensed there were issues she and her father would never resolve. "Those are the stories I want to tell."

"Do you want to write under your real name, then?"

"Oh no." Joan hastened to correct her agent before the other woman took off with the erroneous assumption. "I still want to protect my family's privacy as much as possible. So I'll keep my pseudonym."

"Okay." Heather sounded wary. "Just as long as your family realizes that what happened with the gossip columnists going after you because of your relationship with Ron Montgomery could happen again."

"They do understand that." Joan rubbed her stinging eyes. Nothing as exhilarating or wonderful as Ronald Montgomery would ever happen to her again.

"To paraphrase Frank Sinatra, here's to doing it our way." Christine held her coffee cup aloft as she made the toast, then tapped it against Joan's and Margaret's cups.

"To Ol' Blue Eyes." Margaret sipped her drink.

The three sisters had squeezed into Joan's office after closing The Artist's Haven Friday night. They sipped their ginger ale in silent contentment. Christine sat in the brown guest chair. Margaret settled into a spare folding chair. Joan watched her sisters from her seat behind her desk.

Margaret took a deep drink. "Have you heard anything more from Silas?"

"Not a peep." Christine took another sip of the chilled

soda. "Wedding plans were already in motion for me. We can just continue with you as the bride now."

Margaret nodded her agreement. "Very convenient." She drank more ginger ale. "I didn't think Mom and Daddy would accept our decisions so easily." She looked at Joan. "Although it probably didn't seem as easy to you."

"I was afraid they'd never speak to me again." Joan glanced from one sister to the other. "I was afraid you wouldn't speak to me, either."

Christine nodded solemnly. "You've always been the strong one."

Joan was uncomfortable with the admiration she saw in her little sister's eyes, especially since it wasn't deserved. "No, I haven't."

Christine laughed. "Are you kidding? I'd never even have *dreamed* of writing romance novels, much less *written* them."

Margaret crossed her legs. "Well, I might have dreamed of it, but I'd never have actually done it. I'd have been too afraid that Daddy would react *exactly* the way he did. But you volunteered to tell him the truth about your writing."

"Yeah." Christine faced Joan. "What were you thinking?"

Joan stared into the distance, remembering the evening she'd shown her first published novel to her family. She relived her fear, disappointment, and grief. "I was thinking that I didn't want to lie to my family anymore."

Margaret set her Styrofoam cup on the corner of Joan's desk. "I'm sorry we gave you such a hard time."

Joan shook her head. "That's in the past. You were there when I needed your support the most."

Christine cocked her head, with a frown. "What kept

you going? Why didn't you stop writing? If Daddy had put that much pressure on me, I would have caved."

Joan stared into her cup of ginger ale. "Ron kept me going. He helped me to believe in myself. With him, I didn't feel like I had to be strong alone."

Christine gave her a cheeky grin. "Where is the thrilling author? He usually stops in the store at least a couple of times a week. I haven't seen him at all."

Joan took a bolstering breath. "We aren't together anymore."

Christine's expression went from amused to astounded as fast as the breeze. "Why not?"

"You seemed perfect together." Margaret's tone echoed Christine's shock.

"Looks can be deceiving." Joan forced a smile and inclined her head toward Christine. "I think we've seen that with Chrissie's transformation into Chris."

"So what happened?" Margaret asked, her impatience showing.

"I'm not the right woman for him," replied Joan.

"Did he say that to you?" Christine sounded like she was spoiling for a fight.

Joan rushed to reassure her. "No, I said that to him."

Margaret and Christine exchanged confused looks. Margaret turned her frown on Joan. "What kind of woman do you think is right for him?"

Joan heaved a frustrated breath. She didn't want to relive the painful discovery that Ronald was more interested in her alter ego than the true Joan Brown. But she wanted her sisters to understand why she couldn't stay with him.

"He should be with someone who's more like him. Someone confident, exciting, and interesting. Someone who can mingle with him in his world."

"But that's you." Margaret's eyebrows had climbed almost to her hairline.

Joan frowned at her older sister. "Be serious."

"She *is* serious, Joan." Christine's eyes were wide with understanding. "You may not be used to thinking of yourself that way, but that's the way you are."

Joan shook her head, thoroughly exasperated. "That's exactly my point. Other people aren't seeing the real me." She took a deep breath, trying to rein in her impatience. "What makes you think I've always been the strong one, as you said? What makes you think I can mingle in his world?"

"*You* do." Christine made her answer sound obvious. "You make us think all those things about you by your actions."

Christine's words stopped Joan cold. Her sister wasn't comparing her to Cleopatra Sinclair. She wasn't projecting an image of what she wanted Joan to be. She was interpreting Joan's actions, and actions always trumped words.

"You need to give yourself more credit. You're more than the sum of your parts." Margaret reached over to squeeze Joan's forearm. "Taken together, Joan Brown is a very confident, exciting, and interesting person."

Could they be right? Was she so used to trying to be the dutiful daughter that she'd become blind to the person she really was? Was Ronald right when he said Cleopatra and Joan were the same?

He'd missed her. Ronald stood in the doorway of Joan's office at The Artist's Haven and watched her work. He clenched the small gift-wrapped package in his left hand. He wanted to march to her desk, drag her over it, and shake her for tossing him out of her life and leaving his heart in pieces.

He wanted to yell at her for accusing him of not knowing her. Of course, he knew her. Well enough to know he needed her, that he could never be happy without her. Well enough to miss the scent of her as she slept beside him at night, and the sight of her when he woke up in the morning. Well enough to want to walk behind her desk, kneel beside her, and wrap his arms around her.

Joan stopped typing. She raised her right hand and rubbed the back of her neck beneath her thick raven locks. Slowly, she lifted her head, and her gaze caught his. Her eyes flared with surprise. In their chocolate depths, he saw the same loneliness he'd felt the past week. Did she regret their separation, too? God, he hoped so.

Ronald swallowed hard. "Hi."

"What are you doing here? I mean, I was going to stop by your apartment tonight."

He stopped breathing. "Why?"

Joan glanced at her lap before looking up. "To talk about us."

It helped to know she was nervous, too. Feeling more confident, Ronald stepped from the doorway and entered her office. "Let's talk now. You said I didn't know who you were."

"I thought you were attracted to a figment of my imagination. A smoke-and-mirrors woman."

Ronald stopped on the visitor's side of her desk. The furniture's edge pressed into his thighs, lending him support. He laid the package on the desk and balanced his palms on two of the many piles of papers scattered across her writing surface. "No. I fell in love with a flesh and bones, blood, sweat, tears, and muscle woman."

Joan séemed to collapse deep into her chair. "You can't be in love with me." The words flew out of her.

Ronald arched a brow. His gaze compelled her to deal with him, not to turn away. "Tell me why not."

Joan stood. Her gaze ricocheted around the room. It landed briefly on him before dropping to her desk. "Isn't it too soon? We've known each other less than two months. And you're a best-selling author from New York. I'm a minister's daughter who owns a little art-supply store in Columbus, Ohio."

This was where she'd defeated him last time. This time Ronald treaded carefully. He was after a much more favorable verdict.

"I know who you are. You said you thought I'd seen the real you and liked you, anyway. I don't like you *despite* who you are. I love you *because* of who you are."

"I don't move in the same circles as you."

"Just how glamorous do you think my life is? Most nights I just like to watch TV. I do my own laundry. I even scrub my own toilets."

Joan's smile was weak, but it still gave him hope. "You were right. You've seen me all along. I was the one who was blind. But I'm still afraid you'll get bored with me."

"There are too many facets of your personality for me to ever become bored. The minister's daughter. The naughty romance writer." He glanced at her desk. "The efficient—if unorganized—business owner. And that's just scratching the surface." Ronald reached out, curving a hand around the back of her neck to draw her closer. He gave her a sweet kiss, a brief kiss, landing softly on her lips. "We also have the loving sister, the loyal friend, and the generous lover."

"Does that make me interesting or crazy?"

Ronald chuckled. "We all have more than one persona,

and, depending on what group of friends or family we're with, one personality trait shows up more than the others. That doesn't make us crazy or fake." He grinned. "Just make sure you bring all of them to our wedding."

Her eyes widened. "Wedding? But we've only known each other a month."

"You survived the worst the Montgomery family has to offer and you didn't run for the hills." He sobered. "We've seen each other in some good times, and we've seen each other go through some pretty bad times. I'm not asking you to go to the courthouse with me now. But I know there's no one else I could count on to stand with me during the best and worst times."

Joan blinked. "I live in Ohio. Your world is in New York."

Ronald brushed away a tear as it trailed across Joan's cheek. "We can keep my apartment in New York for business and visits, and buy a house in Columbus. We'll eventually need more room."

She blinked again. "I don't know what to say."

Ronald picked up his gift from her desk and handed it to her. "Say you love me. Say you'll be with me. I want forever with you."

Joan wiped her fingers across her damp cheeks and opened the package with shaking hands. She revealed a framed pencil sketch of two dark lovers reclining naked in the grass. The man's broad back was exposed as he leaned—half sitting, half lying—over the woman.

The figures were surrounded by scattered precious gems, heaps of wheat, waving lilies, grape vines, palm trees and golden goblets. In the background, a stone tower rose. In the foreground, tiny fish swam in a pond.

The sketch was titled "Song of Songs."

Joan looked up, her expression filled with awe. "It's beautiful. Did your agent's friend draw this?"

"Yes, she did." He circled her desk to stand beside her, close enough to breathe in her powder soft scent. "Solomon is a prominent biblical figure who embraced his sexuality. A minister's daughter and erotic romance author aren't mutually exclusive."

Joan stared at the framed drawing again. "This looks like us."

"She said the drawing doesn't get us out of sitting for her, though."

Joan's chuckle wobbled around the edges. She lifted her face to stare deeply into his eyes, tears in her own. "I love the way you see me. The way you see all of me. I want forever with you, too." She lifted the drawing with both of her hands. "My parents can't see this, though."

Ronald smiled. "I didn't buy it for your parents." He stepped closer, lowering his head for a kiss. "We'll keep it our little secret."

Don't miss Patricia Sargeant's

On Fire

and

You Belong to Me

Available now wherever books are sold!

From *On Fire*

"I'm taking you off the fire department beat," Wayne Lenmore announced.

Her newspaper editor's words hit Sharon MacCabe like a leather palm. Hard. Stinging. Totally unexpected. Announcements like this shouldn't come on a Friday.

Sharon searched the older man's drooping features. She was too breathless to be hysterical, too numb to be outraged. She leaned back onto the hard plastic visitor's seat, seeking support. "Why?"

Wayne shifted in his battered blue office chair. It squeaked under his weight. "The publisher is going to assign someone else to the beat. He thinks you're better with features."

Sharon flinched at the implication she couldn't handle hard news. She'd been covering the fire department for the *Charleston Times* for the past six months. The previous beat reporter had left the West Virginia daily for greater fame and fortune. The assignment had taken her one step closer to her dream of becoming an investigative reporter. That's why she hadn't resented the fourteen-hour days, or weekends in the office learning about firefighting and meeting department officials.

She'd worked for years to prove herself capable of handling a hard news beat. She'd finally been assigned to one only to have it snatched away from her.

She gripped the chair's cool plastic arms. "Are you dissatisfied with my work?"

Wayne's pale gray gaze slid from hers. "Your work is fine."

His comment wasn't resounding praise, but neither was it criticism. Sharon clenched her fists in her lap to isolate her shaking. "Then why am I being demoted?"

"It's not a demotion. We're just shuffling personnel."

First, he demotes her, then he lies to her. The ice of shock melted under the heat of temper. "Who else are you shuffling?"

Wayne sat back and his seat screeched again. "At this time, no one. But additional reassignments may come later."

Something was wrong with this picture. Apparently overnight, Gus Aldridge, the publisher, had sprouted some wild hair and stomped her budding career into the ground. What was going on?

"Does Gus have a replacement in mind?"

Wayne finally looked at her. "Lucas Stanton."

Anger thumped in her chest, each pulse reverberating in her throat. "Senator Kurt Stanton's nephew?"

"He starts Monday."

The state senator from Institute, West Virginia, was up for re-election in November. He faced a tight race over the next seven months against his challenger.

What was Gus up to?

Sharon's voice shook as she spoke. "What newspaper experience does the senator's nephew have?"

Her boss sat straighter in his chair. "He received a degree in English from West Virginia State College."

"Oh, come on, Wayne." Sharon's chuckle held more scorn than humor. "You know there's a world of difference between a comp paper and a news story."

"Everyone has to start somewhere."

"I started six years ago transcribing police reports. Why can't Stanton's nephew do the same?"

"Because Aldridge wants him to start with the fire department." Wayne rested his forearms on the stack of press releases and news clippings on his desk. It wasn't quite nine a.m., but already the sleeves of his white shirt were dusted with newsprint.

Sharon swallowed her disappointment. "You told me it was my time to move up after Ernie went to the *Baltimore Sun*. Now you're taking that away?"

Shame joined regret in Wayne's tired eyes. "I'm sorry, Sharon, but Stanton starts Monday."

He spoke with finality. Sharon took a steadying breath. The musty scent of newsprint filled her lungs. Her gaze wandered her boss's office. It resembled a storage locker of newspapers. Rival papers. National papers. Small community weeklies. It was a definite fire hazard.

Wayne's room was one in a row of offices along one wall. Dim, dingy plasterboard formed three of its sides. The fourth was Plexiglas, which afforded the office's occupant a view of the reporters' cubicles. Were people watching them now and, if so, what was their interpretation?

She looked again at her editor. "What about the feature interview I scheduled with the new fire station captain today? And the fire department meeting this evening?"

"Features are your area. You can write up the captain's

interview. And go to the meeting. If anything comes from it, brief Stanton Monday."

Sharon's temper spiked. She counseled herself not to let her emotions take over. Nothing would be gained by creating a scene. "Do you expect me to train my replacement?" Her tone was hard but calm.

"Don't forget someone helped you when you first joined this paper, MacCabe."

"No, Wayne. I worked my way up from an intern. I wasn't *given* someone else's beat to curry political favor."

The flush started in Wayne's neck and rose to spot the scalp beneath his thinning gray hair. He dropped his gaze. "You have your assignment, MacCabe. Take it and be glad you still have a job."

Although muttered, the words stung. Sharon pushed herself to her feet and crossed the fraying gray carpet to the door. She clenched her jaw to keep from hurling words she could not take back.

She turned with her hand on the knob. "This newspaper is putting Stanton's political connections above my experience. How does that serve our readers?"

She turned her back on Wayne's guilty expression.

Sharon walked down the aisle, past the newsroom's gray-and-glass decor, and curious coworkers. Back at her cubicle, she continued to fume as she fired up her computer. A newspaper was no place for political cronyism. Among other things, people depended on the paper for information to actively participate in their democratic society. It shouldn't be used to advance someone's agenda, which was obviously Gus's intent.

"What did that keyboard do to you?"

Sharon looked up at the sound of Allyson Scott's voice. The political reporter stood in the entrance of

Sharon's cubicle, the inevitable mug of coffee cupped in her palms.

"I've been replaced on the fire department beat." Fresh anger spurted into Sharon's veins.

Allyson's hazel brown eyes widened in her tan, heart-shaped face. "Why?"

Sharon shrugged. "Gus wants to please his political buddy. Senator Stanton's nephew starts Monday."

The other woman's jaw dropped. In one fluid movement, she settled her mug on the corner of Sharon's desk and displaced the folders from the guest chair to the floor so she could sit.

The political reporter was a tall, willowy brunette. Her appearance was so feminine and unthreatening that new people at the capitol usually didn't notice her sharp mind until it was too late.

Allyson reclaimed her coffee. "How long has this been in the works?"

Sharon glanced at her watch. She didn't want to be late for her interview with the new fire station captain, Matthew Payton. "I don't know." She jerked open her bottom desk drawer and grabbed her stash of pretzel rods.

"Is this a temporary assignment or is he going to be permanent staff?"

"I have no idea. I was too upset to think of asking those questions."

Sharon bit into one of the pretzels. Low sodium, low fat, very little taste. Once this bag was finished, her healthier eating habits would die an unlamented death.

Allyson leaned forward and touched the back of Sharon's wrist. "I would have been too. This is just so strange."

"I know." She offered the pretzels to Allyson, who declined the snack with a shake of her head. "Gus is a registered independent. Why would he cozy up to a particular politician?"

"Money and power. That's what everyone's ultimately after."

Sharon pulled her oversized, overstuffed purse from her desk drawer and heaved it onto her shoulder as she stood. "It used to be about the news."

Arriving at Fire Station 11 almost thirty minutes later, Sharon followed the administrative assistant's directions to an office at the opposite end of the main floor. The room was devoid of personal effects. If it weren't for the nameplate on the wall beside the door, she wouldn't have known she'd found Matthew Payton.

Charleston's newest fire station captain looked over from his computer as Sharon paused in the doorway. With her reporter's eye for detail, she cataloged his dark brown skin, prominent cheekbones and strong jaw. Full, well-shaped lips softened features so sharply drawn, they could have been sculpted from the mountains that made her state famous.

When he spun his chair forward, the woman in her caught the full effect of his broad shoulders, gift wrapped in a plain, white cotton shirt. He stood, smoothing his royal blue and yellow tie.

His midnight eyes held her gaze for a long moment. Sharon wondered whether he was going to invite her in or if he expected her to conduct the interview from the hallway.

She made herself relax. The drive from the newsroom hadn't done much to improve her mood. She was still seething over her demotion. But this meeting wouldn't go well if she projected that anger onto her interview subject.

Sharon found a smile and strode forward, hand extended. The captain met her halfway and wrapped his long, blunt fingers around hers. His touch was firm and warm.

She tilted her head to meet his eyes. He was at least seven inches taller than her five-foot-five. "I'm Sharon MacCabe. Thank you for allowing me to interview you."

"You're welcome. Have a seat."

Matthew's deep, dark voice was even more compelling in person than it had been during their brief phone conversation. She watched him return to the large, brown executive seat behind his desk. He waited for her to sit before folding his lean body onto the chair. She was curious about the wariness in his eyes.

Sharon crossed her legs, pulling her reporter's notebook and mini-recorder from her bag. "Would you mind if I taped this interview?"

"No, go ahead."

She turned on the recorder, then found a blank page for her notes. "Why would someone born and raised in a big city like Pittsburgh decide to move to a much smaller one like Charleston, West Virginia?"

Matthew leaned back in his chair, propping his elbows on its armrests. "I was ready for a change."

It took a moment for Sharon to realize he wasn't going to elaborate. "What kind of change?"

Matthew paused as though considering her question—or maybe his answer. "The usual. A new place to call home and the challenges of a new job."

"This is your second week on the job. What challenges have you faced so far?" Sharon's hand sped across the page, transcribing his answers even as she continued to ask questions.

"Nothing I can't handle."

The captain's reticence to be interviewed fueled her

curiosity. She was writing a harmless feature. To what could he possibly object? She'd lobbed softballs at him—as they said in the newspaper business—but he refused to relax. She switched her attention from her notepad to her interview subject.

"I'm sure you're up to these challenges, Captain, but could you give us examples of them?"

Matthew again appeared to weigh his response. "Recreating a fire scene is always challenging."

"In addition to being the station's captain, you're also the lead fire investigator. How will the dual roles influence the station's fire inspection procedures?"

"I won't discuss that until we've completely reviewed those procedures."

The interview wasn't going well. Sharon smothered a sigh and went back to the basics: age, rank, and hobbies. How did he like the Mountain State? What tourist attractions had he seen so far? What was he looking forward to experiencing next? With each question, Matthew's answers became more relaxed.

Sharon was pleased with the interview's improvement as her pen flew across the notepad. "What was your job with the Pittsburgh fire department?"

"I was a firefighter."

She glanced up. "A lieutenant?"

"No, a firefighter."

"How did you jump from being a firefighter to station captain and lead investigator?"

Indignation flared in Matthew's midnight eyes. "I had the skills the fire chief and assistant chief were looking for."

"What are those skills?"

Matthew heard the incredulity in the reporter's voice. He also sensed her anger. He didn't know why she was upset; he was the one on the hot seat.

He hadn't wanted to be featured in the *Charleston Times*. However, his new boss, Assistant Chief of Administration Brad Naismith, and Fire Chief Larry Miller insisted the story would help improve the department's image in the community. Deciding to save his energy for more worthy battles, Matthew had agreed to the interview.

The little reporter appeared harmless with her guileless ebony eyes. But he'd learned from bitter experience the press was capable of twisting answers to seemingly innocent questions.

Sharon pushed strands of her thick, dark hair behind her shoulder. She repeated her question. Her soft, Southern accent reminded him of warm summer nights. "What are those skills?"

"I have twelve years of experience as a firefighter."

She arched a winged eyebrow. "Do you have any experience running a station?"

"Ms. MacCabe, I don't have to give you my résumé. I've already earned my job."

"I realize that. But the community has a right to know their fire station captain's qualifications."

Matthew wasn't going to play the public's-right-to-know game. The press had a wicked winning streak compared to both the interview subject and the public whose interest they professed to protect.

He stood. "Chief Miller and Assistant Chief Naismith can vouch for my qualifications. Any other questions?"

The pint-sized reporter rose too. The modest cream dress shifted over her slender figure as she stepped closer to his desk. "Just one. Why are you so defensive?"

He couldn't believe her audacity. "This was supposed to be a personality story, not an interrogation."

Her eyes sparked with anger, and vivid color dusted

her cheekbones. "I wasn't interrogating you. I was asking simple questions."

"I'm sure that's what Woodward and Bernstein said before they brought down Nixon's presidency." He crossed his arms. "Not everyone you meet has a criminal intent."

The reporter's sharp intake of breath let him know he'd hit his target. "I'm not out to get you. I'm just doing my job."

"What is your job, Ms. MacCabe? I thought reporters were supposed to cover the news, not pass judgment."

She stepped back as though he'd struck her. He held her wide-eyed gaze, refusing to regret his words.

Sharon turned from him to lift her oversized purse from the floor. She pulled the strap over her shoulder. "Thank you for your time." She turned, back straight and head high. Long strides carried her from his office.

Matthew's temper chilled with the realization he'd just crossed the media. In a normal situation, he would welcome the attention of an intelligent, attractive woman. But, circumstances as they were, this woman's interest could burn him.

Sharon paused in a corner of the station lobby, shaking with fury. She skimmed her notes. She had pages of inane questions and answers. They were enough for a surface piece that would entertain her readers, but they didn't delve far enough to satisfy her.

She glanced down the hall toward the captain's office. There was a lot more to Matthew Payton, but she wouldn't find out from him.

She stuffed her reporter's notebook into her bag and wove her way past groups of people entering and exiting the government building. Beyond the glass doors of the side entrance, she saw Li Mai Wong,

Brad's administrative assistant, sharing a smoke break with coworkers.

Sharon pushed through the revolving doors and approached the tall, slender woman. She ignored the odor of cigarettes that carried on the late spring breeze.

"Hi, Li Mai. Do you have a moment?"

"Sure." Li Mai drove her cigarette into a standing ashtray. "How'd the interview go?"

"Fine, thanks. But it needs some background." Sharon led her companion to a quieter section of the break area. She leaned against the side of the building, trying to appear more casual than she felt. "What can you tell me about your new captain?"

"He's very nice. He doesn't talk much, though."

"Is he a snob?"

"No, just quiet. He doesn't talk much about himself. But he does ask a lot of questions."

Sharon pounced. "What kind of questions?" *Questions about how to do his job, maybe?*

"He wants to learn about the department. Administrative details so he knows how we do things here."

Sharon nodded. Those were reasonable questions for a new manager. She searched her mind for a way to dig deeper into what the other woman knew about the recent addition to the Charleston Fire Department. Administrative assistants were a great source of information, if you knew the right questions to ask.

She tried a chummy tone. "Matt told me Brad and Chief Miller interviewed him. Did Brad tell you how many candidates they met with?"

"They talked to a lot of people. Several of them were from other states." Li Mai brushed a restless hand over the hips of her wide-legged black pants. The matching jacket hung open over a white shell.

"What was it about Matt that impressed them the most?"

The other woman glanced away. *Bingo.*

Sharon gave her a persuasive smile. "What?"

Li Mai combed her fingers through her short, black hair. The straight locks swung above her narrow shoulders. "I don't know if I should say anything about this."

Sharon held her hand over her heart. "I promise not to tell a soul."

Li Mai looked around, making sure no one was near enough to overhear. "Off the record?" She waited for Sharon's nod. "The assistant chief said Matt's father is a friend of Mayor West."

Sharon's smile froze. "Really?" Another person who was sneaking up the career ladder on cronyism rather than merit. Two in one day.

"Yes. But you have to promise not to tell anyone."

Sharon stood away from the building. "You can trust me, Li Mai. I won't tell anyone."

The fire department's meetings took place promptly at four o'clock in a community center room that looked and smelled like a classroom. Every time Sharon walked through its doors, she had flashbacks of her elementary school.

As she strode to the front of the room, she surveyed her sparse surroundings. Rows of wooden chairs made the space look even smaller. And Sharon knew they never had as many attendees as the number of seats implied.

She took her customary spot in the front and selected a pretzel rod from her bag to quiet her growling stomach before the meeting. As she bit into the snack, she brooded over her horrible day and her options for salvaging her career. Unfortunately, Charleston didn't offer a lot of choices, and she'd rather not leave her hometown.

There were several suburban weeklies, but applying for a job with one of those companies would be a step backward after working for a metropolitan daily. The *Charleston Gazette* and the *Charleston Daily Mail* were the capital city's other daily newspapers. She'd look into opportunities there.

Sharon finished her pretzel and stood to dust crumbs from the skirt of her cream dress. Minutes later, the fire officials filed into the room.

The department served the sixty thousand residents who lived in the thirty-three square miles covering Charleston's hills, and the valleys the Kanawha and Elk rivers created.

Having covered the department for six months, Sharon had made the acquaintance of the fire chief, the two assistant chiefs, and the eleven station captains. The twelve men and two women took seats behind a row of tables that had been pushed together. Nameplates were already in place. Matthew's was shiny and new.

And directly in front of her.

In the hours before this meeting, Sharon had mentally replayed that morning's interview with Matthew. When she'd put herself in the captain's shoes, she'd realized he'd had cause to be defensive. Her softball questions for the puff piece had turned aggressive when she'd asked about his professional background.

Sharon tried a conciliatory smile when she caught Matthew's eyes. His expression remained somber. *Ouch.* She obviously had a long way to go before she could gain the captain's forgiveness. She switched her attention to her notepad.

Under Chief Miller's direction, the meeting moved quickly through the agenda. Sharon took exact quotes when she could and paraphrased when she wasn't able to keep up with the dialogue. This story would be the curtain call on her fire department assignment. She'd make it as thorough and informative as possible. The senator's nephew would have a hard time following in her footsteps.

When the meeting's momentum slowed, she flexed her writing hand and lifted her head. Matthew's midnight gaze snagged her own. There was suspicion in his eyes, as though he was trying to decide whether she was an ally or an enemy. Sharon fought a disquieted feeling as she held his gaze.

She'd already acknowledged that, during the interview, she had projected on to him her anger at being taken off her news beat. She'd been wrong to do that, and she would apologize. However, her behavior shouldn't label her public enemy number one.

Assistant Fire Chief Brad Naismith's voice broke her train of thought. "An electrical malfunction caused Tuesday's greeting-card store fire."

Sharon wasn't a fire expert by any means. But, based on her research, the event she'd witnessed earlier in the week seemed to move too quickly for an accidental blaze.

She glanced at Matthew and saw his questioning frown. Brad's ruling appeared to surprise him also.

The meeting adjourned less than an hour later. As Sharon stuffed her notepad into her large bag, she saw Matthew approach Brad. She slowed her movements to catch snatches of their conversation.

Matthew's warm baritone hailed Brad. "What information did you collect from Tuesday's fire?"

Brad's rural West Virginia roots were apparent

in his voice. "The usual. Heat readings, photos, samples. Why?"

Sharon retrieved her notepad. With her back to the two men, she pretended to review her notes as an excuse to linger while they spoke.

Matthew's tone was casual. "The fire didn't have the characteristics of an accidental burn. I'd be curious to take a look at that information."

Sharon mentally patted herself on the back. It was satisfying to know her suspicions of the fire coincided with those of an expert. She'd spent a lot of hours reading about fires and fire investigations—for a beat that was no longer hers.

Brad sounded irritated and defensive. "The case is closed. My ruling is final."

"I'm not only the station's captain, I'm also the lead fire investigator. How do you suggest we work out our roles for the future?"

Sharon was impressed that Matthew was asserting his position in the station. Maybe the mayor's pet intended to take his responsibilities seriously. She crammed her notebook back into her purse and prepared to leave. She wanted information about the fire, but she wasn't interested in eavesdropping on a power play between the two men. She began working her way past the groups of friends and neighbors still congregating around the room.

Sharon was now in a hurry to return to the newsroom to file her story before dinner. The pretzel rod hadn't satisfied her hunger. Several times during the meeting, her empty stomach had spoken up.

Matthew saw Sharon leave the room and hurried after her. He caught up with the reporter as she crossed the parking lot. He called her name and she turned, her thick, wavy hair swinging behind her.

He jogged toward her, stopping an arm's-length away. "Hear anything interesting?"

The flicker of embarrassment that tightened her delicate features confirmed Matthew's suspicion she'd been eavesdropping on his discussion with Brad. He was still trusting enough to be disappointed that this reporter was like all the others.

Sharon angled her head to the right. "It was a good meeting."

"You know what I'm talking about. Are you going to give your readers the inside scoop on my conversation with Naismith?"

Indignation snapped her brows together. "I'm a reporter, not a gossip columnist."

"That's not an answer."

"I'm not going to report on your conversation with Brad."

A reporter shying from the scandal of intra-departmental discord? Not likely. He could even see the headline: SPARKS FLY IN FIRE DEPARTMENT.

Matthew crossed his arms. "I don't believe you."

"I can't help that."

He watched her tug her purse strap more securely onto her narrow shoulder. He wondered what she could possibly need to haul around in that misnamed suitcase.

Sharon folded her arms. "Off the record. Did Brad agree to your reviewing the information from the fire?"

Matthew hesitated. "He doesn't want to revisit cases he's already closed. We'll start the new investigation procedures going forward."

Sharon smiled, her eyes twinkling at him. "That's a diplomatic answer. I thought the fire was suspicious as well. It moved so quickly."

Reluctant admiration diffused most of his irritation. "That's true. How did you know that?"

"I wanted to know as much as I could about the fire department since it was my beat." She checked her wristwatch. Its thick black plastic band looked awkward on her delicate wrist.

Matthew checked his own watch. It was almost six o'-clock. "It's getting late. I don't want to keep you from dinner."

She adjusted her purse strap again. "I have to stop by the newsroom to file this story."

"You may want to eat first. Keep your energy up for the free and responsible press."

Sharon frowned. "What do you have against reporters?"

His irritation reawakened, the walls going back up. "You have your job to do, and I have mine. I just want to make sure your job doesn't make mine harder."

"You have trust issues, Captain. Have you been burned by the media in the past?"

Matthew froze, furious with himself for saying as much as he had. More than was safe. Sharon's expression held concern rather than curiosity. She searched his eyes as though looking for a door into him. He turned away before she could find it. He couldn't take the chance of a reporter learning anything about his past.

From *You Belong To Me*

"What are you doing here?"

Nicole Collins pitched her voice low in the elegant hotel restaurant. Still, she managed to interrupt the introductions between her literary agent, Denise Maitland, and the two men who stood in front of their table.

Malcolm Bryant turned toward her, a wariness in his cocoa eyes. His chiseled brown face hadn't changed much in the past four years. Perhaps it was even more appealing now, as was his six-foot-plus frame. No, *appealing* was the wrong word. The writer in her searched her mental thesaurus for something more appropriate. *Compelling*, she decided. He was more compelling and more confident. A self-assured stranger in a tailored, dark blue suit.

"I co-own the company that optioned for the movie rights to your book." His deep-sea voice washed over her. It still had the power to sweep her away.

"You own the production company?" She spoke through numb lips.

"Co-own." He inclined his head toward the tall,

well-dressed man beside him. "This is my partner, Tyrone Austin."

Nicole glanced at the smiling stranger before returning her attention to the man in front of her, and the memories of broken vows and tragic loss. She folded her hands in her lap, hoping that would stop their shaking.

"Nicky, what's wrong?" Denise asked.

She turned toward her agent. "Did you know he owned the company?"

"Of course." Denise regarded her with a confused expression on her dark, round face. "Does it matter?"

"It matters." If she had known Malcolm was Celestial Productions, she wouldn't be here.

Nicole scanned the room. Couples and groups of friends enjoyed lunch and quiet conversation. Now and then, bubbles of laughter floated across the silence, then faded away. He had brought her here. Paid for her to fly first class across the country to Los Angeles, back to his territory. Reserved a suite for her in a luxury hotel. Invited her to a business lunch in the hotel's four-star restaurant. And then, once she was lulled into a false sense of security, he'd changed her dream to a nightmare by reappearing—and bringing the painful past with him.

Nicole returned her attention to him as she stood. His gaze tracked her, and his firm lips stopped moving. She hadn't heard a word he'd said.

"I can't do this," she stated.

"What?" Denise half-rose from her chair.

Nicole picked up her purse and walked out of the dining room. She squared her shoulders, tilted her chin, and kept her vision straight ahead. She couldn't do anything about her shaking knees, though. She'd lost her temper—and probably her agent. She hated herself for running away from Malcolm. But she'd hate herself more if she stayed and did something stupid, like burst into tears.

A crowd waited in front of the elevators. The doors opened as Nicole approached. She stepped on and noticed someone had selected her floor. The crowd thinned as the elevator rose, seeming to stop at every floor. Nicole stood, outwardly calm in the center of the packed car, but inside turbulent emotions filled her. Anger. Sorrow. Regret.

Finally reaching her floor, Nicole and several other passengers disembarked and separated in the hallway. She located her room and pulled her key card from her purse. She started to slip it into the security lock when a dark hand grasped her wrist, the long fingers warm against her pulse.

"We have to talk," he murmured.

Malcolm Bryant felt the pulse jump in Nicole's delicate wrist as he leaned over her, his chest against her slender back. He could feel her warmth as he breathed her soft fragrance—a mixture of the soap she used and her natural scent that still stirred him, even in his dreams.

"We have to talk," he repeated.

An older couple stepped from the room across the hall. Malcolm caught their curious stare before they moved along.

"We can stay out here if you want," he murmured into the shell of Nicole's ear. "But we'll probably attract a lot of attention. Personally, I'd prefer to talk in your room. Either way, we will talk."

"Fine." She pulled free of him and pushed open the door. "We'll talk in the room."

Nicole crossed the thick, turquoise carpet, walking past the dining section and small living area to the sliding glass doors on the opposite side of the suite. She tossed her purse on the mahogany conversation table between two matching overstuffed chairs, folded her arms across her chest, and turned to face him.

She was backlit by the window, which offered a glimpse of the sun straining to penetrate the Los Angeles skyline. The cream-colored pantsuit flowed over her, masking her figure. But he could tell from her face that she was a lot more slender, almost fragile. Her thick, nearly black hair was longer and was gathered in a clip at the nape of her neck. Small stud earrings were her only accessory. The conservative, polished businesswoman before him was very different from the free spirit he had known four years ago.

The scene is set, Malcolm thought, strolling into the living area. He shoved his hands into his trouser pockets, biting back the urge to ask how she'd been the past four years. *Business*, he told himself. *Stick to business.* Emotions always got him into trouble.

"Celestial Productions offered a fair market price for the movie rights to *InterDimensions*. And we've agreed to your other terms," he began.

"You misrepresented your company, Malcolm. You knew I wouldn't have anything to do with Celestial Productions if I knew you owned it. Can you deny that?" she prompted when he didn't speak.

"No." He watched resentment darken her catlike eyes. She lowered her arms and balled her hands into fists. Even from across the room, he could feel her vibrating with anger.

"You were probably disappointed when I insisted on meeting Celestial Productions's principals." Her smooth inflection barely masked the throb of fury in her voice.

"No, I wasn't." Malcolm kept his tone reasonable. "If I'd wanted to keep my identity a secret from you, I could have. I didn't have to come to lunch today."

"Then how would your partner have explained your absence?"

"We would have thought of something. The point is, I never hid from you. When your agent asked for information about our company, we gave her everything. You must not have asked to see it. My name was all over those papers."

Malcolm saw the flicker of doubt in Nicole's eyes before she lowered her gaze.

"After you walked out on me, I never thought you would willingly come anywhere near me again," she said. "But Denise told me Celestial Productions approached her."

Malcolm pushed away the guilt her words evoked, reminding himself he wasn't the only one to blame for their relationship failing.

"Nicky, you pushed me away. After—"

"Don't." She held up a slim hand, pain clouding her ebony eyes. "I don't want to talk about it, Malcolm."

He dropped his gaze to hide his own pain. "Fair enough." *Business. Stick to business.* "Ty and I are very excited about the idea of owning the movie rights to *InterDimensions*. We enjoy science fiction, and we'd do a good job with your book."

Nicole turned toward the window. "And you'd give me everything I asked for. Allow me final approval on the screenplay and input on the shooting locations, the cast, and the final cut."

"Yes." Malcolm frowned at the tightness of her tone.

"Tempting." Nicole turned back to him. "But deals with the devil usually are."

Malcolm felt his nostrils flare. Heat rushed into his cheeks. "You've gone too far. I understand this is a shock to you. I had time to get used to the idea of seeing you again. You didn't have time to get used to seeing me. But there's no reason for personal attacks."

"There's every reason." Nicole seemed to gather herself. Her deep breaths lifted her chest beneath the loose-fitting jacket. "Does Denise know about us?"

"Of course not. That's personal. This is business."

She looked troubled. "Malcolm, I can't do business with you. There are too many . . . difficult memories behind us."

"Nicky—"

"Please leave." Her tone emerged between a plea and a command.

Malcolm started to speak, then reconsidered. She was too agitated to continue this discussion. A discussion that hadn't started well and had deteriorated badly. His gaze lowered to watch her hand press against her abdomen. He flinched, and her hand dropped away.

"You're right." His voice sounded rough to his ears. "We both need some space. We'll talk more tomorrow."

"No, we won't. I'm getting a flight back to New York tonight."

He frowned. "Nicky—"

She shook her head, her voice resigned. "Good-bye, Malcolm."

He looked into her shuttered eyes. She'd closed him out as firmly as if she'd locked a door against him. Pleading with her wouldn't remove the barrier; beating against it wouldn't make it go away. He'd tried those tactics unsuccessfully more than four years ago.

He studied her, this remote, composed woman, and wondered with regret how deep she'd buried the Nicole Collins he'd known. And how much of her demise was his fault. A part of her must still be alive, though, Malcolm thought. The part that had created the fantasy world of the *InterDimensions* series with its warm, close-knit family. That was the Nicole he needed to reach. But, he realized, looking into her eyes again, not today. She wouldn't listen to him today. Without a word, Malcolm turned and walked out, shutting the door behind him.

Nicole was shaking so much, she couldn't convince her legs to carry her to the overstuffed chairs. Instead she sank onto the carpet.

Her mind stayed blank for several minutes before clicking back on. But the memories weren't happy ones. She pressed a damp palm to her stomach. Years ago, their lives had been perfect. But then the foundation had crumbled, and she and Malcolm hadn't been able to regain their footing. At least not together.

An impatient fist pounded on her door. Nicole closed her eyes. *Please let it not be Malcolm.* They had nothing more to say to each other.

"Nicky, open up," Denise commanded. "I know you're in there."

Denise. Nicole groaned. *Could we try curtain number three?* Still, Denise was her agent and her friend. She knew the other woman deserved an explanation for her seemingly bizarre behavior. After all, Denise had worked hard to put this deal together for her—at her request. Nicole scrubbed her palms over her face, then pushed herself to her feet and walked across the room on still-wobbly legs. She checked the peephole to make sure her agent was alone, then let her in.

Denise marched across the plush carpet in three-inch, fire-engine-red stilettos. A form-fitting, scarlet dress wrapped her curvaceous figure. She stopped in front of the glass doors and spun back toward Nicole.

"What's the problem? Why did you call off the deal? Do you know how long and hard I worked to pull this off?"

"So this is about you?" Nicole knew from past experience that putting Denise on the defensive was the fastest way to calm her so they could discuss things reasonably.

"You know this isn't about me." Denise frowned, pointing one cherry-red fingernail in Nicole's direction. "But after all the time and energy I put into this deal, I deserve to know why you pulled out of it."

"Because I knew I wouldn't be able to work with the producers."

"How did you know that?" Denise's voice hovered less than one pitch below exasperation. "You hadn't even met them."

Nicole wandered into the living area and sat on the armchair facing the window. Denise was right, Nicole thought. Her agent deserved to know why she had walked away from Celestial Productions's offer. Nicole wondered how much she could tell Denise without revealing the painful details. What would her friend accept?

"You knew Malcolm," Denise accused. "You've met him before. When?"

Nicole sighed. "I met him in college."

"And?"

"And, Denise, the rest is private."

Denise studied her with a shrewd, dark gaze. Nicole hated that look. It made her feel as though her friend could reach into every dark corner of her mind and find out what she'd had for breakfast, how many hours of sleep she'd had, and the date of her last confession.

"So, this is personal?" Denise's understanding tone put Nicole on instant alert.

"Very personal."

"And you're going to let it affect your professional life? Our professional lives?" Denise baited.

Nicole drew a sharp breath and inclined her head. "Direct hit."

It was frightening how well they knew each other's strengths and weaknesses after three years. Her agent knew Nicole wore her professionalism like a shield.

Denise slapped her full thigh in frustration, her cherry-red lips drawn tight. She turned away, running her hand through her close-cropped hair. The dangling globes she called earrings spun.

With a gusty sigh, Denise propped her hands on her well-rounded hips and turned back to Nicole. "Then how about fairness? I put six months into this deal. That's a lot of time and a lot of work. I deserve to know how you think I failed you."

"You didn't fail me," Nicole retorted instantly. "He did. He failed me four years ago." She bowed her head and rubbed her eyes with a thumb and two fingers, furious with herself for the sting of tears.

"Who did? Malcolm Bryant?"

"Yes," Nicole whispered.

"How?" Denise's tone was a perfect blend of confusion and frustration.

Nicole hid her face in her hands, unable to face her admission. "He left me." She lowered her hands and stared at the floor. "Four years ago, he walked out on me. The next thing I knew, I was being served with divorce papers."

The silence was deafening.

"Divorce papers?" Denise breathed.

Nicole lifted her gaze to Denise's wide eyes. "Malcolm Bryant is my ex-husband."

* * *

"That went badly," Tyrone remarked.

Malcolm noted his partner's bland tone and judged the other man had counted to ten a thousand times while they waited for the valet to retrieve his car. Now, as Tyrone inched the car south on the interstate toward their Inglewood office, he apparently considered himself calm enough to discuss the aborted meeting.

Malcolm sighed silently and prepared to relive his most recent failure. "We knew going in we had a fifty-fifty chance of pulling this off."

"We should have called her before she came to L.A.," Tyrone said, repeating his previous argument.

"She wouldn't have come," said Malcolm, restating his previous response.

"Well, she came, took one look at us—or rather you—and walked out. Now what?"

"I don't know."

In his mind, Malcolm imagined warm, laughing eyes growing cold and distant over the years. The Nicole he knew would have listened to him, if not today, then the next day. She had a temper like a summer storm. It rained briefly, and then the sun came out. The Nicole he had confronted today had frozen over. How was he going to get her to talk to him now when he hadn't been able to convince her in the past?

"You're going to have to think of something." Tyrone's voice grew terse. "When we get back to the office, send her flowers."

"I can't," Malcolm admitted.

"Why not?"

"Two reasons. First, flowers wouldn't work with Nicole. This is business." Malcolm paused. "Second, she's probably on her way to the airport by now. Or she will be by the time we get back to the office."

"What?" Tyrone snapped his gaze from the crawling traffic to stare at Malcolm. With his small, rimless glasses, he looked like an angry math professor. "She's supposed to stay through Friday."

"She dropped the deal, remember? Apparently, she doesn't think she has a reason to stay another two days."

"Great." Tyrone struck the steering wheel with his broad palm. His dark face flushed. "That's just great." He sat glaring at the traffic. "You need to fix this, Mal. I don't care how. Just fix it."

"I will, Ty."

"We told the completion guarantor we would get the rights to *InterDimensions* and that we'd make a blockbuster out of it. I know we can do it. With my marketing ability and your creative skills, we can make a hit movie out of that book. But first we need the book."

"Don't worry," Malcolm assured him. "I want this at least as badly as you do."

"And how badly is that?"

Malcolm looked at the palm trees and the bright California sun. "Badly enough to go to New York in February," he said grimly.

He stood on the fringe of the lobby and savored his victory. It was indeed sweet. He'd followed the drama in the restaurant and taken heart from Ms. Collins's abrupt departure. But Malcolm had followed her. He allowed himself to relive his anxiety as he'd imagined Malcolm changing her mind.

He had decided against following them. It was too soon to show himself, and he had believed Ms. Collins still had time to prove her loyalty. He would have taken that opportunity away from her if he had revealed himself. He had made the right decision, hadn't he? She'd proven herself worthy of his family.

He sighed with deep relief as he gazed around the opulent lobby. It was well lit, nearly blinding with white stone walls and white-and-silver, marbled floors. He stood beside one of the half-dozen lush plants that added to the décor with their flamboyant accents.

The area was spacious and sparsely furnished, but still he felt hemmed in by the bodies congregating near him. He felt oppressed by their presence, contaminated by their smell. And the room was far too bright.

With the back of his hand, he dabbed at the sweat above his upper lip, then turned toward the hotel entrance. It was all right to leave now. He had fulfilled his duty to his family. He could return to their bosom, where he felt safe and accepted.

As he walked toward the surface lot where he'd parked his black Jeep, he thought again of his victory over Malcolm and Tyrone. He'd kept watch on Tyrone and Ms. Collins's friend, with an impatient eye on the time. He had begun to second-guess himself, reconsidering his decision to follow them, when Malcolm had returned. He had been too far away to hear what Malcolm had told Tyrone and the woman. However, triumph had filled him at the expression on Malcolm's face. Malcolm kept shaking his head. Tyrone had looked disappointed. Ms. Collins's friend had appeared stunned.

He'd wanted to cheer, pump his fist in the air. He still did as he almost danced to the surface parking lot. Ms. Collins had come to her senses. He wouldn't have to implement his plan after all. He was glad. He would hate to have to hurt her. But he would do whatever it took to protect his family.

More of the Hottest
African-American Fiction from
Dafina Books

Come With Me J.S. Hawley	0-7582-1935-0	$6.99/$9.99
Golden Night Candice Poarch	0-7582-1977-6	$6.99/$9.99
No More Lies Rachel Skerritt	0-7582-1601-7	$6.99/$9.99
Perfect For You Sylvia Lett	0-7582-1979-2	$6.99/$9.99
Risk Ann Christopher	0-7582-1434-0	$6.99/$9.99

Available Wherever Books Are Sold!

Visit our website at **www.kensingtonbooks.com**.